LATE SUMMER, EARLY FALL

LATE SUMMER, EARLY FALL

A Simple Tale About Forbidden Friendship

SAM W. HAWKINS

Library of Congress Control Number:		2009909825
ISBN:	Hardcover	978-1-4415-8242-3
	Softcover	978-1-4415-8241-6

This book was printed in the United States of America.

To order additional copies of this book, contact:
Xlibris Corporation
1-888-795-4274
www.Xlibris.com
Orders@Xlibris.com
68141

DEDICATION

This story is dedicated to my family. First and foremost to Ann, my wife. She is the center of our universe and the most selfless person I have ever known. Also to Malcolm, my son, and his two children Jack and Anna and to Melissa, my daughter, and her husband, Larry, and their family Coleman, Samantha, Taylor, and Tyler. Their misfortune is to have been born in an urban environment, thereby missing all the joys and frustrations of country living.

And finally to my East Texas family, that means all those people who were raised in East Texas and lived in a unique culture in a time when things were simpler and different. They can reminisce like I have.

With these families, I feel like the richest man alive.

CONTENTS

CHAPTER ONE

Prince David stood on the chancel of the great cathedral before the noblemen and women, ready to walk down the aisle to his many subjects who were impatiently waiting outside in the streets to cheer him. He descended the steps of the chancel and moved slowly as the massive cathedral pipe organ bellowed forth a lively rendition of Elgar's "Pomp and Circumstance." He was the prince who had just been crowned king by the high priest of the state church who was now ready to rule his country. The gold-encrusted crown embellished with diamonds and purple velvet and the ermine cape with its golden braid couldn't have looked more regal. He held a scepter in one hand and the royal orb in the other. He bowed to the nobility and guests in the church. He accepted their cheers and well wishes as he paused on his way to the tall doors in the back of the cathedral to the crowds—now almost riotous—waiting to see their new monarch. Slowly the gigantic doors adorned in brass were opened by the ceremoniously dressed guards. David slowly advanced to the portico of the centuries old cathedral to acknowledge tumultuous screams of his new subjects.

What a dream! It was like a scene from a great movie or a great novel. The reverie was incomparable. And so was his active imagination working overtime.

But it was not a dream or a great movie. He had not just been crowned, nor were there tumultuous crowds in the street. Actually, it was David Wilson standing in front of Crawford's Drugstore holding a broom in one hand and a dustpan in the other—not a scepter or orb at all. He had just swept the porch of the drugstore and was looking up and down Main Street in the East Texas town of Kirbyville. His "subjects" were a lonely, mangy stray dog roaming the street scrounging for food and a person running into the post office up the street, presumably to mail a letter before the morning mail went out. Otherwise the street was completely empty—and why wouldn't it be at seven o'clock in the morning? People were beginning to wake up, and soon there would be a bustling street again; but at the moment, he had Main Street to himself.

He turned to the east as the sun was just peeking over the treetops and roofs. The sun's rays caught his profile, showing his light brown hair, resulting in a halo effect and highlighting his peach-fuzzed face. His green eyes sparkled looking directly into the sun and were like matched emeralds. His six-foot-one-inch body was straight as an arrow, but he needed to add weight to his 135-pound frame. This would come naturally with maturity or in the next four years while away at college.

David turned to the west to look down Main Street. He first saw the water tower with Kirbyville, Home of the Wildcats painted on it. The quickly rising sun began to displace the shadows of the buildings all the way to West End, which was the end of Main Street. It brought that part of town to a new day, but the streets were still empty. Across the street from the drugstore was the Palace Theater, more commonly called the picture show. The coming attractions were displayed on brass poster cases put in front of the theater. It was a perfect day. This was his moment. This was his day. This was his town.

It was May 30, 1950, a Tuesday after the night he graduated from Kirbyville High School. He, with his fellow classmates, marched down the aisle of the gymnasium as the school band attempted a version of "Pomp and Circumstances." "David Wingate Wilson!" His name was called several times just a few hours before. And he had proceeded to the stage of the gymnasium to be recognized and awarded scholarships for academic achievement along with his diploma.

The president of the school board and several faculty members had presented David with the Gee Award, the American Legion

Citizenship Medal, the local PTA scholarship, the American History Award, the Science and Chemistry Award, the *Stylus* Journalism Scholarship, and a state Wilbur Davidson Scholarship, which would pay his first two semesters' tuition at the University of Texas. Quite a lot for a seventeen-year-old boy.

Why shouldn't he feel good this morning? He had won more awards and scholarships than anyone in his class of fifty-one students, most of whom had started together in first grade. One of the nice things of going to a small country school was going through twelve years of school together with the same people. Those classmates became real friends over the years. And this class was particularly loyal to each other.

School was finally over—high school, that is. And in just four months, David would be making his way to Austin to enroll in the University of Texas. Already he had begun to refer to it as "the university," like an alumnus. He could hardly wait for September when he would leave this town where sidewalks rolled up at six o'clock each day and move to the state capital where things were bound to be a bit livelier.

Few graduates of Kirbyville High even attended college. Most would get married soon after graduation, go to work in the chemical plants located in Beaumont or Port Arthur, and start their families, thus insuring future classes in the Kirbyville school system.

If one did go to college, he or she would go to Stephen F. Austin State Teachers College or Sam Houston State Teachers College, which were located within a 120-mile radius of Kirbyville. They would end up teaching school somewhere close to their hometown and reverting to the traditional pattern of those who did not go away—getting married and having babies and living a well-predicted life.

You could name the residents of Kirbyville who had gone to UT on two hands. Some of those became professors in large universities; others became doctors, lawyers, or businessmen. None ever came back to their hometown. The University of Texas! The residents of Kirbyville equated the state university somewhere between the center of liberalism or communism—few saw any difference—and Sodom and Gomorrah. Good and caring parents wouldn't let their children attend such places. Baylor University would have been an alternative, but no one went to Baylor. Too expensive.

But this didn't bother David. He was going to UT with his mother's blessings. She wanted to go there when she was younger. His dad was not as enthusiastic. He planned to major in journalism and political science with law school as his final destination.

In a small town like Kirbyville, social activities were limited. During the school year, everyone went to the Quack Shack, a school-sponsored activity, to dance or play games. They did not meet in the summer.

You could go to the picture show four times a week—which most people did since no movies stayed longer than two days. Unlike the local churches, the Palace Theater was a microcosm of the people of Kirbyville—and it was nonsectarian. People went there to have a good time, not to follow a religious doctrine. Activities throughout the town and calendar dates were set depending on what was showing at the picture show. Life often centered around the Palace. It was also a good place to transmit information. In looking across the street, David noticed that this week's fare would be *And Baby Makes Three* with Robert Young, *Tokyo Joe* with Humphrey Bogart, and Errol Flynn in *Montana*. He would watch them all.

Also, during the summer months, you could go to Singletary's Bridge or Trout Creek for a swim in the local creeks. Nearly everyone would go swimming at least once a week. There was a rumor circulating around town that Mr. Jeb Jones, a local businessman, was building a pool north of town. Nobody was sure, and besides, David would be gone before it opened.

There were also several local churches to attend. The Baptists dominated the community with the Methodists a far second behind in local activities. Many Methodist youth attended the Baptist Church's social events but declined to participate in the "circle of prayer" activities. Young Baptists could recite Bible quotations prodigiously when called upon to cite their favorite Bible passage. For the Methodists youth, it was always a race to see who would be first to get to say his "favorite" verse. The only one they knew was "Jesus wept," the shortest verse in the Bible. Other Methodists went to the Baptist Church because their girlfriend or boyfriend was a member. Any time the Baptists tried to "save their souls" however, their attendance began to dwindle. If you were a Catholic, you had to go to Jasper for services; and all other denominations, usually having fewer members, were minor and actually unimportant although they outnumbered the Baptists as a group. Altogether there were at least three dozen churches in the community. But in reality, you were either a Baptist or a Baptist or a Baptist! And although it was not actually approved—or condemned—by the parents and deacons, sometimes the youth would go out and "steal" watermelons from farmers after a night service at the church. It actually was not considered "stealing" by the community since the local farmers planted extra acres to compensate for the loss by these pranksters. And nobody thought anything about it—unless you were caught. The embarrassment was more important than the "crime."

David was Baptist like most other youth. The First Baptist Church had a big Sunday school program, Baptist Training Union called BTU, Royal Ambassadors, and Rainbow for Girls. The hot summer months were always a good excuse for having ice cream socials. Birthdays of teenage members were celebrated with games of volley ball and 42, a popular domino game, followed by ice cream parties.

Television had not found its way into East Texas at this time except in a few of the affluent families—if they could be called that. But there was always radio, which played current music, news, and serials like *The Lone Ranger*, *The Green Hornet*, and *The Shadow*.

There were, of course, the school activities. Football and basketball drew the most spectators. Everybody in town would go to football games in the fall. Kirbyville had rarely gone past district in its history. And so nobody expected them to have a great team. They were more successful in basketball, making it to regional play-offs. But they would always be beaten by Mount Enterprise, a team from the north that only played basketball because they didn't have enough boys to field a football team.

Dating according to many was not necessarily a social activity. It was more of a necessity. But just about everyone took his date to the picture show. Those who did seek companionship found that the best place to "park" was the airport, south of town, or Windy Hill, east of town. The most secluded and private spot to "park" in Kirbyville was Kirbyville City Cemetery, but getting a girl to smooch while parked among the gray and black headstones was difficult and took away from the romantic aspects of dating. It sometimes became a game the boys played. And though everyone might go there, it always seemed to maintain a sense of privacy. Unfortunately, David did not date. He was too shy, perhaps too immature, to be involved with a girl. So this was one activity he had no use, or experience, for. He had been promoted in elementary school, skipping the fourth grade. David was one of the youngest in his class, and most of his classmates were two years older. The football team looked like men by comparison. He was far more comfortable with older guys who had already graduated, his so-called gang. Besides, he had gone to school so long with the girls in his school that they were more like sisters than girlfriends. His mother, Caroline, did not encourage dating knowing that would all come in time.

And finally, if you had an extra dollar, you could always eat out. Usually after a movie or church services. There were three places to get the "best hamburger in town." On Main Street was Lea's Café, south of the red light was Schaeffer's Café and Bus Station, and outside the city limits on south Highway 96 was Turner's Café. Eating out was not common since most people had gardens and grew their own food. Many simply could not afford it. David had friends whose fathers often went fishing. They would invite the gang over for catfish when they caught a big mess. But to a teenager in this town, getting a hamburger, fries, and a malt at one of these local eateries was really better than going to some big city for a real dinner.

David was a movie buff, and he saw every film that came to the Palace Theater. Reading the billboards across the street, he could see that *Father Is a Bachelor* (with William Holden), *The Inspector General* (with Danny Kaye), and Roy Rogers's *The Golden Stallions* were playing next week. He was not keen on Westerns featuring Roy Rogers and Gene Autry, but went anyway. They were always shown on Monday and Tuesday, and he was past the serials that played on Saturday morning. Serials were very important to the youth during the war, especially the ones featuring the bad Japanese spies and organizations. David could not see what was playing at the Owl Show—the late show on Saturday night. Since staying up late was very fashionable, most young people went to the Owl Show and then would drag themselves up with parental help for church the next day. There were no options. The Owl Show would be repeated the following Sunday night.

Main Street had not changed as long as David could remember. Looking eastward, David saw Wright's General Store, which smelled like mothballs; the post office; Parson's Grocery; Southwestern Development Company, a timber company; Lea's Café; and the Santa Fe Depot. Passenger trains stopped coming through Kirbyville years ago, but you could see a train daily, carrying logs to the sawmill or the paper mill in Evadale. Across the railroad tracks at the depot were a number of nigrah homes set apart from white residences by some vacant lots. The houses were more like shacks, but still livable. Most of the colored people lived west of town in what was called the Quarters or Tram Town. Past the depot were more homes, including the lovely Victorian Banks home; and Main Street at the east end split into two streets—one going to Little Cow Creek and Singletary's Bridge and the other winding its way around to Kirbyville cemetery. Both dirt roads were most passable in good weather.

Looking westward, David saw Mixson's Grocery and Dry Goods Store, Newton's Drugstore, Watson's Jewelers, the bank, Western Auto, Richardson's Grocery, Morgan and Lindsey's Five and Dime Store, Beathard's Furniture Store, and Middleton's Beauty Shop. As far as David knew, they had been there since the Creation. Nothing exciting had happened on Main Street since the bank was robbed in the late 1930s. Citizens regaled, however, in telling the local Bonnie and Clyde story although it had been twenty years ago. The business district stopped at the red light, which was the intersection of Main Street and Highway 96. Looking down West Main Street toward the West End, there were only three imposing structures and a variety of residences. The two largest churches were located there: a rather-imposing classical building for the Methodists and a three-story Victorian wooden Baptist church—its architecture never determined. Overshadowing all the buildings was the red brick three-story school with its forbidden fire escape and hazardous playground equipment. Constructed at the turn of the century, it had served as an icon to generations of citizens. And across the street, now being used as the high school, was the WPA-built gymnasium and a classroom structure. Directly behind the high school, separated only by a railroad track, was the sawmill, which provided employment to many residents and polluted the classrooms, as well as the town, continually with its ever-burning slag pit and its screeching saws from the planer and the gigantic saw that cut the tree trunks into rough lumber. It was hardly the place for the quietude of learning—or teaching.

Going south on 96 would eventually bring you to Beaumont and Houston. If you went north, you would end up in Dallas or Austin. David had checked the map often, knowing he would be going that way in September.

You could buy your gasoline at the two filling stations at the red-light intersection, each displaying their hand pumps. Gasoline was usually about twenty-nine cents, but never any gas wars. Main Street continued for several blocks, curving at what was called West End and becoming the farm-to-market Road 1014 to Magnolia Springs and Mount Union—part of the Kirbyville school district—and other communities farther west. Eventually the road would abruptly stop at the Neches River. To get across the Neches River, you had to toot your car horn and wait for Old Mac to cross over on the one-car wooden hand-driven ferry. In wet weather, it was always a thrill to drive your car down the embankment and on the ferry without running off the other end.

Kirbyville was a one-street town like most other East Texas towns. To know Kirbyville, one must know the county in which it was located. Jasper County was one of the half-dozen counties found along the Sabine River, which separated Texas from Louisiana. Culturally, it was an extension of the Old South just past the border where cotton had dominated the economy until the slaves were freed by that scoundrel Yankee president, Abraham Lincoln. Cotton gave way to timber after the First World War. There were almost as many colored people in the county as there were whites, most being descendants of former slaves. Many had taken the names of their previous owners. So many of the older families had a white branch and a counterpoint colored branch. It made it easier for the dominant whites to maintain control over the coloreds as the nigrahs were expected to be subservient to their white counterpart. There were Wingate nigrahs who had descended from David's great-grandfather's family slaves. But the Wingate family, his mother's family, never mentioned one of the ancestors who had several children by a slave woman. This was not a topic of discussion outside the family. In the family circles, it's always a game to guess which one of the white descendants would have kinky hair and which one straight.

Outsiders often referred to Kirbyville as a "resort" town—"last resort." But David was born there, went to schools and churches there, and had his family and friends there. They were the people he knew and loved, and it was like having his own little world. He never felt like he had to defend his residency there. He loved his hometown although he planned to leave soon.

Many nigrahs lived in the rural areas in predominantly colored communities, usually eking out a living on their meager farms. Luckier ones worked in the sawmill or hauled pulpwood for minimum wages. Whatever their employment, colored people's pay was low. That is why all the white women of Kirbyville had their homes cleaned and clothes ironed by nigrah women. Ironing was a minor occupation. When you saw an uppity nigrah—one dressed nicely and driving a big car—you could bet he was a bootlegger, a moonshiner, a gambler, or from a big city. You took a paved street in Kirbyville west of town, but when you got to the city limits and entered the Quarters road, it became dirt and was often miserable when it rained.

The culture of Southeast Texas may be best described as "Old South with a Stetson hat." More Southern than Western. The relations between the whites and coloreds were cordial as long as each side adhered to the unwritten "code." That code was based on the premise that each race must "know his place." There was never a discussion of the moral or legal aspect of this arrangement. "That's the way it's always been" was the excuse used by the whites. No one saw any reason to upset the balance of that relationship. It was challenged only when one party broke the code, which was done by stepping over an invisible line between the whites and coloreds.

Breaking the code would be such things as forgetting to address whites without the prefix of "mister" or "missus," which usually became "mizzz" or "mistah." Nigrahs had to use only the facilities marked Colored. They had to be in the Quarters by sunset. They could buy goods at the local white stores, and the owners would extend nigrahs credit with easy payout plans. This kept them always in debt. Colored people were to have no social relations with the whites, and glances at white women would extend only the time of a greeting or to answer a question.

Above all, whites could not have a "social" friendship with coloreds. You might have played with a nigrah child when you were a toddler, but at a certain point—somewhere around your teens—the relationship terminated. The status system kicked in at that time and made the whites dominant. White adults may have good dealings with nigrahs. However, that invisible line was still there; and the nigrah became subservient to the whites, never forgetting to refer to his "friend" as "mistah" and using "yes, suh" profusely. David knew that when returning to Kirbyville the following summer, he would become "Mr." David to the colored people.

On the other hand, nearly each white family "adopted" a nigrah family. They provided odd jobs for the nigrah males and house cleaning and ironing jobs for the females. The colored children got hand-me-down clothes from white children, once outgrown. Nigrahs might occasionally "touch" their counterpart white family for a small loan, but no ruckus was made about late payment—or failure to repay at all. They would be allowed to work off their debts. Banks would not loan money to coloreds.

Another aspect of the code was how whites and colored people referred to each other in public. There were no inconsistencies. Coloreds generally referred to whites as "whites" or "white folks." Whites used the terms "colored" or "coloreds," "colored people," and "nigrahs." The derogatory word "nigger," for the most part, was used only by persons of low character—generally called poor white trash—or by nigrahs themselves when speaking about their own kind or in jest.

As long as this arrangement prevailed, neither side was offended. Kirbyville never had any racial problems because the code took care of everything.

The most popular spot on Main Street, or more accurately just off Main Street, was what everyone reverently called the hookworm bench. It was on the east side of the Gilbert Building where someone, years ago, had placed a split-log wooden bench. It was here the white male senior citizens and the so-called retired sat for hours whittling on pieces of pine and cedar. David often wondered what those retired men had retired from because as far as he knew, some of them never worked a day in their lives. They had been sitting on the hookworm bench as long as he could remember. Yet these gentlemen were fondly looked upon as they sat, whittled, watched the girls go by, and pontificated about the world and its problems, the weather, or the "good old days." The owner of the building saw to it that all the wood shavings were swept up daily so the men could start a new day with a clean patch of ground. It looked like the only time the men moved was when going home for the day or picking up their Social Security check or going for dinner. Of course, there were other streets; but most activities were concentrated on Main, from the depot to the red light and often on the empty lot beside Mixson Brothers.

There was one exception. Three blocks south of the red light was Schaeffer's Café and Bus Station. In addition to selling "the best hamburgers in town," it also was the bus depot. Each day at nine o'clock in the morning, two Greyhound buses would meet at the bus station. The southbound bus was heading for Beaumont and eventually to Houston where more and more people were going these days. The northbound bus would go to Jasper, Huntsville, and Austin and other points west. Since this was the bus David would take to the university, he was well familiar with the schedule and knew it by heart. For those without automobiles, buses were the only vehicle of transportation—and perhaps escape—from Kirbyville.

Standing on the porch of Crawford's Drugstore observing Main Street, David was reminded he had seen this scene every day for the past four years. He had begun work in the ninth grade when he heard Mr. Crawford was looking for someone to sweep the drugstore each day and haul off the trash. When he became familiar with the merchandise and the use of the cash register, Mr. Crawford let him clerk with the other help and he became quite familiar with the drugstore business. He also became privy to the knowledge of the city's most and least known secrets. He became aware of the town's eccentrics and the idiosyncrasies of many of the town's leading citizens. He knew who was on narcotics or other drugs and who had the habit of drinking too much. David also learned, however, that such information should be kept within the store family and never repeated. It was part of the code.

Now after four years, he was ready for a new adventure. He didn't mind leaving all this behind him. But neither was he ashamed that he had been a janitor in a small-town drugstore. It was a learning experience and a source of income. David loved meeting the public and was quite good at it. He had made wonderful friends. He was able to save money for his college education. Besides, he would have to get a job in Austin to help pay for his living expenses and his working experience might come in handy. It was a foregone conclusion that he would have to work part-time if he enrolled in the university because his years at the university would be a real hardship for his family. And he didn't mind at all.

There was nothing unusual about David. Yet he was not the typical teenager of the day. He was seventeen, one of the youngest members of his class of fifty-one. His classmates were one or two years older, mainly because he skipped the fourth grade and started early. He graduated with honors but was not a valedictorian or salutatorian. He was the highest-ranking boy in his class, but three other girls had grade averages higher than his. But they had no plans for going to college. It did not bother him particularly although he let people know immediately that he took physics, chemistry, and math while they took bookkeeping, home economics, and shorthand; and that made a difference in the averaging of grades. He never added the fact, however, that his physics and chemistry teachers were not truly qualified to teach those courses. But that happens many times in public education in small-town schools. The number of scholarships and awards given him at graduation attested to his academic ability. He was satisfied in knowing that.

David was not athletic in any sense, probably a great disappointment to his dad, Tom Wilson, who was considered by most residents to be the most outstanding athlete to ever graduate from Kirbyville High School. David's six-foot-plus frame and his 135 pounds just was not appropriate for playing football. Basketball and track required students to miss a lot of school, and his mother would never approve of his regular absences. Besides, he preferred the more cerebral activities. This didn't mean, however, he was not active in high school.

He had been the editor of the *Stylus*, the high school newspaper, and had served as business manager of the *Lair*, the high school yearbook. He was an officer in the honor society, president of the drama club, a class officer, and active in dramatic productions. Kirbyville High School had no band or choir programs. That was where David's interests really lay. A band would begin the following year, but only incoming freshmen were allowed to enroll. David would be in Austin by that time, enjoying the famous Longhorn Band. The biggest regret in his life, so far, was his failure to continue piano lessons. In junior high school, he took private piano lessons from Mrs. Bonnice Benson, another one of Kirbyville's unsung heroines and the most sought-after piano teacher. The delightful and effervescent Mrs. Benson never declined a request to play weddings or community events, including the Lions Club Annual Minstrel Show and the Senior Citizens' Womanless Wedding. Even if those requests conflicted with her own plans, she never refused a person's or club's request. Not a person in town could forget her rendition of "Tiger Rag" or "Kitten on the Keys." David loved music but hated practicing. Since the Wilson family had no piano, it was difficult to practice because he had to use the church or school piano. Arrangements were made for him to use those pianos. If he continued, then Caroline would buy one. When David constantly ignored practice, his mother saw no purpose in continuing lessons. His music days were over.

David loved to read but preferred going to the picture show more than anything. The films at the Palace Theater transported him to lands of fantasy and excitement—a long way from Kirbyville. That's why David rarely missed a film showing at the picture show. He could get lost in the world of filmdom. Many times it had been his ticket out of town. He looked forward to the foreign films which he had heard about in Austin at the Texas Theater, and for only fifty cents.

Soon these things would be a part of his past. Several thoughts persisted in haunting him. *Would he miss the comfort and security of work and of home? Would he be overwhelmed in the days to come by the university, the classes, the new environment? Could the graduate of a podunk high school in Kirbyville, Texas, make it at a big university? Would he have enough money in a school where millionaires' sons played and drove big cars?* He could only speculate about the answers to the many questions that crossed his mind daily. But he was willing to take a chance—to pursue new interests and eventually leave all these memories behind him. Becoming a lawyer would change all that.

As David looked up and down Main Street, perhaps his last serious look in life as a youth at the place of his birth, he had feeling of mixed emotions—wanting to stay but ready to go!

CHAPTER TWO

"David . . . Hey David!" called a voice from inside the drugstore.

At first David was startled by the interruption of his reverie. "What?" he blurted out.

"David, you need to get to the back room and unpack those boxes. A lot of new merchandise came in yesterday. We need to mark it and get it on the shelves."

It was Mr. Crawford who wanted to check the invoices on merchandise which came in daily. He never let David check the invoices alone, but together they would check and mark the prices on the items which came in that day. It gave both men a chance to talk about a variety of subjects. Mr. Crawford had no son of his own to engage in father-son discussions.

"Ready?" Mr. Crawford asked.

"Sure," David replied and they headed for the storeroom in the rear of the store where he put his broom and dustpan in their proper places.

The stockroom of the drugstore had one big counter in the center surrounded by shelves on all four walls. All merchandise not on display in the store would be stored in the shelves along with seasonal decorations and any other item not needed at the present time. Beneath the stairway to the second floor of the Crawford Building were stored the prescriptions which had been filled in the past. It appeared to David there must have been hundreds of thousands, perhaps even millions of them, because none were ever thrown away and the store was established in 1905. They had turned brown and brittle and gathered dust, but it was possible to locate any prescription ever filled—if you had time to wait that long. On the counter, newly arriving merchandise would be opened, checked, and marked with prices. Mr. Crawford would determine the price, and David would mark the cost and selling price on the particular item. The remaining empty boxes and other trash would be tossed out the rear door onto the loading dock, and David would take them to the trash bin to be hauled away by the city garbage department later in the week.

Mr. Crawford was undoubtedly the most popular and respected man in Kirbyville. He and his brother, Ben, had inherited the drugstore on the death of their father. Mr. Crawford, whose name was Bryant, managed the business part of the store; and Ben, a registered pharmacist, filled prescriptions in a room at the back of the store.

Mr. Crawford might have been called the Godfather of Compassion. For years people knew that if they needed help, they could always go to Bryant Crawford. He helped them to find a place to live or help in obtaining a loan. His advice was valued by all. He would extend their credit at the drugstore until times got better. He would often put in a good word to a prospective employer when one was looking for a job. Some accounts were never paid, and Mr. Crawford just wrote them as a bad business decision.

He might have been too good—perhaps to a fault. Sometimes he would break the law by helping someone in trouble. Like giving a bottle of cough syrup with codeine to a mother of a sick child without a prescription or a bottle of paregoric for a child with the colic. Paregoric was legally called camphorated opium, and each bottle should have been registered in the narcotics book. Even the few addicts in town knew they could "touch" Mr. Crawford for a bottle from time to time. But no one knew, cared, or objected; and everyone would have supported him should he ever get in trouble with the law.

David's mother had been a classmate of Mr. Crawford, and that was the way David was able to get the job four years earlier. In those four years, David had come to admire Mr. Crawford profusely and often sought out his advice on personal matters. He felt more comfortable talking to Mr. Crawford than he did with his dad, and Mr. Crawford was always willing to listen. David felt that his dad was embarrassed to talk to him; it was difficult to get close to him. Tom shied away from David if there was a possibility that he might be asked for advice. After so long, David just forgot about it.

Mr. Crawford was a family man, but his brother was still single, recently being separated from the navy after serving during the war. Consequently, Ben was fair game for every available female within a radius of fifty miles. Women looked for any excuse to go to the drugstore. And at that time, he enjoyed his bachelor status. Being away in the navy resulted in broken ties with females during the war.

"You mopped up last night with awards, didn't you?" Mr. Crawford asked David. He also served on the school board and was the presenter of diplomas at the ceremony the night before. That made David's awards even more special to him.

"I was lucky," David replied, trying to look modest but not succeeding.

"I was very proud of you, and I know your family must have been extremely happy to see you do so well."

"Thanks . . . And they were." David's face beamed with satisfaction.

"And I know it was more than luck," Mr. Crawford added.

David smiled.

Mr. Crawford stopped marking for a moment and looked at David. "Are you sure you'll be able to make it in Austin? It's a very expensive town." He continued, "Oh, I don't worry about the grades, you'll top out on those, but I know your family's financial situation," hinting that his parents might suffer hardships with him going to an expensive school.

David was not embarrassed by the comments because he knew Mr. Crawford was sincerely interested in his future.

"You know I am going to room with Cleve, don't you?" he asked.

Cleve was Mr. Crawford's half brother by his father's second marriage. Cleve Crawford had graduated two years before David. He had been the valedictorian of his class. He was intensely studious, spending most of his time in the chemistry lab or at his study desk.

His goal was medical school by way of a pharmacy degree, and the only way to get there was by making good grades. He did not date, and he didn't have much more money than David did. Cleve's mother, a widow, taught home economics at Kirbyville High School. David was confident Cleve would be a good influence on him, especially in the studying department.

David continued, "We already have our room—thirty-five dollars a month for both of us—and we can eat at the school cafeteria for about sixty cents a meal." Cleve's previous year on the campus proved very helpful in determining expenses. David was lucky that Cleve was also frugal.

Their rooming house was one block off the campus and one block from the Commons, which was the university student center and cafeteria. He was every proud of that fact—the closeness of their room to the campus. David thought of the time saved and the energy preserved by living in the rooming house on San Antonio Street. The Forty Acres, which the campus often was called, had long expanded to many times, but no shuttle service operated for students. Walking was the only mode of transportation to get to the campus, and it took only five minutes to get to the Commons.

"And besides, I have saved most of the money from my job and from graduation gifts." Then he added, "I have my scholarships which should help, and I intend to find a job, hopefully in the school library, so that I can work between classes." David appeared to be very confident in his ability to financially handle his first year. He had spent many hours thinking about the future problems and working them out.

Mr. Crawford patted him on the shoulder. "Dammit, I believe you can do it!" he said admiringly. "But," he continued hesitatingly, "if you have problems, let me know. I can help you out some." And then he added, "And you can have a job each summer when you are home. I'm counting on your helping us at Christmas and taking inventory after New Year."

David was thrilled at the job prospect and moved by Mr. Crawford's offer. Jobs, even part-time, were especially hard to find in small towns. All he could muster in way of gratitude was a soft thanks.

But both of them knew that it meant much more than it sounded. Mr. Crawford was impressed with David's work. What began as a favor to a former classmate had turned out to benefit both the employer and employee. More important was the friendship which had developed between them.

Having unpacked and marked all the goods that came in that day, Mr. Crawford suggested they return inside the store.

"I need to do some bookkeeping work now, and you can help wait on customers." Mr. Crawford moved toward his office. "Payroll's gotta be done."

David waved his hand in a cavalier swoop, making a gesture to Mr. Crawford to precede him. "By all means, sire, by all means! The payroll first and foremost, Your Majesty."

Mr. Crawford laughed at his eloquent maneuvers. "Has *The Three Musketeers* been playing at the movies lately?" he asked.

Crawford's Drugstore was an institution long before David went to work there. The store itself was like any other small-town drugstore—one large area for merchandise and customer service and a small room in the back for the pharmacy with an office beyond the pharmacy. They were separated by a swinging door on which was an opening for prescriptions going in and medicine coming out. Ben Crawford rarely came beyond the boundaries of the swing doors, so the clerks usually had the customer service to themselves.

There was no fountain. You had to go up the street to Newton's Drugstore for ice cream and colas. But there was a magazine rack, an old-fashioned cigar case with humidor; a section for veterinarian supplies, paint; a large section on patent medicines, gifts, and various other sundry items. Items were stacked on shelves or in cases around the store. Gifts and larger merchandise were found on the open islands in the center of the store. The store was not unusually large, except to David when he spread oiled sawdust on the floors and swept down the aisles and around the islands each day. Then it seemed immense. Oiled wooden floors prevented the spreading of dust. It took David some time to learn where everything was located and what each item—especially the patent medicines—was used for. Once he learned the merchandise, David became a good salesman and somewhat an expert.

The cash register was located in the rear of the store near the pharmacy, and there was a sitting area for those waiting for prescriptions. This area was open to all, except for one Saturday each month when Dr. Mose Wheeler, the local so-called optometrist, would bring his glasses and charts into the store and test his patrons with optometric aids. He used no scientific testing devices. Instead he would give the patient a visual chart to read and then offer pair after pair of spectacles until the right glasses were found. As unscientific as it seemed, David never heard any complaints from his patients.

The post office had once been located next to Crawford's Drugstore, and upstairs, the only doctor and dentist in town had offices, which were directly over the drugstore that was being reached by a well-worn wooden stairway between the store and post office. Old Dr. McKinnon had been the town and mill doctor since Kirby Lumber Company had located in Kirbyville. He had home-delivered every baby in town for almost fifty years. His offices consisted of two waiting rooms—one for whites and one for nigrahs—two examination rooms where the doctor saw his patients on a segregated basis, and a storeroom which contained supplies but might serve as a recovery room when minor surgery was done in his office. Because of this limited arrangement, all baby deliveries were performed in the home of the expectant mother—white or black. People who could not manage the stairway to the second floor would be accommodated in the drugstore below. Major surgery required the patient to go to a hospital in Beaumont or Jasper.

While Dr. McKinnon was a beloved citizen of Kirbyville, his wife did not receive the same adulation. Mrs. McKinnon thought she was a little better than anybody else. When things did not suit her, she had a habit of saying, "Do you know who I am? I am the wife of Dr. W. F. McKinnon!" She also delighted in seeing her name in the society pages of the *Kirbyville Banner*. Most people were not impressed with her position in local "society," but they accepted her—dyed black hair and all—in deference to old Dr. McKinnon who at one time or another treated them all. That also required suffering through hymns at the Baptist Church when Mrs. McKinnon occasionally substituted for the church pianist. David had heard her hit so many sour off-key notes he often wondered if they were on the same page in the hymnal. Mrs. McKinnon got her comeuppance to the delight of most citizens when she had a serious illness and almost died. To evoke as much sympathy as possible, she wrote the news article herself about her illness and surgery—highly exaggerated—and submitted it to the editor of the *Banner* herself. The *Banner*, always desperate for news, printed articles on everything and anything. That was the philosophy of a small-town paper. The news story, which appeared in the weekly paper, did not turn out as Mrs. McKinnon expected. Mr. England, the editor of the *Banner*, apologized for the error; but some citizens suspected it was no mistake. Somehow the article on Mrs. McKinnon's health problems and hospital incarceration got confused with a write-up of a Sunday school ice cream social held the same week. When it appeared in the society column, it caused quite a flurry among the readers. It read:

> *Mrs. W. F. McKinnon, wife of Dr. W. F. McKinnon, local physician, has been incarcerated in St. Elizabeth's Hospital in Beaumont this week recovering from a serious life-threatening illness. She was rushed to Beaumont by ambulance when she was found unconscious in her home last Thursday afternoon. After surgery, she was confined to her private room for recuperation and visitation. Guests for this happy occasion were members of the Disciples Sunday School Class of the First Baptist Church who played games and sang songs. Peach and vanilla ice cream and punch were served to all members who enjoyed the evening of Christian fellowship. The class wishes to thank the hostesses for a lovely evening. The McKinnon family appreciates all cards, remembrances, and food given during her illness.*

The embarrassment of the article equating her illness with a Sunday school party resulted in "convalescent confinement" for Mrs. McKinnon to her home for several weeks following her return until it was no longer an item of gossip in the community. Several readers of the *Banner* requested similar articles in the future.

A similar situation was found in the dentist's office. His name was Dr. Clarence Libby, and he was the epitome Southeast Texas country dentists. Whites would sit in the white waiting room, which had a ceiling fan for comfort. Nigrahs sat in the colored waiting room and suffered the lack of heat or cold depending upon the season. Whites got the benefit of modern equipment and relatively up-to-date techniques and equipment. Still, Dr. Libby called anyone—white or colored—who insisted on novocaine for deadening pain a sissy. There were many sissies in Kirbyville. Colored people were not as lucky as whites. First, they got old and worn-out equipment, cast off from the white side of the office. There was no need to fill cavities for the nigrahs, the only solution to their dental problems was extraction. No nigrah could boast a filling from the Dr. Libby except those made of gold. And all this without the benefit of novocaine—sissy or not! That probably accounts for why there were so many snaggletoothed coloreds in Kirbyville. But no one complained, and such things were accepted in a small East Texas town as part of the code.

Crawford's Drugstore was a microcosm of Kirbyville and possibly any East Texas town. Being located next to the post office and below the doctor's and dentist's office, it was bound to become the congregating place for everyone in town. And it did. Since everyone had to see the doctors at one time or another or buy veterinary supplies, gifts, and other sundries or pay their electric or water bill or pick up their medicine, their paths led to the drugstore, and Crawford's was the crossroads of the community. And along with that came its share of local characters.

It did not take long for David to learn each and every one of the local patrons and their quirks.

"Morning, Uncle Bill," he would often say, addressing Uncle Bill Casey, the blind piano tuner, who knew everyone in town by the sound of their voice.

"Morning, David," he replied.

David marveled that Uncle Bill never misidentified anybody. "The usual, Uncle Bill?" he asked.

"Right!"

And so David would get a paper sack and put a bottle of snuff—always Garrett's—a package of Red Hots, and a copy of the *Kirbyville Banner* into it. He often wondered what Uncle Bill did with the newspaper, being blind and all, but he never asked and Uncle Bill had been doing this for years.

How many times had he waited on Pokey Weller? David wondered. Pokey was a midget, but larger than most of the midgets he had seen in other places. Pokey was well into his fifties when David went to work, but as far as he could recollect, David never knew if Pokey worked or even had a job. Pokey would pick up his parents' prescriptions and have coffee with Mr. Crawford at Lea's Café. Everyone loved Pokey despite his handicaps and accepted him as a beloved member of the town family.

"Damn and double damn!" David would mutter to himself when he saw Mr. J. P. Pitts, the local depot operator and telegrapher, coming into the store. And he saw Mr. Pitts every day when he came by the drugstore to buy his daily cigar. As many times as Mr. Pitts came to the drugstore, David could not help but wonder why he didn't buy a week's or month's supply of cigars or even a box. But that was not the way Mr. Pitts preferred. One cigar per day. By smoking one cigar a day, he could pacify his wife who didn't like smokers.

"Hey, boy!" Mr. Pitts would gruffly order. "Open this cigar case."

David obliged him, wondering why after four years, day after day, he couldn't call him by his proper name instead of "Hey, boy." "Hey, boy!" was a greeting reserved for whites addressing nigrahs. It was part of the code. David resented the insinuation. The man never smiled or had a kind word for anybody. David remembered seeing a sign once on entering a neighboring town. It read, "Welcome to Newton, Texas. Home of 1000 Happy Folks and a Few Old Grumps." *Well,* David concluded, *this is our old grump.*

David was not prone to curse as so many of his fellow students in high school did. With his Baptist upbringing and hearing mother fuss at his father for cursing, he decided it was better to avoid using profanity. However, from time to time, he felt like cursing was appropriate in situations of frustration or disappointment. He used the expression "Damn and double damn" to calm his anxieties and felt that the expression was not offensive to anybody.

There was no one any kinder to the Roberts family than Mr. Crawford. The Roberts might not deserve being referred to as Poor White Trash; but they were poor, uneducated, and not models of good citizens. The Roberts lived north of town on Little Cow Creek, which also served as their bathing facility as well as water source. Baths in cold weather were few and far between, and hygiene was not a matter that occupied much of their time. Their home was a tin, wood, and cardboard edifice that over the years had grown to be a rather-large building. It did require periodic maintenance, however, after a rain. The family consisted of Mr. and Mrs. Roberts and their daughter, Sweetie, and son, Hawk, and his wife. From time to time, one family member or another would do odd jobs around town, but no one could ever really determine if they had a steady source of income. One family venture was to make red rose wreaths from crepe paper and paraffin and sell them on Main Street. Some people would buy them and put them in the cemetery. Others just bought them to help the family out. Surprisingly, they sold many wreaths. Local grocers would give them food from time to time. They had no automobile, and so they were confined to the area between their home and the town. And yet not a soul in Kirbyville was unfamiliar with the Roberts; and the family was always in the drugstore to see Mr. Crawford or the post office to see Miss Bell, the postmistress, or the grocery store offering advice and taking handouts as if they were leading citizens. In a sense, they were the "local yokels" but were accepted as another part of the city family.

Among his most regular drugstore customers was Roy Cooper. Roy was a nigrah in the fullest sense. He was dark black, uneducated, and ill-dressed. He was a pulpwood hauler, that is, one who cut and delivered pine logs to the paper mill at Evadale. He always appeared on Saturdays, usually in dirty overalls and usually with the sweaty smell that accompanied those who labored in the sun all day. David was introduced to Roy one day when he first began to work when he noticed this colored man standing in the middle of the store. David went over to him as he would any other customer.

"May I help you?" he asked.

Without a word and a slight smile on his face, Roy thrust a quarter into David's hand and nodded.

David was puzzled and continued again. "Yes?"

Roy only nodded and pointed to the rear. Roy was not a talker, but David didn't know that yet.

My lord, David said to himself. *What does this man want? He's a mute.*

At that moment Ben Crawford peered through the opening of the swinging door of the pharmacy. "David!" he yelled. "Come back here."

David was glad to get away. It was apparent he didn't know what to do or what the customer wanted. He didn't know sign language. He rushed to the pharmacy.

"That's Roy Cooper," Ben said. "He comes in here every Saturday. He doesn't speak, but this is what he wants." He walked back to the pharmacy cabinet, pulled out a drawer under the typewriter used to prepare labels. Inside the drawer was an assortment of various brands of condoms ranging from the plain to the more deluxe and sensual. It was David's first encounter with the store's stock of prophylactics.

"He give you a quarter?" Ben asked.

David nodded, holding the quarter up so Ben could see it.

"He wants a three-pack box of Trojans." Ben casually put them in a bag and gave them to David. "He's got ten kids but must think that without using these rubbers, he might have twenty."

In turn, David passed the condoms on to Roy and thus began a relationship which occurred each and every Saturday as long as he worked there. It even came to a point that David had some prewrapped for Roy so as to avoid any delay or embarrassment. And David was glad to know where those prophylactics were stored. During the years David worked for Crawford's Drugstore, he learned that Ramses and Trojans were the most popular brands of condoms. He often wondered if there was something Mr. Davis did not tell about Egypt and Macedonia in world history.

Am I going to miss all this when I leave for Austin? David often pondered. He would like to have answered, "Not a bit." But he, like everyone else in town, accepted these and other characters for what they were—part of the town family. And chances were, they would be a part of his memories as long as he had feelings about his childhood and his small hometown.

David had just graduated from high school and would soon be heading to Austin for higher learning. But in the last four years, he had received another kind of education that no other institution could provide. That was an education of humanity as learned from his employment at Crawford's Drugstore. And David was vaguely aware of this, although the full importance had not quite made itself apparent. This would be accomplished with maturity some time in the future when he could look back at the people and events with fond memories.

There was no veterinarian in town, but if you wanted to know about animal diseases or problems or the kind of paint to use, Bryant Crawford was the expert. He could advise you on anything from sore udders and curing mange to mildew on your home. If you were painting and refinishing furniture, he would sell you the right kind of Kuhn paint product to use.

But the rest of the store was the domain of the greatest salesclerk in the city of Kirbyville. Her name was Bessie Fulton, and she could get a customer to buy anything and thank her for it in the process.

Bessie's age was indeterminable. She and her mother came from Kentucky many years ago. From time to time, she would use words which must have come straight from the hills. And consequently, no one knew her background or family, which was one way of categorizing people in East Texas. She married a mill worker from Call, Texas, but now was a widow with a son of high school age who turned down the job David accepted. Bessie was a short person in stature and a frequent user of Lady Lamour's Jet Black Hair Dye. She seemed to have a boundless well of energy, liked to square-dance, and was game for any playful joke that was suggested. She was friendly to everyone, and that's why everyone liked her. David was crazy about her and appreciated her even more when she covered for him the day he attempted to demonstrate the cancan. He kicked his foot into the air, and his loafer went flying across the store into a showcase. Mr. Crawford could never quite determine how that case got smashed, so he passed it off as an accident on the insurance claim.

Mr. Crawford had certain items in the store, for example Nyal drug products, on which he paid a commission to the salesperson. He bought these products in large quantities, and the margin profit on them was high. He encouraged the clerks to recommend those items first. Bessie could always supplement her salary with these commissions. Nobody could match her in the sales department.

Some people might say it was a "con job," but whatever you called it, she was a master in the sales field. That is why Mr. Crawford got such good deals from the Nyal company. He knew Bessie could move the product.

Bessie's personal choice of products was the patent medicines. One could tell her what the ailment was, and she could tell you precisely what kind of medicine to buy. Over the years, she must have sold gallons of Lydia E. Pinkham elixir for women, tons of Cardui laxative, millions of Carter's Little Liver Pills, and tubes of Blue Star Ointment, bottles of Swamp Root, Grove's Tasteless Chill Tonic, and dozens of other preparations. She had the cure for everything from ingrown toenails and severe hemorrhoids to hair loss.

It was Bessie that introduced David to Dixie Peach, Aida, and other pomades generally advertised in *Ebony* magazine. Hair pomades were big in the fifties, especially with nigrahs and teenage white girls.

"When a nigrah wants a pomade," Bessie told David, "tell them that Dixie Peach or Aida is perfect for straightening hair." She winked and continued, "But when the white girls call for it, tell them it is excellent for curling hair." The commissions for selling pomade were good. And there was never a complaint from the customer.

One of Bessie's most frequent customers was Cecil Jones, a local insurance agent and aging bachelor. Cecil was convinced he had a hair problem when his red hair began to slowly fall out. Bessie helped Cecil, very discreetly, to find the right hair preparation to apply to his prematurely balding head. Cecil blamed his hair problems as the reason he could not find female companionship, especially since he had been so successful in his insurance business.

Bessie tried everything she had on the shelves of the drugstore. Cecil's head, however, remained slick as a button. Finally, out of desperation, Bessie suggested her last remedy. "Cecil, honey," she said as seriously as she could without cracking a smile, "I heard that if you rub Preparation H. Hemorrhoidal Ointment on your head, it would help your scalp."

Cecil looked dumbfounded.

"Really." Bessie continued. "It tightens the skin on top of your head and draws the sideburns up nearer the top."

Cecil shook his head in disbelief. But the serious expression on Bessie's face convinced him that she must be telling the truth. Reluctantly, he bought a tube of Preparation H. and quickly left the store. Bessie broke into laughter as he departed. It was meant to be a joke that got out of hand. No one ever knew if Cecil took her advice seriously, but Bessie never sold him a refill; and if he used the ointment, he must have bought it somewhere else. But several weeks later, people swore his hair was getting thicker. He began sporting a new hairstyle. Cecil never revealed his secret to Bessie, but he began to date the new elementary school teacher and finally married her. Bessie took the credit anyway, considering herself a good matchmaker—as well as an excellent solver of medical problems.

High on Bessie's list of sales products was Hadacol tonic, bay rum, and Dr. Tichener's Antiseptic Mouthwash. She sold so much of those products Mr. Crawford started buying them by the cases at greatly discounted prices. Some people became regular customers of those "medicines" which alcohol content exceeded 50 percent. Mr. Crawford warned her that she might be turning them into alcoholics. But since Bessie had never seen them inebriated or dangerously affected by the products, she continued to comply with the customers' requests. This, of course, did no harm to her commissions, which increased at the same time.

Mrs. Bessie was not without flaws or idiosyncrasies, however. David always thought of her like a "diamond in the rough"—a precious stone with a slight flaw. Bessie was notorious for mispronouncing words, especially the names of the products she sold. Trouble was, she sold so much of them the customer often asked for the product by the name she had given it rather than the one given by the manufacturer. That was not her worst habit however.

Bessie never admitted to having a slight hearing problem, although her friends had suggested her life would be better if she wore a hearing aid. Rather than going to that expense of buying one, she would just ask the person again and again until she understood what the customer wanted. When she still didn't understand, she would ask Mr. Crawford if he knew what the product was. And when that did not provide the answer, she would always follow it up with a question. "What's it used for?" That would usually bring results.

One day, however, the strategy did not work out like it should. A female customer no one recognized entered the store, cautiously moved down the aisle, and very discreetly sought out Bessie to wait on her. "Can I hep you, honey?" Bessie asked in her most cordial manner, smiling as she approached a potential new customer. The young lady quickly looked around and, seeing that no one was watching her, answered Bessie, "Yes, I'd like some condoms, please."

"Some what, honey?"

"Condoms, please."

By now it was obvious that Bessie did not know what the customer wanted. So in the most pleasant voice you can imagine, she called across the store to Mr. Crawford, "Mr. Crawford, do we sell condoms?" Then she quite innocently looked at the young lady and asked, "What are they used for, honey?"

By then the customer was halfway down the aisle and was out of the store in a flash. Bessie never saw her again but wondered why. Later that day when Bessie was about to go home, Mr. Crawford took her aside and explained what had happened. He advised Bessie to use a different sales approach in the future.

Bessie was miffed to say the least. "If she had said she wanted some rubbers, there would have been no problem," she retorted. "Who asks for condoms around here?" And with that question, she took her purse, left the store in a huff, and went home. Mr. Crawford just chuckled.

Despite her faults, Bessie was loved by one and all, and David suspected that a lot of Crawford's Drugstore business was due to the attraction of Bessie Fulton and her congeniality. It was for sure that Mr. Crawford would never fire her.

David was on the floor behind a showcase arranging women's toiletries when a customer appeared in the front door.

Bessie moved to greet her before she got halfway down the aisles. This scene had happened before. "Can I hep you, honey?" she asked. Bessie was sometimes wiser than people gave her credit for.

"I'd like David to wait on me, please," she replied.

David cringed and tried harder to be invisible. "Damn and double damn," he murmured to himself. He recognized the voice immediately and moved even farther back, hoping to hide himself behind the Dubarry, Max Factor, and Ponds beauty products hoping they would hide him. But it was too late. She had already spotted him.

"Oh, there you are!" She smiled through the glass case, and his only recourse was to get up and speak to her. "Good morning, Davey."

No one called him Davey. David's mother, Caroline, had named him David after her father, and she was intent he should never have a nickname. When people called him something besides David, she immediately corrected them. She decided years ago there were enough Juniors, Bubbas, Daves, and Daveys in Jasper County. She felt the same way about double names. It seemed that it was part of the East Texas culture to name persons with double names and they carried that name for the rest of their life. She was tired of Joe Bills, Betty Janes, Sue Anns, and Herbert Rays. She tried everything to keep people from calling David that way.

It was Dorie Dean Grimes, known to one and all as Dee Dee, a name she had given herself when she got tired of everyone calling her Dorie Dean.

"Hi," was the only response David could summon up. He felt like a rabbit caught in a snare. Bessie, observing from the rear of the store, knew what was going on. She had seen it before and felt sorry for him.

Dee Dee was what most people would say "from across the tracks," except there were no tracks. She actually lived north of town on U.S. 96 just past the Cow Creek bridge. She was a junior and had been in the drama club with David. She was not unattractive with her olive skin, hazel eyes, and brown hair; but when she smiled, she looked like she had fangs. And with her very slight mustache, any interest one might have in her was wiped away.

Dee Dee wanted to be liked. She tried to finagle David into taking her to the junior-senior banquet and prom, but was unsuccessful. It was probably less her looks than David's inability to relate to girls. He went to the banquet alone much to Caroline his mother's chagrin. She tried to help him find a date but she, too, was unsuccessful. Dee Dee was irritated about being turned down, but she was quick to forgive him. He was the only friend she had.

Dee Dee wanted to be part of the in crowd so badly that she never denied the rumor she *put out* to gain popularity. The male students were certainly aware of that fact. But David was not so sure about that rumor. At least, he never was granted an opportunity to check it out. He wondered what he would do if even given a chance to have sex. If he couldn't get a date to the prom, he surely couldn't get into the pants of a female. Basically, Dee Dee wasn't bad. But she was aggressive, and most men did not appreciate pushy women, especially Southern men. Since she was rejected socially, Dee Dee decided to act the role of a bitch she was relegated to by the community. And she played to the role well.

Dee Dee's problem was her family. They lived north of town on U.S. 96 near Cow Creek where her father had a garage. He was a good mechanic, but his language was abusive and offended many people. Mr. Grimes made no pretense about his dislike of colored people. He didn't follow the code. People felt uncomfortable around him, and he had a reputation for getting drunk in public. The best way of dealing with Mr. Grimes was not to deal with him at all. David never saw Mrs. Grimes.

It was her brothers that determined the status and future of Dee Dee Grimes. Some people might refer to those two brothers as unrefined. Others might excuse their behavior as being prankish and dismiss it by saying "Boys will be boys." David knew better. "They were just plain mean," he would often tell his mother. He had heard of their activities long before he entered high school. They attended each grade twice before finally dropping out before graduation. He had seen them many times cruising around town in an old beat-up car. There was only one way to describe the Grimes brothers, and that was "mean" in capital letters. They had been in trouble with the law but somehow had always been able to beat the charge. People just didn't mess with the Grimes brothers. Howard and Fred Grimes were several years older than their little sister. That was Dee Dee's problem. The brothers protected her like she was Princess Elizabeth. They watched her carefully (brotherly protection, some might say) and anyone who offended or aggravated her in any way would often end up with a black eye, body bruises, or broken bones—possibly all three. And Dee Dee took full advantage of this protection. You learned early to keep out of her way.

David often wondered what he had done to gain Dee Dee's favor. He never tried to curry her favor or attention. He was shy and not particularly good-looking. He was built like a scarecrow, and his sex appeal wouldn't attract an earthworm. And yet she came onto him like a leech. He was kind to everyone, but David finally decided it was common membership in the drama club.

Dee Dee smiled and leaned over the counter, revealing her threatening cuspids and her full breasts to David. He tried to look away. "I seen you at the graduation last night," she remarked. "You done real good getting all those awards. You got more than anyone else."

David was embarrassed about this and replied, "I lucked out, I guess."

Dee Dee knew better. "Oh no," she quickly added, "you deserved every one of them. Davey, you are the smartest person I know . . . You going to college?"

"University of Texas . . . in the fall."

"Texas! My my, how exciting that must be . . . going to Austin and a big university like that. When do you leave?"

David was surprised she knew anything about the university, much less where it was located. "Leaving middle of September . . . Going to room with Cleve Crawford." Why he added that bit of information he did not know. It just came out.

"Oh, I remember Cleve. He's nice. I used to like him too," she added. "Had his mother for home economics. She's so sweet."

—

David interpreted that to mean she had tried to attract Cleve Crawford too, but had been rejected by Cleve. *Lucky guy*, he thought.

"And he'll keep you out of trouble too . . ." Dee Dee continued. "He's shy like you, Davey. I don't think he had a girlfriend when he was in school," she continued.

She was right. Cleve's interest in girls was the same as David's. *Neither one of us could scare up a date if our lives depended on it*, he thought.

"My brothers go to Austin every once in a while to buy cedar posts . . . Maybe I can come out with them and visit ya'll some times."

Damn and double damn, he told himself. David was terrified at the thought of a visitation from Dee Dee—and her brothers. David did not know how she knew Cleve since he was three years ahead of her in school. But he never doubted Dee Dee's ability to get around, and if she said she knew Cleve, he would accept her word.

Mr. Crawford had come from the stockroom and was witnessing David's predicament. He looked at Bessie who had witnessed the whole situation. He chuckled to himself and thought about leaving him there. But that would have been cruel after seeing David squirm and sweat. After observing a few more moments of David's torture, he called across the store, "David, we need to clean up the stockroom."

David was saved! "Guess I've got to get back there and clean up, Dee Dee." He was just about on his way when she interrupted.

"But I came in here to make a purchase," she said.

"Oh?" he replied. "What can I do for you?"

"I need some Kotex."

David was not surprised. Dee Dee had done this before. He always thought she enjoyed embarrassing him, but then again, maybe she just didn't know any better. He gave her the benefit of doubt.

"Hadn't you rather have Bessie wait on you?" he asked.

"Don't be silly," she replied.

He reached for a box under the counter and proceeded to get a sack.

"Oh no, Davey," she exclaimed. "I want the economy size. Like those way up on top of the shelves." She pointed to the big blue and white Kotex boxes stacked to the ceiling. "Super, please."

David climbed to the top of the shelves, retrieved the box, and wondered how many people in the store were observing this scene.

"Anything else?" he said, hoping this was the only item she wanted.

"A jar of Massengill Powder."

David got a box of the female hygienic product from the shelf in record time. *God! I can't believe this.* His composure was almost gone along with any male ego he might have possessed. *She's asked for everything but a box of condoms.*

"What else?" he asked. You could tell he was fully exasperated. He kept telling himself the customer was always right. *Damn and double damn!*

"That's all," she replied. "No, let me have some Midol tablets."

Then looking under the counter near the cash register, he noticed that there were no sacks.

"Dee Dee," he said with a little remorse, "we don't have any sacks to put this in."

Dee Dee was unperturbed. "That's all right. I'll take them like that."

She opened her purse, counted out the exact amount of change that came up on the cash register, picked up the box of Kotex and jar of powder and tablets, and departed the store as quickly as she had arrived. The picture of Dee Dee Grimes with a box of Kotex under her arm and a box of Massengill Powder in her hand walking down Main Street stuck with him several days.

David did not see Dee Dee for the rest of the summer. He was usually gone when she came to the drugstore, but she always asked for him first anyway. But Bessie would remind him that she had been by the store to see him.

David didn't dare look around to see where Bessie or Mr. Crawford or anybody else were. They had witnessed the whole scene and the agony on David's face. They pretended, however, to be preoccupied somewhere else. He retreated to the stockroom as quickly as his feet could take him there. *Thank goodness*, he thought, *no one saw me.*

The stockroom was a mess since he had not cleaned or picked up in two days. There were many empty boxes and packing straw and paper everywhere. He began to pick up the trash and stack the boxes on the loading dock. The drugstore received merchandise two or three times a week, and the storeroom was always piled with boxes.

David was, however, still caught up in the jubilation of his graduation night's activities and the reveries of his days in Crawford's Drugstore in spite of Dee Dee Grimes. Standing on the loading dock in the rear of the store, he remembered an incident which took place two years ago on that exact spot but one which no one—absolutely no one—ever knew about. He would rip his tongue out before he told this secret.

Kirbyville, Precinct 2 of Jasper County, had no stock laws. The city council never found it necessary to pass an ordinance prohibiting livestock from wandering up and down Main Street from outside the city limits. As a result, it was not uncommon to see cattle walking down the street, especially in the earlier part of the day, leaving their "calling cards" in the form of manure piles all over Main Street. No one liked it, but no one was willing to alienate Mr. Nance Wiley who owned the cattle. So the cows wandered into town, drank at the city pond, and then proceeded to stroll down and mess up Main Street. Often they would go down the alleys behind the store looking for fresh grass. They developed an appetite for cardboard boxes—always in the trash bin—and consequently would spend the day munching on their newfound meal between the buildings.

One day as David was loading the trash on the loading docks, Mr. Wiley's cows came sauntering down the alley, leaving their stench behind them. He had seen them do this dozens of times before and stepped in the "cow dabs" many times, but for some reason, today it angered him immensely. Maybe he got tired of cleaning up cow manure.

Almost instinctively, David went back into the store room and found a bottle of High Life. High Life was the common name for carbon disulfide, a chemical used as a fumigant to kill weevils in grain

---

41

or beans or sometimes was poured down the holes of insects to kill them. However, High Life, when put on hairy skin, burned like fire and was terribly painful, though temporarily. He filled a veterinarian enema syringe full of High Life and quietly crept back to the loading dock. The cattle never noticed him, being too interested in the grass around the loading dock. Without startling the animals, David slowly sprayed the High Life on the cows closest to the dock. It took a few moments for the chemical to take effect; but when it did, those bovines first snorted, then bellowed, and then took off like a wild herd, their tails erected as if flags, running down the alley and turning toward Main Street. The rest of the herd followed.

At that precise moment Mr. Huntley, an elderly gentleman who had been sitting on the hookworm bench whittling like the others but had decided to go home for dinner, was crossing the exit of the alley. He came face-to-face with a herd of bellowing and stampeding cattle, urinating, defecating, and heading for Main Street.

The old man could think of only one thing. And thus he ran down the street, yelling to the top of his lungs, "Mad cows! Mad cows! Run for your life!"

The cattle swept past the men on the hookworm bench, who by now were standing on top of it as the cows surged past. They, too, agreed the cows had gone mad. Traffic came to a standstill on Main Street as the cows headed out of town and back to the sanctuary of their ranch. The incident was soon over, but it was a topic of conversation for several days. David never told anyone about the origin of the Great Cattle Stampede. Old man Wiley never knew what happened to his cattle as the High Life evaporated, leaving no blisters. David continued to remain silent about the incident, but he was secretly pleased that within six weeks, the city council passed an ordinance declaring the open-range stock law was over. It had been on the agenda many times, but no one in town wanted to alienate the ranchers. All livestock must now be contained within appropriate fences. Kirbyville was free at last!

David had to get back to the task at hand. *And stop this day dreaming*, he thought. During those moments of thinking about the past, he did not notice that he had company using the common trash bin in the alley. As he began to take the boxes to the garbage container, he spotted a young nigrah boy. He did not look like most of the nigrahs David was familiar with. Primarily, it was his lighter skin—much lighter than most colored people who came into the store. His nose was much thinner than most nigrahs whose noses were indeed broad, and his lips resembled those of white people. He had the beginning of a very thin, but nicely trimmed mustache. He was well over six feet tall, athletic in stature, with muscles rippling in the sun as he lifted boxes and sacks and threw them into the trash bin effortlessly. Sweat was running down his face, but through the sweat, you could see his coal dark eyes watching every move David made. He had the physique of a college track star—lithesome and fleeting in appearance. Despite the sweat covering his body, he was the picture of perfect coordination, very natural. It was apparent this man was an athlete and a good one. His hair was cut in what the local coloreds called the zampudas-style—short and to the skin. It was the fashion of the day.

As he approached the bin, David smiled and greeted the nigrah with a pleasant hey.

At first the boy just nodded and tried to look away, paying more attention to disposing the trash than acknowledging David.

"You new around here?" David asked, trying to break the silence.

"Yeah," was the terse reply.

"Who you working for?"

"Parson's."

Parsons's was a grocery store between the post office and Lea's Café, just down the street from the drugstore. It was owned by the old man and run by his two sons. Most of the people who lived in the east end of town shopped there.

"I'se started this moanin'," the young boy added. "Gonna be heah for the summah, I'se s'pose."

"Well, it looks like we'll be seeing a lot of each other then," replied David. Throwing a box on the pile, he continued. "My name is David Wilson, and I work for Crawford's."

"I'se knows who yo' is."

David was shocked. "How do you know me?" he asked.

"My mama told me."

"Who are you and who is your mama?" Curiosity was beginning to get the best of David. He did not like people knowing about him and he knowing nothing about them.

"Well, my name is Toye Lee Johnson, and my mama's name is Allie Mae Johnson. She work at Lea's Café. She's the chief cook and bottle washa' . . . and she waits on the coloreds when they come to eat." Nigrahs, by law, had to enter the restaurant by the back door that was accessible from the alley.

The name was not familiar to David. He remembered seeing a nigrah woman at the back door of the café many times, usually taking a smoke break. His puzzled look prompted Toye to continue.

"She worked for yo' mama and daddy when yo' was first born." At that moment, Allie Mae stepped out the back door of the café to take a few drags on a cigarette. "There she is," he said, pointing toward his mother standing by the back door of the café. She gave a slight wave.

David immediately could see Toye Lee took his facial characteristics from his mother whom he resembled a lot. But his skin was considerably lighter.

That explained why David was not familiar with Toye Lee's mother because his mother had not had help in years, except occasional ironing jobs.

"You live around here, Toye Lee?" David asked.

"Ovah there, across the tracks." He pointed in the direction of the depot at the end of the business district, indicating the wooden shacks along the dirt road running parallel to the railroad tracks.

Coloreds could live in two places in Kirbyville. One was the place to which Toye Lee pointed. There were a few houses, a café, and some kind of two-story building referred to as the hotel. Most nigrahs lived in an area referred to as Tram Town or the nigrah Quarters, more commonly called the Quarters. It was located west of Kirbyville just outside the city limits, not qualifying the residents for city utilities, namely water. Each house had its own water well in the backyard, but no sanitary tests were conducted there. The Quarters had electricity provided by the REA, a rural electric cooperative; but many residents still used kerosene lamps, which were cheaper. The streets of the city were maintained by the city and were paved; but once over the city limits line, all streets became dirt, maintained by the county and were truly bad in rainy weather. Like a lot of the white's houses, the area was also characterized by outdoor toilets—"privies"—mostly two-holers. Anyone with a three-holer was considered extravagant. This never made sense to David anyway. Where do two people use the bathroom at the same time? The Quarters consisted of a couple of hundred residents living in ramshackle houses, a run-down schoolhouse, a café-store, and a building generally called Pete Parker's Place. Pete's was supposed to be a café and meeting place for the residents, but most of the whites suspected it was a place you could buy beer in a bone-dry county. Law officers never raided Pete's because they bought beer there also. David had never gone to Pete's, nor did he know of anyone who had. But every time he drove past it, he wondered about the blue lights and the music coming from its interior.

Toye Lee and his mother lived in one of the shacks along the railroad tracks on the east side of town.

"Your daddy live there too?" David asked.

"Naw. He dead." Toye replied without emotion. "He passed when I was a baby."

David had never had a conversation with a nigrah male before except as a customer in the store. Few came in except to buy medicine or pay their utility bills. That did not include the many that came in like Roy Cooper to get their week's supply of those items found in the drawer in the pharmacy. David didn't count them because the contact was so short. He knew more female coloreds because they worked in the homes of his white friends as domestics. Talking at length to a nigrah was a new experience for him, and he felt rather comfortable talking to a person of another color.

"You go to school?"

"Yeah, I'se guess yo' could say I'se does."

Toye's answer piqued David. "Why do you say that?"

"You evah been to West Kirbyville High?"

"No." David had seen it from the road but never had an occasion to go to the school. "Now, what would a white boy be doing in a nigrah school?"

"Yo's right! . . . Or a colored boy in Kirbyville High School?" he continued. "Well, the school's is in the Quartahs, and they's got no bus that run from my house to the schoolhouse," Toye Lee answered. He was referring to the fact that if the students who lived on the tracks wanted to attend school, they had to find their own transportation to the Quarters. There were no busses for colored students. And the most common way of getting there was about a thirty to forty-minute walk each morning. And that wasn't bad except of days when the weather was bad, and then students just stayed home. The other problem was having to go by the sawmill and be engulfed by smoke and covered with cinders from the burning slag pit. Whites had the same misfortune if they walked to school, only in the opposite direction The high school was almost directly across the railroad sidetracks from the mill. David had passed the sawmill many times on his way to see his grandmother and was quite familiar with the ashes and cinders that covered the city. Kirbyville had not yet entered into the period of clean environment.

"And then they's days the teachah's jus' don't show up or the roof leaks or not enough kids shows up and they just turn out for the day." Evidently, attendance was not as important to the colored school as it was at the white school.

West Kirbyville High was a product of the WPA days. It was a wooden building now in a great state of disrepair, and the paint on the walls had disappeared years ago. Teachers were often substandard—untrained—and teaching supplies almost nonexistent. It was a common practice to give textbooks, maps, mimeograph machines, and similar equipment and supplies, including library books, to West Kirbyville High when the in-use date expired or the equipment became obsolete at Kirbyville High. West Kirbyville High was legally supported by tax money, but since nigrahs paid little taxes, they got little in return.

Few students ever reached the twelfth grade in the nigrah school. Girls would drop out early to go to work as maids for local women get married, or to have babies—but not necessarily in that order. Some often moved to Beaumont or Houston seeking a better life than they could find in the Quarters. But the big cities overwhelmed them, and they came back and lived in poverty. By the time males reached eighteen, they, too, were long gone. Many would go to work as a pulper, cutting wood and taking it to Evadale to the paper mill. Some would go to work as manual laborers at Kirby Lumber Company located just up the road from the Quarters. If a person was really lucky, he would hightail it to Houston, join the army, and make a career of it. These were the ones who were most successful, although the U.S. military still practiced segregation there also. Joining the army was the dream of many of the nigrah youth.

"How old are you, Toye Lee?"

"Almost seventeen. Yo'?"

"I'll be eighteen later this summer. We're pretty close to being the same age," David replied. "Only a year apart."

"Right, old man."

"What grade are you in, Toye Lee?" asked David.

"I'se think I'se be called a jun'yah." Toye Lee seemed somewhat unsure of his status. "I'se don't know how many credits I'se got. Maybe not enough."

"I graduated last night in the gym. Planning on going to college next fall."

"I'se seen all them cars last night. Nevah been to no graduation," Toye Lee replied. "And prob'ly nevah will. Matter of fact, I'se don't know many people who graduated at all." It was if he might be predicting his future for colored students.

As David and Toye Lee went back and forth from their stores to the trash bin hauling trash, they made small talk or smiled or chuckled. Both seem to enjoy the company of the other.

"You into sports, Toye Lee?"

"As much as I'se can be." Toye Lee explained he played football and basketball. There ain't no real track program. "I'se play baseball in the summah."

"I figured as much by the looks of those muscles," David commented, pointing to Toye Lee's biceps. "Man, you are in good shape!"

"Dat's the only part of school I'se likes," Toye Lee added. "But yo' know, nothing's regular in sports at West Kirbyville. We doesn't have no real sports program . . . or schedule. We doesn't have no reg'lah coach. And the equipment is piss-po'. Yo' knows we's only gets the leftovahs from yo' school. We's in a district which may or may not play a game. And we's sho' don't have transpo'tation to the games."

David sort of held his head down in embarrassment. "I've always heard that . . . I don't really care for sports myself."

His reply aroused Toye. "Then why the hell do you go to school if yo' don't want to play spoa'ts?"

"I'd rather be involved in the academic and literary activities . . . Look at this body. Does this look like an athlete to you?" David mimicked a body builder in pose.

To this, Toye had a singular and exasperated reply, "Shit! That's sissy crap."

As they jostled each other, Toye Lee noticed the back door of Lea's Café open. From within, a woman stepped out again onto the back porch, still smoking another cigarette.

"Oh, that's my mama now." Toye Lee ran to see what she wanted.

The woman had motioned for him to come to the café. David looked up and gave a slight wave that she returned. Allie Mae Johnson was much younger than David's mother—probably in her early or middle thirties. She was darker than Toye but had his broad smile.

Lea's Café had two entrances. For whites, you could enter the front door from Main Street, and there were neat booths and chrome stools at the hardwood counter for the customers. Colored people had to go around the building at the end of the block and enter the rear through the alley. Facilities were not as nice, being the castoffs from the front dining room when it was remodeled. Allie Mae was the "chief cook and bottle washer" and the only waitress for the nigrah customers. She got to eat there free along with Toye Lee. Her pay was minimum, but it was a steady job, and with it she supported herself and Toye Lee. She was much better-off than most colored women. And they lived only three blocks from the café.

When Toye Lee returned, he was carrying two neatly wrapped packages. "Mama sent this to yo'," Toye Lee said, giving David one of them while displaying his broad infectious smile.

Inside the carefully wrapped packages were hamburgers with all the trimmings, still hot from the grill.

"She thought we might like an afternoon snack."

David was more than happy to take advantage of this pleasant gift. "Thanks, Toye Lee," he said. "And thanks to your mama." He turned to wave at Allie Mae, but she had retreated to the café.

As they wolfed down their hamburgers, Toye broke the silence. "I'se got a deal for yo'."

"What's that?" David asked.

"What yo' say we's meet here evah day so's we can have us a little rest break?" He continued. "Mama will get us some hamburgers or whatever is on the stove at the time. One of my jobs is to check the bruised fruit in the produce cooler and take it out if it looks too ripe. They's lots of still good fresh fruit that's throwed away evah day. Why not eat it instead?"

David was interested. Fresh fruit, even vegetables, sounded good to him. He, like all teenagers, had an insatiable appetite; and he was ready to strike a deal.

He hesitated. "But what can I contribute to the party?" he asked. He had neither food nor fruit. "We do have Pangburn's candies that we discard every once in a while like at Christmas, Valentines, and Easter. But I can't think of anything else . . . maybe some nuts."

Toye Lee looked at him, then grinned. "You can supply us with them 'thangs.'"

Perplexed and assuming that "thangs" were "things," David asked, "What things?"

"Them thangs in the draw' under the typewritah!"

David thought for a moment, and then it dawned on him. "Rubbers?" he exclaimed. "You mean those rubbers?" *How did he know where the rubbers were kept?* David thought. *Where there's a will, there's a way, I guess.*

"Yeah! Yo' got it!"

"But what in the name of heavens do we need rubbers for?"

Toye's reply was somewhat peeved, biting and incredulous. "Yo' dumb ass, what the hell do yo' think we's needs them for? We's goin' to blow them up and send them up as weathah balloons."

David felt and looked like a fool. *Why did I ask a stupid question like that?* he asked himself. In matters of sex, David was absolutely out of his element. The extent of sex was limited to a book he read in the ninth grade called *The Amboy Dukes* and the sex education he got from his biology book in high school. The school board had seen that the most graphic biology books were not adopted. Obviously, this was not a problem with Toye Lee who looked like a ladies' man.

"Okay! Okay! I forgot I was talking to a stud."

"Yo' right, brotha!" And with that answer, Toye Lee flashed the biggest and brightest smile David had ever seen. "And don't yo' forget it."

David regretted his naïveté. But Toye Lee could see right through him in such matters. And he understood David's predicament.

It was agreed. Toye Lee would provide the food, and David would provide the prophylactics. *How many would he need?* David only hoped no one saw him as he extracted a pack of condoms from the drawer from time to time. *Will this go on all summer?* he asked himself. And he presumed it would. He remembered an earlier time when he got some condoms for Glenn Michaels, a friend of his. Ben Crawford spotted him reading the labels on the boxes. He told his brother, and somehow Bessie found out about it, and David quickly developed an unearned reputation as a ladies' man. They kidded him for weeks after it happened. He was embarrassed every time they brought it up.

Standing there looking at Toye Lee, David suspected that Toye Lee was a real stud. He didn't bother to tell him that the condoms he got would be for Toye Lee only. What use did he have for them? David was still a virgin. He couldn't even get a date to the junior-senior banquet, so sex was not on his agenda. But those facts David decided to keep to himself.

The afternoon was quickly coming to an end, and the cleanup was complete. It was time to get back to the store, finish up his other chores, and get ready to head for home.

"Gotta go, now, Toye Lee," David said.

"Me too."

"See you tomorrow, I guess."

"Yo' bet." Toye Lee winked, which was followed by a big grin. "And don't forget . . . them thangs. I'se can use them as soon as I'se can get them."

As David was moving toward the store, he told Toye Lee, "I'll see you later. Guess I'll see you all summer. Do you like movies?"

Toye Lee nodded and made his way back to the grocery store.

"Damn and double damn!" David muttered to himself as he entered the store and closed the door behind him.

David had a routine he followed each day before going home. *What a creature of habit I am*, he would chide himself. Every day the same. Every day. Then he would remind himself that that would be a very good practice when he went to the university. If he could get his study habits down to such a routine, he would have no problems. Besides, he kept telling himself, it sure makes the job easier the next day.

He prepared a can of oiled sawdust to be spread on the floor the next day. He emptied the waste baskets, careful not to get any of the discarded pharmaceuticals on his hand. And finally he checked the bottles and pill containers in the pharmacy to make sure there were plenty for tomorrow. And it wasn't coincidental that his eyes glanced across the typewriter and the drawer that was below it. The condoms were there waiting for him. *Not yet*, he said to himself.

This had been a long day for David despite the busy daily work activities. First, of course, there had been the excitement of the graduation ceremonies the night before. Then the intimidation and embarrassment brought about by Dee Dee Grimes. And finally, the afternoon visit with Toye Lee Johnson. That was a new experience for him. Never before in his life, as far as he could remember, had he engaged in a plain conversation with a nigrah. David had played with some nigrah children when he was a child, but that was a long time ago. He wasn't sure what he would talk about when he met one. It wasn't as bad as he thought it would have been. *And I think I might come to really like Toye Lee*, he told himself. *Just don't break the code—or at least, don't get caught.* That sounded like a challenge.

If you came to work at seven, you could leave at five. Bessie insisted on coming at eight o'clock, so she stayed until six. And this was perfectly all right with David, who was an early riser.

"Bye, Bessie,' he yelled as he headed toward the front door. "And thanks for trying to save my butt this morning from Dee Dee,"

Bessie waved. "Bye, honey, it was the least I could do. We'll see you tomorrow.

"Bye, Mr. Crawford."

"So long, Mr. Honor Graduate!" Mr. Crawford answered. He had a real knack of making you feel good, and David left with a chest of pride.

Chapter Three

David was in no particular hurry to get home, so he decided to stop along the way and maybe even have a Cherry Coke at Newton's Drugstore. First, however, he would run next door to the post office, get the mail, and speak to Miss Bell, the postmistress. A female postmaster was considered unusual by many people; but Miss Bell, an old maid, and her family had been government employees for so many years no one in Kirbyville gave it a second thought. Miss Bell was another one of those institutions that made the town unique.

Miss Bell was at the customer window and spotted him immediately. "Congratulations, David."

"Thanks, Miss Bell," he replied.

"Here's a little something for one of my favorite friends." She handed him an envelope, obviously a greeting card. "Best wishes on college. You will do well."

David was really surprised by the gift, and he surmised that since it was a card, there was probably money in it. *More money for my bank account*, he thought.

There was no mail other than an advertising flyer, which promptly found its way into the trash can in the lobby. As he left the post office, he noticed that Dan Compton was changing the billboards of the coming movies at the Palace across the street. David didn't really care to go to the picture tonight—Mondays and Tuesdays were days when the Westerns were shown, and he had never been a fan of Roy

Rogers. In fact, he was past those Gene Autry—Smiley Burnette—Lash LaRue—Bob Steele days. But he was curious about the coming movies. The bill of fare for later in the week looked pretty good with Lucille Ball and William Holden in *Miss Grant Takes Richmond* at the Owl Show Saturday night and Spencer Tracy and Jimmy Stewart in *Malaya* showing next week.

As he proceeded up the street, he noticed that there were still some old-timers sitting on the hookworm bench. In Kirbyville you went "up" the street to the red light and "down" the street to the depot.

"How you fellers doing?" he yelled at the whittlers. David saw some of them beginning to close their knives. They, too, were beginning to hear the call of suppertime.

They waved as he walked by.

Newton's Drugstore was always a gathering place for the young people. It was second only to the Quack Shack, a weekly dance club for teenagers, in popularity. It had no pharmacy but did have a good fountain—the only one in town—and a jukebox. Most of the school students came by during the day after school. David looked through the window to make sure Dee Dee Grimes was not inside, planning to go home if she was. But she wasn't in sight, so he decided to stop.

"Give me a Cherry Coke, please," he yelled to Miz Mabel, the attendant who was working the counter that day, as he sat down at one of the small marble toptables. "Put a dip of vanilla ice cream in it, please."

Miz Mabel was very accommodating, and within minutes, David was swigging on the best drink in town. What a marvelous effect a drink can have when you are tired and your throat is dry. He nursed his drink like it was a vintage and expensive wine.

Miz Mabel was another legend in Kirbyville. A middle-aged widow, she had raised three children and now was waiting for the end of her life. She always spoke to David and truly acted like she was interested in his activities. She reminded David of the hostess of a saloon in a Western movie. Always there with a heart of gold. And he could see that heart of gold beyond all her miseries. But the lines across her parchmentlike face told of her life and disappointments—the Depression, war, marriage, and booze. *What a woman!*

"Ready to leave, David?" she asked.

"In September," he replied.

"Well, the best of luck and have a good time. Come back to see me."

"Miz Mabel, you know I will. This town wouldn't be Kirbyville without you."

"You better."

No much going on here, he discovered. The only action was around the jukebox where some junior high kids—loaded with nickels—were playing a round-robin medley of "Chattanooga Shoe Shine Boy" then "If I Knew You Were Coming, I'd Baked a Cake," which then changed to "Music! Music! Music!" and ended with "Rag Mop." The music was loud and so were the teenagers.

This is driving me crazy, he told himself. Gotta get out of here. So with one last gulp, he finished his Coke and headed home.

David's home was four blocks past the red light and one block north on Harris Street. It was a small bungalow-style house built in the 1930s. His parents had bought this place shortly after their marriage with the help of his mother's father, Judge David Wingate. It was the intention of his parents to sell this house in a few years and move to a bigger and nicer place on some tree-lined street in a good neighborhood, but as time passed, that idea became more and more remote and finally forgotten. Caroline still dreamed of a new house. The house would be ready for a paint job in another season or two; but David's dad, Tom, avoided committing himself to a specific date. The yard was large for a small house, and it was David's chore to keep it mowed with a push lawn mower, one of his least favorite activities. David's grandfather had planted some fig, plum, and pear trees in the backyard; and in season, they bore fruit profusely. At one time there was a small garden in a corner but no longer in use. The grass had covered the rows and mounds, and mowing was a real problem. David's mother no longer canned vegetables or preserved fruit. It would have been economical for them, but when her interest waned and she finally stopped, no one really cared anymore and her canning days were over.

David entered the house and yelled at the same time, "Mother! It's me. I'm home!"

A voice from within answered, "Hi, honey! I'm in the kitchen. Come on back."

"Hi," he replied.

David strode across the kitchen and gave her a peck on the cheek that she had turned toward him. He often felt foolish doing this, thinking that he was too old to play this little pecking game, but his mother insisted on being kissed at every greeting and departure. And it was easier to do than to cause a commotion and hurt her feelings, which he would never do. At he same time, he was scanning the room to see if he could locate the cookie jar. He couldn't find it.

Rebecca Caroline Wingate Wilson was a striking woman—in her own way—in spite of her tousled hair and being up to her elbows in lard and flour.

"I was working on dinner when your father called to let me know he would be late tonight," Caroline told David.

"Why?" David asked. Coming home late was not unusual for Tom Wilson.

"Some equipment broke at the planer, and it had to be fixed before work tomorrow. He shouldn't be too late."

And then with a sort of acknowledging smile, she added, "And no, we have no cookies in the house." She was aware of his subtle search around the room. "But I'm making some now, and they'll be ready in a few minutes."

"Great!" was David's only reply. He smelled the aroma of the baking cookies coming from the oven. His favorites were Grandma Wingate's old-fashioned tea cookies. Caroline used a family recipe, and nothing was better than tea cookies and a glass of milk. Every cook in East Texas had his/her version of tea cookies. That went along with other customs in East Texas of swapping recipes.

At forty-six, Caroline was older than the mothers of other students in David's class. Few people remembered she had a child in school ten years ago. It was hard to distinguish the gray hairs from the flour in her head, but she definitely was turning gray. Her friends told her a trip to Middleton's Beauty Shop would made her look years younger. Caroline rejected the suggestions, claiming that coloring one's hair was deceptive and against nature—even God. She preferred the natural look even though it made her look older. She was the only daughter of Judge David Wingate, a former local Justice of the Peace and the person for whom she named her son. Caroline had been named after her father's grandmother, Caroline, and adamantly insisted on being called Caroline. And never Carrie. Even her husband, Tom, was told never to call her Carrie. She hated nicknames and was determined that David would never become Davey or Dave or any other cutesy variation of that name. She relented later and let Tom use the name of Dave, but no one else.

You couldn't call Caroline a beautiful woman. If the poet or novelist had to write a description, they would say "stately" or "eloquent" or perhaps a "woman of character" or "distinguished," but not beautiful. She would be a perfect model for any artist who was creating a picture of a pioneer woman looking westward. She was steadfast and enduring. Many people saw "reliability" as her greatest characteristic. Or "perseverance." She had always been a frail person since early childhood. And that frailty had given way to the lines that had begun to inch their paths across her face. Caroline had a wounded look in her blue eyes, like she had missed something along the way and was hoping to get it back. Often, without being aware of it, she seemed to leave reality and drift away to some place in another world or another time. And her eyes would moisten a bit. It had been very noticeable to Tom and David since "the accident."

Caroline had enrolled in the Kirbyville school system in 1909 and concluded her student days in 1920, being named valedictorian of the class of 1920. She was not a popular girl in school, but she commanded the respect of all her classmates. If they wanted the answers to questions and problems, they knew they could go to Caroline for the answers. That help was not called cheating. Instead it was referred to as "helping each other," and it was a way for Caroline to be included in the female students' social circle. She had been active in all literary activities, honor society and was named by her classmates as the Most Likely to Succeed. She had not begun to date yet, probably because of her parents. Any contact with a boy had to go through Judge and Mrs. Wingate, along with an examination. To boys, it was not worth it.

To her it was not a matter of going to college. The question was which one and what major? Medicine? Business? Law? Education? Academics? To heck with tradition. The choice was hers. Her ability and education had opened vistas to her that very few women enjoyed. She was encouraged by her father, the judge, who, failing to have a son, gave Caroline all the fatherly attention and advice he would have given a boy—one of which was to stand up and not be intimidated.

Caroline enrolled in Stephen F. Austin State Teachers College in the fall of 1920. Most of her daylight hours were spent in the classroom or the library. Her social life was limited, not by choice, perhaps, but more likely because she gave the appearance of an intellectual Iron Maiden. She had suffered this "curse" in high school, and when she found it difficult to relate to males, she retreated to the academics. Basically, boys were afraid to ask her out, generally fearing of getting an encyclopedia rather than a date.

That is, until she met Tom Wilson. He was also an earlier graduate of Kirbyville High School class of 1918 and unquestionably the greatest athlete to graduate from that school. In those days, he led both football and basketball teams to the state play-offs, a feat never accomplished before his graduation. His fans followed him like a film celebrity. And there were so many would-be girlfriends, some people jokingly referred to them as his harem. It was an assumed fact that he could have any female he desired. The residents of Kirbyville looked at him as the town's greatest hero—their Jim Thorpe.

To say Tom Wilson was good-looking was an understatement. He was like a Greek god and sometimes acted like one. Girls, in one word, simply called him "gorgeous." His six-foot-plus frame could move like a poem in motion. His blonde hair and dark blue eyes attracted looks from anyone who passed him. His muscles rippled in tandem as he moved his body in any direction. His attraction even extended to older women who had to hide their feelings but couldn't.

But why would a big high school and college football and basketball hero give any attention to a lowly freshman? She didn't exist in his universe until she entered Stephen F. Austin State College and their paths happened to cross. And then it was quite by accident.

They were both sitting at a study table in the main library one evening—she studying for a test and he checking the parade of females and reading a sports magazine. It would be a lie that say she didn't notice him. Not when every girl in the library came by and spoke to or batted their eyes at him. She brushed it off as wishful thinking knowing her luck with the opposite sex. Potential boyfriends seemed to sense her dislike for the intellectual capacity of jocks.

Then he noticed a copy of the *Kirbyville Banner* lying on her books.

"Where'd you get that?" he asked, pointing at the paper.

"It's my hometown newspaper," she replied.

"You're from Kirbyville?"

"Yes, I am."

"What class?"

"Class of 1920," she answered.

"That's my hometown too!" Tom was beginning to get interested. "I graduated in 1918." He moved his chair closer. "What is your name?"

"Caroline Wingate."

"The judge's daughter?"

Caroline nodded. "Granddaughter." She was surprised he was familiar with her grandfather's name.

"My name is Tom Wilson, and I'm on the football squad."

"Oh!" she replied. She didn't dare look like those other drooling females, but she had been one those girls in high school and college who swooned over him like all the others. She told herself to remain calm as her heart beat frantically and her face turned pink.

After that, Caroline and Tom were inseparable. She would attend his practice sessions and never miss a game. He got tickets that put her on the fifty-yard line directly behind the lumberjack bench so even during a game, she was always there. She was his date to every school dance and pep rally. And just being with him made her the envy of every girl on campus. She loved the belated attention she was now getting.

And the big question around the campus on everyone's mind and, for the females, the universal questions were "How did she snag him?" or "What's she got that I don't have?" For the males, the puzzle seemed to be "What does he see in her when he could have anybody on this campus?" They were interesting questions that seemed to have no answers. Tom and Caroline could care less about what others were saying. It was a unique relationship that people had yet to figure out. It was a strange relationship but one which seem to have a solid foundation.

Being a consort of Caroline Wingate did not hurt Tom either. First, she was the judge's granddaughter and that added a little class. As a male, he was flattered by Caroline's hanging on every word he uttered and the attention she paid him. She filled a certain void in his life that he had missed somewhere along the way. That was her intellectual character and her studiousness. He came to rely on her steadfast presence. It was so unlike the frivolous behavior of the many lightweights or butterfly beauties he had known before he met Caroline. Best of all was her willingness to help him with his studies. Secretly, she wrote and typed his papers and insisted he spend time in the library. They never admitted to the fact, but most people suspected she kept him eligible during the football season. The coaches surely did not object to his dating a brain. Caroline couldn't take his test, of course, but she prepped him for test using his somewhat-skimpy notes along with her own knowledge of the subject. Caroline had a problem deciding what a physical education major was supposed to know. From her experiences in high school, they did not know much of anything—except football plays and football statistics.

On many occasions, Tom would throw up his arms in exasperation. "I just can't do it!" he'd yelled.

And Caroline, in her own stern and calm way, answered, "If you can learn those football plays in that play-diagram book, you can learn math and English as well." And they would start again. Whatever the techniques used, Tom's grades improved drastically; and with the records he was setting in the conference, he was a shoo-in for all-conference and possibly small college all-America. That would be his ticket to a good job in some business owned by a lumberjack football fan alumnus, and he would settle down into a comfortable life in a large town—maybe Dallas or Houston.

More and more there was talk of marriage immediately after graduation or perhaps the end of the football season. Tom gave Caroline a diamond engagement at the beginning of the football season. And being students without employment and sources of income, the response of those whom they showed it to was a subdued "Oh, isn't it sweet!" The conversation quickly ended, and the admirer was on his or her way. But Caroline was as proud of that ring as much as she would have been if it had come from the maharajah of Bangalore.

The dream came to an end in the third quarter of the Sam Houston College game when Tom was gang-tackled, resulting in a broken hip and fractured leg. That ended the season for him as well as his football and sports career. With the loss of his scholarship, Tom withdrew from school in the spring and returned to Kirbyville to face the many disappointed residents.

The injury turned out to be permanent and resulted in a slight, but detectable, limp which he carried with him the rest of his life. At first, life was miserable for him; but he was offered a job as section boss in the planer division—that turned rough boards into smooth lumber—of Kirby Lumber Company, and the wounds and disappointments of his misfortune became less acute and finally disappeared.

The experience was equally painful for Caroline. She was miserable without Tom on the campus. She was no longer welcomed without Tom. Her mind began to wander frequently, and her interest in school and maintaining high grades also dissipated.

She completed the semester, but on her next visit to her parents, she made her startling announcement. "I will not be returning to school next semester," she announced without hesitation. "I no longer have any interest in college."

Her parents were aghast but had long suspected that it would end this way. They had trouble in accepting the closing of her college career. Her parents had such high hopes for her future.

———

"I'm just wasting your money and my time to continue," she tried to explain to her parents, "especially the way I feel now."

She saw the disappointment on her parents' faces but knew they would support her whatever her decision was. Knowing this, Caroline made another announcement. "Tom and I are engaged and plan to marry as soon as we can make the necessary arrangements!"

Judge and Mrs. Wingate had nothing against Tom. In fact, they liked him a lot although they had hoped Caroline would have finished college and then had met and married someone else—someone new from another town. All families needed new blood. Wasn't that the purpose of sending a daughter off to college?

Tom would have preferred eloping and getting married by the Justice of Peace in Merryville, Louisiana. "No waiting and two bucks," he assured Caroline. "An hour and half from here!"

But Caroline had promised her folks that she would have a church wedding with all the trimmings. She was very conscious that weddings were as much for parents as for the bridal couple, possibly even more. Her daddy was not to be deprived from showing off his little girl, his daughter—now bride—to the community and his new son-in-law. Mrs. Wingate insisted on going the full course—showers, lunches, bridal parties, and everything else connected with a wedding. She was so hopeful Caroline would ask to wear the same wedding dress that Mrs. Wingate and her mother had been married in. Caroline did.

The *Kirbyville Banner* described it as the "wedding of the decade." And it was, indeed, something that the guests would remember for years to come. The First Baptist Church sanctuary was packed with people as the invitation was extended through the paper, the church, and the mail. The church sanctuary was adorned with cascades of beautiful white stephanotis, gladioli, and long-stemmed roses; the attendants looked resplendent in their matching peachy attire; the parents glowed with pride—first with their daughter and second knowing they had pulled off the social *coup* of the year. Even Caroline, plain as she was, looked radiant and was most gracious to the compliments she received, especially for the three-generation wedding dress she wore. For once, her reservedness gave way to nuptial giddiness and true happiness. She was so in love.

The couple honeymooned in Galveston, staying at the Galvez Hotel along the beach. Though short, they took advantage of the three days as fully as they could, especially enjoying the shrimp which was always a delicacy to a Southeast Texas resident and hard to get in Kirbyville. They were tempted to go to the Balinese Room, but resources and good sense limited them from going to the gambling casino operated by the Maceo brothers—suspected of being part of the Mafia.

Tom swam in the surf, still turning heads on the beach as he ran into and out of the waves. Caroline wouldn't go near the water, but waved from the hot sand and her umbrella. She noticed the attention Tom was getting but reminded herself not to worry. *He belongs to me, so hands off.* She tried to immerse herself in a book, but she was more interested in preventing getting sunburned and the glances of the onlookers.

Within weeks after their return to Kirbyville, the young couple had made arrangements with Mr. Conn, president of the bank, to secure a loan to buy their first home. Judge Wingate had guaranteed payment should they default on their mortgage, and from time to time, he also would make extra payments in order to pay it off quicker. The judge also helped them pay for their first furniture.

"Eight hundred and fifty dollars!" exclaimed Tom. "We got a real deal on this house." He sounded like he had made the bargain of the century.

Caroline was equally proud of the house on Harris Street. It was painted white with a brown roof and was a bungalow-style so common in the 1930s. Two bedrooms, a living room and separate dining room, plenty of closets, a big back porch, and a kitchen with a pantry that was as nice as any in town. And perhaps best of all: running water and indoor plumbing. She was an immaculate housekeeper and was learning to become a good cook, thanks to the six cookbooks she got as wedding presents.

"I think this batch is just about ready," Caroline announced, referring to the cookies she had been preparing. She no longer had to use those cookbooks to make cookies. She had memorized the recipe after years of practice.

—

"They smell wonderful," David added. He moved to help himself to the tea cookies.

"Ice tea or milk?" she asked. "Watch out, they're hot!"

"Milk. I'll have tea for supper."

It was a pleasant scene. She baked old-fashioned tea cookies and showered him with the kind of affection that only a mother could give. And the son appreciated her efforts by letting her have her way, which she would have done anyway despite his objections.

"All right," David said abruptly, shattering the domestic reverie. "Time for your test."

Caroline was well aware of what was coming. Almost daily, David would test his mother on current events. She was supposed to report what was going on in the world and who was who. David didn't know how she did it because he never saw her read a newspaper or magazine or listen to the radio, but Caroline always was well-informed about national news. And it was a way for David to catch up on the news as well without reading the newspaper himself.

"Oh, great Queen of the World News," he jested, "what great things hast thou heard today?"

Bowing deeply to the Great Inquisitor and pausing momentarily, Caroline began her discourse on the current world scene.

"President Truman played the piano at Mrs. Mitchell's party in Washington today. And it more and more looks like General Eisenhower will be drafted to run against President Truman. Three senators in Washington are hogging the headlines. They are Senators Kefauver, Morse, and McCarthy."

Caroline hesitated a moment and added, "And a man by the name of Nixon won the nomination for Senate in California. He's running against some woman. Poor man, looks like he needs a shave. And he has shifty-looking eyes." She searched her memory for other events. "Queen Mary celebrated her eighty-third birthday. Nash Auto Company reveals its new models, and Kaiser introduced a new concept in automobiles. A rocket reaches the height of 106 miles after being launched from a ship, and there is a communist uprising in Southeast Asia." She stopped her news review momentarily by adding, "I don't really know what communists are and why we are concerned with them in Asia. We just got out of Asia—at least the Pacific. We surely don't need to get involved there again."

In the style of Luella Parsons or Hedda Hopper, Caroline proceeded with the news. "And now the latest news from Hollywood . . ." Caroline always added filmdom tidbits because she knew David was such a movie fan. "Elizabeth Taylor marries Nicky Hilton, son of a wealthy hotel owner. Claudette Colbert is voted most popular star in Hollywood. Ava Gardner, Frank Sinatra, and bullfighter Mario Cabré are making headlines in Tinseltown. And Ingrid Bergman and Robert Rossellini introduced their new son in Rome."

Running out of news, Caroline concluded her report by adding, "And that, Mr. and Mrs. America and all the ships at sea, ends today's world report.

"Aha!" David exclaimed. "You forgot sports," he immediately reminded her, hoping he had stumped her on sports items.

Caroline hastened to amend her report. "Pancho Segura beat Jack Kramer in a tennis match as Gussie Moran paraded around in lace panties. And the Boston Red Sox beat the St. Louis Browns 29-4 in a game which went over seven hours. Finally, Citation won the Golden Gate Handicap . . . There! Are you satisfied now?"

David was utterly amazed by his mother's ability to recite current events. Especially the sports news since she never cared about sports. "You win again," he announced, yielding to the extensive knowledge his mother displayed. "I wish I could retain information that easily when I'm at the university. It would be great for tests."

"Just concentrate. I'm not worried about your studies," she replied. "You will do well. You got good study habits in high school."

She never told David about it, but sometimes Caroline secretly wished she had finished college with a degree in history and social science. Often, she thought how nice it would be to teach social studies in the local school. That secret dream would never be fulfilled. Caroline turned to continue her preparation of supper, and David reached for another cookie when the thought suddenly occurred to him.

"Mother, I met a person today who said he knew you, at least, his mother knew you.

"Who was that, honey?" she asked. Caroline continued stirring her pots, adding spices, and moving the pots around on the stove.

"His name is Toye Lee Johnson, and he works at Parsons'.."

Caroline stopped for a moment to listen to David and then continued her cooking.

David proceeded to tell of his discovery. "He's colored and he started working today. I talked with him on the loading dock, and we put out trash together."

Caroline slowly turned around, her eyes indicating an inward search for the identity of Toye Lee Johnson. "I just can't seem to place him, honey."

"Well, he said his mama worked for you when I was a baby." David was trying to help jog her memory. "She works at Lea's Café in the back. Allie Mae? Allie Mae Johnson?"

Caroline had never had help. They couldn't afford it. And being seventeen years ago, the name just didn't ring a bell. "Just can't place her."

She started to turn toward the stove again but hesitated and then looked David straight in the eye. "Wait a minute," she said slowly as if she were getting a signal. "There was a young girl your father hired to keep you when I was in the hospital. She stayed here at the house until I came home. Mama and Papa stayed during the day, but she kept you during the night."

David saw something that he had never witnessed before. Although she was looking directly at him, Caroline was gazing past him, miles past him as if into another world. It was a vacant look into a world of emptiness. It was as if she were trying to put pieces of a puzzle together in her mind but not succeeding.

"And I think her name was Allie Mae Johnson. Slim? Good bit younger than me?" She was searching. "Must have been fifteen or sixteen at the time."

David nodded. "I saw her behind Lea's today. She looks to be about early thirties." He wondered. *Could this be the same woman that he saw today?* "But if she was Allie Mae Johnson then and Allie Mae Johnson today, why didn't she change her name? Toye Lee's name is Johnson too."

Caroline, trying to solve the mystery, replied in nigrah dialect a phrase she had heard all her life from the coloreds, "Honey, we's jus' takes up and don't botha' to find a preacha'."

"Toye Lee said his daddy was dead," he insisted.

Caroline only shrugged.

The conversation had triggered memories of a time she had long suppressed and never wished to recall. But now they were all being revived and being brought right into her kitchen in front of her son. It was "the accident" all over again. And how she tried to forget it over and over. The events of the past had come back to haunt her once more. Caroline stood there as she recalled those earlier years.

Not long after she and Tom were married, Caroline discovered she was pregnant. A mother at the age of twenty-one! She could handle it. Tom had a job. They had a new home. She was learning how to cook. Why not? She needed something to keep her busy now.

She went to old Dr. McKinnon as all expectant mothers were supposed to do. Get weighed and examined. Obtained literature on prenatal and postnatal care. Being a novice to motherhood, she had to rely on others with more experience than she had.

Dr. McKinnon, already in his sixties, had been the company doctor at the sawmill but had resigned and opened an office above the drugstore. He was your only choice, and his only nurse Lola took care of relatively minor cases. At night and on the weekends, he would see patients at his home on Main Street, the largest home in town.

The examination over, the doctor left the examination room but returned when Caroline had redressed. He was concerned. You could tell by the expression on his face.

"Caroline, I have cared for you since you were in grade school. Your daddy and I were good friends for years. I am familiar with your medical history."

She nodded in agreement. And she suspected he was about to say something to her which may not be pleasant.

The doctor continued. "You have never been a healthy girl. We've had some scrapes in years past. I can't reverse your pregnancy, but I have to warn you that there might be some real problems during your pregnancy. Your body is not strong enough to carry a baby well."

Without hesitation, Caroline assured the doctor she would be very attentive to her condition. "I want this baby more than anything in the world. And I will have it whatever happens."

"Wingate stubbornness in you," he added. "Just like your daddy. Don't worry, we'll work it out. But you will have to obey my instructions carefully."

She nodded. "As always."

Nothing more was said by either person. Caroline hastened home to tell Tom the good news.

Tom Wilson was ecstatic at the prospect of becoming a father. There was no doubt it would be a son. In his mind he saw a father-son combination in every sports activity they undertook. "He'll be Kirbyville's greatest athlete, replacing the king himself," he said, chuckling at his own abdication.

On hearing the news, he promptly went to a closet and found an old football and basketball now deflated with age.

"But what if it's a girl?" asked Caroline.

"Boys always come first in the Wilson family," he paused a moment. "But if not, *she* will be the greatest girl athlete in the history of KHS and we shall reign as king and queen! Basketball, volleyball, softball, track." The list seemed endless. "But let's talk only about boys from now on."

Caroline so wanted to please Tom. She was as devoted to him as ever, and she prayed for a boy at every opportunity. She bought boy's outfits in a way to tempt Mother Nature. The discomfort and pain she suffered were far overshadowed by the excitement and anxiety of her husband's desire for a child. This knowledge sustained her during those difficult months waiting for her baby.

The pregnancy was not as bad as Dr. McKinnon had dreaded. The delivery was another story.

The baby was late. When notified that she was ready, Dr. McKinnon came to the Wilson home, prepared to stay until the delivery—all night, if necessary. He called his midwife-assistant to meet him there. The doctor didn't like inducing labor, but considering how large Caroline had become and how frail she was, he thought about it. He preferred natural birth procedures. He was used to those little ones just popping out when they were ready. The bed and bedroom of the patient were no place for complications.

He was spared early inducement when Caroline finally went into labor. She was in labor for almost twenty-four hours—too late for a caesarean section. Caroline pushed and pushed, but the little head would not move. The sweat from her body soaked into the bedsheets, which had to be replaced.

"I think you'll have to use forceps, Doctor," the midwife said.

You could tell by the grimace on her face that Caroline had intense pain. But she made no outcries—only some muffled grunts and contortions.

"Give me another push, Caroline," the doctor begged, hoping to avoid the use of forceps.

Caroline complied. There was a slight movement. Then another and another.

"It's coming, Doctor," reported the midwife.

Caroline gave one last push, and the newborn arrived as if nothing had happened.

Dr. McKinnon thrust the baby into the midwife's arm as he noticed fresh blood spurting from Caroline's body. "She's hemorrhaging!" he exclaimed. The doctor worked on the new mother for two hours. Little was said between him and the midwife as they worked to stop the bleeding. The baby had been put aside when the emergency started.

"She's stopped . . . finally," he announced. He patted an exhausted Caroline on the head gently. "Go to sleep, honey." Dr. McKinnon arranged her head to make her more comfortable. "We're out of the woods." The doctor wiped his brow. This might have been his most difficulty delivery—certainly one of the most important. He sat down in a rocking chair, prepared to stay until he was sure Caroline was all right. "Wonder if I could get a cup of coffee?" he asked.

The midwife moved toward the kitchen.

"No," the doctor responded. "Clean that baby up and show him to his daddy . . . Then get my coffee."

Tom was right. It was a boy—nine pounds, thirteen ounces, and twenty-two inches long. And the doctor commented, "It is one of healthiest babies I have ever delivered!"

You would know it when you heard him squall. What lungs! His cries filled the house.

"Signs of a natural-born leader!" Tom remarked.

Tom and Caroline had never seriously discussed a name for their new son. They had been more concerned with her health and the problems of delivery. When the doctor asked the name of the new one for the birth certificate, without hesitation, Tom proudly announced, "Thomas Autrey Wilson. Autrey was my mother's maiden name."

Caroline was taken aback. "I didn't think we had decided on a name yet," she said.

"But, honey, all the first sons in my family are named Thomas Wilson. Just like I was . . . and my dad . . . and his dad . . ."

Deep down, Caroline was immensely disappointed. First, because she had not been consulted by Tom. Second, she hoped that her firstborn would be named after her father, the judge. Especially since he had been so helpful to them in getting started in their married life.

But she yielded, as usual, and the doctor penned the name on the certificate. She couldn't deny her husband at possibly the greatest moment of his life. And Thomas is a traditional name, she kept telling herself.

As much as Caroline disliked nicknames, the baby became Tommy almost immediately, and later he was called Little Tom by everyone—except his mother. Little Tommy was Big Tom's baby—his pride and joy! To Caroline, Tom acted like his son was his sole possession, but she ignored it by telling herself it was only fatherly pride and ego. Tom took over his upbringing within days of his birth. That is, the carrying him around and showing him off and playing games. Already Tom had bought a baseball and bat. But when it came to diapering, bathing, and feeding him, he was Caroline's child. She loved such things but would say to herself, under her breath, "Typical male!"

CHAPTER FOUR

From the first day you could instantly tell who the child looked like. His father would never be able to deny whose child he was—even if he wanted to. Tommy had the physique and good looks of his father even at this early age. And with that physique, Tom prepared to groom young Tommy to be the greatest athlete to ever come out of Kirbyville, Texas—maybe the state itself.

Tommy had every kind of ball and equipment available at the time. And uniforms to match. There were none of the traditional toys like trucks, tricycles, and planes. Tom never bought books, puzzles, or educational toys. Caroline tried to, but they "mysteriously" disappeared. She also tried to set aside a time each day to read to Tommy, but somehow one thing or another seemed to get in the way and interrupt this activity.

"Honey, I don't think we need all these sports items," Caroline protested. "He outgrows the uniforms so quickly. His room is cluttered already." She especially was displeased with the sports posters which adorned each wall in Tommy's room. "And our budget can't include all these things . . . every month. Honey, we have to be more prudent with our money."

But budget was the last thing on Tom's mind when Tommy was concerned, and consequently Tommy's collection continued to grow.

There was the incident about the pets. "Every boy needs a horse and a dog," Tom announced one day to Caroline.

"Where would we put a horse?" Caroline asked incredulously. "And what kind of dog, pray tell?"

"I've already asked your daddy if we could stable a horse at his farm and he said yes," Tom answered with a smirk. "And what kind of dog do you think? . . . A hunting dog!"

Again, Caroline could only protest. But Tom had already made a deal on a horse. And in a few days, he brought home a young pup that had all the makings of a squirrel dog.

"Look at that pup," he said. "Isn't he the prettiest thing you ever saw? His mama was a good hunter." He scratched the underside of the black puppy, which had rolled over and was enjoying the petting. "I think I'll call you Nubbin."

"Nubbin?" Caroline asked. "What kind of name is that?" She bit her lip secretly but maintained her silence. *What good would it do anyway*, she asked herself. *His mind was already made up.*

The Wilson family expanded with the addition of a black dog of mixed origin, which was supposed to be Tommy's companion and the best squirrel dog in the county.

By the time Tommy entered school, his athletic reputation around town was already being established. He was enrolled in every sports activity that the city sponsored. Everyone wanted him for his team, but Tom guided him to the ones that had the best chance of winning. The town was already looking forward to Tommy reaching high school and possibly the state championships. He had physically matured far beyond any other child of his age, and his athletic future looked bright. Tom was not exactly standing on the sidelines those years either. He pushed Tommy hard to excel in everything.

Between the time of school opening and Christmas, Tom became more and more assertive. He made all decisions affecting Tommy by himself, without consulting Caroline. These ranged from his general purchase of clothing—only masculine outfits—to whose parties and what activities he would attend. "No fancy outfits for my boy," he reminded Caroline. "And no dances!"

At first, Caroline was reluctant to say anything because her decisions and opinions tended to be somewhat minor. But as the fall progressed, with her abstention, Tom became more and more dominant. The issue came to a crisis on Christmas Day, a few months before Tommy's seventh birthday. Santa Claus had arrived and departed the previous evening. Under the Christmas tree in the living room was a pile of neatly wrapped packages. Caroline and Tom were in the kitchen having a cup of coffee, waiting for Tommy to wake up and open his gifts—to see what Santa brought him.

Things were going well for Tom at the mill, and the bonus check Tom received would permit them to buy a few extra presents. And also, Caroline thought, to pay off some bills if she could get her hands on it first. Since Tommy's birth, Tom had taken more control of the family finances.

"Merry Christmas, sweetheart," Tom whispered, reaching across the table and gently touching her on the arm.

"And to you too, honey," she responded.

"This has been a good year for us. Your health is good. Our furniture paid off. Looks like I'll make section foreman sometime this year. Tommy's doing well in school. This year has been a good year for the mill, and next year promises to be better."

Caroline agreed. She still thought Tommy was given too many liberties and not enough responsibilities. He wasn't the top student in his class as she would have preferred, but she had come to live with the arrangement and complained about it only to herself.

"I think he's up," Tom announced abruptly. "Let's go in the living room."

Tommy was indeed up and in the living room before his parents arose from the table. They could hear him tearing paper as he opened his presents. All presents, that is, except the one in the corner, partially hidden by the Christmas tree.

Tommy was admiring all the things that Santa had brought to him when his dad exclaimed, "What's that present over there in the corner." Tommy had overlooked that one in his excitement to open those more accessible. And reaching behind the tree, Tommy retrieved the last present, which was in a long and narrow box.

Even Caroline was curious about this one because Tom had not mentioned another present to her. She had not noticed it, nor had she had anything to do with its presence under the tree.

"Honey, where did . . ." she didn't complete her question.

"Shhhhhhhh." Tom placed his finger across his lips. "Looks terribly important, son," he added.

Tom was bursting with pride and could hardly wait for Tommy to unwrap the gift.

When the paper finally fell from the box, Tommy shouted with jubilation. "Wow!" he shouted. "A Red Rider automatic pump BB gun!" He never looked more excited or happier in his life than the moment he held the gun in a firing position and pointed to an imaginary target.

Tom, acting like another child, shared his joy and excitement.

The expression on Caroline's face was different, perhaps you might call it shock and anger at the same time. She had never expected Tom to give Tommy a gun at such a young age.

"Thomas!" her voice was quivering. "Whatever possessed you to..."

Her question was interrupted by Tom's assurance. He knew how Caroline felt about guns.

"All Wilson men get their BB guns the first year they are in school." He quickly turned to Tommy and asked, "You are going to be very careful with this gun, aren't you, son?

Tommy nodded. "Yes, sir."

"And we will only shoot at tin cans and trees," Tom added, "not birds or animals or any living creature." He knew so well how Caroline felt about protecting wildlife. "And only in the woods or far away from people? Right, Tommy?"

Again, Tommy responded with a "Yes, sir."

Caroline had heard these arguments many times before. And she knew that it was impossible to police the use of guns completely. And East Texas tradition was on Tom's side. Amendment II of the American Constitution was sacrosanct in East Texas.

"What if he shoots someone? Or shoots himself in the eye or somewhere?" She could imagine the most gruesome scene with Tommy and his gun.

"I'll always be around, and he can only shoot when I am with him." Tom tried to assure her. "Now let's put it away and let him play with his other toys."

Caroline was not satisfied. She was furious by now, but like so many times before, she withheld her anger. *Why change now?* Tom had always prevailed in decisions about Tommy. But in her mind, she had a plan. The BB gun might just disappear one day or be put away and forgotten where it was. And with Tommy's other activities, maybe no one would notice. Mothers have ways of handling problems that sometimes require cunning as well as brains. She saw the scenarios as a plot of a Nancy Drew mystery novel—*The Case of the Disappearing Gun*. And for the moment she was satisfied.

Caroline immersed herself in activities that might give other women the rigors. She continued to sing in the church choir and was secretary for the Sunday school department. Her spotless home was often the meeting place for the historical society that seemed to have more "society" than "history." She served on several city committees and never turned the mayor down when he needed volunteers. But it was her activities dealing with the school system that took most of her time. She was PTA chairman in Tommy's class that year and all the previous years, almost fighting to get the position. She chaperoned every field trip the students took. She worked as a volunteer in the library. But her favorite activity was substituting for ailing teachers. It was the closest thing to having a full-time job in the school system, and becoming a professional teacher had always been her secret wish. And though she could never bring herself to admit it, working in the school kept her near her son. Tommy seemed to become Tom's property at home, but at school, she had him to herself.

The truce—if you could call it that—between Tom and Caroline on raising their son lasted until Tommy's ninth birthday. For the first time, they had a real disagreement. Some people would probably not call it a fight, but to Caroline and Tom, it was nothing less. It was never a verbal disagreement—neither person ever said bad or unkind things about the other—but the feelings and stern looks it provoked could clearly be seen and felt.

On that day, without prior consultation with Caroline, Tom gave Tommy a .410-gauge automatic rifle. The wounds and hurt feelings that had been festering for three years were once again opened by a real gun.

Caroline was visibly upset with Tom. "I thought we had settled the gun issue with the BB gun!"

"Honey," Tom retorted, "I know how you handled that situation," referring to the gun that disappeared. "I've seen the box in the back of your closet." Tom had never mentioned the matter because Tommy actually had been too busy with other events, and shooting a rifle at cans didn't seem as important as football. "But he'll soon be old enough to get a hunting license and experience the thrill of his first squirrel or buck."

Caroline was unmoved.

"Thomas, he is too young for that kind of gun," she firmly replied. She actually meant any gun.

"Everybody else's kids have a gun." To him the argument didn't seem to require an explanation. "Nobody's a man until he goes into the woods on a hunt. Caroline, honey, you can't imagine bagging your first squirrel or your first deer. My boy is *not* going to be the only kid in Jasper County without a gun or who hasn't gone hunting! It's just part of a boy's upbringing." He was emphatic about this. *How many fathers in Southeast Texas had gone through this rite?*

Caroline was just as determined. Tommy was her child too, a fact Tom seemed to forget. "But he's only a child. He can't shoulder the responsibility of owning a gun. He acts like a gun is a toy."

Tom reciprocated with another argument. "I'll keep the ammunition in my bag so he'll only be carrying an empty weapon."

"Sure. It's always the *unloaded* gun that kills."

It was apparent that neither of them were willing to change his mind on the gun issue. Caroline was willing to concede in order to keep from losing the battle completely.

"What if he waited until he was twelve? Would you go along with that?" she asked.

"And be the laughing stock of every daddy in town?"

Caroline never agreed to anything thing, but since the argument was going nowhere, she left it there and turned her attention to something else. Tom also saw it was not wise to push it any further. In fact, he wouldn't mention it unless he absolutely had to.

The day soon came for the first "official" hunting trip. Tom had shown Tommy how to carry and operate the rifle. He had demonstrated the procedure over and over. And he kept close watch over the security of the ammunition. Only he could issue the shells. Tom made his announcement at breakfast that Saturday morning.

"Tommy and I are going up to the old Wingate farm in the morning. Heard the squirrel were running all over the place."

Caroline stiffened but made no comment. She didn't have to. Her eyes expressed her feelings, and Tom quickly got the message.

"We'll be right off the road in that stand of trees where the pig pen used to be. We'll be back before lunch. You go to church, and when we get home, we'll all go to Schaeffer's Café for lunch. Schaeffer's steam table was the town's drawing card for church members on Sundays and a place for getting all the gossip in town. In a way, it sounded like a bribe knowing how difficult it was for Caroline to rush home after church and prepare a meal, but it was not.

Caroline still maintained her silence. She knew that he intended to go regardless of what she said. She didn't want Tommy to see them arguing. And Tom knew how she felt about this whole affair, and he wasn't about to stir up any more trouble than he had to.

Next morning before six o'clock and still somewhat dark, Tom and Tommy, along with Nubbin, who by now had grown large and turned out to be a pretty good squirrel dog, packed their gear, including a little midmorning snack, and headed for the old Wingate farm.

"Now, son," Tom carefully reminded Tommy. "Remember everything I told you. Everything we went over and over."

"Yes, sir." Tommy was careful, but excitedly cuddling his empty gun by his side.

On arriving at the farm, Tom gave Tommy ammunition with a precaution. "Don't put these in your gun until we get to the pig pen . . . and hold your gun down."

Again, Tommy nodded; but already he had slipped a shell into the chamber of his gun without being detected by his dad. He would show his dad what a big boy he was.

"The best hunting was on the other side of the fence in that stand of oaks and pines" Tom pointed to a place several hundred feet away. Heading for the fence in front of the stand of trees, Tom again restated safety precautions. They proceeded to cross the meadow. Nubbin was running back and forth trying to stir some kind of wildlife.

"Now, lean your rifle against the fence post and carefully crawl over the fence. Watch me. Like this!" Tom slowly put his feet on the wire, swung himself over and retrieved his gun from the fence.

"See?"

Tommy followed him exactly, being very careful to play it safely. He was on top of the fence with a hand on a post about to jump down. But Nubbin, finding himself about to be left on the opposite side of the fence from his masters and finding no gap to squeeze through the fence, decided that he had to jump the fence also. As Nubbin tried to jump the fence, Tommy's gun slipped from its resting place on the fence post, hit the ground, and discharged.

In an instant there was a yelp, an explosion, and a cry of pain from Tommy who grabbed his chest as blood began to spurt from beneath his shirt.

"Oh my lord!" screamed Tom, rushing to the fence. Seeing Tommy crumpled on the ground covered in blood, he threw his gun aside. "Get out of the way, Nubbin." He pushed the dog who was obscuring his view aside. Tom felt sick to his stomach. He climbed—almost jumped—back over the fence and dropped beside Tommy, unsure what to do. "Tommy? Tommy? Can you hear me?" He bent low over the small body. There was no answer. But Tom could feel life in the quivering body. Thrusting his arms under the child's small frame, Tom picked him up and began running toward his car all in the same movement. He was there in what seemed like an endless moment. Nubbin was right behind him and into the car. Tom jumped in the car after placing Tommy in the backseat and was on this way back to town. Tom's face had become colorless, and his chest felt tight, like he was about to smother or vomit. He was only a few miles from town. There was no heavy traffic to fight, and Tom was back in town in a few minutes.

"God," he said aloud. "Please let the doctor be at home."

Dr. McKinnon did not open his office on Sundays but would see patients in his home office in case of emergencies. Tom's foot pressed the accelerator to the floorboard of his car as he turned left at the red light on Main Street. From there, Tom arrived at the doctor's home in less than a minute. Dr. McKinnon saw him from the window and rushed to open the door. Tommy's blood-spattered shirt had already begun to dry. The limp body was now motionless as he moved up the sidewalk and into the small office.

Dr. McKinnon motioned for Tom to put the boy on an examination table. "Please wait outside, Tom," the doctor said. There was no one to assist him in his examination. Tom tried, but the doctor again ordered him out of the office.

After few minutes, the doctor opened the door and motioned for Tom to come inside. His face told Tom the news he was dreading to hear.

"I'm sorry, Tom," he began. "It was too late to stop the bleeding. He's gone."

The doctor called the funeral home, and Tom prepared to go home to tell Caroline. If ever he wanted a drink, it was now. This would be the hardest thing he had ever done in his life.

The news of Tommy's death spread through Kirbyville quickly. Friends began to arrive almost as soon as Tom got home. The ladies from the missionary society at the church assumed the responsibility of preparing food and invaded Caroline's kitchen like a silent army.

If floral tributes are an indication of love and sympathy—and in small East Texas towns that is how one measures the magnitude of the departed's importance—Tommy's service was the biggest funeral in the history of Kirbyville. Flowers banked the casket and all around the chancel and up the aisles on each side of the church sanctuary. People had squeezed into every pew, and some were moved to the choir loft. Those arriving late were left to stand on the sides of the church or in the foyer of the church or go to the balcony. There were no close out-of-town relatives to wait on, so the service became a personal community-family event.

By the time of the funeral service, Caroline Wilson had become an inanimate object. Tom had taken Dr. McKinnon with him when he broke the news to her, and she had been sedated since then. At the funeral, she sat motionless, only staring at the small gray metal casket topped by a spray of pale pink roses. Tom guided her through the service and led her from the sanctuary when it was over. The reality of the accident finally hit her as the casket was slowly lowered into the newly dug hole on the Wingate family plot of Kirbyville City Cemetery. At that moment, Caroline seemed to give up life itself. Tom hired a neighbor to sit with her during the day, fearing she might hurt herself if she were left alone. There was even talk that she might have to be committed to an institution. Dr. McKinnon made daily calls to check her condition and monitor her medication. Since Tommy's birth, Caroline's health had gradually declined, but only the doctor was aware of her condition.

Then for some reason which Dr. McKinnon could not explain, things changed. In the weeks that followed Tommy's burial, Caroline's health began to slowly improve. Ladies at the church called it a miracle. People around town looked upon her convalescence with amazement and expected to eventually see her return to her natural self. Caroline's resiliency was a topic of conversation in many homes.

It was Tom who felt so wretched during this period. He had seen Caroline fall apart and become a person he had never known—almost a vegetable. He could imagine what she must have been thinking in those dark days of depression, and he intensified the situation by taking full blame for all that happened. "If only . . ." became a phrase that haunted him daily. *If only I had not bought that damn gun. If only I had to listened to Caroline. If only I had checked the ammunition chamber before we crossed the fence. If only . . . if only . . .*

Caroline did not blame Tom for Tommy's death. She never mentioned it. What would be the purpose of that now? In fact, she rarely talked about it although he could sometimes hear her late at night weeping as she sat at the foot of their bed. Tom loved her more than ever because of this. After a while he, too, forgot the burden of blame that he had placed around his neck like a noose for the last few months. And although the country was in the severest depression in the history of the United States, Tom felt that they had begun a new life together and his love and devotion for Caroline was greater than it had been during their entire marriage.

CHAPTER FIVE

One evening, months later, Tom and Caroline sat in their backyard enjoying the last rays of the setting sun and eating a bowl of homemade ice cream. Shadows quickly disappeared as millions of stars began to peek down on earth. Already the daily nocturnal concert from the dozens of insects had started, and bats were in great abundance, seeking dinner. Because of the heat and dry humidity, there were no mosquitoes, making backyard sitting a pleasure. Things were going great for Tom at the sawmill, and she had pretty much gotten over her illness, at least visibly. Both of them had readjusted their lives and had settled into a pleasant and comfortable, but childless, lifestyle. Caroline—while greatly improved, still showed the effects of the ordeal of the past months on her face—looked at Tom. He was puzzled by the peculiar look she had as she turned to speak to him.

"Honey," she said, seeking his attention. She put her hand on his arm and gently ran her fingers up and down. Tom was flattered.

"Yes, dear?"

"I want another baby!"

"What?" he asked. He wasn't sure he had heard her correctly.

"I want another baby," she repeated.

Tom was totally shocked. He never expected to hear those words again. He didn't know how to respond to a statement which he knew by the tone of her voice was a demand. "But your health!" he hesitated, looking for excuses. "Do you remember what Dr.

McKinnon said when you were pregnant with . . ." He didn't complete the sentence when he realized what he said and the cutting look she shot him.

"With Tommy?"

Tom lowered his head, ashamed he couldn't look Caroline in the face or say Tommy's name. "Sorry."

"It's all right, honey," she assured him.

"And your age? You're thirty-one, or is it thirty-three now? Don't you think that might be too old?" It was Caroline's health and Dr. McKinnon's warning that worried Tom—not her age.

Caroline did not like to be reminded of her frailty.

And he added, "And I'm thirty-four . . . sorta late to start again, don't you think?"

"Thirty-four is not old, Thomas Wilson. And if I had a child before, why not again." She paused, then continued, "I feel a lot different now. Better . . . I have matured . . . no longer a naïve, flighty bride. I've had a shattering experience since the accident." Caroline still could not bring herself to say "Tommy's death."

"I know things are a little tight now—financially—and bonuses at the mill are not likely this year, with the depression and all. But from the look of the bellies of a lot of women here, there are going to be a lot of Depression babies. Unemployed men often are the cause of population increases." Caroline had a sly smile.

"They stay at home too much, and then you know what happens— more babies," she added.

She continued. "But you have a job. I can substitute at school . . . They are always needing substitutes. At least for a while." She knew pregnant women were not allowed to teach in public schools. "One more mouth to feed wouldn't cost much more. I'll promise to watch the budget and save where I can. And just having a small one around the house again, honey, that's the best medicine one can have."

What could Tom say? His reluctance melted away with her impassioned words. Her arguments lacked good sense—at least logic—but how could he deny her? If he did object strongly, he becomes the villain again, a role he would avoid at all costs. And she would go ahead and do it anyway. Women have a knack for that! And deep down, he reminded himself that he needed an heir to carry on the family name. At least, if it's a boy. And he was sort of anxious to get back into the sports world. And if it was a girl, it would be less important than before—but he could still dream. But most importantly, he was not passing up a chance to share a bed with Caroline again.

"You win," he finally said, throwing his hands up in surrender. "When do we start?"

"Soon." That old sparkle had returned to her eyes. And with a devilish expression on her face, she was off to wash the dishes in the kitchen. "Maybe tonight," she yelled back at him.

Now Tom was more than ready to hit the sack.

It was the whistling of the tea kettle on the stove that brought Caroline back to reality. She caught herself reliving the memory of a tragic event that seemed so many years ago. As much as she tried to erase it—or at least camouflage it from her memory—it was always there waiting to challenge her sanity. And sometimes the least mention of a word or a name or a place brought the sadness and pain back to her. But things were so much better now with a second child and a devoted husband. And now her main objective was to get supper ready for her two men.

"David, honey, would you hand me those dishes behind you? We need to set the table for supper."

I don't have time to think about an ugly experience, she kept reminding herself. She hadn't thought about the accident in some time and didn't wish to bring it up now. Especially with David in the kitchen. She looked at David, thinking how his birth had revitalized her life—and her marriage. He was not familiar with the story, and as far as she was concerned, he would never hear the long and sordid episode. Not if she could prevent it. David's knowledge of his brother's death was very sketchy, and since his parents never mentioned it, David never bothered to ask. Tom told him what little he knew about it. But Tom, like Caroline, chose to forget it as much as possible. And David didn't seem interested enough to pursue knowing more about it. He could tell, however, when his mother was thinking about Tommy by the pained and distant look on her face, which would occur from time to time.

Trying to forget her reverie, Caroline changed the subject to something more pleasant. "Mrs. Allen came by this morning."

"Really? What did she want?" he asked with real curiosity.

Mrs. R. C. Allen had been David's English teacher for four years in high school. And his favorite. A teacher who taught one class through high school was unheard-of. New teachers always got freshmen and sophomores. Experienced teachers continued teaching literature in the eleventh and twelfth grades. Mrs. Allen had requested taking a class through the whole high school cycle. It was sort of an experiment for her. She had exposed David and his classmates to the world of literature. And before it was all over, she had gotten those students involved in *Macbeth* and *Hamlet* and begging for more. David never cared for *Beowulf* or other early British literature, but the other authors fascinated him. Through Mrs. Allen, students came to appreciate poetry. Her specialty was grammar and diagramming sentences. But after graduation, David felt he was ready for English 301 at the University of Texas, the course that wiped out more freshmen than any other course. Mrs. Allen also was sponsor of the *Stylus*, the school newspaper. David, as editor, would see her several times a day during the school year. It was her influence that led him to select journalism as a comajor for prelaw. David could honestly say her influence was greater on him more than anyone, except his mother. Mrs. Allen bumped Mr. Crawford to third place.

"She came by to tell me how proud she was of you and your accomplishments last night . . . I suspect she was responsible for getting you the English Award." Caroline was a great admirer of Mrs. Allen because she knew what a good and dedicated teacher she was. They shared a similar teaching philosophy—basics and no fooling around. "And here's an envelope she left." She handed David three or four envelopes. "The others were from neighbors who had dropped by or were given to me in the store."

"Hot dog! more money," he exclaimed. "I hope."

Sure enough, his assets increased by fifty dollars. And calculating his savings in the bank, he announced, "That brings the total to fourteen hundred and twenty-five dollars. Along with my scholarships, that will get me well into the year. Especially after I get a part-time job."

Caroline was very proud of her son and was living vicariously through him. Her first choice had been the University of Texas when she graduated from high school. She settled for Stephen F. Austin State Teachers College instead to please her mother. She was determined that her son would get the best education in the state. She had secretly begun to put aside some grocery money to help him pay tuition. Tuition was only twenty-five dollars, but there were other fees and expenses. Sports activities, cultural events—especially plays—and several other activities were included in the general fees, and she thought he should take advantage of everything the university offered. She wanted to have enough put aside to pay the first year's bills. Textbooks were probably the most expensive item in a college education. David hoped he could buy books that were used.

"I wonder if we should get you some furniture—second-hand stuff—for your room?" she asked.

David was quick to answer.

"Mother, it's only a furnished room in a rooming house near the campus. Cleve said there were two beds, two desks and chairs, a dresser, two lamps, an old wardrobe, a heater, and a bath. That's all we need. Rent is $17.50 per month . . . each. What would you expect for $35 a month?"

"Spartan simplicity decor?" she asked. "No pictures, no accessories to put around?"

"Rooming houses don't make the pages of *Better Homes and Gardens*," David replied. "You can give me some sheets, blankets, towels, and a pillow." He stopped to make a mental inventory. "That should do it! Nope, I need a clock. That will be my accessory."

Caroline was not all that happy knowing David would be in a very plain cubicle without any of the amenities of home—like a cell.

"What about a radio?" she asked. "Even prisoners are allowed to have radios."

David had forgotten about a radio. He nodded vigorously. "By all means."

"That's all anybody has," David added, "and think of moving it all back and forth each school year. Remember, I'm not a frat boy with a big car to zip around town in."

Caroline was convinced, and she dropped the matter.

"But," David continued, "you can send us some care packages from time to time. Like those cookies over there. And maybe some cheese crackers?"

"I've already checked with Mrs. Lola, and we've worked it out." Caroline and Mrs. Lola, Cleve's mother, already had made plans to send goodies periodically to the boys. They would not starve.

"The university made the front page this morning?" Caroline was putting the finishing touches for supper.

"Sports?" David asked. He was well aware of the extensive athletic program at the university.

"No. The *Enterprise* had an article on the *Sweatt* case. It's gone to the Supreme Court now."

Heman Sweatt, a colored man from Houston, had sued the University of Texas for denying him admission to the law school. The nigrah activist groups had taken his case and had appealed to the High Court. It had caused a lot of demonstrations and bad feelings around the state—and the university. Caroline was a lady of the South, but one would more likely call her a daughter of Jesus than think of her as a Southern belle.

"Looks to me like people could put aside their prejudices and live by the words of the Lord," Caroline commented. Her face reflected the disgust she had for the treatment of nigrahs by whites. "Separate drinking fountains, separate toilets, separate schools—well, separate everything doesn't make sense in this day and age. We fought a civil war to solve that problem, and it looks like the losers were the winners after all. Our Wilson and Wingate ancestors fought in the Confederacy, but they were following a lost cause. And during the last war . . . how could we treat them like that after they fought the Germans and Japanese? . . . How could Christians be so uncaring? The Bible says love your enemy as well as your brother."

"You'll never find that love in this town," David quickly added. "As long as they stay in their place and do what the whites say, that's when the whites will love the colored people."

Caroline looked at David in amazement. "You sound just like everybody else in this town . . . like your daddy. I thought I taught you better!"

David had never had any relations—or problems—with nigrahs but as a product of the Southeast Texas culture, he was well aware of the invisible line that separated the whites from the coloreds.

Caroline continued her discourse. "I hate that word! What is 'place'? What is your 'place'? What is mine? Nigrahs might be poor and uneducated, but they're God's children too. And you're not going to see nigrahs and whites in separate mansions in heaven."

David had heard this discourse before. He couldn't agree or disagree with her because his association with colored people was so limited. *Maybe, I can learn more now that I have met Toye Lee*, he thought.

"Thank goodness, it's not as bad as it was in the days of the Klan?" Caroline was reminiscing again. "Papa used to talk about their activities in Newton County."

"Papa Wingate was in the Ku Klux Klan?" David was shocked.

Caroline nodded. "But only for a short time."

"But he was a judge."

"It was long before he was a judge—when he was a young man. In those days every man joined the Klan or people distrusted you. So Papa just fell in line with all the young men then. But after the lynching, he got out—and in a hurry."

David was even more intrigued. "What lynching? I thought those things only happened in Western movies."

"I don't remember the details, but a young nigrah man was taken from the jailhouse, a noose put around his neck and tied the rope to a car and driven around the courthouse square until he died."

"What did the nigrah man do, for heaven's sake?"

Caroline was searching her memory, but nothing seemed to appear. "I just can't remember. But I'll bet you it was something minor by today's standards. We are supposed to have laws that take care of those matters."

David was amazed and somewhat sickened to hear about the incident. It turned his stomach to think that such a thing had happened in the next town and involved his grandfather. But he suspected that he had only heard a small bit of the Klan activity in that county.

"I would have never guessed Papa was a part of that!" he said sadly.

"Well, honey," Caroline assured him, "he wasn't a part of it. He was there when it happened. I doubt he could have done anything. And probably wouldn't if he was smart."

"But he was a judge."

"And he was a fine judge. He wasn't proud of his membership in the Klan, and he let everyone know he didn't approve of their activities. That's why he got out. And he always said that part of his life would never affect his decision as an officer of the court. Everyone liked him, and he never had an opponent when he ran for office. Nigrahs respected him and felt he was always fair in his decisions. In fact, his was the first funeral that nigrahs attended. They sat in the balcony of the church, of course, but several colored people paid their respects."

At that moment the telephone rang and Caroline went into the living room to answer it. David could hear her speaking to someone but could not hear the conversation.

"That was your father," she announced on returning to the kitchen. "He's finished the repair job at the mill and will be here in about thirty minutes." She moved to restart the gas under the pots on the stove.

"Why don't you go into the living room and listen to *The Shadow* until I get supper ready?"

David had a curious look on his face. "Why do they call it supper around here and the other part of the country it's called dinner?"

"Remember you're in East Texas, and that's the way it is. Everyone has breakfast, but we have dinner at noon and supper at night. It's the culture around here."

"Like having black-eye peas and cabbage on the first day of the year?"

Caroline nodded. "And introducing people by who they're related to . . . and eating peas with a knife . . ."

"Like Papa Wingate?" David asked, remembering his grandpa, the judge.

She giggled as she remembered her own father would line up peas on a knife before eating them. "We just live in a different world." She thought for a moment. "What do we always say when we say good-bye to someone?"

David immediately responded, "Ya'll come."

She continued, "People here have a real problem pronouncing certain names, like Carthage and Shreveport. And we must be the only place on earth wherein the name Jordan is pronounced Jurden." Caroline was beginning to think of all sorts of East Texas customs. "And remember that the number of floral tributes were considered the importance of the deceased . . . Just Southeast Texas, I guess. And friends sit up all night with the body of a deceased person." David rose from his chair. He didn't listen to the serials very much since he started working. But he went anyway. "Okay. But it's the *Lone Ranger* on Mondays and Wednesdays and the *Green Hornet* tonight." Few people had to be reminded that radio serials came on at six-thirty every night."

Caroline and David heard Tom before they saw him. First, when the car came to a screeching stop in front of the house, then when he shut the door to the car, and finally as he stomped up the steps, strode across the porch, and opened and slammed the front door.

"Those damned slant-eyed, yellow-skinned bastards!" he yelled.

By that time Caroline was in the living room to see what the ruckus was all about. She saw the anger on his face but did not have an inkling what the trouble was.

"Honey?" she asked "What in the world are you screaming about? What has happened?"

David was already in the living room as Tom entered the door. He looked scared because he had seen that his dad's anger sometimes explode into a real fit of rage. He didn't say anything, but his expression was one of great curiosity but mixed with fear.

Tom answered, "Haven't you heard the news? It's been on the radio all afternoon."

Caroline was still in the dark. She hadn't listened to the news since early that morning, and her perusal of the *Beaumont Enterprise* had been very cursory that day. She didn't see anything unusual at the time. She usually listened to the radio station for the noon news, but with everybody dropping by this morning and trying to do her chores, she had forgotten to turn it on.

Tom could see she was unaware of the day's activities.

"There are communists uprisings all over Asia. The Reds in Malaya have seized the rubber plantations. The Chinese are gathering on the border, threatening to invade Korea." He paused a moment, catching his breath, then continued. "Senator McCarthy is right. Those damned communists are everywhere."

Caroline led Tom into the kitchen and steered him into a chair. His face was still flushed with anger.

"Thomas, you need to settle down and cool off. This is not good for your health. Would you like a cup of coffee or a glass of water?" Nobody, but nobody, ever called him Thomas except Caroline. But to him it had a soothing effect although he hated being addressed that way.

"Ice water." He wished it was a big shot of whiskey.

"Only five years after the war and we are heading for another fight. The Chinese—our allies during the war and now our enemies. Bastards!"

Caroline tried to calm him, but he was on a tear. "Don't talk like that before David," she asked as if David had never heard profanity before.

Tom continued. "I wish I could have fought in the Pacific Theater. I would have taken them out then when we had a chance. I'd volunteer right now if they let me go. I hope President Truman doesn't sit on his butt and let them get away with this!"

Tom was too old to be drafted in World War II. He would have never been eligible anyway because of his football injury. He still walked with a limp, which became more pronounced the older he got. But the spirit was there, and he surely would leave for the military today if he could.

Except for his limp, Tom was in excellent shape, that is, for a man in his fifties. He had been attentive to keeping in shape ever since his college football days. Six feet two inches, he stood as tall and erect as he had at twenty. His full head of hair had not begun to gray like Caroline's, and it sometimes bothered both of them that some people thought she was older than he was. The wind and sun had tried to take their toll, but his face had resisted beautifully, and the wrinkles so noticeable on Caroline's face had not yet made their way onto Tom's. And his broad smile was infectious as it had always been.

Whether he was walking down the street or just having a conversation with a friend or acquaintance, Tom's physique, with his boyish charm and devastating smile, seemed to exude a message that few could mistake. He could still turn a female's eye. "There may be snow on the rooftop, but there's still fire in the furnace," he would always jest. And many of the female gender believed him and would have offered themselves to him if they thought he was interested. Infidelity was never on Tom's mind, nor would it ever be. He was still crazy about Caroline and always would be.

Tom was devoted to Caroline. It had never crossed his mind to look at another woman. He was still amazed that she had given him a second glance in college days, much less married him. He was a nobody—just a jock—and she was so smart and gifted. She came from one of the leading families of Kirbyville and had the prospect of becoming anything she desired. And yet she gave up college, married Tom, and made him the happiest man alive.

If such a title existed, Tom would be declared the most popular person in his hometown—Mr. Kirbyville. Even Mr. Crawford would concede this. To many, he was still the athletic hero he was when he was in high school. All-district in football for three years, all-region for two years, and Most Valuable Player in basketball, holder of the state record in the 100-yard dash, all-state baseball team—Tom was the hero of past glories of the Kirbyville school system. The school had never seen the glories of athletics like those in Tom's years as a student. The trophies he helped to win, though tarnished and corroded, still remained in a place of honor in the trophy case outside the principal's office at high school. David had seen them every day. And often some townspeople wondered why some of Tom's athletic ability didn't rub off on David. People had expected Tom to do well in college—and he would have—except for the football accident which brought his sports career to an end.

Tom was not terribly upset about losing his football scholarship once he got over the initial shock of his injury. And never being a real ambitious person, it didn't bother him to return to his hometown. Officials at Kirby Lumber Corporation gave him a job—perhaps a delayed reward—as assistant crew leader in the planer section of the mill. He had gotten promotions and pay raises periodically. His life was perfect when Caroline also came home and they made plans to marry. He had his love and was back in the place where people adored him—where he was king! Kirbyville was like another appendage to his body and existence. It was part of him and always would be.

Kirbyville provided everything he needed or desired. Next to his wife and son, his most cherished possession was his 1949 four-door black Ford sedan, which he lovingly called Geraldine. He never revealed where he got that name, and nobody was going to ask. It was the first new car he had ever purchased and the first vehicle of any kind since the war. The old car he had driven during the war was just about to fall apart, and he still shuddered at the thought of using ration stamps to get gasoline. He gave Geraldine as much attention as anything. Tom was an avid hunter—squirrel and deer—during season and liked to get together with the boys for some poker or 42. As much as she tried, Caroline could never get him too involved in the church although he would go occasionally, but he preferred to spend his Sundays in the woods. He found God in the trees and meadows of the countryside—in the flowing streams and cloudless skies. He had been active in the city sports programs, but since the accident, he had withdrawn from them completely. The church officials offered him a chance to coach the softball team. He declined, however, suspecting it was a subtle way of getting him to church so they could "save his soul."

Understandably, Tom's greatest civic interest was his membership in the Kirbyville Volunteer Fire Department. It was an organization that had rigid rules about attendance and practice and yet always had a waiting list of men wanting to become firemen. David often wondered why so many men were so anxious to be invited into the fire department and why so few left. He had always assumed it was men who reverting to their pyromaniacal desires of childhood. All boys, even David, loved to play with fire, especially campfires. As he grew up and the world began to reveal itself more clearly, David learned the truth. The fire department had a good truck and excellent equipment which members were more than willing to maintain in top condition. They had won several awards for being a top-notch volunteer fire department. They practiced every Monday night, being reminded by the wailing of the fire siren, and many members went there throughout the week to "work" on equipment or "do" paperwork. Upstairs at the fire station was a large room, perhaps better known as the lounge. Within the room were some refrigerators and a wet bar. Members went here to drink beer or liquor and to play poker or 42. Kirbyville and Jasper counties were bone-*dry*—that is, alcoholic beverages of any kind were illegal. The people had voted down "going wet" several times. Baptist. Of course. Local ministers often preached sermons on the evils of liquor and the sins of gambling, perhaps another reason for Tom to avoid getting involved with the church. But everyone in town knew the truth and accepted the behavior of the firemen and what went on in the fire station. They just looked the other way. So many owed a debt of gratitude to the department no one had the nerve—or really wanted to—to say anything about the drinking and gambling that was going on upstairs at the fire station. Another way of showing their gratitude was buying tickets to the annual chili supper and attending the firemen's street dance on Fourth of July. The money raised by the events permitted the fire department to operate in the black.

Slowly, Tom had begun to unwind. The water had cooled his body, and being home had a similar soothing effect. The smell of the food whetted his appetite. After a day at the mill, he was ready to sit down and relax. He thought of going to the fire station, but he had been there the day before. It was an evening to stay home and be with his family.

"Supper's ready," Caroline announced.

David added quickly, "And so am I!"

They took their respective places and began to reach for the food spread before them on the table.

"What have you two—" Tom started to ask, but was stopped by Caroline by putting her hand on his arm.

"Let's have grace first," she said. And they bowed for the blessing of the food. Tom was never comfortable during grace although he had heard it hundreds of times. He always felt Caroline was directing her prayers toward him because of his lack of participation in the church. Caroline said a very short prayer.

"What have you guys been doing today?" Tom asked although he knew perfectly well what they had done. "It's sure been a scorcher today, hasn't it?"

"Several people came by today to congratulate David," Caroline answered.

"And they brought money," David added.

"How much to you have now, son?"

"Getting close to fifteen hundred dollars."

"You could just about buy a car with that," Tom added.

"Thomas!" Caroline blurted out without even thinking.

"Oh, honey, I'm just kidding. I wish I could help you out more—and I will when I can."

"Dad, I'm going to make it just fine. I know you would. Don't worry." David was sincere in his reply. He knew that going to the university would be his own responsibility.

"My boy's going to be a tea-sip." Tom was kidding him now. He might have preferred David go to Texas A&M, but if David was satisfied—and Caroline happy, very happy—it was all right with him. He really had no part in that decision anyway.

David never liked the name tea-sip because it was insulting to a student at the university. But he dismissed the thought immediately because he knew those persons who used the term were jealous. It was only another way his dad teased him.

"Maybe you and Mother could come out for a football game this fall. I bet I could get some tickets, and you have Geraldine who'll get you there without problems."

That thought appealed to Tom. All the sports magazines had predicted that the Texas Longhorns would be in the race for the national championship. Only Oklahoma University loomed as a formidable opponent. And Tom's old love for college football had never died.

"We'll see." Tom decided that the prospect of going to Austin for a weekend had merit, and he would pursue the matter later. "By the way," Tom continued. "I heard some of the boys at the mill talking about a nigrah enrolling at the university. Did you hear about it?"

"Mother mentioned it to me earlier this afternoon," David replied. "There's something about it in the *Enterprise*."

"Why can't *those people* go to Prairie View college where they belong instead of stirring up trouble in Austin. Prairie View's got a good program for nigrahs."

Caroline was quick to interject her opinions. "*Those people* have as much right to go to the university as David does."

"But Prairie View was set up for nigrahs. And they will be with their own people there."

David could see the beginning of another argument that he would like to head off if he could. "But it's only for the law school," he added.

"Son, what you don't know about colored people is if you give them an inch, they'll take a mile. I see it all the time at the mill. Law school today, then graduate school, and finally undergraduate school. And the standards go down, and the problems go up. Nigrahs will start to date white girls—then marriage and then all hell breaks loose. One of these days . . . just mark my words . . . they'll try to get into the public schools. Just wait and see. Integration won't work!"

Caroline was already exasperated. "Honey, that's not fair."

"You've got to let nigrahs know where they belong. It's like drawing a line." Tom drew an imaginary line across the table with his finger. "They are on one side, and you are on the other. They understand. Once the line is drawn, then each side can go about its business knowing each other's place."

David followed this conversation but made no comment. He never had to deal with nigrahs directly like Tom did at the mill—every day.

"Let's change the subject." Caroline saw she was getting nowhere but angry with this argument.

But Tom continued. "All I'm doing is telling David to be careful in Austin. Don't get too close to the coloreds. Be on your guard at all times. Watch your pocketbook. Lock everything up. Understand?"

David nodded but still had no idea what all the commotion was about."

"Honey," Caroline said again, trying to tranquilize the situation, "David met a boy today at work who says his mother used to work for us. I've racked my brain, but for the life of me, I just can't think of who she is."

Tom continued to eat and asked with his mouth still full of food, "What's her name?

"Her name is Allie Mae Johnson, and her son is Toye Lee Johnson."

"She works at Lea's Café," David added, "and Toye Lee works at Parson's Grocery."

Tom thought a moment, shook his head, and answered, "I don't remember anybody by that name, and I don't think we ever hired anybody with a child." He mulled the name over again in his mind. "Allie Mae Johnson? . . . Nope! . . . Doesn't ring a bell with me either. Do you think it was someone who ironed for you?"

Caroline never liked ironing. And Tom was a little particular about his shirts. That is why they would get someone in the Quarters to iron his shirts sometimes.

"Toye Lee said she worked for us when I was a baby," David replied.

Again, Tom searched the inner reaches of his memory. "Your folks came over and kept David when you were in the hospital. Your grandmother babysat him during the day when I was working. That was for about two weeks as I recall."

Caroline thought back to that time, and things began to come back to her. "That's right. I remember now. But who stayed with David when Mama and Papa had to get back to the farm in the evening to take care of the cows?"

"Wait a minute!" Tom exclaimed. "I do remember hiring a girl from across the tracks to come in and stay with him. Seems to me she was about fifteen or sixteen. Maybe a little older."

"And didn't you set up a roll-away bed in the baby's room so she could sleep next to him at night?" asked Caroline.

"You're right. She stayed with us until we brought you home from the hospital."

David was listening to the conversation but had not said much up to this time. "That's her. She's probably in her early thirties—maybe her middle thirties. She cooks the food and waits on the colored customers in the back of the café."

"I don't think I have seen her since then," Tom added.

The mention of Caroline's hospitalization triggered a series of memories Tom tried to suppress through the years. They only reminded him of those painful and anxious events he tried to erase from his life. But like a bad dream, he had to wake up to make it go away, but the dream would reappear another time in another dream.

The events starting with Tommy's accidental death, then Caroline's health problems and depression following the funeral, and concluding with the many problems of her second pregnancy were like a murky panorama to Tom who tried to remove them from his memory. Those images came and went, not always clear, but never completely blotted from his mind. They were things he would have long forgotten had it not been for the fact that they were reflected in Caroline's lonely eyes and the faraway look that sometimes appeared on her face. Tommy's death was the first blow to Tom's perfect world. He recalled over and over the scene of the falling gun and his desperate race to Dr. McKinnon's office. He recalled the pain that he felt when the doctor looked at him and shook his head. Worse still was the memory of having to tell Caroline the tragic news and her collapse on hearing it. A million times he blamed himself for the accident and apologized to Caroline for taking Tommy on that hunting trip. He often told himself how different things would have been if he had listened to her.

Caroline never blamed him for Tommy's death. But as much as she tried to console him, he couldn't absolve himself. Every time Tom saw a father and son engaged in athletic activities or heard the boys at the mill tell of their recent hunting trips, it would remind him of that fatal day. He could suppress it temporarily, but it always returned like the shadows of the night.

Caroline's physical deterioration made things even more tense. How happy he was when she began to pull out of her depression. He would have done anything to have her back to the same Caroline he knew on the day they married. When Caroline began to improve and return to her old self, Tom thought they were finally on the way to recovery and better days were ahead. Her vacant gaze into an unknown place indicated to him that things would never be the same, yet he was encouraged by her attempt to restore the life they had before. It was at this time Caroline announced she wanted another baby.

Tom was startled at her announcement. He remembered how difficult her first delivery was. He recalled Dr. McKinnon's warning about another child and how dangerous it could be to both the mother and child. He was reminded of his own mental anguish and how the whole ordeal had temporarily sapped his sanity and physically his energy.

"Honey," he had told her, "remember you are over thirty now and you know that your health is not"—he was very cautious to not say the wrong words—"not perfect." But in her eyes he detected a will of iron that was unlikely to change.

"I know the dangers. And I know all the arguments you can give me," she said. "But for a woman, being a mother is the most important and satisfying thing that can happen. Without children, life is empty. God fulfills a woman's destiny when he gives her a child."

"But God doesn't ask one to abuse his body or endanger his life," Tom was quick to assert. "What about the possibility of an adoption? Dr. McKinnon often delivers babies that the mothers don't want or can't afford to keep them."

"But they're someone else's . . . They don't have Wingate or Wilson blood in their veins . . . or genes. We would be taking a chance to adopt some unknown baby. I want to see my child . . . mine . . . grow up, have friends, go to school, go to college, get married, and have children of their own. I want to be a grandmother to *my* own grandchildren—not someone else's."

Tom knew Caroline was right—or at least he knew how she felt. A son—or a daughter—sired by someone else would not be the same. He would have never known if he had passed his own characteristics to the next generation. Yet the health factor still gnawed at his conscience. The thought of losing Caroline was more than he could bear. He winced at the thought of carrying the burden of another guilt trip. Tommy's was more than he could sometimes bear.

Tom looked into Caroline's eyes, still empty from the months before. They still reflected the sorrow she carried for the son she had buried in the Kirbyville cemetery east of town. But the look on her face now was a look of determination. When she wanted to, Caroline could be a strong woman. And perhaps that determination of her spirit would offset the frailties of her body. How could he refuse her?

Tom consented somewhat reluctantly to try to have another child. Both knew the desire to have a child would not guarantee one. But when both parties were willing, it might happen.

Caroline's second pregnancy was difficult from the start. Dr. McKinnon had given her a list of things to do and not to do. He suggested a lot of bed rest—off her feet as much as possible. There was no diet problem as Caroline ate relatively little, but always healthy foods from local gardens. She sometimes spotted. She would forget and lift something that was too heavy. But on the whole, she was very careful.

In the months before David's birth, Tom became a nervous wreck. But he also acted like a different man. He would call Caroline during the day from the mill. His church attendance improved. He performed additional chores around the house to relieve Caroline of the strain. He practiced his skill at cooking but never produced any gourmet meals. He was somewhat hesitant about touching her or hugging her for fear of hurting her or the baby in some way. His time at the fire station diminished to about half the time of what it had been before.

Caroline would get irritated by this behavior because she felt he was creating a schism between them—some people might think there was something artificial in their relationship. She assured Tom her body was not that delicate.

"I'm not a porcelain doll or a fine antique," she would remind him. "I don't intend to break and fall into a hundred pieces. Put you arms around me . . . and feel this baby."

To Tom, though, she was like a fine piece of china. And as much as he would have liked to sweep her up in his arms or tumble in the bed with her, he kept his distance or at least was very cautious about his touch. It was as if Tom had encased her in a glass dome and put her away on the shelf in the living room for nine months. He was madly in love with her, but it was a vicarious kind of love.

Old Dr. McKinnon was as anxious about the baby as Caroline and Tom were. He knew Caroline's poor physical condition and had seen the worry on Tom's face every time they met. Wherever he saw either of them—in the office, at church, in the grocery store—he would always encourage them. Optimism worked better than fear. "We're going to do the best we can," he promised them. "I might have to move in the house with you, but I'll be there. Now you two just don't worry."

Tom and Caroline were consoled—to a point. The thought of the doctor moving into their home was humorous. But if that's what it took, they were more than willing to have their house become a clinic.

Dr. McKinnon was more concerned than he admitted. He was comfortable when the pregnancy was normal and the mother was healthy. That was not the situation in Caroline's case. He delivered babies in the home—in the bedroom. It was not the right environment if there were complications. There were no instruments or equipment for emergencies. He was not even prepared for that in his office above the drugstore. When he foresaw a problem or had an emergency, he would have the patient transferred to the hospital in Jasper nineteen miles away. But in Caroline's case, he couldn't decide whether to go ahead and move her to Jasper or wait until the baby came and take his chances at home. Unknown to Tom and Caroline, he wrestled with this dilemma for weeks.

———

It was near the end of the day when Tom was shutting the planer down for the day that he got a telephone call from Dr. McKinnon's nurse. The doctor, early in Caroline's pregnancy, had decided to use a nurse rather than a midwife. A nurse would be more apt to handle emergencies than an unskilled helper.

"Tom, we're at your house already, and it looks like Caroline's gone into labor. I think you ought to come on home as soon as you can," she said.

Tom rushed to his car. *Geraldine, get me home quickly*, he thought. He only lived a few blocks from the mill, and in less than ten minutes, he was running up the steps of his house.

"Settle down," Dr. McKinnon warned him. "No need to panic." He could feel the tenseness of the scene—the strain of the situation had begun to etch lines on Tom's face. "We're going to be here for a while. She just started to dilate, so you're in for a long evening."

Tom's supper was tasteless. He tried reading the *Beaumont Enterprise*, but his mind was not functioning—even on the sports page. He looked around for things to do, but Caroline's immaculate housecleaning provided nothing. He called Caroline's parents but did not want them to come over yet. *I can't sit here and watch them wring their hands all night*, he told himself.

Around midnight, activities around the house began to pick up. First there were groans and then screams. With all the movement from one room to another, Tom could only stand and look helpless. He had no idea of what to do. Movies always had the hero boil lots of water. Tom saw that all four burners had pans of boiling water—ready if necessary.

"Looks like we're in business!" yelled the doctor. "Tom, don't get in the way. I have enough to do without taking care of you."

Tom was in agony. He didn't remember anything like this with Tommy's birth. He tried to think back but realized he didn't remember anything at all. Tom paced the floor for what seemed to be days. He could hear Caroline's grunts of pain coming from the bedroom. Tom knew she was trying her best to keep from screaming. Tom heard the muffled conversations of the doctor and the nurse, sometimes sounding more like a shouting match than a conversation. At times it was more than he could bear. He moved toward the bedroom door for a glimpse of Caroline in her bed.

"Not now, Tom!" the doctor shouted. He came to the door once with blood on his jacket and gloves. "Sit down, Tom. Relax. Get yourself a drink of whiskey . . . anything! Just keep out of our way!"

Tom panicked. He would have lighted a cigarette, but he didn't smoke. His whiskey was at the fire station. He realized this was too much to bear alone—even for him. By now he knew he should call the judge and his wife. They could be there within the hour. He called and hoped that he would not fall apart before they got there.

It was almost daybreak when Dr. McKinnon opened the door holding a small object wrapped in a blanket.

Tom and Judge and Mrs. Wingate immediately moved toward the doctor whose face showed an expression of relief.

"Tom," the doctor said, adjusting the blanket around the child's head, "I want you to meet your son."

The word "son" did not register with Tom at first. He peered over the doctor's shoulder, looking for his wife. "Caroline? What about Caroline?" he asked.

"She had a hard time, Tom." The doctor saw the terror on his face. "It was a breech baby. Caroline lost lots of blood."

"What's a breech?" Tom was completely baffled by that comment.

The doctored continued, "The baby comes out feet first rather than head first. It is always very difficult on the mother."

"And Caroline?" Tom asked. "Is she all right?"

"She's exhausted. The loss of blood has left her weak. She's resting now . . . it's best not to arouse her."

Tom interrupted. "But is she going to be all right?"

"If she rests and doesn't hemorrhage, I think she will pull through." Dr. McKinnon looked Tom in the eye. "You need to get some help to watch the baby. We'll have to get it on formula pretty quickly. Caroline can't nurse it. I'll be carefully watching her. The nurse is here too. I have all the confidence in the world that things will work out."

Caroline's parents had already volunteered to do whatever was necessary. Together they would find someone to come to the house

---

103

and care for the baby when Caroline was unable to do it herself. And they would also babysit during the day.

Tom would have cried had he not been scared out of his wits. But the reassurance of the doctor and the willingness of his in-laws gave him the hope that Caroline would recover.

"My advice now," Dr. McKinnon continued, "is to let her get rest, and get some yourself, and put this whole affair in the hands of God. The baby is healthy. He is a fine boy . . . perfect health. He's going to be all right. Our job now is to get Caroline back on the mend."

"A boy!" Tom uttered to himself. Then aloud he announced, "A healthy boy!" He finally realized he once again had a son. He had secretly wished for a boy but never mentioned it to anyone. Tom pulled the blanket away from his newborn son and gazed with the pride of a new father. At that moment all the anxieties and agonies of the past few months seemed to melt away and the picture of a new life before him transported him to the realm of ecstasy.

Looking at his in-laws, Tom exclaimed, "My son . . . My son!"

The judge, not forgetting his relationship to this newly delivered package, added, "And my grandson—and don't you forget it! He already has the look of an attorney—perhaps a judge." He was beaming with pride.

Interrupting the men, Mrs. Wingate added, "And don't forget me. I'm the grandmother." Mrs. Wingate took the baby from the nurse's arms. Gently tucking the receiving blanket around the baby, she unconsciously muttered, "Oh my goodness . . . He looks exactly like Little—" Catching herself as she glanced at Tom, she didn't complete the sentence. "Isn't he beautiful?"

Caroline's parents adjusted their schedules so that they could keep the baby during the day. Since the judge's schedule depended on the cases before his court, it presented no problems for him either. Mrs. Wingate was tickled pink to be grandma again. The judge had to go back to the farm in the evenings in order to feed the animals and milk the cows. Mrs. Wingate volunteered to stay around-the-clock, but Tom wanted to help Caroline himself if he could. When he came home from the mill—and he left as early as he could—he checked the baby carefully. He learned to change diapers. He served Caroline meals cooked by Mrs. Wingate. He discovered another new skill—washing dishes. He could boil bottles and wash diapers as well as any mother. He also became proficient at preparing baby formula.

This was a side of Tom that Caroline had never seen—but neither had Tom. He was proud of his new accomplishments.

"How are you at mopping and sweeping?" Caroline asked in a weak, whispering voice one evening. "Could I hire you?"

"Damned good, ma'am," he answered like he was being interviewed for a maid's job. "But I warn you now. I don't do windows . . . or ironing."

Caroline's recovery was slow but steady. The loss of blood had made her weak, but mentally, she was alert although her body did not respond as quickly. She nursed the baby for some of its feedings but relied more and more on formula for his nourishment. It appeared she would make a full recovery, but everyone expected a long recuperation. Dr. McKinnon was more relieved than pleased with her recovery.

For several days after the baby's birth, Dr. McKinnon would drop by and check mother and child. He was amazed how well the baby was doing and was pleased with the progress Caroline was making. He wouldn't call it a miracle, but he often remarked that the Wilson family was indeed lucky.

On one of his visits during that time, the doctor made an important announcement.

"I want you two to be the first to know my good news!"

Caroline and Tom could not imagine what he was about to tell them but were anxious to know what it was. The last several days had made them feel like family.

"Well, what is it? Tom asked.

"A former resident of this area has just graduated from medical school in Louisiana and wants to return here to begin his practice. He and I have agreed to form a partnership and build a new clinic for this community."

To Tom and Caroline, the news was startling. Perhaps more of a shock. There had been no rumor about this circulating town—a town where very few secrets are kept.

"The Mixson family has donated the block behind their store so we can build a twelve-bed clinic with all modern equipment to go with it, including an x-ray machine. One of the best things will be an operating room where baby deliveries can be made in a clean and up-to-date facility. And a place for mothers to recuperate."

Tom and Caroline did not have to be told the significance of his announcement. But the doctor added the comment anyway.

"We won't have to go through the ordeal like the one we went through with you." The doctor was so pleased with his announcement. "And I can move out of that loft above the drugstore. Looks like my final years will be spent in a decent clinic."

The news of the new clinic was one of the most electrifying and welcomed announcements ever made in the community. People had long dreamed of such a facility but never realized that it would actually happen. Kirbyville was not a town that a young and ambitious doctor would choose to set up a practice. Doctors still made house calls there. The town looked with great anticipation for the new doctor and his new clinic.

One evening as the doctor was making his nightly house calls, he turned to Tom. "You never told me whether you wanted the little one circumcised or not . . . Did you ever decide?"

Before Tom could answer, Caroline blurted, "Yes!"

"No!" exclaimed Tom, almost as quickly. He felt that such a procedure was a brutal thing to do to a baby. And it robbed him of his manhood.

Caroline reaffirmed her decision. "Yes," she repeated.

Tom could tell by the stern look on her face she would have her way.

"We can do in the office when you're up and about," the doctor said.

Tom was hurt. "I always thought this was a father's decision—not one for a woman."

"It's a family decision and I have decided yes!"

Tom was beaten, and he knew it. The matter ended with him muttering, "Okay, but I hope he isn't teased too much about being a Jew."

"In Kirbyville?" Caroline asked.

As Dr. McKinnon was preparing to leave, he noticed the certificate in his bag. "Oh, by the way," he commented. "Did you know we never officially named the new son. There was so much commotion that night and the days after we forgot to complete his birth certificate."

He took the paper from his bag and removed the cap of his fountain pen and began to write. Let's see . . . County? . . . Date? . . . Time? . . . Sex? . . . Date of birth?" The doctor completed the blanks that he knew the answers to. "Legitimate or illegitimate?" He continued to fill in the blanks on the birth certificate. "Name of father . . . Name of mother . . . Here it is . . . Name of infant?" he asked as he turned to Tom for the name.

Before Tom could respond to the doctor, Caroline announced in a weak but very clear voice, "David Wingate Wilson!"

Tom was startled. "Honey, I kinda thought—" He didn't finish the sentence.

Again she repeated, "David Wingate Wilson."

Tom was silent.

Dr. McKinnon slowly spelled out the name. He moved slowly in case Tom stopped him or suggested another name.

"D-a-v-i-d . . . W-i-n-g-a-t-e . . . W-i-l-s-o-n."

Caroline spelled the name very slowly and clearly for the doctor to write.

Dr. McKinnon looked at Tom and, seeing no disagreement or correction, folded the paper. He put it in his bag. "I'll file this tomorrow, and the county will send you an official copy."

As Tom assisted him out the door, the doctor said, "The judge would have been pleased to have a namesake. I'll see you folks tomorrow."

Caroline knew Tom would immediately come back into the room to discuss the name, and she was waiting for him.

"Honey," he began, "I kinda thought we ought to name him Samuel after my mother's dad. We never really discussed this, you know. Do you think we acted to hastily?"

Caroline's voice was now a whisper but a determined one. She was still weak, and the effort had emotionally drained her of energy. She looked at Tom and declared, "Thomas Wilson, that baby is mine and don't you ever forget it."

CHAPTER SIX

Taken aback by her assertiveness, Tom could only ask, "What?"

"I suffered pain you could not know. I almost put my life down for that child. My emotional future is dependent on this baby. Thomas, that baby is mine."

"But, honey, he belongs to both of us. We're his parents."

"Of course, he is, and I'm sure you will love him as much as I do." She hesitated for a moment and, after a deep breath, continued. "Like Tommy was yours. I let you name him, I let you make all the decisions about his life. I never objected to the toys or presents you gave him although I wanted to. You mapped his whole future the way you wanted it to be. You set the course of action in his life. You had your chance. Now I want mine."

Tom was flabbergasted. "What do you mean?"

"I intend to develop David's mind, not his body. I will give him educational toys and not fill his room with dozens of footballs or basketballs or any other kind of sports equipment. If he has an interest in sports, then he may pursue it, but it will not be forced upon him. He will not be given a horse unless he wants one. I shall encourage him to be active in the literary events of school and work toward the goal of a college education. He will be encouraged to participate in all activities and clubs in the school, and we will be active in the PTA. And under no circumstances—and I mean no circumstances—will he ever be given a gun or any other kind of weapon whatsoever."

Tom stood in silence. Speechless. Stunned.

Caroline then concluded her proclamation, "Do you understand? Do you agree?" A long moment passed before an answer.

What were his options? How could he say otherwise? As much as he was hurt, Tom nodded in consent.

"I want to hear it."

"Yes, I agree to let you raise David"—the name David sort of stuck in his throat—"with an academic background. And any decision or request from me will have to be approved by you beforehand."

Tom felt like he had symbolically signed the most important verbal contract of his life. He didn't feel good about it, nor did he hold any resentment. He would always be there to share in David's life. It was like buying a round-trip ticket on the *Titanic*. There were mixed feelings about the arrangement. Tom had mixed feelings about the arrangement. But someone else would be setting the agenda and pulling the strings. Tom thought for a moment. She was right. He had dominated Tommy's life with little help from her. He had never thought about that before. And he consciously did not mean to. And she did have a right to raising a child where he had failed.

Caroline was exhausted by their conversation. She still was not feeling well, and their conversation was also emotionally draining. "Thomas, I'm so tired. Please let me get some sleep now. I feel so worn-out." Shortly, Caroline was sound asleep and Tom was left alone to reflect on her pronouncements.

Tom was at the mill when he got the telephone call. For several days he had thought about the agreement he had made with Caroline and about the future that he had sentenced David to. As he mulled these over in his mind, he could not decide whether it was good or bad, right or wrong. But his love for Caroline prevented him from reneging on his pledge. And who was to say it was a bad deal? So what if he didn't become Kirbyville's greatest athlete? There were many things much worse, so he tried to put the thoughts out of his mind and get on with his job.

The mill clerk relayed the message to Tom by telephone in the small office near the planer.

"Tom, Judge Wingate called and told us to get this message to you. There has been an emergency, and Caroline has been rushed to the hospital in Jasper. Dr. McKinnon went with her to the emergency room. Mrs. Wingate is keeping the baby at your home, but they thought you ought to go to Jasper immediately."

Tom was speechless, and he felt like he might throw up. *God, I don't want to go through this again! I'm not sure I can take it again.* Crises were beginning to dominate his life.

"Tom? Tom? Are you there?" the clerk asked, searching for a reply.

"Yeah, I'm here. Call the section chief and tell him what's happened. He'll cover for me. I'm on my way to Jasper. Thanks for calling."

Dr. McKinnon was conferring with the hospital staff physicians when a distraught Tom arrived. Spotting him coming down the hall, the doctor said, "Here he is. He's the husband."

The doctors introduced themselves to Tom, who was more interested in finding what was happening and locating his wife.

"Caroline hemorrhaged this afternoon," Dr. McKinnon informed him. "She was up lifting the baby after giving it a bath when it happened. We couldn't stop the blood flow, so we rushed her here. Her blood pressure is very low, and she's not responding to treatment." He had warned her continually to stay in bed and let somebody else do the lifting.

"Where is she?" asked Tom.

They pointed to room nearby.

Tom moved in the direction of the room, but the doctor stopped him.

"Tom, she will need blood transfusions. Do we have your permission to give her blood?"

Tom nodded his consent. "Of course. Do anything necessary."

By now he spotted the judge.

"It happened so fast, Tom," the judge said. "The doctor thought he could stop the bleeding, but it was too much. The ambulance came immediately, and we got here in less than an hour."

As they were talking, Mrs. Wingate joined them. She was distraught, and you could see she had been crying. She tried to look brave but was not very successful.

Tom was surprised to see her there. "I thought you were keeping the baby," he said. His statement was more of a question.

Wiping tears from her eyes, Mrs. Wingate replied, "And leave my baby to suffer up here without comfort. I got Granny Mixson's cook's daughter to come over."

This announcement would have alarmed Tom had it been anybody else's daughter than Sparrow Wright's. Sparrow, whose name was pronounced by everyone like "spare," had worked for the Mixson's for years, raising their children and grandchildren as well as her own. Tom could think of no colored person he would trust more.

"Her name is Allie Mae," Mrs. Wingate continued. "She's been around children all her life . . . And Spare is just across the alley . . . Spare says Allie Mae is as good a cook as she is and helped to raise her brothers and sisters."

Tom doubted that she was as good a cook as her mama, but he was relieved that help was found so quickly. "Will she be able to help us out for a few days? . . . While we're in the hospital?"

"She said she would, and if you liked the arrangements, she could have a meal prepared in the evening for you."

"That sounds good to me." Tom was so thankful to have that matter taken care of. "Thanks, Mama Wingate."

Mrs. Wingate smiled as much as she could under the circumstances and now was happy she had found she could be of service to Tom.

Tom looked through the glass panes of the emergency room section. He could see Caroline in the bed with numerous tubes and needles piercing her delicate and lifeless body. The nurses had begun the blood transfusion. It pained him just to look.

Tom spent the rest of the night in the waiting room next to the emergency section. There was no change in Caroline's condition. Nurses kept coffee available for him. The next day, he stayed near her room, taking breaks only to get something to eat or go to the restroom. The hospital food was tasteless. But it didn't matter much to Tom since he had almost lost his appetite. The men at the mill had heard of the emergency, and all volunteered to cover for him and share his duties. People in the community called their home for an update, and the prayer circle at the church met to offer prayers. A list of possible blood donors had already circulated through town. And more than enough had volunteered to donate blood.

You could see the toll the ordeal was taking on Tom. He had never looked as bad in his life as he did that second night at the hospital. His masculine vigor, so characteristic of Tom, had been transformed in the movements of an old man. He lost all sense of time, and his speech had begun to turn to erratic mutterings. His eyes had lost their soul. And his stubbled face showed no character.

Early in the evening, the hospital doctor approached Tom. From the expression on his face, Tom feared he was bearing sad news and stiffened his body, prepared for the worst. Did he really want to hear what the doctor had to say?

"Mr. Wilson?"

"Yes, Doctor." *Here it comes. I can't take it. I can't live without Caroline.*

"Some of the color is coming back to Mrs. Wilson. She's not in pain, but she is still comatose. It's still too early to predict what will happen."

The news did not help Tom feel any better. Yet no news might be good news. Looking through the window, he saw her frail body still ladened with all sorts of life-saving devices.

"Mr. Wilson," the doctor continued. "I know you are exhausted. You haven't slept in two days. Why don't you go home, take a good hot bath, and get a good night's sleep. You can't do anything here but wait. Our staff is very reliable. Besides, the break will be good for you. We have your phone number if we need to get in touch."

Tom was hesitant to even think about leaving. But the doctor was right. In the last two days, he had paced the floor and nothing else. He had never felt so helpless or useless in his life. And he was about to collapse. Even black coffee had no effect. What the sleepless nights had not done to upset his system, the hospital food had.

"Are you sure, Doctor?" he asked.

"Absolutely."

It didn't take any more encouragement from the doctor. Tom drove back to Kirbyville hoping that he would not fall asleep at the wheel of the car on the way home. It was a long and lonely nineteen miles.

When he arrived at his home, he discovered the Wingates had just left heading home to get some rest and take care of the animals at the farm. The house was in immaculate order. Allie Mae must have been psychic because she had prepared a meal which was hot and ready to serve. He looked at the pork chops, mashed potatoes, fresh tomatoes, turnip greens, black-eye peas, and cornbread. After two days of institutional food, it looked like a Roman feast to Tom. Just the pleasant surroundings of his home had a therapeutic effect on him. He greeted Allie Mae like a long-lost friend.

"I know you're Allie Mae . . . I'm Tom Wilson."

"Yes, suh. I'se knows who yo' is."

Allie Mae had none of the African features that characterized most colored girls. Her nose and lips were thin, more Caucasian than nigrah. Her dark eyes were piercing. Tom could tell she was younger than she looked, but he could never tell the age of colored people. They all looked alike to him. Her skin was medium brown, and although her hair was curly, it wasn't kinky and could be combed. Tom thought she would be right at home on an Ethiopian or Egyptian royal barge sailing down the Nile River—a Cleopatra of the ancient world. When she spoke, however, you could tell her education was limited—probably a school dropout. She was pure nigrah.

"How's the baby?" he asked. He was already on his way to the bedroom to see his new son who had somehow been forgotten in the past few days.

"Oh, Mr. Tom," Allie Mae answered. "He be just fine. He such a sweet baby. No problem at all. Just sleep all the time 'cept when he be wet or hungry." Allie Mae was good with children even as young as she was. She said she had learned that raising her own brothers and sisters. She was very proud of the way she had taken over.

Tom looked at his son for several moments. He was trying to reacquaint himself with his heir. Little David slept unperturbed by his admiring father. For a precious moment, he had the baby all to himself.

"Mr. Tom, I'se also moved my bed in heah so 'se could be with him at night. He don't cry none, but if he do, I'se right next to him."

"You're a jewel Allie Mae." Tom was very relieved to see how she had taken over, and a lot of his fears were immediately allayed.

"I'se got suppah ready, Mr. Tom, whens yo' ready."

"Allie Mae, I'm starved. And it sure does smell good. I think I'll take a hot shower before I eat."

Allie Mae headed for the kitchen, and Tom got some clean clothes and departed for the bathroom.

God, it was good to be home, he kept telling himself. For a moment, he forgot the problems and events and things that had happened in the last few days and concentrated on being back in the sanctuary of his own home. The hot water rippled across his back and untwisted his man taut muscles. Here he was safe. Here he was comfortable. Here was his own little universe. Only Caroline was needed to make it complete.

Allie Mae was indeed a good cook. If she was only half the cook her mother, Spare, was, then Spare must be a gourmet chef. She told Tom she had learned it cooking for her brothers and sisters. It might have been soul food. But it was good for Tom's soul as well as his stomach. After his supper, Tom retreated to the living room. *If I smoked*, he thought, *I'd light up a big cigar right now and just sit here.* But Caroline had seen to it that no one smoked in her house. And Tom had given up the habit years ago to keep peace in the family.

But Tom, having second thoughts, told himself he could have a drink of good whiskey. He had a bottle of Wild Turkey in his locker at the fire station. He never drank anywhere except the fire station where it was hidden from the public eye. He didn't worry about being caught because he knew the community would overlook it anyway. And everyone else did it—even the Baptists. But if he could just have one now, life would be nice. The picture would be complete. *Maybe there's a bottle around here*, he thought, unless Caroline, in her zealous Baptist spirit, threw it away.

As soon as Allie Mae finished cleaning the kitchen, Tom went into the pantry. He moved the cans and boxes around searching for what he hoped would be a bottle with a little liquor left in it. Not finding any there, he searched under the cabinets. When he pushed some old washing powder aside in the pantry, he found a half-full bottle of bourbon whiskey. *Thanks, Lord.* You could tell by the thick layer of dust on the bottle it hadn't been opened in ages. Nevertheless, he wiped the bottle, opened the cap, and poured himself three fingers of the whiskey. It was still good—even aged.

By his second drink, he had come to the conclusion that life had reversed itself and things looked better all the time. He felt like that old Tom Wilson that used to inhabit his body. Even in the midst of a bad depression, happy days were here again. He had come home. And it was good—no, it was fabulous!

The next morning Tom was aroused by the telephone ringing.

"I'll get it!" he yelled in case anyone else was up.

"Mr. Wilson?" the voice asked.

"Yes, this is he."

"This is the Dr. Singletary at Jasper General Hospital."

Tom's heart stopped for a moment. The knuckles on the hand holding the telephone turned white. He had a sinking feeling in his stomach. His voice quivered.

"Yes, Doctor?" He was afraid to say more.

"Mr. Wilson, your wife has awakened from her coma. Her color is good. She's able to talk. And she says she's hungry." The doctor hesitated. "I believe we have passed the crisis and are out of the woods."

Tom made no effort to stop the tears. By this time, he was so weak that had a breeze gone through the house, it would have blown him over. "Thank God. Thank God." There was a moment of silence—perhaps a short prayer. "I'll be up as soon as I get dressed. Thank you so much, Doctor."

Within a week or so, Caroline was on her feet, feeling well and ready to be dismissed. Her return to her home was a town event. It seemed that everybody wanted to drop by and welcome her home. Tom tried to screen her visitors because she was still weak. But it was difficult not to show their happiness at being home. Many people sent food, and Lock's Flower Shop made daily deliveries.

Judge and Mrs. Wingate greeted her with little David in their arms. It was like seeing her baby for the first time. Caroline took David from her mother and gave him a big hug. She made no efforts to hide the tears running down her cheeks. It was a moment in Wilson family history that each member would remember in his own special way.

As Tom brought things in from the car, Caroline surveyed the domain she had left so abruptly. "This house is perfect—no dust, no dirty clothes, not a pot or pan out of place."

Mrs. Wingate quickly spoke, "It was Allie Mae. She's been a jewel—the baby loves her. Tom didn't need us as long as she was here."

"I can hardly wait to meet her, Mama. When will she come by?"

"Honey, she told me last night she had been offered a job in Beaumont." Mrs. Wingate hated to break the news to Caroline. "And since you were coming home today, I told her to take it—at least check it out—before someone else got it. You know how hard it is getting jobs during this Depression . . . especially for nigrahs."

Caroline was disappointed. "I hope to meet her soon and tell her how much I appreciated her help." Caroline sat on the empty roll-away bed beside their own bed. "Maybe I can do something for her one day." Caroline never met Allie Mae but could keep up with her through her mama, Sparrow. "I hope Tom paid her extra for all she did."

Tom, who had been listening to the conversation in another room, interrupted the ladies by saying, "I paid her more than enough . . . I'll get this bed out of here right away." He pushed the roll-away toward the front porch. He was so glad to be home again with his family.

Within a few weeks, Caroline was up and about doing all the chores that she had missed while she was away. Now she had an additional one—caring for that little son who was growing like a weed. She had no serious illness after that, although Dr. McKinnon checked her heart on a biannual basis. She knew she would never have another child. Caroline wrote many thank-you notes for the food and flowers. She thanked her friends for their prayers. She never ceased to thank Dr. McKinnon in her own prayers. He had almost become her second father. But most of all, she regretted that she had never seen or met Allie Mae for the biggest thanks of all. *Maybe*, she convinced herself, *our paths will cross one day.*

Things were like they used to be. That was a long time ago—almost eighteen years. The Depression was over; and they had gone through World War II, rationing, the draft, Gold Star Mothers, and all the things that came with war. Tom's disability exempted him serving in the army. Otherwise he would have enlisted early in the war. They were fairly comfortable—no bills or debts at least—and there had been no significant health problems for anybody since Caroline's stay in the hospital. Tom remembered those good days and tried to push the bad events from his memory as much as he could. Now all those he loved were sitting with him in the kitchen.

Tom pushed the plate away from him and drew a cup of coffee closer. "Mrs. Wilson," he said, "that was a delicious supper."

She responded with a smile and a "thank you."

"Larrapin," David added.

"Larrapin?" Caroline asked. "What does that mean?"

"I don't have the slightest notion. It's a word that Bessie at the drugstore uses when something taste good," David answered. "I think it's one of those words her family used when they lived in the hills of Kentucky."

"Can I interest anyone in going to the picture show?" Tom inquired. "I think there's a Danny Kaye comedy running tonight. Got some pretty good reviews. Boys at the mill liked it."

"No thanks," David was quick to answer. "I think I'll go over to Sug's house and play 42. He said several of the guys were coming by later tonight."

Caroline, too, begged off the invitation. "Honey, I don't want to leave all these dishes in the sink, and I don't think we can make it on time if I clean up first." She looked tired. Caroline could work all day and look utterly exhausted. Tom could work all day and come home full of energy and ready to go.

"Why don't we go another time?" she asked. "You can read the *Beaumont Enterprise* while I'm cleaning up and then maybe we could sit out in the backyard and enjoy the evening breeze."

"Sounds good to me."

David left, and Caroline and Tom enjoyed the pleasures that only an older couple could appreciate. Lightning bugs were beginning to fly in the backyard. They looked like sparks from an unseen campfire swirling toward heaven. The fragrance from Caroline's rose garden wafted across the porch and into the yard. The hoot owl that visited the Wilson garage each evening was warming up for its nightly serenade. With the crickets, it became a nocturnal duet that Caroline and Tom had come to love. Tom put his arms around Caroline and drew her close to him, and she in turn lovingly kissed his arm. It was one of those moments when silence said it all.

CHAPTER SEVEN

To a young man who was waiting to leave Kirbyville and move to Austin and the state university, the days were incredibly long and hot. To David, the routine got monotonous. Home. Work. Play 42 with the gang. Home. Sleep. Work. Picture show. Home. Work. He felt like he was a prisoner of the calendar. Life was not as boring as he seemed to make it. He ran around with his friends—the gang. They played 42 almost every night or so. The Palace Theater had a change of movies every other day, and the cost of going was only fifty cents—not prohibitive for a young man saving his money for college. This week, patrons had an opportunity to see *Dear Wife* with Joan Caulfield and William Holden. But the films everyone was talking about were *The Asphalt Jungle* starring Sterling Hayden and featuring a new face in Hollywood named Marilyn Monroe. Science fiction fans looked forward to *The Next Voice You Hear*.

David saw Toye Lee every day. They would wave or yell at each other as they dumped trash. Toye Lee would bring the overripe fruit from the grocery store, and they shared expired pastries and milk from time to time. Allie Mae would often look out the back door of Lea's Café, wave at the boys, and sometimes bring them a sandwich or hamburger. However, she never came close enough for David to introduce himself or talk to her. With all the food David was getting, he often did not go home for lunch, choosing to eat food from the store and café instead. When that happened, he could talk to Toye Lee a little more at length. Already Toye Lee had asked David to get some of them thangs from the drawer in the pharmacy three times—the economy size. He had never seen any of Toye Lee's girlfriends, but there was no doubt in his mind that they existed, maybe a harem. Until David met Toye Lee, he had never known what the guys called a stud. He had prepared a story for the day he had to go back to the pharmacy and withdraw another package of condoms—Trojans or Ramses—from the drawer. His biggest concern was whether the pharmacist believed him when he said they were for someone else. Perhaps, he thought, but he'd better just take them when no one was watching.

For the older generations, times were normal. Hot and dry. Long ago they had realized that they would be in Kirbyville for the rest of their lives. That wasn't so bad. They rarely left except to go to Beaumont to shop or out of town on vacation. Unlike the youth, they enjoyed the long days and breezy nights. Caroline spent hours singing in the church choir; she did volunteer work in the community and took care of her men. Since school was out for summer vacation and David had graduated, she was not involved in PTA anymore since it stopped in elementary school. She would sometimes substitute as teacher for her Sunday school class and usually attended Sunday evening services, but always alone!

Tom stayed busy working as a volunteer fireman after he got off from the mill. Besides the regular practice on Monday nights, there were hoses to clean and trucks to maintain. And those activities culminated with a session with the boys in the lounge upstairs and having a drink or two. Occasionally he and some friends would go fishing at the dozen lakes in the area or on the Sabine River. His family was particularly fond of river catfish. He was always anxious for the arrival of fall and hunting season. That was one topic, however, he never mentioned around the house anymore since the accident.

While the city of Kirbyville was suffering from a case of the summer "slows," this was not the case on the world scene. The *Enterprise* carried limited coverage of world news, but the citizens of Kirbyville realized that soon things would be in a state of turmoil—again.

Tom Dewey announced to his supporters that he would not seek the Republican presidential nomination in 1952. He had lost face after he "won" the election of 1948 and people—Republicans—wanted a new face and a winner and no more embarrassment.

To Caroline, that was good news. "He shouldn't after he blew it two years ago. I agree with Alice Roosevelt," she told her friends. "He does look like the bridegroom on a wedding cake. The party needs a candidate with some warm blood in his veins . . . and something new to offer." She continued to hear General Eisenhower's name mentioned as a potential candidate and was pretty well convinced he would get the nomination. He had personality even though he had no political philosophy. Republicans couldn't resist picking generals. She shuddered at the thought that they might call General MacArthur from Korea to run. *Lord, help us from his making two messes rather than one.* But that was two years away. She was thinking like a political analyst or that might be her Democratic upbringing talking to her. It made no difference to her since she had voted Democratic since the days her father first took her into the polling booth on election days. There were no known Republicans in the county. As a matter of fact, the Republicans, seeing their party's having no chance of victory, nominated the statewide Democrat candidates, hoping they might get something from the ruling party. If there were Republicans, they operated underground. Kirbyville voters had no individual voting booths—only the tables in the school library. Marking a ballot could not be called secret since a lot of other people were voting also at the same table. It was another social event, and talking about the candidates at the polls was not considered a felony that the law said it was. Everything they did was illegal. Who was going to report them? The nonexistent Republicans? Tom voted only when prodded or coerced by Caroline. Since he might vote *wrong*, Caroline often went to the polls alone.

Civic duty to Tom was warning *blind* Americans of the apparent communist infiltration in the United States. That was a subject that could really get his temperature up.

Senator Joseph McCarthy continued to point fingers at people in Washington with accusations of being communists or communist sympathizers. He also was blaming Hollywood celebrities for subversion.

"Witch hunt!" Caroline cringed at the thought of the despicable senator from Wisconsin. "Why are people so intimidated by him and his methods?" The senator truly disgusted her. "Why people believe him and his lies is something I don't understand."

Tom had another opinion. "He's a great American doing what the president and those other weaklings in Washington's ought to do . . . He should be the presidential candidate."

"And I would be out on the streets working for his opponent," she said just as quickly, "whoever he was."

But it was the events in Southeast Asia that became the concern of the American people. Korea had been invaded from the north and rejected the orders of the United Nations to cease fighting. President Truman ordered the defense of Formosa with American troops. Seoul was abandoned and fell to the communists forces. In June, President Truman had ordered General Douglas MacArthur to South Korea and troops would surely follow. The UN supported the cause of South Korea, but by late June, the communists had already crossed the 38th parallel. Russia in the Security Council was using its vote to thwart the will of the majority. To many, it was just a matter of time before the United States was involved in another global conflict. The draft would have to be reinstated in order to get personnel to fight. And that was so soon after World War II.

Caroline started reading the newspaper daily and would turn on the radio more often than she usually did. "The whole world's gone crazy again. This is not our fight!" she exclaimed.

Tom completely supported the Democratic administration on its Korean policy, although he preferred stronger action. "Someone has got to push those gooks. If not us, who?" He laughed at the news that North Koreans had formally objected to the use of the term "gooks" to describe them. "Gooks . . . chinks . . . slant-eyed bastards, yellow sons of bitches from hell. What the hell? We'll call them whatever we want." His profanity always bothered Caroline.

To Caroline, the UN involvement meant one thing—the United States' involvement. "We'll be fighting with the most men and paying the largest amount of money to cover the costs. It'll be us pretty much alone."

Tom had to agree with her on that opinion. But he saw the costs justifying the action.

David and Toye Lee still talked each day while they went about doing their chores. Their friendship had gotten to the point they could kid each other and horse around the alley. But until now, they had never done anything away from the store or around town.

David was the first to make a suggestion. "Toye Lee?" he asked as he pitched a cardboard box onto the trash pile. "Why don't we do something different sometimes—together."

The suggestion immediately raised all kinds of doubts and thoughts for Toye Lee. "Like what?"

"Well, like going out . . . to a movie . . . Or to get a Coke. Or something."

Toye Lee was surprised. "Yeah. Can't you see a white boy and a black boy hauling ass around town together . . . or sitting in the picture show together."

David was quick to explain. "I know we can't go to the show and sit together or get a Coke at the same counter. But we can go somewhere where we can't be seen. Or get some drinks and sit in the car."

"In this nosey town?" Toye Lee asked.

"Yes. If we are careful." David began to see the silliness of it. Husbands who cheated on their wives and slipped around thought they were getting away with it, but usually everybody in town knew about it. The same was true of wives. The gossips of Kirbyville knew something on everybody. David knew for sure that the mother of his friend, Sug, marked her calendar nine months after a couple married. Weddings were community events—everyone being invited. So were births. There were some local ladies who like to keep account of the *premature* babies born to the newlyweds. *Early* babies were always a good topic of conversation at the missionary society or the quilting circle. And there were many.

Toye Lee was still not convinced. He had seen times when nigrahs—right or wrong—got blamed for breaking the code. He remembered an incident where the wife of the Church of Christ preacher got the hots for the church's colored janitor. She was also the church choir director, despite the fact that the church prohibited coloreds the use of musical instruments. Their affair was discovered when she was noticed spending more and more time checking the music in the choir rehearsal room. The matter caused an uproar in the church and even more so in the community. It ended when the minister was *called* to another pulpit. "Called" meant the minister got a better job offer somewhere else or he was in trouble and had to get out of town in a hurry. The couple abruptly moved away. The colored janitor was driven out of town by an unruly committee of church elders who resembled the Klan without their bedsheets or burning crosses. Whenever and wherever this topic came up in the months that followed, the citizens, especially the church members, would always embellish the story about the preacher's wife with an additional phrase: "She was a Yankee, you know." That seemed to take some of the sensationalism out of the scandal and smoothed over the indiscretions. The event was taken seriously by the Baptists and Methodists who became more careful of their indiscretions. Everyone in town knew who the drinkers, the philanderers, the debtors, and the "ladies of the night" were, but accepted it as a matter of fact.

Toye Lee still wasn't sure this would work.

"Look," David suggested, "let's give it a try. I'll choose a place, and then you choose a place. We can do it at night or out of town. Dad lets me use the car sometimes, and we can get away from here."

To have a set of wheels appealed to Toye Lee even if they belonged to a white man. His resistance began to crumble.

Tom would let David drive Geraldine from time to time. College boys from Kirbyville didn't buy cars until after they graduated. David never felt a right to have the car when he wanted it. That's why he always asked. But Tom was fair about the use of the car, and when David wanted it for some special reason, he could usually get it. Transporting a colored boy around town was not so exciting to David. His dad would strongly object. Therefore, his passenger would remain anonymous, especially to Tom.

Toye Lee was wavering. He had to weigh the prospect of having a new friend—a white boy—with the possibility of having his ass whipped by local thugs if he got caught. It was not an easy choice to make.

"All right," he finally said. "Yo' first."

David was enthusiastic about the new venture. He would start with a simple excursion, and maybe things would progress to more interesting events later in the summer.

"We'll go to the picture show," David announced.

Toye Lee winced.

"What's the matter?" David asked.

Toye Lee had problems sitting for two hours at a time in the hot balcony. His energy far exceeded his patience.

"Look," David assured him, "as many movies as comes to the show every week, there's got to be something you like. Do you like comedies? Dramas? Action?"

He offered the bill of fare for the next week. "Red Skelton in *The Yellow Cab Man*. He's always good. *The Traveling Saleswoman* with Joan Davis. She's crazy."

A movie David was dying to see would be playing soon, but he hesitated to mention it. "Broderick Crawford is starring in a picture called *All the King's Men*. It won the Academy Award, but it might be too serious for you. It's based on the life of Huey P. Long."

"Who he?" Toye Lee asked.

"He was the governor of Louisiana in the thirties. Got assassinated." David thought the picture might have racial overtones, so he suggested something else. "There's a good action film coming I know you will like. It's called *Twelve O'Clock High* with Gregory Peck. It's a war picture with lots of drama."

"Is it about the army?" Toye Lee asked.

"Well, about the army air force in World War II."

"Let's see that one. I'se like to see army shows."

They made plans to meet in front of the picture show next Thursday night. They would pretend they didn't know each other. They would buy their own tickets, sit in the separate white or colored sections, see the movie, and then meet behind Lea's Café and then go get something to eat. They would order their food to go and eat it in the car.

Nigrahs entered the Palace Theater by two stairways on each side of the ticket booth. These stairways led to two small separate balconies on each side of the projection booth. Whites entered by the two main doors downstairs. David was careful to choose a seat where he could see Toye Lee out of the corner of his eye. From time to time, he would look up. Toye Lee reciprocated by tossing a piece of popcorn at him. He laughed each time he did this. Toye Lee's smile was infectious, and at certain times, it could melt a person's resistance. David often wished his own personality was a little more congenial and effervescent—more like his dad rather than his mother. The balcony sections were always noisier than the downstairs sections. The colored people didn't mean to be raucous, they were just enjoying the movie. The whites often wondered what went on upstairs with all the chuckling and dragging and stomping of feet. No one, however, ever went to the balcony. It was off-limits to whites and against the code.

After the movie, Toye Lee and David met behind the café. David had been able to get the car that night, so they had wheels. Toye Lee was impressed with Geraldine. New cars were still unique because Detroit had not yet filled the demand after the war. Tom Wilson treated his vehicle like a member of the family. He kept it spotless and always full of gasoline—just in case!

"You like the movie?" David asked.

"Yeah. I'se going to join the army someday and get into some action. Maybe a little travel. At least away from this dumpy town."

This was the first time David had heard Toye Lee say something about the town in a derogatory manner.

"You ever been anywhere, Toye Lee?"

"Man, I'se ain't even been out of this heah county!"

David was surprised to hear that. "Not even to Beaumont?" he asked, referring to the city sixty miles away.

"I'se said this county," Toye Lee repeated. "I'se a real hometown boy!" He laughed when he said it. "When yo' don't has wheels, yo' doesn't go nowheres."

"Well, my friend, you are going to go to Newton County tonight," David notified him.

Newton County was just a few miles east of Kirbyville and primarily a farm county. "We are going to the Hawthorne Community, and I'm treating you to the best watermelon you have ever eaten."

Toye Lee looked puzzled.

"You do like watermelon, don't you?" asked David.

"Do squirrels have a tail?" Toye Lee hesitated a moment after looking at David. "Dumb ass, of course I'se likes watermelon. Ain't we s'posed to?"

Toye Lee punched David in the ribs. He just broke the code first by getting in the front seat and then by touching a white boy.

As they drove toward the county line, David told Toye Lee the plan. The Hawthorne Community was an area where several members of the Hawthorne family had settled years ago. They were farmers. Each year they planted several acres of watermelons—some for sales, but primarily for the family and friends. It was customary for the farmers to plant extra hills of watermelons, knowing that the teenagers would come out and *help* themselves to them. By local standards, this was not considered stealing but a part of growing up in the county.

"You now are in Newton County, Toye Lee." David crossed the county line.

Toye Lee smiled, and now he was a traveler.

As they approached the farm, David spotted the watermelon patch. He quickly cut off the lights. As they emerged from the car, David motioned to Toye Lee to be quiet.

"Do you hear anything?" he asked, hoping he had not aroused the sleeping farmers.

There was complete silence except for the chirping of the evening crickets and the breeze moaning through the pine trees.

David continued. "We're going to climb through that fence and find us a good melon. Take only what you can eat. Don't be wasteful."

It only took a few minutes. David found his melon quickly and broke the stem. Toye Lee found two that looked good to him. Unable to decide, he announced, "I'se take both and don't play favorites."

After returning to the car and putting their melons in the trunk, they drove down the road to Singletary's Bridge. That was a popular place to go swimming in the day, and there were some picnic tables to eat on.

Toye Lee looked at David. "If us niggers done this, it be's called stealin'. When whites do it, it be just a prank."

David had no response.

Toye Lee was enjoying this. He acted like a kid who was pulling a fast one on someone, especially white folks. "I'se got a knife." He pulled a pocket knife from his pocket and sank it into the melon.

David usually just dropped the melons and ate the heart. But this was more civilized.

"That's quite a weapon," he commented.

"Carry it with me ever'weh's I'se goes."

"My mother would never let me have one."

"My mama say to carry it always. Might come in handy if I'se get in a fight."

"Damn, Toye Lee!" David exclaimed. "You could kill a person with that thing."

"Yo' right! But so far, I'se clean."

David gave Toye Lee a penetrating look. Then he shrugged. He looked like he wanted to say something.

"What?"

"Nothing . . . nothing."

"I'se knows what yo' thinkin'," Toye Lee blurted. "Yo' been tol' all yo' life that us niggers like watermelon and carry knives . . . 'cause we likes to fight. Now yo' seen it . . . and prob'ly believes it . . . guess yo' believe we be's natu'l tap dancers too. We just got that rhythm from our ancestahs in Africa . . . ain't that what yo' thinkin', David?"

David did not move or say a word.

Toye Lee looked at David who looked away. "That what all whites think 'bout us, ain't it?"

"Shit! Toye Lee!" David was miffed. "You going to drop all the problems of nigrahs on me . . . and make me feel bad . . . no way. Go blame the South . . . or the Klan . . . but don't think how white people think about nigrahs is my fault . . . that old dog won't hunt."

"Well, fo' yo' information, it ain't true. I'se really don't like watermelons all that much, and I'se can't dance a step. If I'se got rhythm, it's in my hips, not my feet." Toye Lee looked more serious than angry. "But I'se does confess . . . and please don't go and tell yo' white friends . . . I'se does loves moon pies and RC Cola." He bent over, laughing as he said it. "Likes we's s'posed to."

In the conversation, David did not mention his ancestor Robert Wingate brought two hundred slaves from Mississippi to East Texas in 1852. They had been emancipated on June 19, 1863, now called Juneteenth, but it was best that Toye Lee not know this information.

David had begun to feel uncomfortable by Toye Lee's comments. When he realized Toye Lee was pulling his leg, he was embarrassed. "Damn and double damn," David replied. "You turd!"

Toye Lee just cackled.

David and Toye Lee returned to town about an hour later. David drove across the tracks to Toye Lee's home. It was dark, so they assumed Allie Mae had already gone to bed.

"You choose our next venture," David told Toye Lee.

"I'se be's thinking about it." Toye Lee already had an idea in mind. "I'se see yo' tomorrah." He chuckled, then laughed out loud.

"What's the matter?" David asked.

"I'se nevah knowed white boys . . . *lifted* things in the night. Yo' whites always say we's the ones that steal . . . Now I'se knows bettah."

David decided that it was not worth explaining what they had done was not considered stealing. Logically, he thought, stealing is stealing, whatever the object. Degrees of stealing made just about as much sense as "being a little bit pregnant."

"Get out of here," he said as he pressed his foot to the accelerator. "Good night."

"Night," Toye Lee responded as he ran toward his house. "Don't let the bedbugs bite!"

David drove home. The evening had been a first for him. He had discovered that nigrahs had feelings too. All the things he had been told about colored people were exaggerations. He liked Toye Lee and was curious to know what plans he would make on their next time out.

CHAPTER EIGHT

David had not dropped or deserted his other friends. In fact, they never suspected that he was seeing a colored person. David wondered what they would say if they did know. He continued to go to the picture show and play 42 with the gang. His church activities took precedence over all other social pursuits. The gang knew that Caroline often expected him to help her at home and they never bothered to memorize his work schedule; so he could always say he was at home, at work, or at church and no one would question his absences. Actually, David didn't feel what he was doing was wrong. But would people understand? Better that they didn't know than try to explain it to everyone, especially his dad.

One Saturday a week or so after their movie experience, as David and Toye Lee were dumping trash behind the store, Toye Lee announced his plan. "We's goin' fishing."

David was not a fisherman. He had put out some trotlines with the gang when they spent the night at Crawford's camp on Cow Creek. It was only a chance to get away and play 42. Fishing, like hunting, was not on David's agenda. Many times before, Tom had wanted to take David with him when he and the boys went to the river. He yearned for the opportunity of taking his son out and showing him some fun. All the other fathers did it, why not him? But he never had the courage to ask Caroline. Being turned down was worse than asking. He was trying to honor the bargain he made with Caroline eighteen years ago—no guns. Besides, he had already discovered long ago David had no interest in guns or sports.

"Sounds great!" David exclaimed. "But I don't have any fishing gear." Then he remembered they sold hooks and lines in the drugstore. "But I can buy some inside."

"Yo' doesn't need a thing. I'se got everything we's needs," he was told. "All yo' has to do is meet me here tomorrow after church."

Sunday was a beautiful day, but like all days in a Texas summer, it was miserably hot. After church, he told his parents he was going out for a while. They never asked for specific details unless he wanted to tell them. Toye Lee was waiting on him behind the drugstore.

David was somewhat apprehensive meeting in the daylight behind the drugstore. "Don't think anyone will see us?"

"We goin' slip right down this alley, cross ovah the tracks, walk behind those shacks ovah there," he explained, pointing to the homes of those nigrahs who were on the east side of town. "The creek is right behind the houses, and we walks up the creek to my favorite fishin' hole."

"Where's the tackle?" David asked, realizing that Toye Lee was empty-handed. He expected him to have a box of some kind with fishing gear.

"Got it in my pocket," he responded, patting his pants pocket in the rear. "Let's go!"

They quickly crossed the tracks and disappeared between the houses and into the woods. David hoped no one saw them.

"The creek's just ahead." Toye Lee was leading the way. "We turns left right up heah."

Despite the soaring temperature, the vegetation and shade from the trees on both sides of Little Cow Creek was thick and lush. The creek was small compared to others farther from town. It was an all-year stream which sometimes flooded in the winter and spring but was still enjoyable in the hot summer because of the heavy foliage. It was a refuge from the blistering summer heat for the plants and animals that depended on it for survival. "This is wheah the animals come's to drink," Toye Lee added.

Toye Lee led David down a worn, narrow, but distinct trail running along the creek bank. Sometimes he would have to push overhanging

—

vegetation out of the way to pass. And bushes and plants would whip back and hit David in the face.

"What are those plants, Toye Lee?" David asked, pointing to some broad-leafed bushes with purple berries.

"Pokeberry plant. Berries be's poisonous, but you can eat the leaves. Yo' never had no poke leaf salad?"

David shook his head. *Must be some kind of nigrah food*, he thought. "And those?"

"Mulberry bushes. Makes good tea."

David recognized the dandelions with their heads of yellow blowing in the breeze. They would soon turn into puffs of seed that the wind would take far and wide and again become a nuisance in somebody's yard.

"Yo' can make beer with those dandelions," Toye Lee added. "See them vines in the trees?" He pointed toward the trees. "Them's muscadine vines. Best wine yo' can make. They's be bearin' in the fall. Maybe we's come back down here and make some wine fo' yo' when yo' come home from school." Toye Lee was amazed by David's lack of knowledge of the various plants and shrubs. "Boy, wheah yo' been all yo' life? I'se thought everbody who be's raised in Texas knowed about them. Didn't yo' take biology in school?"

"I've never been in the woods much," David volunteered. Toye Lee was more a botanist that anything in the botany books at school. "That's poison ivy," Toye Lee cautioned as he saw David reach toward the vine. "That will cause yo' misery."

David quickly withdrew his hand. He remembered the time he got into some poison ivy on his grandfather's farm. Dr. McKinnon first diagnosed it as the *itch* which people associated with "poor white trash." There had been several cases of itch and lice at the school. Decent people didn't have those *diseases*. David's entire family had to take the *cure*, which included rubbing their entire bodies with a sulfur salve. After two weeks of the cure and it didn't clear up, the doctor realized it was poison ivy and changed the medication. Those were two of the most miserable weeks in his life. Afterward, they had to burn the clothes they wore during treatment—and what a smell.

"And them's chinky-pins," he said, pointing to the small trees with strange-looking prickly nuts on the stems. "Squirrel's crazy about them . . . and piney woods rootahs."

"What's a piney woods rooter?"

"Wild hawgs . . . and if yo' evah see one comin' yo' way, yo' bettah shimmy up a tree quick . . . or lose yo' leg."

"Any of those hogs around here?"

"Sometimes and snakes and scorpions."

David had heard of chinquapins—could even spell it but had never seen one. "I'd like to try one of the nuts." But the thought of a wild pig in the area encouraged him to continue down the trail right behind Toye Lee as close as he could get.

"See that tall tree over there?" Toye Lee asked, pointing across the creek. "Them's possum persimmons. Good to eat when ripe but will draw yo' mouth up when eaten green." He puckered his lips up to illustrate the point. With his lips puckered, he added, "Yo' evah want to have some fun, give 'em some green possum persimmons. They be whistlin' 'Dixie' then." He chuckled at the thought of some unsuspecting person biting into a green persimmon.

The botany lesson would have continued, but they had arrived at the fishing hole. It was larger than the rest of the creek with high banks on each side. On the trees hanging over the banks were ropes which were used for swings. An oak tree had fallen in the creek years ago, and the remaining log was to the side of the swings.

"Looks like a swimming hole too, Toye Lee."

"I think some white folks come up here sometimes. But they usually go to Singletary's Bridge or Trout Creek. Can't fish if they's someone swimmin' out there." Toye Lee reached into his pockets and retrieved two Prince Albert tobacco cans. In one were some hooks on a line. In the other were some earthworms which he had dug earlier that morning. "Now look around and see if you see a pole. If we don't find one, I got my knife and we'll cut one down."

Fortunately, there were several poles left by previous fishermen, just right for fishing off the banks. Toye Lee threw David a hook, sinker, and cork all rolled up into a small ball.

"Just tie it on the end."

David tried but it slipped.

"I'se bet yo' can't even bait a hook, can yo'?" David had never baited a hook but didn't know how was he going to do it without Toye Lee knowing it.

He was spared the embarrassment when Toye Lee reached over, picked up a worm, and ran the hook down its middle. "See? Nothing to it!"

David looked as the worm shrank from the intrusion of the fishhook into its stomach. He winced. It was different from baiting trotlines with pieces of calf liver.

With the hooks now ready, Toye Lee was ready to climb down the embankment. There were logs and cypress knees around the slope leading to the water's edge. And some limbs reached out over the water.

"Be careful now. Yo' might slip and fall. Or hit yo' head on them roots or that big log ovah there," he warned, pointing to a huge tree that had fallen into the water years ago. "I'se doesn't want to do mouth-to-mouth on you if yo' fall in," he added, jabbing David in the ribs. "Besides, yo' ain't my type." Toye Lee cackled out loud.

David was attentive to the instructions and got down the embankment without difficulty.

"Now just throw your line ovah there," Toye Lee instructed David, pointing to a spot that looked deep and foreboding.

David followed instructions precisely. He was now ready to pull in the mother of all perches, but nothing happened—not even a nibble. He moved his line around to another spot.

In the meantime, Toye Lee had thrown his line in the opposite direction, got a strike, and pulled in a nice-sized sunfish. "I'll make a stringer out of a limb." He cut the branch from a shrub and made a homemade stringer and put it through the fish's mouth. In a matter of minutes, he had put his hook back into the water. Again, the line bobbled, and he pulled up another fish.

"My lucky day!" he exclaimed. "Ain't yo' got a bite yet, David?"

"Nothing."

While David was shifting from one foot to another, Toye Lee was pulling still another perch from the stream that flowed south into the Sabine River miles away and finally into the Gulf of Mexico.

—

David couldn't decide whether he was angry or embarrassed at his prowess as a fisherman.

Toye Lee tried to soothe his ruffled feelings. "David," he blurted, "yo' know us niggers is just natu'al-born fishermen. Got generations of training. Yo' know . . . in the jungle."

David was amused and smiled at the comment then almost instinctively threw his head back and laughed. "Sho' 'nuff," David answered, mimicking Toye Lee.

"See that blackberry on that vine over there?" Toye Lee asked, pointing to a branch over David's head. "I'se bet I'se could catch something with that on a hook."

"Crap! Whoever heard of fish eating berries?"

Toye Lee reached over David's head and picked a firm blackberry from the vine. "Not too juicy or it fall off the hook." With a flourish, Toye Lee threw the hook near a log with several branches protruding from the water. He sat very still.

David was about to chide Toye Lee for being a smart-ass when he noticed the line dip under the water. "You got a bite!"

"'Coa'se. I'se does."

The line disappeared at the same time Toye Lee jerked on the pole. Up came the line and a nice bass.

"Biggest one so far," claimed Toye Lee, who was obviously proud of his catch. He thought how they would smell in a frying pan.

David was at a loss for words momentarily. He shrugged his shoulders and acted like it was just an accident. "Lucky, butt."

Toye Lee's smile turned to an outright laugh. David was dealing with an old hand at fishing now. Only he didn't know it. Toye Lee didn't tell David that he had fished here many times before, always coming home with a mess of fish for supper. "And I'se wants yo' to know that I'se doesn't like gar or buffalo fish. I'se knows what yo' whites say 'bout us, but it ain't true." Toye was referring to the expression made by whites that only nigrahs ate gar and buffalo fish—fish considered by whites to be trash fish.

Within an hour, Toye Lee had caught enough fish for a mess. He never took more than he could eat at one meal.

"Let's take a break, David."

They climbed back up the embankment and found a grassy spot in the sun to sit on.

"Does yo' know how to scale fish?" But David's expression had already given Toye Lee the answer. "Damned, yo' white boys doesn't know nothin'."

He was joshing David who took it in good spirits. After all, Toye Lee was right.

"At least there's one thing we can do as good as you can," he commented.

"What's that?" Toye Lee asked curiously.

"We knows how to drink RC Cola and eat moon pies," David retorted in a nigrah dialect.

They both fell back into the grass with a roar of laughter. As they lay looking at the sky, David heard what he thought was some kind of strange music.

"Do you hear that, Toye Lee?" he asked.

"Shhhhhh." Toye listened for a moment.

"It's music coming from up the creek," David added.

"Must be New Jerusalem Primitive Baptist Church," Toye Lee answered.

"Who are they?" David asked.

"It's a little church over neah the highway. I'se bet they's having a baptizin'."

"Can we go see it?" David was very curious now.

"Yeah. But we's bettah be quiet. Don't make any noise. They's like they's privacy."

As they quickly walked up the trail along the creek bank, the singing became louder and louder. You heard the words of the songs now and then and comments of the preacher. Soon they could see movement through the foliage. They moved very carefully toward the ceremony but hid behind the trunk of some gigantic magnolia trees and yaupon bushes.

The congregation was standing on the banks across the creek. They were singing and clapping their hands and invoking the blessing of the Lord. Those to be baptized were wearing long white robes and were standing in a line awaiting their turn to be immersed. The reverend was also in a white robe with a golden belt, standing in the middle of the stream. As each person waded to the preacher, there would be a prayer before he was immersed.

"Lord, take this sinner to your breast and make him whole. Cleanse his body and protect him from Satan. Now go and walk with Jesus for the rest of your life," the preacher proclaimed. The immersion followed.

On coming from the water, the congregation sang and shook some kind of rattle and clapped their hands. The congregation was shouting in joyous unity. "Hallelujah! Praise Jesus! Amen!" They clapped their hands as they shouted. They undulated, moving back and forth like the golden rods in the breeze behind them.

Toye Lee whispered to David, "They's got the ghost?"

"The what?"

"The Holy Ghost. Yo' dumb ass!"

"Why don't they use the baptistry for this?" he whispered to Toye Lee.

"Because, Mr. White Boy, they's ain't no baptistry in the church. Not all these churches have them fine things yo' white churches has."

David had been baptized—in the church. It had no real meaning for David. Everyone his age had joined the church. It was more of a social thing with little spiritual meaning. He thought to himself that this was much more in keeping with the spirit of the church. Like John the Baptist baptizing Jesus in the Jordan River. The New Jerusalem Church was more in keeping with Jesus's tradition than his own church. He was fascinated by what he saw. The baptism ceremony was over in a matter of minutes, and the congregation retreated to their cars in their white, but dripping robes. The preacher had concluded the ceremony with a resounding amen, to which every member had responded with a louder amen.

"Do you go to church, Toye Lee?" David asked as they walked back to the fishing hole.

Toye Lee was reluctant to answer. Then he said, "Sometimes I'se does."

"This church?"

"Naw, I'se goes to Pilgrim's Rest African Methodist Church . . . in the Qua'tahs . . . My mama go lot mo' than me . . . She believe in God . . . not sho' I'se does."

"Why do you say something like that?" David asked, not believing what he heard. "I thought everybody believed in God."

"If they be's a god, why do he let colored people be treated the way they is?" It was a question that David could not answer. "God is fo' white folks . . . not for us niggers . . . Just look around and you'll see who gets all the blessings of life. Yo' evah seen a pic'sha of a black god or a black Jesus?"

David decided to end the conversation that was getting too philosophical for him. It was hard to argue the valid points Toye Lee was making.

Toye Lee and David were still discussing the baptism event when they returned to the fishing hole. The afternoon had turned into a sweltering day, and the swimming hole looked like an oasis, though dirty.

Toye was the first to comment on the heat. "Is it just me, or is it really hot today?"

David answered, "It's just plain hot. Must be over a hundred degrees by now, and this is only July." They could look to three more months of this sweltering heat.

"Well, we's can fix that right now," declared Toye Lee.

"We can? How?" David was curious.

"We's goin' swimmin'."

It was a good idea, but David had not thought to bring or wear a swimsuit. "You bring a suit?" he asked.

"Naw. Yo'?"

David shook his head. "Then what are we going to wear?"

Toye Lee was half-undressed before he answered. "Has yo' ever heard of yo' birthday suit?"

David hated gym class because he felt uncomfortable undressing around his classmates. He rarely undressed in the gym, and now he was about to disrobe in front of a nigrah. That is why he spent so much time working on the school paper rather than taking PE. "Good lord, Toye Lee, we're practically on the highway!"

"Put yo' clothes in a nice little pile over there under the tree." Toye Lee pointed to a spot which would be readily accessible if they had to make a quick change. "Then grab a rope and jump in."

Toye Lee was completely naked by now, his clothes scattered around in less order than he suggested. His tan body was the epitome of physical perfection, his muscles rippling with each movement—like Jesse Owens running in a race. He found a rope on a low-hanging limb of an oak tree and swung out over the creek and let go. *Splash!* He hit the water with a thud.

David looked like a child who had lost its mother in a department store. He had heard of communing with Mother Nature but wasn't sure he liked it.

"Come on in, fraidy cat," Toye Lee yelled from below the embankment. "Yo' got a problem?"

David moved like a film in slow motion. He slowly took his clothes off—still embarrassed—and laid them near the tree. David felt the hot Texas wind hitting his body. He grabbed the rope and swung to the middle of the creek. He had never done anything like this in his life and was still apprehensive about it. *And with a nigrah.* But when he dropped into the refreshing water, he changed his mind. He thought of the song by the Sons of the Pioneers on the Bewley Chuck Wagon Gang radio show. "All day I ride the barren waste, without the taste of water . . . Cool, clear water . . . ."

The water was far from being clear, but he now could appreciate that song.

"I've got church tonight—and the young people are having an ice cream social," David announced.

"Yeah," Toye Lee agreed. "I'se think I'se go ovah and see a girlfriend myself."

David wondered how many girlfriends Toye Lee had. Many, he suspected. "Anyone special?"

"Naw. I'se loves them all as long as they let me get 'tween theys legs. That's why I'se need them thangs so often."

"You prick!" David yelled at Toye Lee.

"That's me!" he replied, followed by a loud whoop. "A big one!"

After the swim, they gathered their clothes. After dressing, Toye Lee went to the edge of the water to retrieve the mess of fish he had caught earlier.

"Want these?" Toye Lee asked.

As much as he liked fish, David declined. "You take them. I bet your mama is a good cook—especially with fish. And besides, how would I explain where I got them?"

"She sho' is. Maybe yo' can come ovah sometimes for catfish and hushpuppies."

"Maybe so," David replied.

Both knew that time would never come for them to have a catfish supper together. Summer was almost half over, and David would soon be gone to Austin. And Toye Lee's future was questionable.

But each had enjoyed the day and the company of the other. And neither thought they had broken the code again that day. *Is the code broken if no one knows about it?*

CHAPTER NINE

July is always hot as hell in Kirbyville. Heat waves rose from the torrid streets and sidewalks making residents suffer twice. Air-conditioning was for people who had money, so most people had to rely on a good oscillating fan, especially a GE model, which never wore out or broke down. And there was also ceiling fans. After the sun went down, people would retreat to their backyards in hopes of getting some evening breezes. If you had a car, your air-conditioning was provided by opening the windows and sticking your head out the windows. Going to the creek, especially Cow Creek at Singletary's Bridge or Trout Creek near Powell's Store, was still the best and most common way of keeping cool. Ice cream socials were common in the churches, and one could always fall back to the watermelon patches on a hot night.

David and Toye Lee saw each other every day as they discarded the boxes and garbage from their respective stores. If their bosses noticed them meeting or spending too much time in getting these chores done, they didn't say anything about it. It was hard to speculate where this friendship was going, if indeed it was going somewhere. They came from two culturally different backgrounds. Yet because of that, David and Toye Lee enjoyed each other's companionship and began to trust each other more. They felt free to discuss things which usually were never permitted between whites and coloreds. They were disappointed that this friendship could not be brought out into the open. They did not like the secret or coincidental meetings that transpired, but each was acutely aware of the consequences of forgetting one's place in this rural setting. The code prevailed.

David became more aware of he social injustice found in American society. He read the articles in the *Beaumont Enterprise* of how the nigrahs were challenging the policy of college segregation. The *Sweatt* case was often covered by the media. The *Enterprise* pretended to be unbiased in its news reporting, but David saw that was not the case. Other states were also in the throes of civil unrest with legal challenges to the segregation system. The University of Virginia refused to admit Gregory Swanson, a colored attorney, to its law school as a graduate student. The Alabama legislature was protesting the national government's involvement in a state's right to regulate its own educational system. The University of Missouri had been ordered to admit three nigrahs to its campus. In Oklahoma, coloreds were suing to be admitted to the state university. David often wondered what he would find when he entered the University of Texas in September. How odd, he thought, that white attorneys did not hesitate a moment taking nigrah clients and their money, but fought viciously to keep them from entering their law schools. Lawyers, the same profession that swore to uphold the Constitution of the United States, forgot to apply it to their own members. David wondered what his position would be on the issue when he opened his law practice one day. Whatever it was, it would be a situation that was new to him and the people back home would never understand, especially his dad. *Do I dare go back to Kirbyville to open my law practice?* The chances looked remote.

It didn't bother David much that Toye Lee had no real interest in the protests of the people of his race. Once he began to know more about Toye Lee, he realized what a vacuum he and the other nigrahs of Kirbyville lived in. He didn't for a moment think they were happy people, accepting the conditions in which they were born like Hollywood's portrayal in Shirley Temple films. After talking to Toye Lee and observing the coloreds in the stores or on Main Street, he could now see an undercurrent of discontent. But he also saw the inability or unwillingness to do anything about it. Knowing one's place had become so ingrained in the people of Southeast Texas—almost instinctive—that it seemed to be more basic than the Ten Commandments. Whites lived in a world of very subtle subjugation while the coloreds lived in a society of fear, ignorance, and futility. And who was going to change it?

Toye Lee's world was more of a dream than one of reality. David saw Toye Lee's interests consisted of three things. Sports, cars, and girls. Of course, he always talked about joining the army—something he wanted more than anything. One would not notice this at first, but during those days in July, David realized that Toye Lee was quite informed on what was going on in the sports world. How he obtained this information, David never discovered. Toye Lee never mentioned reading the *Beaumont Enterprise*—or any other newspaper—or being a regular reader of a news magazine. If he had a radio, he never mentioned it. Nevertheless, his knowledge of baseball and many other sports was uncanny. His interest in automobiles was strictly from a wishful point of view. Neither he nor his mama, Allie Mae, had a car. Prospect of owning one was remote. Living just across the tracks from their workplace negated the need for transportation. That was also the reason for their isolation in this small East Texas town. But Toye Lee was a great admirer of new car models—the ones seen on the floor of Conn's Chevrolet or Bean's Ford dealerships and the ones pictured in current magazines. He lived for the day that he would have some wheels of his own to drive out of town and never come back.

Toye Lee's exploits with girls were never really discussed between David and Toye Lee. David was still very immature in these matters; and Toye Lee, realizing this, never brought up the subject. Well, perhaps sometimes because he had asked David to get him some "thangs" from the drawer under the typewriter in the pharmacy. It embarrassed David to have to get them, but he had agreed to do so. Actually, David did not appear to be remotely interested in the conquests or escapades of Toye Lee and his lady friends. And that was probably a good, friendly way to maintain a relationship between two completely different individuals.

It was not the adventures of two teenage boys and the cultural barriers that affected their friendship that was the most talked-about matter in Kirbyville that summer. During the month of July, the focus of conversation was still Korea and the prospect of the United States getting into a fighting war again. Only five years had lapsed since the end of World War II, and people were still recovering from the effects of that war. It seemed like the Pacific area veterans has just gotten home, and it was starting again. Rationing was over, but not the memories of it. Some items were just beginning to be plentiful, but prices had begun to increase noticeably. David remembered Tom mentioning knowing so many people making so much money in the war plants but not having anything to buy. Some workers, he mentioned, would have paid thousands more for a car than it was worth just to have one. But no automobiles were made for the public, and the twenty-one-gallon limit on gasoline imposed by rationing didn't take a person too far. Many families were still grieving the death of sons who did not come home from the war or the millions that had died in the Nazi death camps. Even Kirbyville had a number of Gold Star Mothers. Americans objected to their burial of their sons and daughters on *foreign* soil. They insisted their bodies be brought home. And despite these strong feelings, all signs pointed to the fact that once again, the United States was on the fringe of another armed conflict.

In rapid succession, one event after another led to the conclusion it was only a matter of time. President Truman had authorized General MacArthur to send ground troops to Korea, and they arrived in Korea very soon afterward. Citing the Korean invasion as an "act of aggression," forty-four United Nations members backed a resolution declaring help for Korea. Truman asked Congress for money to build an H-bomb although General Leslie Groves was not sure one could be built. People had not yet realized the full impact of an atomic war but only saw Nagasaki and Hiroshima as shortcuts to victory—and justifiable in every sense. Kirbyville had a veteran who had worked on the plane that dropped the Nagasaki bomb. It was not known to many, however, and he rarely mentioned it. As a matter of fact, many veterans tried to avoid discussing their service in the military. It was an emotional disaster. And David was aware of some residents who had been wounded and those whose airplanes had been shot down and they were captured by the Germans.

Now atomic weaponry was being suggested for Korea. Four U.S. battalions completely withdrew across the Kum River and retreated forty-five miles in nine days. Congress gave President Truman draft powers and the right to call up National Guardsman and reservists. Once again it looked like young men would have to register at the age of eighteen, and some veterans would be recalled for new duties. The American air superiority helped to slow the Red aggression, but the pilots of the F-80s had great respect for the Korean Yaks, though made in Russia. All agreed that more power was needed. General MacArthur was appointed as the UN commander, and the UN flag was flown alongside of the U.S. flag. The draft system was gearing up to send out a call for more personnel, and Camp Pendleton and Fort Ord in California became the training place and springboard for troops going to Korea. And while these events were transpiring, the Soviet Union was boycotting the activities of the UN while accusing the United States of "pushing us in an open war."

One afternoon while taking a break from their jobs, David asked Toye Lee, "Toye Lee, how old are you?"

Toye Lee was surprised by the question since he knew David was aware how old he was.

"Almost seventeen," he replied. "Yo' knows that."

"Well, I do, but I was trying to figure out when you would have to register for the draft."

"What's the draft?" Toye Lee was curious.

David tried to explain. "Now that it looks like we're going to war again, every male has to go to his draft board and register when he's eighteen."

"Why's that?"

"All young men between the ages of eighteen and thirty-five can be called into active duty with the service."

David really had Toye Lee's attention now.

"Yo' mean that theys could make yo' go into the army?" Toye Lee wanted to know more.

"That's right," David replied. "Unless you can get a deferment."

"What's a deferment?"

"'Defer' means to postpone or put off. Sometimes when a person is in college or in an important job—like engineer or doctor—they don't have to serve or they serve after they finish college."

"What about people who work around here? Can they be deferred too?" Toye Lee asked.

"I doubt it." David could see the puzzling expression on Toye Lee's face. "Unless they have a physical disability. Or for some religious reason like being a pacifist—a person whose religion opposes war."

"Shit!" yelled Toye Lee. "I knowed it . . . I knowed it . . ."

"What?" David asked.

"This heah draft ain't fair. If yo' go off to college or got a good job, yo' can be passed ovah, and they's draft po' folks or niggers like me." You could see the anger on Toye Lee's face. "And besides, what religion s'pports war? That be the case, we all be paci-pacif—"

"Pacifists."

"Yeah, yo' got it." Toye Lee continued. "Besides, it look like eveahbody would want to serve his country and wear that uniform."

David admitted the draft system favored whites and the affluent. He remembered his history teacher tell about a conscript paying someone to go fight for him during the Civil War. Toye Lee saw bias immediately.

Toye Lee continued, "So it's okay fo' me to get my butt shot off while yo' sits in college or has a job—making good money and having a good time back home."

David agreed with a nod.

"Same old story, ain't it?" Toye Lee blurted. "Whites gets the gold mine, and we's gets the shaft."

David thought for a moment, counting the weeks. "I guess I'll have to register soon. Number 18 is coming up right away."

"Where do you go to register?" Toye Lee asked.

"You can actually sign up at the post office by filling out a card. But our draft board is Number 100 in Orange, Texas."

David didn't look forward to the day of committing his future to Uncle Sam. Basically, he thought of himself as a compulsive civilian.

Or was he just scared? His mother had already begun to fret about his military conscription. She had already lost one son. He could see the worry in her eyes. But he was not about to try to avoid it like some others in town had tried. *I'll never shoot off my big toe like the Wendt boy did*, he told himself. *Or try all sort of gimmicks to fail the physical exam—like sleeping with a bar of soap under each armpit causing the temperature to rise excessively high.*

Toye Lee was quick to admit that he really didn't oppose the draft. "I'se wish I'se was eighteen, and I'se go with yo' to the board. Yo' lucky to be eighteen already. Does yo' think I'se could lie about my age?"

David was quick to inform him that "lying is a federal offense. It's called perjury." David knew that penalties would not be that severe but chided Toye Lee anyway.

"You want to go to jail instead of the army?" David got serious for a moment. "When you lie about your age in the army, they send you to Alcatraz Federal Prison . . . You know . . . the one out in San Francisco Bay. If you try to escape, you become shark bait."

David watched Toye Lee's eyes get big. "Sharks especially like dark meat."

Toye Lee's eyes got bigger still.

"Is that what you want?" asked David.

The military appealed to Toye Lee but jail or sharks? "No way!"

Toye Lee still didn't realize David was kidding him. David maintained his serious composure. Maybe this was a way of keeping him in school.

Break time was over. Both boys knew it was time to get back to work. Toye Lee left pondering how to lie about his age and still be allowed to join the army.

Before going, however, David yelled to Toye Lee, "Tomorrow's Sunday. Get some drinks and chips together. I'm going to take you to the top of the world!"

"Where that be?" Toye Lee asked. "Where we's goin'?"

"You just be here. Three o'clock."

CHAPTER TEN

Next day David went through the Sunday rituals. Get up. Eat breakfast. Make up his bed. Sunday school and church. Then lunch that his mother always prepared late Saturday or early Sunday morning—unless they ate out, which was rarely. It was his responsibility to clean the table and wash the dishes. Caroline had always insisted that everyone do chores around the house. David helped his dad with the yard work and then minor housework. Tom was never pleased to see his son don an apron and push a broom or mop around. Or wash and dry dishes. To him it was unmanly. But he never said a word about it or complained to his wife. He always seemed to find an excuse to be exempted from household chores. Caroline never mentioned it to him, but she was determined that David would help around the house however sissy it might look. *He'll be a good husband one day*, she told herself. And Tom, remembering their agreement, remained silent while biting his lips.

Tom had already given David permission to drive the car that afternoon. Geraldine looked real spiffy with her wash and wax job. He missed church that morning with the excuse of having the car ready for David.

"Where are you going?" Tom asked.

"Just around town—nowhere in particular," David replied.

"Try to avoid dirt roads if you can." Tom knew how country roads could mess up a clean car quickly. He also knew that most roads around town were dirt roads—even the road to Singletary's Bridge—so he wasn't expecting a clean car to be returned. "And avoid high center roads." They were hard on transmission systems and axels.

"I'll try!" yelled David as he grabbed the keys and headed for the automobile.

Caroline came to the door as David was getting into the car. "Be sure you're back in time for Baptist Training Union tonight."

David waved and replied "Yes, ma'am."

David picked up Toye Lee behind the drugstore, and the two headed east down Main Street. At the end of Main Street, David turned right onto a dirt road.

"This go' to the cemetery, don't it?" Toye Lee asked.

"Yep."

"Why we's going to the cemetery?" Toye Lee was a bit nervous, and his heart palpitated a little faster. Nigrahs had great fear—and respect—for the dead.

The cemetery was a favorite parking place for lovers. They were always sure of privacy unless the city constable happened to drive by.

David only smiled. The car crossed the wooden bridge, and in moments, they were near the gate of the cemetery. Actually there were two cemeteries. Plots were available to anybody—as long as they were white. On the left was the Bean Cemetery—free to people who couldn't afford a burial site. The gravesites were closer together, and the headstones were not as pretentious. On the right was the Kirbyville City Cemetery where lots were sold. But lots were cheap. Sometimes it seemed that families tried to outdo each other by the size of the marker—the greater the headstone, the more beloved and important the departed. The thought of a free cemetery—a pauper's field, so to speak—was repugnant to a lot of people, so most people were buried in the city cemetery. This was where the Wingate family plot was. David's grandparents, Judge and Mrs. Wingate, were buried there; and he assumed that one day Tom and Caroline would take their place alongside the other family members. The Bean Cemetery had plenty of *residents* however. Neither boy questioned the policy of a segregated cemetery. Whites assumed that nigrahs preferred their own cemetery like they preferred their own chuches and undertakers. It was just part of the code.

"Toye Lee," David said, "I'm going to bring you out here at night and show you some eerie sights." David's voice slowed to a spooky sound.

Toye Lee was not comfortable listening to him.

"See that vault over there?" David pointed to the imposing Mixson family mausoleum in the middle of the cemetery.

Toye Lee nodded.

"I hear at midnight all those ghosts come out and dance around it. I want to come see for myself."

"Not me, brothah!" Toye Lee emphatically said. "Yo' be coming by yo'self." Toye Lee would not admit to being scared, but it was evident that he had a great respect for letting the dead remain dead. "And I'se wouldn't park heah neitha . . . Don't need love that bad."

David laughed and drove on. He turned left at the cemetery road and headed east toward a community called Adsul. Adsul had been the center of logging activities years ago and had provided trees for thousands of feet of timber cut and planed by Kirby Lumber Company—his dad's employer. But over the years, when the timber was finally cut—and not replanted—the community had practically disappeared.

At the end of the Adsul road, David turned left and drove onto a state highway. It was paved, and so far, not much dust from the roads had settled on Geraldine.

"We're almost there!" David announced.

"Wheah?"

Before David could answer, the rock entrance of the E. O. Siecke State Forest No. 1 appeared. He turned the car to the left and entered the gate, crossing the cattle guards with a burring sound. "This is the number one forest experimental station in the state of Texas," David replied.

E. O. Siecke State Forest facility had been a CCC project during the Great Depression. David and other members of his third-grade class rhythm band had played to a group in 1942 in the pavilion. It was here that all kinds of trees, forest products, and forestry techniques were tested. There were hundreds of acres of pine saplings at various stages of growth. There had been experiments using various fire lane techniques. Some plots had scars of fire burn and other remnants of insect infestation. There must have been hundreds of miles of roads and trails in and out the plots of trees, and it would not have been unusual to get lost in this gigantic forest. It was at this facility that pine cones were gathered and the seeds turned into seedlings and distributed throughout the state.

Toye Lee looked disappointed. "I'se thought yo' said we's goin' to the top of the world."

David veered off to the right of the main road. "Hang on to your drawers a minute," he told Toye Lee, "if you're wearing any."

Toye Lee smiled and winked but commented, "I'se doesn't wear any, theys just get in the way." He chuckled again.

Another mile or two down the dirt road, they came upon a fire watchtower. David did not know how tall it was—in terms of feet—but it was the tallest fire tower in the state.

"There it is," he said, pointing to the top. At the top was a small cubicle or cabin with windows completely around it. It was the place that foresters sat and watched for fires, not only in the state preserve but on private land as well. The view extended for miles to other counties and even to Louisiana.

They got out of the car after parking it under some trees and shrubbery so as to not draw attention.

"Get our drinks and chips," David reminded Toye Lee.

They walked over to the gate that led to the stairs that zigzagged back and forth to the top of the tower. Toye Lee stopped abruptly when he saw the big and very clear sign by the gate. He read it slowly, "No trespassing."

It read, "Trespassers will be prosecuted. Keep out! Danger! Texas Forest Service."

"What kind of mess have we's gotten' into now?" Toye Lee asked David. "Man, this place is off-limits to us." Toye Lee had seen signs like this all over town as a warning to coloreds.

———

151

"Don't worry," David assured him. "The forester goes to our church, and I know for sure he and his family are on vacation in Colorado. Come on."

The gate was not well secured; and all you had to do was to scoot around it, crawl over a bar, and you would be on the stairs in a moment. Toye Lee was still not sure about this. Whites could break the law and get away with it. Blacks were usually prosecuted to the fullest. But if David was going to climb it, so was he and he would be first to reach the top.

Standing on the ground looking directly up at the tower was imposing. It looked much taller up close than it did from the road. *Was this so smart after all? Can I climb that thing? Should I back out now? And lose face with Toye Lee? No way!* David had to show some kind of bravery or be kidded by Toye Lee.

"If yo' waitin' on me, yo' draw's is a dragging'! . . . If yo' has any on," Toye Lee yelled as he rushed up the steps. He climbed up the steps like a mountain goat in heat, and in a matter of seconds, he was several levels above David who already was beginning to pant. Toye Lee continued to climb up the steps, careful not to slip. David slowed down considerably—making slow but steady progress.

"C'mon, slowpoke!" yelled Toye Lee from somewhere above David who now realized his own physical abilities were somewhat limited. He realized then that he should have been more attentive in his high school physical education classes.

Toye Lee was at the top before David got halfway. He was laughing at David's slow progress.

"I'm coming. Hang on!" David yelled.

As David approached the top, Toye Lee had already made himself comfortable. The tower cabin itself was locked, but the walkway around it was wide enough to comfortably sit and spread out if desired.

"I guess you think you are some kind of stud 'cause you can hop up these stairs like a goat?"

Toye Lee laughed. "I'se always knowed white boys can't jump. They's can't climb either." He had to rub it in.

David had no retort.

"But that's okay," Toye Lee continued. "Not all whites are weak like you. Look at Jack Walsh, he's white."

"Who in the hell is Jack Walsh?" David was completely mystified.

"He was the man in Trenton, New Jersey, who lifted weights the other day. Set a new record."

Once again David was impressed with Toye Lee's uncanny reservoir of sports information. "Dammit, Toye Lee," he blurted, "if you can remember all these things about sports, why can't you do the same with history or English or science?" He shook his head in disbelief. "You would be a good student. I bet you could be the top student in your class if you tried . . . and got off your ass and rested your pecker."

In all the joshing around and kidding with each other, Toye Lee and David momentarily forgot where they were. When they finally realized they were "on top of the world"—overwhelmed by the magnificence of their surroundings—they were both speechless by the view that lay before them. It was like being on the rim of the Grand Canyon on a perfect day near a perfect sunset. The Texas summer day—although blazing hot—displayed a panorama of subtle colors splashed as far as the eye could see. Reds, oranges, and yellows mingled with the various shades of greens etched by the blacks and browns of tree trunks; and shadows gave the forest an unbelievable kind of beauty—and mystery. The blue sky above, laced with fleecelike clouds, was like a canopy to the horizon until it touched the green and became one. Sitting on that deck far above the ground was like being on a magic carpet soaring over a vast empire of verdant subjects.

Toye Lee interrupted the silence. "Maybe this really be the top of the world," he exclaimed, "at least my world."

"Don't you wish God would let us spread our arms like wings and fly out there like eagles?" asked David. "A pair of majestic birds in all their grandeur . . . just you and me out there . . . together."

"Yeah! And fly and fly and fly"—Toye Lee held his arms out like wings and pretended to fly—"and nevah come back!"

Then regaining his composure and returning to reality, Toye Lee continued. "But that ain't the way it work."

"What do you mean by that comment?"

'Oh, yo' be an eagle all right . . . with its head of white feathers and proud beak and broad feathers. But . . ."

"But what?"

"I'se ain't sure God would let me fly at all. And if he do, I'se wouldn't have a great white head. God make me a buzzard . . . black, dirty, with a ugly bald head. I'se just be there to clean up the crap that someone else left." Toye Lee looked David in the eye and, as quickly as David, looked away.

David knew what he meant and didn't want to pursue this topic any further.

"Ever fight forest fires?" David asked. He changed the topic quickly.

Toye Lee nodded he had. "In the woods behind our house. Almost set the house on fire once."

"Then you know how hot those damned things can get."

"Yo' ain't kidding. And so much work to put it out."

"The forest service watches for fires around the area—and tries to stop it early . . . if they can. See . . . a man sits in there and looks in all directions." David pointed to the small cabin where the forester sat.

The forest service as well as the major land owners like Kirby Lumber Company and Champion Paper Company learned years ago that all fires were not started by errant lightning. The woods were full of squatters and moonshiners. In the past when the timber companies tried to remove those intruders from their land, the intruders retaliated by setting the woods on fire, destroying hundreds of acres of timber. It didn't take long for the companies to realize it was more economical and prudent to let them *squat* on the property and give them an acre legally, rather than remove them and face a forest fire. That strategy also applied to people who cut their pine, cedar, and holly Christmas trees on public or private property. Trees were like open game in East Texas, they belong to the one that cut it first. No one bought Christmas trees in Kirbyville. Planting additional acres of trees offset the loss of trees appropriated by person or persons unknown during the holiday season.

"Look over there!" David pointed to the horizon. "There's Kirbyville. See the smoke from the sawmill slag pit?"

"And there," exclaimed Toye Lee. "That must be Newton in the next county. Damned! How far do yo' think that be?"

As they looked in each direction, they tried to locate landmarks of each area. It was a magical jigsaw puzzle. The water tower in town was most easily seen in the panorama.

This reverie was brought to an abrupt end with Toye Lee announcing, "Where's the food? I'se hungry."

It was time for a snack and return to reality. As they were eating their candy bars and chips and drinking their Cokes, David hesitated momentarily, as if he were withdrawing the question, but then continued. "Toye Lee, a year from now you are going be where I am today. Out of school at a crossroads trying to making a decision about your future. What kind of plans are you making?"

Toye Lee was surprised by David's question. He thought the answer was obvious. "What kind of chance do yo' think a colored boy from Kirbyville, Texas, has? Look at yo'. Yo' talks about college knowing yo' will go—no question about that. For us, getting out of high school is not even sho'. What is yo' dream, David?" Toye Lee was being evasive. He continued, "I spect that most girls will not graduate. They's goin' to have babies."

"Yours?" asked David.

"Not this time," Toye Lee answered. "As far as I'se knows . . . 'member yo' got me those thangs to stop that."

It was true, as David had gotten so many condoms from the drawer in the store and the guilt feelings he had sometimes overwhelmed him.

David did have a dream. There was never any doubt that college was in his future. His mother had made plans for that years ago. His scholarships and savings and the prospects of summer employment assured him that he could return each term. David gazed out across the vast wilderness below him, trying to say what he would like to do.

"I want to be a lawyer someday," he continued. "But before I go to law school, I'll have to get a bachelor's degree, so I'm going to major in journalism and political science. Course, if I don't make law school, then I can fall back on either working on a newspaper or teaching school—maybe government work. I think I'd like being part of a big law firm in Houston or Dallas. And maybe one day I could run for or be appointed to a judgeship somewhere. Like my grampa."

"Yo' grandaddy is one of the few men in town that colored folks thinks of as bein' fair and a good man. But to a nigrah, a lawyer is a person who takes yo' case—and yo' money—but don't care whether he win or not. They send white folks bills, but for nigrahs, theys has to pay up front. Coloreds don't like lawyers."

David wanted to know more about Toye Lee's hopes for the future. "You might think about college. You're good in sports—maybe a scholarship to Prairie View or some other nigrah college."

"Yo' talkin' to a boy who might not even finish school next yeah'. Not many do. Besides, yo' know I'se isn't too smart—yo' gotta have some grades if yo' want to pass. White people can go to college just about any area in the state of Texas. But what choice do black folks have? Prairie View and some small private church school like Wiley College."

David tried to encourage him. "Prairie View is a part of the A&M system. A degree from there would be good, and they have a good athletic program." David didn't think his argument was getting anywhere with Toye Lee. "It's still not too late to do well in your senior year."

"Heman Sweatt," Toye Lee continued, "couldn't get into the University of Texas law school because he was a nigrah. They went so far as to build a law school for coloreds in Houston just to keep him out of the University of Texas . . . What about that, Mr. UT man?"

David was surprised that Toye Lee knew that fact.

Toye Lee commented again, "Prairie View was set up for coloreds who couldn't go to Texas A&M—a white college. Ain't no colored person from this town evah gone off to college. In fact, I'se can't think of anybody who has gone off—period—and done anything 'cept Ivory Joe Hunter. And when he left, he stayed gone . . . lucky butt."

Ivory Joe Hunter was a local colored man who had moved to Hollywood years ago, entered the musical field, and was enjoying current popularity with a record called "When I Lost My Baby I Almost Lost My Mind."

Toye Lee had played the record many times. "He stay around heah very long, and he sho' 'nuff lose his mind." Toye Lee chuckled at what he said.

"Everybody can't make it in the music business," David replied. "But there are other ways of being successful."

"What be's success?" he quickly inserted. "Success to yo' is money. Or a good job. A college degree . . . Meetin' a nice gal and gettin' married. Or livin' in a big house on Tall Timber Lane. Going on vacations or maybe even having two cars."

David saw a great deal of truth in what Toye Lee said.

Toye Lee continued, "That ain't going to work for me or any nigger. We can't wish for them things." Toye Lee hesitated for a moment and looked into the space before him. "Success to me be gettin' out of this black hole called Kirbyville, Texas. Success be goin' somewhere where yo' treated like a human being and not a hired hand. Success be able to go to the picture show or café and enterin' the front do' like the whites . . . a place which don't remind yo' twenty-four hours a day that yo' better stay in yo' place and never cross that invisible line between whites and coloreds."

Toye Lee was wound up now. "Success be livin' in a house that don't leak—with glass windows—and has 'lectricity and indo' plumbing. It be sayin' what yo' believe without havin' yo' face smashed in or yo' teeth bein' knocked out . . . fightin' back without bein' thrown in jail or beat up by a mob . . . or killed. Success be havin' a school where books and equipment is brand-new—and not hand-me-downs from the whites . . . us havin' teachers that is qualified so yo' can graduate and get a half-decent job. Success be bein' able to talk to anyone whatever color they's skin is. Success is havin' paved streets in the Qua'ters and not sinkin' to yo' knees in mud when it rain. And they's a lot mo'."

Toye Lee's forehead was beaded with sweat that glistened when he looked to the west, his lonely-looking eyes peered across the treetops to the horizon. "Success be buying yo' groceries on credit instead of always paying cash. Success be goin' down to the bank and gettin' a loan on my own name without some white man cosignin' fo' me. It be buyin' a car—not no new car . . . just a decent car—from a white man and not havin' to spend a lot mo' money gettin' it fixed right. I'se likes to think success be saying just what I'se just said to yo' without feah' of losing my life."

Toye Lee was quiet. He looked exhausted. Looking at the majestic view before him, he concluded, "We can't find success in this town . . . in this state . . . this country. We won't find success in my lifetime . . . not real success . . . maybe nevah!"

David was beginning to feel uncomfortable. "Toye Lee, I've never felt that way. I think of you as my friend."

"I know you try, David," Toye Lee continued, looking away in to distance, "but deep down, that line is still there 'tween yo' and me. Yo' can't step ovah it—or yo' won't . . . Or maybe yo' just be afraid to!" Then turning and looking David straight in the eye, he added, "It's almost ovah now 'tween us."

"What's almost over?" David insisted on knowing what he meant.

"In a few weeks, yo' be leavin' for college. Going to the University of Texas. A place no nigger is allowed to go. Gonna get a education. But when yo' come back, it ain't gonna be David and Toye Lee anymo'. It's goin' to be Toye Lee and Mr. Wilson. Or maybe Toye Lee and Mistah David. I still be Toye Lee, and you become mistah . . . . That line now become visible."

David thought for a moment, and he had to agree. He had seen it happen too many times before. When white young men and women reached a certain point in their life, the coloreds started referring to them as mistah or miz. And though they had played together as children or their mamas had been their nannies, the nigrahs were expected to refer to them by formal address.

Toye Lee was not angry when he spoke. Neither was he blaming David for the system of segregation. In his own way, he was trying to explain the difficulty of breaking out of a culture that had kept million of nigrahs down for generations.

"Are you mad at me, Toye Lee?" David asked.

Toye Lee gave him no answer.

"Look at the choices I'se got, David," Toye Lee added. "I'se can stay here in this town and get a job like I'se has now. Or do odd jobs. If I'se could buy a truck, I'se could haul pulpwood to the paper mill or logs to Kirby Lumber Company. Who gonna loan me money? Without a truck, I'se be a pulper or mill hand on some section like yo' daddy's. Money's po', so I'se prob'ly end up in the po' house anyway. If I'se move away, I'se still ain't no better off. Still don't have no trainin', so I'se ends up doing same thing in some big city. Rent and groceries is high. Don't make enough money to live on. So I'se goes to the po' house . . . or jail. Whites get married and moved into a nice house. Or get a loan from the bank to build one. No bank's gonna lend a nigrah no money to build a house. So we's has to find some shack that nobody's livin' in and call that home—or move in with our parents. Most nigrahs nevah own a piece of property in they's life. Maybe we's rent but nevah own. How do all this sound to yo'?" Toye Lee was now looking David straight in the eye.

David was shocked at what Toye Lee had just told him. He had never heard a colored person express his feelings like this. The system never permitted it. It was part of the code. But as Toye Lee spoke, David could remember specific examples of every point he made. Toye Lee's assessment of the situation was accurate as far as David could tell. He had never had the courage or interest to look at the issue directly. When he did, it hurt him. Then David asked, "So what now? How are you going to change the way of life here?"

Toye Lee continued, "Hell, David, I'se never be able to change things the way they's be now." Toye Lee admitted. "Wouldn't even try. This town is set in concrete. But I'se can get my butt out of heah."

"But where?" David asked.

"David," Toye Lee continued. "I'se hears yo' whites talk about World War II. And now everybody talking about Korea. And how we's gonna have to suffah again. They says how bad war is with all the killin' and dyin'. They talks 'bout rationin' and not havin' all the nice things that make livin' bettah. Well, war sound good to me . . . What I'se got to lose if I'se ain't got nothin' to lose in the first place?"

David was stunned. "Good?" Again he asked incredulously, "War is good?"

"That's right. As long as they's war, they's an army or navy or some military service. And that's my ticket out of Kirbyville. I'se doesn't have to go to college. Man, I'se don't have to graduate from high school. They takes yo' in when yo' turn eighteen. And I'se s'pect I'se can lie about my age. Don't have no birth certificate. Yo' goes in the army, and they trains yo' for a special job. You gets a skill now. Might train me fo' a job when I'se gets out. Army service improve yo' score on civil service test. Post office hires vet'rans."

David quickly interjected, "But they're still often grunt jobs—jobs nobody else will do. Or jobs you can't use in civilian life."

Toye Lee continued. "But a lots do. Military police can go into police work. Cooks can work cafés. Motor Pool mechanics can learn about cars and have theys own shops. Truth is, lots of folks stay in the army for a lifetime. Pay is bettah than anything around heah. They gets promotions and raises. But most of all, they's treated different than the way we is heah. I'se could make it up to sarjant."

David had heard that *treatment* might not be as good as Toye Lee imagined. Then he added, "The army's segregated too. Remember during the war there were nigrah units—completely colored."

"Sho', but President Truman has already changed that. But," Toye Lee insisted, "they still be somebody. They's has some pride."

David had to agree.

"In the army yo' gets to travel. Around the U.S. and ovahseas. I'd like to go to Japan or to Germany or France. I'se hears that those gals ovah there likes us *night fightahs*." Toye Lee laughed as he used the phrase often used by Europeans to define colored soldiers.

"And I'se bet I'se looks like a million dollahs in a unifo'm!" Toye Lee pretended to strut on the platform high above the ground. "My mama be so proud of me," he added, flashing his uncanny smile. "And I'se help my mama with my paycheck."

"And you might go to Korea, too, and get your ass shot off," David added.

"Better than gettin' it shot off around heah for nothing by some nut in a bedsheet. And if I'se be killed, I'se could be buried in Arlington cemetery in Washington—like white folks—not on that little clay hill ovah there called Evergreen Cemetery." He pointed in the directions of the Quarters'. "Besides, I'se might meet Curt Simmons somewhere in my travels."

"Who in the hell is Curt Simmons?" David asked.

"Curt Simmons, Mr. College Boy, is the pitcher for the Philadelphia Phillies who was called to active duty the other day."

"Well, pardon me, General Johnson . . . for my ignorance."

"The day I'se turns eighteen—or befo' if I'se lie 'bout my age—yo' gonna see this heah nigger get on the bus and take his black ass to the army recruiting station in Houston . . . yo' can bet on it!"

David shrugged hopelessly but did not comment. He wondered if he should give Toye Lee some friendly advice. He hesitated, then went ahead and say what he wanted to. "Don't sell yourself short, Toye Lee. You've got more on the ball than you give yourself credit for . . . but—"

"But what?" Toye Lee asked abruptly.

"You need to improve your speaking."

"What yo' mean?"

"You sound like a person talking a language somewhere in the land of Uncle Remus and Amos and Andy . . . You sound just like a . . . a . . ."

"Nigger?" Toye Lee asked.

"Yes." David was glad Toye Lee used the word instead of him. "Even in the army, good English helps you get better jobs—just like in business." David thought of times past when his mother enrolled him in Mrs. Ora Hendon's elocution and diction class. He remembered the preciseness of Mrs. Hendon's pronunciations and the roundness of her words. It was silly then, he recalled; but it helped in high school, especially in the literary events and dramatics.

"I'se never be able to speak as good as yo', David," Toye Lee remarked.

"But you can try to improve, can't you?"

There was no comment from Toye Lee.

"Right?" David asked again. "Right?" he asked again.

Toye Lee finally responded in his very exaggerated dialect, "Ah's gonna try mah best, Massa David. Honest, Ah is. Ah's gonna try to sound lak yu's white folks. Sho' 'nuff . . . Just ax anybody . . . Thankee suh! Thankee suh!"

"You prick!" yelled David.

Toye Lee leaned over and gave a big and loud laugh. "That's me."

Seeing that he was not offended, David joined in the levity.

High above the ground, the boys enjoyed the pleasure of the fresh summer breeze. Knowing it was still scorching below on the ground, they could feel the tower sway slightly as the wind blew. For some time, they noticed a flock of buzzards flying around in circles over a spot near Call Junction, several miles away. They watched a dozen brown hawks as they darted back and forth in the sky chasing insects and each other. They thought about what they had just discussed and realized this was a good place to get away from the problems of the world and just feel free.

"Wonder what this place is like at night?" asked Toye Lee.

"I never intend to find out," David answered. He could imagine the difficulty he would have climbing in the dark. He looked at his watch and then the sun that had begun its descent.

"Think we better go? It's almost six o'clock."

"Yep. I'se think we bettah haul ass. Want to race down?"

David rolled his eyes at the suggestion. He could see that Toye Lee was game for anything athletic.

"You go ahead and catch me if I fall," David suggested to Toye Lee.

"If yo' fall, I'se just meet yo' on the ground—latah."

The descent from the tower was much faster than going up. The boys slipped around the locked gate and slowly moved to the car.

"I'se hope yo' ain't mad at me for what I'se sayin' up there, David," Toye Lee said somewhat apologetically. "I'se nevah told anybody about how I'se feels about being a nigrah. David, please don't yo' say anything about what I'se say today."

"I understand what you said, and I wished I could do something about it, Toye Lee," he replied, defeated by the code. "But I think we better keep it to ourselves, don't you? Friends don't squeal on each other."

"Damned right."

They headed home before it got dark.

"Time for me to go to church, I guess," David said, just making conversation.

"Yeah," Toye Lee replied. "Time for me to go talk to one of my gal friends too."

"Yeah . . . Sure. You go talk to her. You do a lot of talking. I bet you're some kind of conversationalist. One of these days, there's going to be a little Toye Lee running after you after one of those conversations."

Toye Lee's only reaction was a broad smile revealing every tooth in his head. "Nevah got no complaints."

CHAPTER ELEVEN

August—like July—in Southeast Texas is almost unbearable and even hotter, and, as always, was the daily conversation of the residents and sometimes the only conversation. The weather was big on everyone's mind. It came every season. There are cloudless days without rain for weeks. Gardens wilt and foliage begins to dry and drop to the ground. Many of the creeks dry up, but Cow Creek and Trout Creek were still and deep, but had stagnant and warm water. Cattle were also affected by the hot days. Their output of milk was lower and if they resorted to eating bitter weeds for food, because of the lack of fresh grass, their milk was also bitter. Farmers are wary about plowing their horses for fear that they might have a heart attack. Dogs sleep in the cool spots in the soil under the front porches of the houses, too hot to bark at strangers passing by. Evening brings little relief since the temperature drops only a few degrees. And there are the problems of insects. During the day, you fight gnats and sand fleas and scratches from the day before. No one seemed to be exempt from their bites. At night, the mosquitoes take over the backyard and buzzing and droning like miniature helicopters. Sitting outside was courting disaster and misery. Everyone complained, yet it happened every summer right on schedule and people knew what to expect. Weather was the topic of conversation most of the time, and the people became weather experts.

Such was the case in Kirbyville in August 1950. There was little one could do to truly be comfortable. Few people had air-conditioning except the Palace Theater, but that respite would only last for an hour and a half. You could go to Singletary's Bridge on Cow Creek to swim, but there were so many people there you would only find a spot to cool in, but there would be no swimming. Henry's Drugstore had just opened for business with the only fountain in town. Everyone was going there to sample their frosted Cokes, malts, and banana splits. Watermelons were available both in the stores and in the fields, and many pounds of watermelons which had a cooling effect were consumed. People would get their wooden ice cream freezers out of the closets or garage and turn out gallons of delicious homemade ice cream with flavors to suit the most particular taste. The energy spent in turning the handle was well rewarded. In the local churches, you could always pick up a cardboard fan, compliments of Stringer Funeral Home, in the foyer and fan himself through a fiery sermon. There was plenty of ice tea consumed and colas, but nothing was as tasty as fresh water from a hand-dug well. Problem was, very few people in town had wells now. General Electric and Westinghouse would be happy with the citizens of Kirbyville for buying every conceivable model of oscillating fan they produced. But they were a poor substitute for the spring breezes which now had been turned into blistering summer winds. Everyone griped abut the weather—a topic constantly on the tongues of just about everybody in town. But they accepted those long hot summers as a given fact and hoped that Crawford's Drugstore would not run out of Arrid deodorant and Evening in Paris cologne. They longed for the fall and winter, which on its arrival led to a discussion of how cold it was and how nice it would be to have spring and summer again. No one liked the weather of Southeast Texas.

It was on such an evening in August that found the Wilson family at home. Tom came home at his regular time, and there were no fireman chores that night. He wanted a bottle of cold beer from the refrigerator at the fire station, but it was too hot to go there and he really didn't want to go anyway. Caroline also had a free night. There were no meetings of the various committees she served on. Prayer meeting and choir practice had been held earlier in the week. No one had died in three weeks; a death in a small town always prompted the local ladies to prepare food for the bereaved family and often required they go to the funeral home, or perhaps the home of the deceased, and sit with the family through the night. As chairman of the committee, she had not yet begun to make plans for the refreshments to be served at the church revival in two weeks. David came from the drugstore—it had been an uneventful day there—took off his shoes and shirt, and immediately helped himself to a Coke while he sat down under the fan. He made no plans to go out with the gang that night, to play 42 or go to the picture show. *Bride for Sale* with Claudette Colbert was showing, but he had seen it the night before. The gang made plans to go to the Owl Show Saturday night when *Holiday Affair* with Robert Mitchum would be playing.

But it was a special day in the history of the Wilson family. David was celebrating his birthday—his eighteenth—and Caroline was determined to make this one very special. She had asked David if he would like to have his friends over for supper, but David was somewhat adamant in declining the offer. Since he was a small boy, he had always cried when people sang "Happy Birthday" to him, and he decided some years ago that birthdays for him would only be family affairs.

Caroline had asked him earlier what he wanted for his birthday dinner.

David was not hesitant about his request. "Fried chicken, mashed potatoes, butter beans, and fried okra," he said. And then added, "And fresh rolls . . . lots of them." He could eat a dozen of Caroline's rolls without flinching.

"And for dessert?" she asked.

Normally David would ask for peach ice cream with homemade pound cake, but on this day, he asked for a raisin pie. He usually got raisin pies at Thanksgiving and Christmas.

"That's a strange request," his mother replied.

"I know, but I'll be gone soon. To the university. Do you think they serve raisin pies in the Commons cafeteria there?"

"I doubt it," she answered, knowing how so many people disliked raisins and probably even more had never heard of raisin pie. To many people, cooked raisins looked like dog ticks—and not very palatable. But she had an old family recipe from the Wingate cookbook of pre—Civil War recipes.

David appreciated his mother's attention to his birthday and all the trouble she went to prepare his favorite foods. Still, the fact that in six weeks he would be living in Austin and enrolling at the university dominated his thinking. The anxiety and the apprehension of such a change alternated in his thoughts about his future. Still, leaving for the university was the most important thing on his mind these days.

"Supper is ready," Caroline announced. "Everybody get washed up."

Tom and David did not have to be told twice. They were at the table quickly. Caroline took her seat at the end of the table. Tom's hand was reaching for the plate of fried chicken, and David already had a roll on his plate.

"But first," she said, "let's say grace."

Tom withdrew his hand and looked embarrassed. Together they joined hands as Caroline continued. "Lord, we thank you for the many blessings you have given us. For our health. For the security of our home. For the food which thou has put before us. And today, Lord, we thank you for our son, David, who will soon be leaving us when he begins a new pursuit in his life. Give him the courage and wisdom to meet the demands that will be placed on him in the days to come. Keep him safe and return him to us with thy protection. Now, bless this food to the nourishment of our bodies and us to thy service. For it is in Jesus's name we pray. Amen."

There was a simultaneous amen from Tom and David. Tom's was muffled as he seemed more interested in nourishment than he was praying.

"Thanks, Mother," David said. "I'm probably going to need all the help I can get." He chuckled.

"I expect you to go to church each Sunday," Caroline added.

"Yes, ma'am," David assured her, but deep down he knew this would not happen—not every Sunday.

They filled their plates with the food Caroline had prepared.

"You don't have to pile it so high," she chided the men. "You can have seconds."

David and Tom chuckled as they downed the food.

"Now," Caroline continued, picking at the small portions she had placed on her plate, "what news does anyone have to report?"

"I guess you heard about Uncle Bill Casey's passing?" Tom asked.

David was surprised. "No!" Uncle Bill was the blind piano tuner who pecked his way to the post office each day with his walking cane. David had seen him hundreds of times during his employment at the drugstore. "You know, he was sort of an institution around here. I'll miss the old man."

"Did you see the *Banner* today?" Caroline asked.

David and Tom shook their heads.

"It's sort of funny," she continued. "In today's edition was the first mention of Korea and what's going on in the Far East."

"What's funny about that?" Tom asked.

"Well, it's been in the *Enterprise* for weeks," she answered. "And it's been the talk of the town by a lot of people."

As usual, David remained quiet, enjoying his food and listening as his parents discussed world events.

"People don't like to think about war. Remember it's only been five years since our last one," she said.

The men said nothing.

"But if people are not aware of what's going on, they must be living in a cave somewhere," Caroline continued. "Already prices are going up." She paused a moment. "I hope that we don't have a shortage of goods like we did last time."

Tom and David were too busy eating to comment.

"President Truman has assured us that there will be no rationing."

Tom had heard this before.

"And the profiteering," she added. "Everybody's got to make money when there's a war at the expense of others."

David stopped eating. "They told us in government class that there's no official war until Congress declares one," he interjected. "Has Congress acted yet?"

"Not yet," Tom replied. "Leaders are calling it a police action. But when someone is shooting at me, I'd call that war. Congress can kiss my . . . foot. Trouble is that the United Nations is making the decisions, but it's our boys who are doing the fighting and dying. Look at that pitiful number of troops supplied by Thailand, Turkey, Britain, and Australia. My god, that's not even a full division." He was obviously perturbed by the inactivity of other UN nations in assisting American troops. He hated the UN with a passion.

"Well, at least President Truman has promised not to use the atomic bomb in combat." Caroline was looking for a positive point in the conflict. "And the president has said he will integrate the armed forces. It was part of his platform in the last election."

That comment caught David's attention immediately, but he said nothing.

"Damned bastards!" Tom yelled. "If it was up to me, I'd blow their damned butts to kingdom come with a lot of A-bombs!" His face was turning crimson. "I wouldn't want to be in a company of nigrahs. Doubt they even know which way to shoot, although they all got guns."

"Thomas?" Caroline exclaimed. "Do you have to use such profanity—and at the table!"

David looked at his father and chuckled to himself. He liked to see his dad provoke his mother.

Tom found renewed energy when talking about the Korean conflict. His eyes sparkled, and he was interested in what was going on in Southeast Asia. He didn't look at war as a good thing. Yet in his discussions and comments, he acted as if he had been shortchanged when he was exempted from serving in World War II because of his age and the limp he received in that football injury in his college days.

"I was talking to some boys from the chemical plants the other day," he said. "The government is beginning to take those warships in dock at Orange out of mothballs and get them ready for action again." He was referring to the great fleet of World War II ships which had been mothballed and docked at Orange, Texas, and deactivated after the war.

The Gulf Coast industries, which included ship building and the petro-chemical industry, flourished in crises and military activation. Probably half the middle-aged people who lived in the Kirbyville area were now connected with those industries and making a good living as a result of the United States' policy of policing the world.

"Gonna be a lot more jobs now that the plants are gearing up for another war," he continued. "David, I'll bet you could get on at one of the plants and make lots of money."

"He probably could," snapped Caroline, "but David has other plans."

Tom continued his discussion of the world events. "The selective service has issued a call for one hundred thousand draftees in September and October. Some seventy thousand doctors are to report in November and a large number of marine reservists have already been called to active duty."

"I do swear, Tom Wilson," Caroline said, obviously upset with the way the conversation was going, "you like all this fighting, and killing, and preparing for war."

"Honey, I don't like war. Nobody does. But I don't like those foreign countries pushing us around. I don't like them treating us like aggressors. Look how we carried the burden—men and money—during the last war. Now they are criticizing us and picking on other countries. Korea. Russia. China. Remember China. Used to be our ally. We saved it from the Japanese and gave it aid. Now they've turned on us. Goddamned communists!"

"Thomas!" Caroline protested again.

"Now those communists are beating our butts and pushing us around like we were a bunch of pansies. It's time we did something about it."

Tom reached across the table and slapped David on the shoulder. "You agree with me, David?'

David was startled at first, being preoccupied with eating his third piece of chicken and the integration of the armed forces still interested him. He waited for his dad's question or comment. His mouth was full.

"David, you ever think how exciting it might be to wear the uniform of the United States military? To have the honor to fight for liberty—for democracy? . . . For freedom? . . . To face our enemies and kick some ass?" Tom's adrenaline was flowing rapidly now. He was really waving the American flag now.

"You mean to kill, don't you?" asked Caroline. "To be part of some action where thousands, including civilians and children, are killed and millions are dispossessed from their homes and families? And when it's over, nothing as been accomplished?"

Caroline was a mild-mannered woman, but she did have very definite opinions on war and fighting. She was distressed that Tom should even bring up the matter, especially before David. She had been on the committee that accompanied old Dr. McKinnon when he delivered the telegram notifying the family that their serviceman had been killed or wounded in action during the war. She had seen enough grief for a lifetime in the last war. If Tom could see the face on those mothers, he might have a different attitude about fighting. *Those poor Gold Star Mothers*, she thought, *and I could be one of them.*

David did not have an opinion on Tom's question. "I never thought about it, Dad. I was only eight when the Pearl Harbor was attacked. I don't think kids my age think about it too much today."

David and all the youth of Kirbyville had played soldier during the war. They had divided into the Allied and the enemies and had elaborate battles all over town in the street and woods. But their weapons had been sticks or pieces of lumber carved like guns. And grenades were tin cans or ice cream cups filled with sand. And no one was ever hurt. Even at age of eighteen, it was not a matter which required serious discussion though it had some romance about it like all wars do. Wars were always romanticized by movies and novels.

"That's just like the generation today!" Tom blurted. "You forget our history too soon. Patriotism doesn't mean much to you and your generation!"

But Tom was again on a lofty discourse now, and the more he thought about it and discussed it, the more he got carried away with his patriotism.

"But to wear the colors of the United States. To be a member of its fighting forces. To feel like you were doing something really—I mean really—important like saving the country." Tom was swelling with pride. He continued, "Fighting has been part of our history forever. Look at the American Revolution, the Civil War. World War I. Don't you remember Woodrow Wilson saying we had to save the world for democracy?"

Caroline was quick to interrupt. "But, Tom, Korea is not our fight. It's an internal matter in a part of the world so remote from us that very few people knew about this country before this outbreak."

"But if they want to start it, by god, we'll finish it. We never lost a war yet!" Tom was on his soap box now.

David had remained silent during most of this discussion. He consumed his food and followed the arguments of his parents; but his youth, information, and inexperience prohibited him from entering the discussion with real arguments. What he did realize from his dad's comments were the similarities between Tom's discourse and the statements made by Toye Lee that Sunday when they sat on the platform of the fire tower in the state forest. Uniform. Respect. Serving one's country. It all sounded familiar—same song, second verse!

"I don't think this will be a long conflict," Tom said. "When we get our troops there, we should take care of those gooks in a few months." Tom sipped his tea and continued. "And we have all the war material in place from the last time."

"I hope you're right," Caroline added. "The first soldier killed in military action was reported last month by the Pentagon. His name was John Birch. They are estimating a figure of about 2,600 deaths so far."

"Honey, when you have war, you have deaths and casualties. It's a given fact," Tom reminded her.

"But don't you sympathize with the parents of those killed in action in a land so far away and so different from ours. Where our interests there are questionable?"

"Course I do," Tom added. "But that is the price of preserving democracy . . . keeping peace."

Caroline could not answer that rhetorical question. She did recall an article in that week's edition of the *Banner*. It had affected her deeply, but she had tried to forget what she read. Now she brought it up again.

"Jasper County had its first casualty this week."

That did get David's attention.

"Who?" Tom asked.

"A boy from Magnolia Springs. I can't remember his name, but he was in the army medical corps." She turned to David and added, "You know those medics are right up on the front line during combat."

"Was he a nigrah boy?" Tom asked.

Caroline nodded that he was, but Tom made no reply to her nod.

She continued, somewhat concerned by Tom's disinterest, "But that nigrah mother would feel the same way that I would if my son were taken away from me in enemy action."

"Guess you didn't hear about Clem Franklin?" Tom asked.

"Is he part of the Franklin family in Call, a community south of Kirbyville?" she asked.

Tom nodded.

Caroline waited to hear what Tom was going to say.

"He was wounded in action last week in Korea."

"Is he going to be all right? Was it serious?" she quickly asked.

"He died. Family got word this morning," Tom added.

A sudden pain raced through Caroline's body. She caught her breath. "I used to work with his mother in PTA. Why, that boy just dropped out of school two years ago. I knew he had moved away but didn't know he was in the army. He couldn't have been over nineteen . . . David, he was about your age, wasn't he?"

Caroline's face was etched with grief. "I'll have to fix some food and take to the family."

David had sat listening to the discussion. He vaguely remembered the boy but had never really known him. He shrugged. His only comments were, "A white boy and a black boy?"

But what really mattered to David was the memory of what Toye Lee had said that day on the tower. He had mentioned the draft always favored the white person and those with resources to go to college or get "critical" jobs. Nigrahs and poor people were more likely to be drafted—and killed—than others. Toye Lee was right.

David was reluctant to mention it at this time, but he decided it was as good a time as ever to bring the subject up. "Folks," he began as they both looked to see what he was about to say, "I registered for the draft this week."

For a moment his parents' facial expressions froze, especially Caroline's. It was not something they had expected him to say.

"Oh my goodness," Caroline finally was able to say, catching her breath. "You do have to register by your eighteenth birthday. I had completely forgotten that."

"Well, it didn't amount to anything. I went to the post office, and Miss Bell gave me the card, which I filled out and sent to Draft Board 100 in Orange."

Draft Board 100 had announced through the *Banner* that it was calling twenty-eight males to report to the army processing center in Houston in September. Already some of the inductees had received their greetings.

Caroline was the first to comment on David's news. "Well, we don't have to worry about that now. You will be eligible for a deferment while you're in college.

"As long as he makes his grades," Tom added, "and doesn't flunk out."

"I have no doubt David will be an honor student. And by that time, hopefully, the war will be over and we won't have to concern ourselves with such matters."

Nobody noticed it, but Tom had an expression on his face that might indicate that he would reject the deferment and serve if he were drafted. He still had some feelings about David going to the university—so far away. Lamar College was much closer. He still thought of the time that David could have been the town's greatest athlete— not another college student. But he kept his thoughts to himself.

"Well, enough of that kind of bad news," Caroline said, changing the subject quickly to a more pleasant topic. "Let's talk about more cheery subjects."

Tom was quick to give his two cents' worth of news. "The Census Bureau has announced that the population of the United States is 150 million people. Texas has jumped 19 million since the last census." He laughed at the drastic change in topics. "And more importantly, the local barbers have announced a price change in haircuts and shaves. Haircuts are now seventy-five cents and shaves are fifty cents, David."

The news was hardly earth-shattering, especially since David was not shaving yet. "Bet they're more in Austin . . . probably at least a dollar," David replied.

Quickly Caroline came to the rescue of the conversation that seemed to be going in a strange direction. "I mean like birthday cakes and birthday presents."

"Oh yeah," David said. He had almost forgotten they were celebrating his special day. Recalling the previous discussion of the draft and Korea, he added, "Funny, isn't it?"

"What?" asked his mother.

"Today, I'm old enough to fight but not old enough to vote!"

"Or drink!" Tom added.

Caroline gave Tom a cold look.

"Don't you think that's ironic in a democracy?" David asked. "Maybe the ones that declare wars should fight them."

"Never happen," Tom responded. "Not with our politicians."

Caroline had gotten up from the table and was busily puttering around the sink. Sheepishly, she made a confession to David.

"David, honey, I prepared the raisin pie for you as you wished. But it just didn't look like a birthday cake with candles and all, so I made your favorite chocolate cake too."

She carried a beautiful chocolate cake adorned with eighteen candles to the table. The small flames were dancing to and fro, and the aroma of the cake was a treat to the nose. After placing the cake before David, she returned to the cupboard and produced a pie with one candle, also lighted and flickering as the electric fan oscillated its monotonous way, trying to blow it out. With both desserts before David, she began to sing "Happy Birthday," joined by Tom.

David felt the tear in his eye, which he quickly wiped away; and with a deep breath, he blew the candle flames out. *I am too old for this crap.*

"You can send us some goodies like these anytime you want to," he announced to his mother. David had already heard how great care packages from home were for the college student.

—

Caroline beamed with pride. "Now which do you want?" she asked. "I'll take a piece . . . of each!"

She cut him an extra big piece of the cake and pie and put them before him. Then she left the kitchen and walked toward her bedroom. David heard the closet door open and close. Then as quickly as she disappeared, she returned. Caroline was holding two beautiful tan-colored pieces of matching Samsonite luggage.

"These are for you, Mr. . . . Joe College," she announced.

David was surprised and delighted at what he saw. He had wondered what he would take his clothes in when he boarded that bus to Austin next month.

"Gosh, Mother . . . Dad. These are really nice. And Lord knows I really needed them. I was about ready to get some tow sacks to carry my things in." David laughed at the thought.

"This is what I thought we would do." Caroline sat down again and began to outline her plan for moving his things to Austin.

"We can get some large boxes from the drugstore and pack things like blankets, towels, pillows, winter clothes like sweaters and coats. And some soap and toothpaste and such. We'll ship them a few days before you leave and hope they arrive about the same time you do. Let's see, 2214 San Antonio Street. Right?"

David nodded. That was the correct address.

"Then your good suit, everyday clothes, socks, underwear, and such we'll put in these bags, and you can carry them with you on the bus," she continued. "I'm a very good packer, and you'll be surprised how much I can get into a suitcase."

Tom interjected his question. "But can he carry them? They look awful heavy."

David had no intentions of taking a lot of clothes with him. For one reason, he didn't have many. But khakis and blue jeans were universal attire on college campuses, and he had enough of those. Since he did not plan to pledge a fraternity—even if he wanted to—he would not need any fancy clothes.

Tom did not have much to say during their conversation. He watched with interest—and pride—but remembered the promise he made to Caroline many years before. He left it to Caroline to plan and handle David's college activities. He prepared to make an exit as quickly as possible. Tom decided he needed to check on the fire truck at the station.

Caroline was bubbly with excitement. "I've made arrangements at the bank for your own checking account. You'll have to go with me to the bank and transfer your money. If I'm careful, I think I can put twenty-five dollars a month in your account—at least enough to pay your rent—and if you can find a part-time job, I think we'll have enough for the first year."

David was overwhelmed with her preparations. He was not quite sure he understood everything she had done, but he was grateful she had helped.

Caroline continued. "If you write a check and your account has insufficient funds, I have made arrangements with the bank to deduct it from our account so you won't be guilty of writing a hot check."

That was good news to David. But he was determined to be very careful and frugal with his finances because he knew his parents also lived on a tight budget and had to watch their spending too.

"I think we'll be in pretty good shape," Tom added. "And I'm due for a raise around the first of the year."

The day, so far, had been a great success. The birthday dinner was exactly what David wanted. He was thrilled to get much-needed luggage. And the planning for his trip to Austin and his financial situation was working out beautifully. And now there was only one other thing for David to attend to.

"I can tell you how to make this the perfect birthday," David said. He was groping for a way to present it to his parents. He wasn't quite sure how they were going to react to his request. And he certainly didn't want to disrupt the harmony of the day.

"Oh?" Caroline answered. She was curious.

Both parents were looking at him, waiting for him to speak his piece.

"Dad," he asked reluctantly. This matter was more pertinent to his dad, but his mother would have the final say in it. David continued, "Dad, do you think that sometime in the next two or three weeks you can let me borrow Geraldine and take the gang to Galveston?"

"Galveston?" his mother asked.

"Well, I thought it would be like a final vacation before I left for school. Well, maybe not a vacation, but a chance to get out of town for a day with the gang. And I have worked all summer without a break." David planned to work until the weekend before he left. He needed the money. But since he was off on Sundays, he thought it reasonable to drive down to Galveston for the day.

"I was thinking about a Sunday. Leave early and come back late in the afternoon."

Already Caroline had a worried expression on her face. "Honey, you have never driven anywhere but around here. Do you think you could drive in that heavy city traffic?"

"I know I could. Besides, I got to learn some time. Better there than Austin."

Tom was also concerned about David's safety—and Geraldine's welfare. "I thought that's where your class went on senior day," he said.

"It was, and we had a great time. But we were chaperoned and didn't get to do everything we wanted to. And besides, this would be with the gang and not the whole senior class."

"Like what?" Tom was curious.

"Like riding the Ferris wheel and roller coaster at Stewart's Beach," David answered, "and eating seafood. Remember we took a picnic lunch and ate on the beach that day. I've looked at a map, and we can go through the Big Thicket on state highways all the way to Galveston, so I'd only be driving in the city for a short time."

Tom remembered his visits to Galveston and the fun he had. And he felt every boy ought to experience the thrill of that old shaky roller coaster. He doubted that David and his gang would visit Post Office Street—the red-light district—like he did in his youth. "Got enough money?"

David nodded. "Plenty." He knew it wouldn't take much that day, maybe twenty or twenty-five dollars, plus gasoline.

Tom looked at Caroline. She was already worried. It was a mother's instinct when the cub left the lair. But neither could think of a reason why David shouldn't go.

"I think it would be a good trip for you," said Tom. "But only under one condition."

Damn and double damn! he thought to himself. David knew there would be a catch, and his disappointment showed on his face. "What?" he asked reluctantly.

"You must wash the car when you return and rinse all the sea salt off."

"Sure," he answered, so relieved at such a minor matter.

"Geraldine does not want rust spots on her belly and fenders," Tom cautioned him.

Caroline quickly added, "And promise that you will be careful." Caroline was not as anxious to let him go as Tom. But she reminded herself that in a few short weeks he would be gone for much longer than one day.

Tom saw this as the first sign of the cutting of apron strings. He was glad. Maybe it would open the door for him to have more time with his son.

David was excited about this trip. But he felt a deep sense of guilt. He had lied to his parents. It was not the gang that he planned to invite, but Toye Lee. He knew his dad would never agree to let a nigrah take a trip with him to Galveston—or any where else, especially in the front seat. And he would have to live with this lie. His parents were so good to him and had done so much for him he hated himself for the deceit. And as he had heard many times before from his elders, they would eventually find out. You can't keep secrets in a small town. He'd have to face the music then. And with Austin just a few weeks away, maybe they would have forgotten about it when he came home for Thanksgiving—or Christmas. So he proceeded with his plans for Toye Lee's first big trip.

Chapter Twelve

David could hardly wait to announce his plans to Toye Lee. He was truly excited.

Next day he purposely went to the loading dock in hopes of seeing Toye Lee around the garbage bin. But it was only after lunch when he had to throw out trash did he finally see Toye Lee talking to his mama at the café. He motioned for Toye Lee to come over. Toye Lee ducked into Parson's Grocery for a moment to get a bag of trash and then ran to meet David.

"Where you been all morning?" asked David.

"Mostly in the sto'. We's got a big shipment of produce this mo'nin', and I'se had to put it out. Why yo' ask?"

"I've got some good news!"

Toye Lee abruptly stopped David before he could tell his good news.

"Shhhhhh," Toye Lee said. He put his finger to his lips.

"What's the matter?"

Toye Lee reached into his trouser pocket and withdrew a small package. It looked like it had been wrapped in paper and string from the meat department. In pencil he had scribbled "To David from Toye Lee, Happy Birthday" on the package.

"What's this?" David asked.

"Yes'tiddy your birthday?"

David was taken by surprise. "How did you know that?"

"A little bird told me," answered Toye Lee. He put the gift in David's hand.

"Oh, Toye Lee. Why did you get something for me?" David was embarrassed. He didn't even know Toye Lee's birth date. "You didn't have to do that—but I'm glad you did."

Toye Lee was anxious for David to open his present. "I'se always thought numbah 18 was special. S'pposed to be a man now. Old enough to go into the army with no permission. C'mon . . . open it up!"

David fumbled with the string and slowly unwrapped the paper. "Damn and double damn!" he exclaimed. "This is great," he responded to Toye Lee, whose broad smile was overbearing.

It was a black onyx-colored Schaeffer fountain pen with a clip and point made of 20K gold. David had never had a pen so nice.

"Toye Lee," David continued. "This is really neat . . . How did you know . . . what I needed?"

David abruptly stopped fondling the pen. "Wait a minute. You didn't . . ."

Toye Lee knew what David was thinking and about to ask. Quickly he blurted, "No, I'se didn't take it from the case. I'se bought it with my own money at the drug sto'."

David remembered admiring it in the display case in the drugstore. Sheaffer was the best. But it was too expensive for him to buy at the time. He had decided to use the old one he had used in high school. "It's really beautiful, Toye Lee. And I didn't have a fine one like this. I ought to be able to take good notes with this beauty."

Toye Lee's eyes sparkled with pride. You could tell by that broad smile how proud he was. He was so glad that David had not received one for his graduation.

Changing the subject, David asked Toye Lee, "Got a little money?"

Toye Lee was perplexed at the question. "Why?"

"You got a bathing suit?"

"Why yo' asking these questions?"

David was ready to tell Toye Lee his news. "I talked to my parents last night about borrowing the car and taking a little trip. Next Sunday or the one following, I want to take you to Galveston."

"Galveston?" Toye Lee asked, his face somewhat shocked but curious.

David continued. "I want us to get up on a Sunday morning and drive to Galveston and spend the day. You say you never been anywhere, so this is a good chance to get away for a day before I leave for Austin and you go back to school. I'll be the tour guide, and you'll be the tourist."

Toye Lee was intrigued. "How much money?" he asked.

"Probably about twenty-five dollars. We'll have to buy some gas. And some hamburgers or hot dogs. Gotta eat. And something to drink. Cokes."

"Don't yo' mean RC Cola?" Toye Lee asked. Both boys chuckled.

"And it will cost a little for the rides," David continued. He didn't want to let Toye Lee know about the roller coaster until they actually got to Galveston.

"What rides?"

"You'll see when we get there," David answered.

"I'se think I'se can cover that," Toye Lee said. "But I'se ain't got no bathing suit. Nevah needed one."

"Well, you can't go running around the beach bare-ass naked like you do in the swimming hole up the creek."

"Got some cut off blue jeans," Toye Lee replied.

"They'll do. Wear your regular clothes, and we'll change in the car after we get to the beach. And bring a towel to dry off with. What about your mama?" David was still not sure how much Allie Mae knew about their relationship. David had wondered how many friends she might have mentioned his name to.

"Aw. She don't care. She gotta work anyhow."

"You ready to have some fun?" David asked.

"Yo' bet!"

So it was set. David would pick up Toye Lee behind the café on Sunday morning at eight o'clock. This would be before people were out on the streets going to church. They would go south on Highway 96 by way of the Call road. David was so intent on getting up and getting away on Sunday he was willing to forego the Owl Show with the gang on Saturday night. Even if it meant missing Gary Cooper, one of his favorite actors, starring in *Sergeant York*.

As planned, David met Toye Lee in the alley behind the café. Toye Lee was ready to go. His cutoff blue jeans were wrapped in a towel which had seen better days. But neither boy seemed to care what they looked like. They wouldn't see anybody they knew, so what the heck? As soon as Toye Lee jumped in the car, David handed him a road map. "I'll be the driver," he said, "and you'll be the navigator."

"What's a navigatah?"

"The navigator reads the map and tells the driver which direction or which road to take to the final destination."

"Shit!" Toye Lee exclaimed. "I'se ain't evah even seen no road map, so how can I'se read one? How is I'se s'pposed to know that? This heah thang look like a pic'sha of some kind . . . how do yo' read a pic'sha?"

David had looked at the map many times before that day and knew perfectly well how to get to Galveston. But he liked to tease Toye Lee, and he was going to have some fun today. "Well, what the hell *do* you know?"

"Well, I know Gil Hodges hit four home runs for the Brooklyn Dodgers in their 19-3 win over Boston."

David tried to look exasperated. "How is that going to help us find our way to Galveston, Mr. Baseball King?"

Toye Lee shrugged his shoulders.

As they sped down Highway 96, David announced that he would tell him about the towns and some of the history of the areas they would pass through. He didn't want to sound like this was an education trip. But he remembered that Toye Lee had never been out of Jasper County, and there would be some interesting sights to see along the way.

Pointing to a dot on Highway 96 on the map, David said, "See that dot there? That's Kirbyville. That's where we are now. Now come down a bit, that line is the highway, and you'll see Buna. Right there. When we pass through Buna, I want you to see if there is something unusual about that town."

Toye Lee became attentive to seeing what David was referring to. It was like playing a game. His eyes went from one side of the road to the other. Then, as David knew he would, Toye Lee saw what David meant for him to see.

"Goddamn!" was his first comment. "I'se seen places with blue lights, but I'se ain't nevah seen no house with blue spots."

Sure enough, there was a white house covered with blue spots. It was probably the only interesting thing in Buna.

"Nobody knows why the owners painted a house with blue spots," David said, "but everybody in Southeast Texas has seen or read about it. There was an article in the *Enterprise* about it."

They were through Buna in a moment and were on their way to Silsbee. Crossing the Neches River, David slowed the car to point out another frequented business. "See that building? That's Frank Arnold's honky-tonk and liquor store. Hardin County is wet."

"Wet?" He did not understand. Toye Lee looked outside to see if was raining.

"It means you can legally buy and sell alcohol beverages in the county," David answered.

"Don't make no diff'rence to me. We's makes our own stuff."

David continued, "Everybody who wants to get liquor or beer has to go to Silsbee. That's where Kirbyville people buy their beer and whiskey. Lot of the kids at school go dancing there. Never did myself." He didn't mention one of his old classmates worked there now. Within minutes, they were stopped at the red light at the crossroads in Silsbee. "Not much here except the sawmill. It's bigger than the one at home." Although it was Sunday, the slag pit from the mill was burning like it did twenty-four hours a day; and as they drove through downtown Silsbee, Toye Lee and David could see—and smell—the smoke that hovered over the city most of the time.

"Look like this damned town on fire. Look at all them cinders." Toye Lee could see the smoke swirling from the slag pit. "Bet it be hard to keep a car clean 'round heah."

They went west from Silsbee as quickly as possible.

"Our next town will be Kountze." Toye Lee was trying to find it on the map. David could tell he was successful by the smile on his face. He was getting the hang of how to read a map. Kountze is the beginning of the Big Thicket.

"What's the Big Thicket?" Toye Lee asked.

"It's river bottom land for miles and miles. There's places in there that men have never seen. Heavy undergrowth and big trees. Some hundreds of years old. Lot of swamp there and probably lots of alligators and other animals, especially wild pigs."

"Ain't ever seen a gator," Toye Lee said.

"Not at the creek?"

"Naw."

"Let me tell you friend," David added with an expression that sounded like a warning. "This is not the place for you nigger boys to get caught. The people here would just about as well shoot you as to look at you. I heard they used colored boys for alligator bait."

Toye Lee began to feel uncomfortable. He had heard about some of the stories about how colored people were treated in Hardin County. It was an area where the KKK was alive and still active. There were rumors of lynchings from time to time. Toye Lee became suspicious of his surroundings. As they sped along, David pointed to the heavy Spanish moss hanging from the trees and the water in the swamp which oftentimes came right up to the highway. He didn't see any alligators, but once he spotted a piney woods rooter running among the palmetto bushes.

David continued his discourse on the Big Thicket. "I've heard stories about green lights that often are seen in the sloughs and swamps around here. Nobody can explain it, but there's sort of a green eerie light that moves around." Then David made a low oohing-moaning sound like a ghost. "Want to come down and look around some time?"

Toye Lee's eyes got big. "I'se think we's bettah get out of," he suggested. "And fast!"

Kountze was soon behind them as they sped south. The midmorning sun assured them that it was going to be another scorching day. They passed a highway sign indicating that Sour Lake was fifteen miles ahead.

"Sour Lake," Toye Lee said aloud, reading the sign as the car sped on, "that's a funny name."

"Not if you lived around here," David replied. "This is oil and gas country. The undergrowth had begun to thin out and die. The land is getting flatter. There are so many oil and gas wells around here they have soured the water. Good drinking water is harder to find than oil. You might have to drill a dozen times before you get decent drinking water."

Toye Lee was looking to see what David was talking about.

"Look over there, Toye Lee," David said, pointing to a place ahead of them. "See those oil derricks? And to the right of them, you can see the piping of the gas wells. Look at the black areas around the well where the crude oil has oozed out and killed the grass and weeds. He pointed to an outdated pumphouse."

"Bet the owners has lots of dough."

"I'm sure they do. But look how their land is messed up. And sometimes they'd rather have a good water well than all the crap around the wells."

Toye Lee could care less about environmental problems.

David looked at his watch. "Want to stop here for a Coke and some tater chips?" David had spotted a filling station just ahead.

"Sho'. Why not?"

They had driven with all windows of the car rolled down, and the car stilled smelled of smoke from the sawmill in Silsbee and the gas wells of Sour Lake. David was hoping it would have disappeared when they got back home. It was hot, and it would feel good to stretch their legs. And they might as well make a pit stop while they were there.

"Maybe just to be safe, you should sit in the backseat," David mentioned apologetically.

Toye Lee understood perfectly what David was suggesting and jumped into the backseat promptly. "Like this?"

"The next towns we'll be passing through are rice-growing areas. You eat rice, Toye Lee?"

"When my mama fix it."

"Well, this is where it comes from. Look on the map. See Nome, Winnie, and Stowell?"

Toye Lee was getting better and better at reading a map now. "Right here," he said, pointing to the three towns mentioned.

Soon they were in the middle of a rice country. The land was as flat as a pool table. It was a pretty sight to see the wind whip the maturing grains of rice during harvest season, but these crops were still green.

"People around here have an expression about the flatness of the land," David commented as he looked at Toye Lee.

"What is it?" Toye Lee asked.

"When the cows pee, the area floods."

Toye Lee smiled at the joke but was more interested in looking at his map and the surrounding countryside. On this first trip, he was not going to miss a thing.

"Can you see the water canals?" David asked, pointing out the window. "They fill those terraces up with water in the early rice season and leave it there until the rice is ready. Then they drain the fields and let it grow."

Toye Lee, however, now was more interested in the specks in the sky which quickly turned to some kind of darkened cloud. "My god almighty," he exclaimed. "Them's birds. Thousands of them. Maybe millions." He raised his arms as if he were aiming a rifle at the birds. "Bam! Bam! Bam! Gottcha!"

"They're rice birds," David told him. "Farmers don't like them. They're like grackles—you know, those old dirty blackbirds we have at home? They're awful messy and hurt the crop."

Toye Lee took another imaginary shot at them.

"There are a lot of geese and ducks here in the winter. They migrate from the north on their way south to escape the cold weather and to hatch their young. That's when you have the hunters out. You ever hunt duck?"

Toye Lee shook his head. "Don't recall evah seeing no wild duck."

Hunting duck and geese—like hunting deer and squirrel—had no appeal to David. His dad went hunting quite often, but he never asked David to go with him. David was always curious about that since all the other dads took their sons with them. But he never asked about it. David had suspected there was some kind of secret between his parents relating to guns. But he didn't bother to ask about it. And he never saw the purpose in killing innocent animals. Sitting in a boat on a cold and rainy morning was something he would leave to the more ambitious sportsmen. He had heard lots of tales about frozen duck hunters. A nice warm bed sounded much nicer.

—

David held his hand out the window as if he was trying to scoop some of the air into the car. "We should be coming up to Highway 87 pretty soon, Toye Lee. When we do, we'll turn right and be very close to Bolivar Peninsula. That's where the beaches are."

Toye Lee checked it out on the map. You could see how anxious he was getting by the way he constantly looked down the highway in anticipation of the next town.

Within minutes, they saw the road sign indicating that High Island was just ahead.

"That's where we turn," David announced. "The highway parallels the Gulf."

He turned the car to the right and headed west. As they left High Island, the Gulf of Mexico rose before them with dirty sandy beaches, washed up kelp, and lapping waves with a vista that seemed to extend to infinity.

"There she is, Toye Lee." He pointed to the Gulf of Mexico.

Toye Lee's mouth dropped open, and he was speechless. Finally he spoke. "Good god almighty . . . I'se ain't nevah seen nothing like that in my whole life . . . Look at all that water! Looky there at them ships," he said, pointing to the oil tankers on the horizon. "What's them orange things bobbing up and down?"

"They're buoys. They show how deep the water is so boats won't ground on the sandbars."

"We goin' get out there in them waves?" Toye Lee asked. He was both anxious and apprehensive. "Little bigger than Cow Creek, ain't it?"

"A little," David answered with a laugh. "We're going to turn right up there, a Crystal Beach.'

As they approached the city of Crystal Beach, they noticed signs pointing to the left. Some said Private Beach. Others said Public Beach. Finally, David chose a road, turned left, and headed straight to the water. It was a public beach, but few people were out that early in the day; and he noticed that if he drove down the sandbar far enough, they would be completely away from the few swimmers who had ventured out that morning.

"We have to go in the water here because the public beach in Galveston is segregated," David explained.

"Ain't everything?" Toye Lee retorted.

David nodded and gave a slight smile.

"We gonna drive on the sand?" Toye Lee asked.

"Yep."

"We won't get stuck in the sand?" He remembered some of the sandy hills around Kirbyville and how people were always needing help in being pulled out of the sand when they went fishing.

"No, it's firm," David assured him. "This looks like a good place to stop." David parked the car with the windshield facing the water.

To Toye Lee, the view was breathtaking. Directly behind him was a salt grass dune that helped to stop erosion and blocked the car from the highway. And lots of beer cans, paper, and pop bottles were scattered on the beach.

"What do you think, Toye Lee?"

"Beautiful." He was completely overcome by the vastness of the gulf. Toye Lee was having a hard time taking all this new experience in. It had just about overwhelmed him.

"Then what are we waiting for?" David asked. "Let's have some fun."

They took turns changing their clothes in the backseat of the car. David put on his blue bathing shorts that had lasted for several summers, but this would probably be the last time he would wear them.

Toye Lee donned his cutoff blue jeans which had faded years ago but would come alive again once in the water. "Think we's could go in naked?"

"Just try it and see," David responded. "Nude beaches are for California or France . . . not Texas. Your ass would be grass, and they'd have the lawn mower."

They walked toward the water as it swept across the sand, pebbles, and shells. The sand tickled their toes. Unlike the blistering sand of Singletary's Bridge swimming hole, it was cool and soothing to the soles of their feet. The gulf breeze made things very comfortable despite the blazing sun.

David stopped abruptly. He looked toward the horizon with an expression of concern. "I'd better warn you now, just in case."

"In case of what?" Toye Lee wanted to know.

"I don't think there will be any sharks today because this isn't shark season on the coast... But just in case they came back early..." David didn't finish the sentence.

"Sharks? They got sharks out there?" Now Toye Lee was beginning to get concerned.

"Oh, hell, don't worry." David continued to walk toward the water. "But . . . if you feel something wrap around your legs, don't panic for God's sake . . . It's probably just an octopus, and if you call me in time, I can probably pull you in before it pulls you out to the deep water."

Toye Lee's eyes looked like saucers. He froze too and was about to turn and head back to the car. "Is yo' pullin' my leg? . . . Yo' is kidding, ain't yo'?"

David looked directly into Toye Lee's eyes and detected an expression that was something between complete absurdity and intense fear. "This is the mating season for octopuses, and they sometimes grab a hold of your legs and do a little humping. You said you like a little pussy. Now you can get all you want. Octo-pussy!"

David was surprised to hear such words coming from his mouth. He never talked like that before he met Toye Lee. But with that remark, David let out a cackle that could be heard up and down the beach. "Gotcha!" And then he ran to the edge of the water and then jumped into the waves.

Toye Lee was shocked. He had never heard David speak like that before. Toye Lee, realizing how stupid he must have looked hanging on every word, could only think of one thing to say, "Asshole!" He started chasing David across the beach and into the water. And once again—as loud as he could—he yelled, "You damned white asshole.!" When he got close to David, he tried to dunk him and the horseplay began.

"Yo' tryin' to piss me off?"

"Better to get pissed off than pissed on," David replied.

—

They pushed each other back and forth trying to splash the salt water on each other.

It was past noon when David finally sat down where the waves were washing onshore. Toye Lee plopped down beside him tired but happy. David fell backward into the lapping tide. As he lay there for a few moments, he looked at the blue sky above him. Finally he spoke. "As bad as I hate to leave, I guess it's time to get out and change back into our clothes."

Toye Lee was not as exhausted as David was. He was having too much fun. "Does we's have to? Seems like we's just got heah."

"The day's not over, and I've got other plans. I'm hungry. We've got to get something to eat."

Toye Lee agreed. That sounded good to him.

David continued, "And then we're going to drive over to Galveston Island and look at the sights."

"Galveston's an island?"

"Yep. And it will take a while to get over there."

"Why?" Toye Lee asked.

"Because we have to take a ferry from the mainland to the island." David felt like this would be another experience for Toye Lee.

After dressing, they drove back down the beach to the road they had entered and headed toward the highway. David turned left and drove toward Galveston. Crystal Beach was strictly a tourist town. There were hundreds of beach homes for white weekenders and many beach cabins for rent. Also, there were many cafés and other eateries, most of which served some version of seafood. Purely tourist places.

"I said we would get some burgers or hot dogs, Toye Lee," David announced, "but I changed my mind. We're going to have some seafood."

"How 'bout some fried shark and octopus?"

"Yo' is kiddin', I'se hopes."

Toye Lee was game for the meal, but curious as to how David planned to do it. "Whites and coloreds don't eat together anymo' heah than theys does at home." He had noticed the absence of nigrahs on the beaches and in the town. "I'se sticks out like a so' thumb."

"We're going to find us a little joint that serves food in a basket and you eat outside under an umbrella." He was looking ahead. "Like that one just ahead." He pointed to the sign which read Mabel's Seafood Shack.

"What do you want?" he asked Toye Lee. "Shrimp? Snapper? Oysters? Gumbo? Gar? Buffalo fish? Looks like Mabel has got it all."

David was asking a person who had eaten two animals that swam—sun perch and river cat. "Nevah ate any of them things," he answered with a shrug. "Maybe I'se should get the oysters. I'se heard they put lead in yo' pencil."

Without changing expression, David was quick to reply to that statement. "Well, it's for damned sure you don't need that. You have enough lead already." He looked at Toye Lee. "If you had any more lead, you would have died of lead poisoning years ago."

Only a muffled smile. "What yo' goin' to have?"

"Shrimp." That was one of the purposes of the trip. He could never get enough shrimp. "Look, let me order for both of us. You sit here until it's ready. Then I'll yell at you."

Toye Lee was agreeable to that suggestion. He looked for a table that was out of the way and partially hidden.

Inside David placed his order. "Two large double fried shrimp baskets, extra fries, double order of Texas toast, and two large glasses of tea."

"Here or to go?" Mabel asked. She looked to see who the second party was.

"Here . . . Outside."

When the food was ready, David took his trays outside and spotted Toye Lee under one of the umbrella tables. David had picked up some catsup on his way out, so they were ready to dine.

They ate their food voraciously—like they hadn't eaten in days. Toye Lee carefully watched how David consumed the shrimp, careful not to eat the crusty tails.

"What do you think?" David asked.

"Larappin . . . real larrapin . . ." It was about the only words he could get in between bites.

"Larrapin? . . . What does that mean?"

"I'se ain't got the shittiest notion . . . yo' uses it all the time so I'se thought I'se would too."

They ate the rest of the meal in silence, except for the sounds of munching or slurping and occasionally the lapping of the water on the jettys.

Toye Lee broke the silence. "Man, that was good . . . real good."

"You're going to have to try some other kinds of seafood," David replied.

"Anytime, brotha. Anytime."

CHAPTER THIRTEEN

They were on the road again, speeding down Highway 87 following the sun which was beginning to drop in the west. As they drove, Toye Lee watched the waves spill onto the shore on the left side and the oleanders in full bloom on the right. The Gulf breeze tossed the salt grass to and fro, and the few palm trees that lined the highway swayed as if they were dancing to some unheard tropical tune.

"What's that?" Toye Lee asked, pointing to the horizon.

"Bolivar lighthouse," David answered. "It was built years ago to warn ships that they we getting near shore."

As they approached the lighthouse, they could see that it no longer functioned for there was no light beaming. And because it had not been painted in years, it was beginning to rust badly—the result of the salt air, hurricanes, and winter storms.

Toye Lee's eyes were fixed on the lighthouse until it was out of sight. "I'se seen a pic'sha of one of them in our literature book at school. I'se thought they was found up north somewheh."

David pointed to the cars parked ahead on the road. "There's the ferry entrance. We'll stop here until the next ferry leaves." He parked the car behind the others in line. "Let's get out and see what's going on."

That was fine with Toye Lee since he was already out of the car anyway.

The sign ahead over the entrance gate indicated that the ferries ran every half hour. Looking at his watch, David announced, "We've got about twenty-five minutes. Let's look around."

Toye Lee was already ahead of him wandering curiously here and there. There were some Coke machines on the porch of a Bolivar café. But both boys were attracted to a beer joint—Tavern, it said on the sign—from which blaring music was coming.

"Want a beer?" David asked, knowing perfectly well that they were both underage and would never be served. He had never drunk beer much less bought it.

"Sho'. I'se love to have a cool one," answered Toye Lee who had purchased beer at Pete Parker's Café in the Quarters in Kirbyville, but he also realized that no place was going to sell beer to minors—or at least a colored boy. But that fact did not keep them from looking inside the tavern. "Saint Louis Blues" was playing on the jukebox, and through the smoke, they could see all kinds of neon beer signs over the bar. The bar was empty.

Almost simultaneously, their eyes dropped to the machines that lined the walls.

"Is that what I'se thinks it is?" Toye Lee asked.

"It is."

Slot machines flashed their multicolored lights trying to attract customers. The boys moved swiftly to that side of the room.

"I'se thought these machines was illegal," Toye Lee remarked.

"I think they are, but this is Galveston County and the law looks the other way here. The Maceo brothers have got this county in their pockets." David was referring to the Italian family that was rumored to be connected to the mob.

He knew it was illegal for minors to play the slots, but he was going to do it if no one stopped him. David reached into his pants pockets and withdrew his change. Selecting a nickel, he slipped it into the one-armed bandit and pulled the lever. The wheels turned. Nothing. He did it again. And again. But no jackpot. "Damn and Double damn! What luck!"

Toye Lee was transfixed by what he saw. He reached into his pockets and felt for some coins. He found a couple of nickels. Just as quickly he inserted one of them into the slot machine. Two cherries and a bell but no jackpot. Holding his last nickel up to David, he said, "Well, this is it . . . Thomas Jefferson, baby, do yo' stuff." Slowly in somewhat of a little ritual, he waved the coin in the air and then inserted it in the machine and pulled the lever. The wheels spun in what seemed like an eternity. Then they stopped. One Bell, Two Bells, Three Bells. Toye Lee held his breath. Then a click on the machine, and the rush of money. Nickels came pouring into the winner's tray, and Toye Lee and David both reached out to stop them from spilling on the floor. The winner's label on the slot machine indicated that three bells returned ten dollars.

When Toye Lee had filled his pockets, he motioned for David to fill his also. "How many nickels is that?" he asked.

Calculating as quickly as he could, David answered, "Two hundred."

"What is I'se gonna do with two hundred nickels?" Already he began to jingle with each step he took. "Let's put some back into the machine. Maybe we can win again."

But at that precise moment, the horn from the ferry blasted and interrupted the silence. David could see the ferry approaching and knew the cars would soon be loading.

"Gotta go. Ferry's here," he announced.

They left the tavern immediately, their pants hanging a little lower than when they entered. Each step toward the car sounded like a Turkish belly dancer performing before the caliph. David began to sing a song, "We got coins that jingle, jangle, jingle. As we go merrily along."

"I'se sho' is glad we doesn't have to run a race right now or climb a tower."

David shook his head in agreement and added, "We'll put these in a paper sack I have in the car."

They returned to the car, and David started the motor. The car was quickly guided onto the ferry with the assistance of the attendants. They were parked near the rear of the ferry. Within minutes, the captain gave a blast from the horn, and the ferry pulled away from its berth. Across the bay you could see the skyline of downtown Galveston and the other ferry heading their way.

—

"Get out," David told Toye Lee. "We could go on the upper deck, but I imagine there would be lots of people."

So far, neither boy had noticed any of the passengers looking at them in a peculiar way. They had almost forgotten that they were not supposed to be seen together or riding together in the front seat of the car. Legally, they were breaking the law. But how did you segregate races on the ferry? And if people were not concerned about a white boy and a nigrah boy riding together, why should they? Galveston's population was half nigrah, and the code was more lax here.

"Let's go to the front of the ferry. You can see a lot from there." David was already wiping the sweat from his brow. The sun was at its hottest at that moment, and both boys had begun to sunburn.

As they stood there enjoying the Gulf breezes and holding on as the ferry tossed to and fro on the waves, David pointed out some of the local landmarks. "There's the coast guard station, Toye Lee," he said, pointing toward the cutter that was docked at the main building. "They do the rescue work in the Gulf and bay. You can see downtown Galveston straight ahead. See those buildings to your right? That's the University of Texas Medical School. That's where doctors get their training."

"Is that whe'ah yo' be goin'?'

David answered, "No, I'll be in Austin."

The experience was almost too much for Toye Lee. He ran from one side of the ferry to the other. Then he spotted something in the water. "Look, David, I think I'se sees some whales." He pointed to the animals swimming alongside the ferry.

"They're porpoises, Toye Lee."

Toye Lee was fascinated by the antics of the mammals and the grace with which they swam. The animals jumped up, dove into the bay, and made strange sounds, at least, strange to Toye Lee.

David went to the car and returned with a paper sack in his hand. "I want to show you something, Toye Lee."

He reached into the sack and withdrew a piece of bread.

"Where did you get that bread?"

"I saved it from lunch."

Then breaking off a piece of bread he threw it up over to one side of the ferry. Immediately one of the seagulls that were following the ferry swooped down and caught it in its beak and flew away. David threw another piece up.

"Let me do it!" Toye Lee said.

David gave him a piece of bread. Toye Lee broke off the bread and threw it up over him. The gulls swept down, and one was successful. Toye Lee laughed as the birds screamed at each other. He threw another piece up. And then another.

David was a little nervous at Toye Lee's actions. Finally he said something about them. "Look, Toye Lee, you need to throw the bread over the side of the ferry." He pointed to a spot off the bow of the boat, above the water. "Don't throw it directly above you . . ."

Toye Lee either did not hear him or chose to ignore him. He continued to throw the bread directly above him.

"Toye Lee!" he yelled. "If you throw that bread up like you are doing, you are gonna . . . ooops, too late!"

In the flurry to get the bread, one of the birds dropped his "calling card" on Toye Lee's head. A white dab on a black head.

Toye Lee felt it drop. And he now knew what David's warning was about. All he could muster was a muffled shit.

"Yep, sure is," David muttered, "seagull."

David reached into his pocket and found a Kleenex that he handed to Toye Lee. Toye Lee wiped his head, but instead of removing the gull poop, he wiped it into his black hair, which now had turned gray.

Toye Lee spent the rest of the trip in the colored restroom trying to clean up seagull poop. There were plenty of paper towels, so it just took some time.

The ferry horn blasted again. David, who was standing outside the restroom door, pounded on the door and announced, "Toye Lee, we're docking. I'm going to the car. Meet me there."

By the time the gates were opened and the other cars driven off the ferry, Toye Lee was back in the car and they were on their way.

As they drove from the ferry, David could not refrain from teasing Toye Lee. He looked at Toye Lee's head, pretending the gull droppings were still there. "For a moment," he said, "I thought you were getting prematurely gray."

—

Toye Lee was not amused.

They were off the ferry now heading toward downtown Galveston. Time was beginning to become a factor. Yet David wanted to point out some of the local landmarks. He wondered if Toye Lee would ever come this way again. And he remembered that he had told his dad they would be back late.

Pointing to the cluster of cream-colored buildings on the right, he announced, "That is the main campus of the UT Medical School. Remember, we saw it from the ferry." He laughed for a moment and continued. "It's located on Post Office Street."

The street meant nothing to Toye Lee.

"That's the red-light district in Galveston."

"What's a red-light district?"

"It's where the prostitutes live . . . and do business."

"What's a pros-ti—"

David interrupted, recognizing Toye Lee's limited vocabulary. "Whores!" He paused. "Dumb ass. You know what they are, don't you?"

"Why didn't yo' say so in the first place?" Then he smiled and said, "Everbody been to the ho' house . . . has yo'?" He chuckled, knowing the answer without asking. "One of my favorite spoa'ts."

They turned right at Broadway Avenue, the main street which ran the length of the island. David didn't want to sound like the director of a Gray Line tour group, but he felt it was one of the most interesting streets in Texas and filled with lots of history. Along the way, he pointed out some of the big Victorian homes, often sitting next to run-down dumps. Many had seen better days. Nigrahs had begun to move in the dilapidated buildings. Even still, the street was elegant and the palm trees and the flowering oleanders enhanced its attraction.

"Galveston used to be the biggest town in Texas—and one of the richest. Lot of money-people lived in those homes."

Houses probably weren't the most interesting things to Toye Lee, but he acted interested. "Some of them look likes castles," he said.

David continued, "It was here in Galveston the Yankees announcement that slaves in Texas were free. That was on June

19, 1865. That was two years after President Lincoln signed the order."

"Juneteenth?"

"Yeah," was David only reply.

"Yo' think we was freed then?" Toye Lee asked. "But don't yo' believe it. We's still be's slaves today. And yo' knows that."

David pretended to be looking for street signs.

Along the way, David pointed out the memorial statues commemorating the soldiers of the Civil War and the First World War. He then slowed the car to look for a particular home. He found it and brought the car to a stop.

"That's my favorite," he said, pointing to a three-story brick-and-rock house with intricate iron fret work. "It's called the Bishop's Palace." He would have liked to take another tour, but the sign stating Whites Only on the porch made that impossible. He didn't say anything, but Toye Lee saw it anyway.

"Who was Mr. Bishop?" Toye Lee asked.

David was amused. "There was no Mr. Bishop. This home was owned by a businessman in its earliest days. When he died, it was given to the Catholic Church as a residence for the bishop of this diocese . . . this area. A bishop is the main man for the Catholics in Galveston." A nigrah Methodist boy from Southeast Texas was not likely to know any Catholics.

"Catholics?" Toye Lee was unfamiliar with the Catholic faith. "Them's the ones who gets on they's knees in church and eat fish on Fridays and wiggle they's hands with beads?" Toye Lee searched his memory for more information. "And theys preachahs wear funny-looking clothes—all black with a white collah'?"

"That's right." David saw that was just about all he could say to identify that group. "And the men are prohibited from marrying."

Toye Lee expressed a moment of shock.

"Is yo' kiddin' me . . . man, that's tough. And the women? . . . They looks like penquins?" Toye Lee continued.

"Yep," David answered.

"Yeah, I seen them in movies. What they do if they be cripple in they's knees or gets arthritis?" Toye Lee was quiet for a moment.

"I'se eats fish on Fridays, and I'se sho' ain't no Catholic. I'se eat fish any day of the week if it be river cat."

David turned at the next light and headed for the beach. "We are coming up upon the seawall," he announced to Toye Lee. "It was built after the Great Storm of 1900, which killed six thousand people."

"Damn!" Toye Lee was impressed by the figures.

"This town just about washed away. The city raised houses, built the seawall, and filled in the space with sand and dirt. Now the water can't get to the houses. But they still have hurricanes."

Even Toye Lee was amazed by the sight of the engineering feat.

As they approached the water, houses on both sides disappeared, and before them in panoramic splendor was a full view of the Gulf of Mexico. The seawall stretched for miles on each side, and below it were sandy beaches and rocky jetties.

"This is why people come to Galveston." David pointed to what looked like thousands of people frolicking on the beach.

"Ain't evah seen so many people," Toye Lee commented.

"You can see why Galveston's a tourist city. Not much here in the winter." David turned right.

"There are some other places I want you to see." David was driving along the seawall and trying to locate some of the places of interest. As they sped westward, David would point to local landmarks. "That's the Galvez Hotel. That's where my parents spent their honeymoon, I think. If you got money, you can stay there, but most people stay in those motels along the beach. Across the street is the Balinese Room jutting out into the Gulf. People come to gamble here—blackjack, craps, slot machines."

"Can we's go in, David?" The words "slot machine" immediately got Toye Lee's attention.

"Whites only . . . and adults only."

"Coa'se. I'se ought to know bettah."

David tried to reduce the disappointment by saying, "Probably don't have nickel machines. More likely to have fifty cents or dollar slots. And you have to dress pretty nice."

Toye Lee was relieved. He couldn't afford that even though he had two hundred nickels in the backseat.

"Bob Wilkins told me when we were on our senior day trip that the Balinese Room was run by the Maceo brothers. And if you got in trouble with them, they would take you out back, throw you over the railing, and you would float out to sea . . . and become fishing bait," David told his story.

Toye Lee lost interest immediately.

They drove on for several minutes observing the various restaurants and the many souvenir shops. Every store seemed to have seashells for sale—and other tourist gimmicks.

"Now, here's a place that you might like," David said as they approached a number of wooden buildings which surrounded a grassy quadrangle. "This is old Fort Crockett—a training camp during the war. Also the home of the soldiers who protected the island from enemy invasion."

"Was they's invaded?"

"No, but the government couldn't take a chance. See those bunkers over there?" He pulled up in front of one of the concrete bunkers which were covered with sod and sea grass. He stopped the car. "Get out."

The boys climbed the bunker and entered the tomblike building from the back. Inside the cold and damp structure, they noticed the thick concrete walls. On the side facing the Gulf were gigantic slits in the wall. It was dark inside, the only light was coming from the slits and the entrance. "There was artillery here which scanned the water in case some enemy ship approached." David pointed to the bolts on the floor which at one time had anchored the cannon. "The enemy never invaded, of course, so they didn't have to use them. But I heard that a U-boat that's a submarine was spotted in the Gulf once early in the war."

Toye Lee was intrigued, and he tried to imagine how it was set up during the war. He looked out the slit at the Gulf below. "Neat."

"Watch out for snakes and spiders. It's so dark you can't see where you're stepping."

"I'se seen enough," Toye Lee announced. He quickly moved to the entrance.

David had forgotten Toye Lee's fear of snakes.

"David, you think I'se be stationed here when I'se join the army?" Toye Lee asked. He envisioned an assignment in Galveston as a good one. There were lots of things to do here—particularly the slots.

"No. It's used only for army reserve training now." David thought for a moment. "And I don't think there are any colored units in Texas anyway."

That reminded Toye Lee that even if he joined the army—which he was determined to do—he might be with all nigrah units and they were located up north. "Yo' right!"

They had seen all the sights that David had planned except the special one. David had purposely postponed seeing it until the last thing. Even he was a little excited about going there and curious as to know how Toye Lee would react when he saw it. "I'm going to take you down to Stewart's Beach now, which is on the opposite end of the island. Couple of things I want to do." But he warned Toye Lee before they arrived there. "Stewart Beach is a white beach. Nigrahs have their own beach farther on down. So we have to be a little careful. And for God's sake, don't ogle the girls—that's the best reason I can think of for a lynching."

Toye Lee was not surprised. He had already seen so much segregation today that he could hardly be disappointed.

"But," David continued, "the midway is open to everybody, but it's separated. We just can't ride together."

"What's a midway?" Toye Lee asked, still completely ignorant of what was about to happen. "And what we gonna ride?"

"Just wait. You'll see."

Stewart's Beach was several miles down the seawall. As they drove along, David pointed out the things they had seen and commented on other activities or buildings along the way. He was not as anxious to get there any sooner than he had to. And already he began to feel the queasiness in his stomach.

They had no trouble finding a parking space on the beach. By now Toye Lee had spotted the midway and all the rides available to the swimmers. His eyes were big and his excitement was obvious.

"Is that a rollah coastah?" he asked, pointing to the humpedlike structure which went up and down, here and there—and out over the water.

"And that is a Ferris wheel," David replied, indicating the big wheel next to the roller coaster. "We'll ride it first."

Both were somewhat apprehensive about the swinging gondolas on the Ferris wheel that were clearly marked White and Colored. They bought their tickets and waited in line until their turn came. It was busy, and every gondola was full of people by the time David and Toye Lee got to the loading ramp. The one that stopped first was marked Colored. As it filled up, the attendant announced, "Room for two more."

Toye Lee didn't know what to do. He could get on, but what about David?

Biting his lip, but very decisively, David stepped forward and told the attendant, "I'm in a big hurry. I'll ride with them." He acted nonchalant about it as he took his seat. But in the back of his mind, he was wondering what his dad would say if he had witnessed that scene.

"Everybody fastened in?" asked the attendant. He had given David a curious second look when he climbed aboard.

You could tell by the arch of his eyebrow that whites didn't normally ride with nigrahs. *Must be a Yankee tourist*, he thought as he snapped the gate and started the Ferris wheel.

David was not really comfortable wedged between two colored boys. *What if they pulled a knife on me*, he wondered.

By contrast, Toye Lee was enjoying it tremendously, laughing at what he was observing, chatting with his fellow passengers. David was now the minority—at least for the moment—and Toye Lee enjoyed seeing him squirm. But David was not going to say or do anything about it, and besides, Toye Lee would take care of him if there was any trouble. And very shortly everybody was screaming and laughing, and the embarrassment was soon forgotten.

The ride was exhilarating, especially the cool sea breezes which blew when they were riding on top. After two rounds, David pointed to two spots on the horizon. "See that big building over there?" It was several miles away toward the west.

Toye Lee nodded.

"That's the hangar at the old blimp base in Hitchcock. It was a gigantic facility which was built to house blimps which were used to patrol the coast during the war," David added, "looking for submarines."

Toye Lee was curious. "Is they's any blimps there today?"

"No. It's been closed since the war."

The wheel was down now, and he had to wait until they rose again to point out the other site. When they were once more on top, he pointed in another direction. "See that smoke over there?"

"That refinery with all them smoke stacks?"

By this time all the riders were following David's conversation and looking in the direction he pointed. He had become a tour guide after all.

David continued, "Those are the refineries at Texas City. That's where the ship blew up, and over five hundred lives were lost three years ago. The town was blown to bits."

"Looks like a lot of people died around here at one time or anothah . . . Flood and explosion. This place be's dangerous," Toye Lee responded. The other riders shook their heads in agreement.

When the ride was over, they moved toward the roller coaster. David moved very slowly as they approached the ticket booth. He bought two tickets. This was not his kind of thing.

As the roller coaster came to a stop, the boys moved to the rear. Again, signs indicating White and Colored were posted. Toye Lee saw how they could resolved the problem. "Yo' sits here in the last seat for whites, and I'll sit in the first seat for colored. We's be together—just two separate cars."

David saw the sense in that arrangement. "Good plan." He got in his seat, fastened his belt, and clamped his hands around the bar in front of him. Toye Lee was too busy checking everybody and everything out before they started.

As the cars slowly moved away from the station, David could feel his heart beating faster and faster. *Why did I do this?* he asked himself. Toye Lee was having the time of his life. By the second dip, Toye Lee had joined all the others in holding their hands in the air and waving them as they descended. David's hands were holding on for dear life, his knuckles around the bar turning white. He hoped that he wouldn't throw up. And if he did, Toye Lee would get the full effects of it.

When the roller coaster came to a halt, David offered a small silent prayer. *Thank you, Jesus, for saving me once again.*

Toye Lee was off the train in a moment and in David's face. "Let's do it again! . . . Please, David, just one mo' time?"

Never had David seen Toye Lee was excited or having so much fun as he was at that time. How could he refuse? Reluctantly, he gave Toye Lee some money to buy tickets and prepared his stomach for a second trip. He thought of all those bottles of Pepto-Bismol on the shelf at the drugstore and how he would love to have one.

God, I wish I had a big dose of that now. Or maybe some paregoric. I'd take anything now.

The second ride was as horrible as the first for David. And for Toye Lee, it was even better than the first. David made a promise to God at that moment. If God would let him survive this ride, he would never get on a roller coaster again. *Really, God, I mean it.* He was desperate for any solution to his nausea.

When the roller coaster stopped, Toye Lee looked at David. "One mo'?"

David could hardly speak now, but he emphatically refused by shaking his head. "We need to be heading home. It's getting late."

Toye Lee could see the sun setting in the west. And he knew David was right. So he did not ask again. Walking down the exit ramp, Toye Lee noticed David's face and his slow movement.

"David," he said, flashing his pearly white teeth, "yo' looks a little green."

David did not tell him how close Toye Lee came to having a lap full of puke.

The ride back to Kirbyville seemed to take twice as long as the trip to Galveston. David finally got over his queasiness, so they stopped along the way for a burger and Coke. He had certainly not wanted food on his descent from the Ferris wheel. They retraced the route they had taken earlier in the day, but with evening shadows now appearing, nothing looked familiar. They engaged in conversation from time to time, recalling the day's events or they would point out something interesting along the way. But there were long moments of silence with each boy reminiscing about the day's activities and perhaps wondering about the future. Both realized that the summer was ending with fall and school just around the corner. You could tell by the look on their faces that it had been a pleasant and rewarding—but different—day. Toye Lee's life prior to this day was confined to the boundaries of Jasper County. It was still remarkable to David that Toye Lee's life had been so limited; and he was proud that he had been able to open the door, however slightly, to a boy's world which heretofore had been restricted to a small Southeast Texas town. And after some thought, he realized that his world, too, had been opened as well by the experience.

"You want to stop and check out the Big Thicket on the way home, Toye Lee."

Toye Lee's expressions told David everything he needed to know. "Maybe next time."

Toye Lee just smiled.

"You went through five counties today, Toye Lee," David remarked. "Now you live in Jasper County, and we went to Newton County earlier this summer. Why, you only have 247 more to go."

Toye Lee looked so proud. "How many counties do Texas have?"

"Two hundred fifty-four."

David continued, "Take that map home and look at it. You can look up those counties later."

Toye Lee was proud to have his first map, but all he could say was a weak "thankee." The expression on his face told a lot more.

They drove into Kirbyville after dark but not too late. Geraldine had made the trip without problems—no breakdown, no flat tires—and there was still gas in the tank. David would fill it up tomorrow and wash. David also knew his parents would be worried since they were arriving later than he had told them. Yet schedules and plans can never be made or predicted with accuracy, and he knew that once he was home—and in sight—his parents would be relieved. Nor would they chastise him for being late.

They found Main Street almost deserted. Except for a few cars in front of the Palace Theater—a few people had chosen to see *Sergeant York*—there was no activity. People were either in church or at home, some listening to the radio. But in either case, David bet they were trying to keep cool. Until now, neither boy had remembered how hot it was or had been all day. But their faces would tell them tomorrow.

David turned down the alley and drove to the back door of Lea's Café. It had already closed for the day. David turned off the motor. Both boys just sat there, looking in space, relieved to be back home.

Toye Lee made no move to open the door. The best he could do was to utter a long and drawn-out sigh.

Finally, he broke the silence. "Davey . . . ," he began.

Dave? Davey? Nobody had ever called him by that name in his life except Dee Dee Grimes, and she didn't count. His mother had never permitted anyone to call him anything but David. She had corrected his father several times when he slipped and used a nickname. And to other people, she would straighten them, telling them to call him David. But he liked the name Davey. It sounded warm—and close. It had a friendly feeling about it.

Toye Lee began again, "Davey," he hesitated again. "This has been the best day in my whole life. I'se seen a lot. I'se done a lot. I'se learned a lot. I'se don't think they's as much in those books at school than all the things I'se learned today. Yo' be a good teacher. Damned good!"

David felt a little uncomfortable with the praise.

"I'se doesn't know how to thank yo'."

There was silence for a moment, and Toye Lee continued. "Yo' has treated me like a white boy today, and I'se doesn't know if that be good or bad. I'se think it be's good. But it sho' could end up in trouble latah . . . if somebody finds out about us. But yo' took a big chance of takin' me out in public. What can I'se say?"

"You don't have to thank me, Toye Lee. I had as good a time as you did. It wouldn't have been near as much fun without you . . ."

"Yeah, but yo' been places and done different things. I'se nevah got far from this town until today. I'se knows next yeah when I'se turns eighteen and join the army I'se be goin' somewheah—and doin' things—but until today, I'se nevah felt like a real person. Nevah thought I'se was somebody or thought that I'se could make a place in the world. Now I'se does. Now I'se knows they's other people like me. They got problems—evahbody do—but now I'se figure I'se can handle my problems a lot bettah. And when I'se get out of basic training, I'se gonna travel mo' and do mo' things so my life ain't so empty and so I'se won't sound so stupid." Toye Lee hesitated a moment, not sure he should say it. "Yo' has changed my thinkin' about white men. They's some good ones among those that be bad."

David didn't know what to say. Then he broke the silence. "Toye Lee, you're not stupid. I think so many people have told you that, you believe it now. You just haven't had the experiences or the breaks I've had. But as you get older and get out into the world, you're gonna be as smart as I am—or smarter! You are already smarter than me in many ways . . . like women and sex and common everyday things. And when you get out into the world, maybe you can help others get out of the hole that our society has put your people in."

Toye Lee knew what David was saying. "I'se sho' hope yo' right. I'se gonna try."

Changing the subject, Toye Lee continued. "Davey, I'se can nevah top what yo' has done today—I'se ain't even gonna try. But it be my time to plan something for yo'."

David interrupted. "You don't have to do anything. I've got to start getting things together before I leave for Austin, so I may not have time to do anything."

"Nope! I'se ain't gonna let yo' get off the hook that easy. What is yo' doing Sat'dy?"

"I'm working 'til eight o'clock. My night to work late."

"That's fine. But yo' be free after work?"

David nodded.

"Can you get yo' car?"

David wasn't sure, but he thought he could arrange it.

"Okay," Toye Lee said, "I'se wants to give you a goin'-away party.

"A party?"

"Just yo' and me—and nobody else."

"Where?"

"That's my secret and my business. Yo' just be ready and leave the details up to me. All yo' has to do is to be present."

David was already concerned. *What did Toye Lee have on his mind? He sure had a devilish look about him.* David could tell by the big smile on Toye Lee's face. But how could he back out? If this thing got out of hand, there could be a lot of trouble—from everybody.

"I'se don't 'xactly know what I'se gonna do—details latah. But don't ax me 'cause I'se ain't tellin'. Okay?" Toye Lee edged a little closer to David.

David felt like he had no choice now. To back off would be chicken, and he didn't want to disappoint Toye Lee. He could see how important it was to him. So with some misgivings, he answered, "Okay." He gritted his teeth and hoped for the best. *I hope this is going to be better than that roller-coaster ride.*

Reaching over in to the backseat, Toye Lee picked up his damp blue jeans and towel.

"Don't forget your winnings," reminded David. "Broke the bank in Galveston!"

They laughed.

Toye Lee reached for the sack, but it dropped out of his hands. Feeling around, he found it and brought it forward and held it up. "Big winnah from Kirbyville."

David laughed. "Don't spend it all at one time."

Toye Lee opened the door. "Pick me up at nine o'clock . . . yo' knows whe'ah." He patted David on the shoulder. Then almost instinctively, he put his arm around David's neck and gave him a hug.

David flinched for a moment. And reciprocated with a pat of Toye Lee's back.

"See, it ain't that bad, is it?" Toye Lee asked.

David nodded but said nothing.

The barrier was broken at last. The code for David was gone.

Then a moment later, Toye Lee got out of the car, said good-bye, headed for the tracks, jangling from two hundred nickels, and disappeared into the darkness.

David sat there for a moment before starting the car. He had a feeling which he could not describe. But he didn't know how he felt. He had just been embraced by a nigrah—one of the greatest infractions of the code. And it was no different than any other hug. Why shouldn't friends—and Toye Lee was his friend—be able to express those feelings for each other? But as he pondered the idea, he knew that this must be his secret to be shared with no one. As he started the car and headed for home, David wondered what was to come next Saturday night.

"Damn and double damn," he muttered to himself.

But first he must get home with Geraldine and assure his parents that everything was all right. It had been quite a day. He would report the gang had a good time. And the gang would keep his secret.

CHAPTER FOURTEEN

The next day as he was leaving for work, Tom Wilson reminded David that he should wash the salt off the car. David remembered his promise and said he would do it as soon as he got home. He noticed the puzzled look on his dad's face.

"Anything wrong?" he asked.

"Not really," his dad assured him. "Where did all those nickels on the back floor come from? They were everywhere."

Taken aback for a moment, then answering, David said, "They must have fallen out of the gang's pockets." He hoped that would be a good-enough explanation. Then he wondered to himself, *How many were there?*

David spent the next several days trying to guess what activity Toye Lee might be planning for Saturday night. Toye Lee appeared to purposely avoid him. He didn't throw out trash at the same time David did, and when David did spot him at the grocery store, Toye Lee ignored him and quickly ducked into the storeroom. It was all very peculiar to David. *What is that pissant up to now?*

David had made arrangements with his dad to have the car on Saturday night. He and the gang were going to the Owl Show, and it wouldn't be over until about one. That would give them plenty of time to do whatever Toye Lee had planned. David was thankful that his parents never attended the late Saturday night movie. His mother claimed it was too difficult getting up next morning for church. His dad just fizzled out by then. Because they would not be at the picture show to notice his absence, David felt safe.

The week was uneventful. A lot of back-to-school merchandise arrived at the drugstore. David and Mr. Crawford spent several hours unpacking Red Chief tablets and composition books, Sheaffer pens, Ace pencils, ink, paper clips, and every other kind of school supplies imaginable. This was a big time of the year for merchants, and they had to be ready when school started.

Mr. Crawford asked him about his plans for Austin and when he would be leaving.

David had found some sturdy boxes in an earlier shipment which he took home to pack his quilts, sheets, pillows, and other things in. They were packed and labeled and ready to ship. So far, everything was going smoothly and he seemed to be right on schedule with his plans for moving.

"I'd like to work up until the weekend before I leave," David told Mr. Crawford. "That Saturday before I leave on Tuesday."

"Fine," replied Mr. Crawford. "I'll have your check ready, and remember, I can use you on the holidays when you come home. And I want you and Cleve to take inventory for me right after Christmas. And plan on working next summer if you are back in town."

David appreciated the offer. He knew that he really wasn't needed on the workforce. That Mr. Crawford could get a nigrah to sweep the store much cheaper. Mr. Crawford hired him as a favor to his mother.

Mr. Crawford continued, "I wish you would consider pharmacy as a career. You know a lot about the business already. You know Ben and I won't be here forever. You could take over the store one day. Find yourself a nice girl. Get married. Raise a family. This is a good town for families."

David agreed, but his future was already planned. "I've always wanted to go to law school since I played around the courthouse when Papa was the judge."

He was referring to his grandfather, Judge Wingate, who would often take him to the Justice of Peace court, which was located on the ground floor of the jailhouse. And the idea of a girlfriend and marriage seemed too remote at that time. He never dated—couldn't even get a date for the junior-senior banquet and dance, unless he counted the offer by Dee Dee Grimes that he turned down. Somehow, he struck out with girls. Maybe in Austin, he thought, his luck would change. But deep in his thoughts, he knew that was not likely to happen, at least anytime soon.

David and the gang played 42 on Wednesday night and planned to go to the picture show on Friday night. They were looking forward to seeing *Sunset Boulevard* with Gloria Swanson, an actress they had never heard about but the film got good reviews. Still, it was Toye Lee's mysterious plans that occupied his attention most of the time. There was not much to do in the first place, and they had done everything David could think of at least in Kirbyville. Toye Lee didn't have a car. *What in the heck is he up to?* He kept turning this question over and over in his mind. Yet he had that feeling there was something special in the offing.

Saturday's anxiety was only broken by sweeping the store early that morning and waiting on customers during the day. He wouldn't get off until eight o'clock that evening.

Finally the day ended. It had been like an eternity to David. The sun set although it was still light outside. He had checked the locks on all the doors and windows of the store. Security was essential at the drugstore since there were many narcotics on the premises. He and Ben Crawford, the pharmacist, checked the safe and began to turn out the lights—except the night security light which was always on. It was a routine he had done dozens of times, but tonight, it seemed to take much longer than usual; and David swore Ben was purposely dragging his feet getting out of the store this evening because he knew David had other plans.

"Good night, David," Ben said, finally locking the front door.

"Good night." David quickly walked down the sidewalk and was at his home in ten minutes. He took a quick shower. Caroline had left a sandwich and some chips on the stove. There was tea in the refrigerator. On the table where it was sure to be seen was a note from his mother. It read, "We have gone to Mixson Brothers to watch the election returns. Keys on the hall table. See you in the morning. Don't forget Sunday school."

David had forgotten Saturday was election day although he noticed an unusual number of people assembling on Main Street. County returns would be posted on a large blackboard outside Mixson's Grocery and Dry Goods Store. It was a special runoff election in the Democratic Party. Republicans didn't bother to hold primaries in Jasper County since they were so few and nobody saw any point in going to the trouble to nominate or vote for a Republican. The culture of the Civil War still prevailed in East Texas. As a matter of fact, no one even admitted being Republican. This election—for state representative—was important to the people of Kirbyville. A local young man who was the son of the editor of the *Kirbyville Banner* had dared to file against the incumbent in the first primary and had come in second. That in itself was unusual since the incumbent had run unopposed for years and no one ever ran against him. He thought he was unbeatable. This year he was forced to campaign—his first in years. Since no candidate had a majority, the top two candidates were in a runoff in August. Many local people were watching the outcome of this election because if their candidate won, two things would happen. First, it would break up the Jasper County courthouse gang that had dominated Jasper County politics for decades and had kept all the power and funds at the county seat. Second, it would shift the balance of political power to south county and give the cities of Kirbyville, Buna, Call, and Evadale more say in county business. Those cities especially wanted more road money that seemed to be trickling into the pockets of the Jasper road commissioners.

It was a local custom for the people of Kirbyville to congregate in the parking lot of Mixson's Grocery and Dry Goods Store after the polls closed. Merchants had put up big tally boards, and as the election returns from around the county were phoned in from Jasper, volunteers would post the votes by the appropriate candidate and precinct. That is how people learned who were the winners and losers. Otherwise, it would be five days before they discovered the winners as reported in the *Banner*. It was also a social event and nearly everybody in town attended, even David, if he didn't have other plans. Mixson Brothers kept their store open during this time so drinks, chips, and candy bars were available for the people waiting for the election results.

The election reminded David of what he had said several weeks before. He and thousands like him could be called into the military service—and possibly die for their country. But they were still too young to vote for or against the ones who would send them into combat. He would be out of college before he got a chance to exercise the "privilege" of voting.

David was relieved his folks were not home. He could avoid answering any questions they might ask. And although the voting tally boards were a half block from the Palace Theater, he knew his parents would be gone before the Owl Show began. He had told them he was going to the Owl Show and did not wish to be caught in a lie. After his shower, for some unknown reason, David put on his good clothes. Normally, he would have worn khakis or blue jeans. But from the tone of Toye Lee's voice, the plans seemed a little special, so he wanted to be dressed in case it was. It was almost nine when he drove out of the garage. The house loomed dark even though he left the porch light on. He didn't lock the door because he didn't know if his parents had their keys to the house. Besides, nobody locked their doors in Kirbyville anyway.

Toye Lee was waiting. David was amazed that he was dressed too.

"New shirt?" David asked.

"Mama bought it for back-to-school."

"Looks good. Like the colors."

David was making conversation until he was told where to go. He had bought clothes from Mixson Brothers, the only dry goods store in town, for years and knew how limited their stock was. But their merchandise was good—and cheap—and that's what the people in town were looking for. When you had a big family, you had to be very economical, and Mixson Brothers was the place to shop.

"New pants too," Toye Lee replied. From the smile on his face, you could see how proud he was of his new duds.

—

David looked at him, waiting to get directions. Toye Lee said nothing.

"Well?" he finally asked.

"Well, what?" Toye Lee replied, stringing David along.

"Are you going to tell me where to go?"

"O-kay. Yo' ready for yo' going-away party?" Toye Lee was having fun with David who was beginning to lose his patience.

Toye Lee began his directions. "Drive back Main Street and head for West End. Go around the curve and get on Highway 1018."

"That's the Magnolia Springs Road. Goes on to the Neches River. We going to the river?" David was curious. "Sheffield Ferry?"

The highway came to an abrupt stop at the riverbank. From there, you would have to take a little one-car, hand-drawn wooden ferry across before you got on a paved highway again on the other side. The next town would be Spurger and then Woodville.

"The ferry's not open at night."

David wouldn't get on the ferry in daylight since any driver faced the risk of running off the ferry into the river, so he certainly wouldn't use it night. The ferry had no protective railings to stop cars. Old Mac, the ferryman, was a customer at the drugstore. He was the ferry master in the day and a put out trotlines for catfish at night. His home was more of a fishing shanty on the banks of the Neches River than a typical home. David had never seen him wearing a pair of shoes. But there were tales that Mac was not always reliable. Sometimes he would be available and sometimes not.

"Mac can't see at night, so he doesn't run the ferry," David told Toye Lee. "But he's on the county payroll."

"I'se knows that, dumb ass. We's goin' that way, not to the ferry."

David was relieved. He was able to breathe a little easier.

They turned on Highway 1018 and drove a couple of miles. It was dark now, and the side roads were hard to see.

"Turn here," Toye Lee directed him abruptly, causing David to almost miss the road.

"Damn and double damn, Toye Lee!" David shouted as he strained to get Geraldine back on the road. "You're going to cause us to flip over."

They drove for another mile or so. Coming around a curve, they saw a building with several cars parked out front.

"Better park around on the side so nobody see yo' car."

The building defied description. It had a porch with some Christmas lights dangling from the eaves. There was a sign above it, but you could not read it in the dark. The front part of the building was one story, but it looked like in the back there was an upper floor that looked like it might have been added later. The building had two entrances. If you went to the one on the left, you would enter a small grocery store. David could see the partially stocked shelves and display islands as he walked up the steps.

"What's going on here, Toye Lee?" David asked nervously.

"Use the do' on the right."

David opened the screen door and cautiously stepped inside. "Where in the hell are we?" His voice was now demanding.

Pointing to the tables and counter, Toye Lee announced, "This heah is Mr. Pete Parker's Café and Grocery Sto'."

David first realized they were on the back side of the Quarters, but they had come a route which he had never taken before. The name Pete Parker was not unfamiliar to him. His dad had mentioned the name Pete Parker before. Tom had always said Pete owned a honky-tonk in the Quarters. But this looked like a café.

David had heard the family story about Pete Parker often told by his parents. When David was about four or five years old, he decided he was going to Beaumont. He announced his departure by train to Tom and Caroline. They thought how cute he was and chuckled at his plans. Caroline got her Kodak from the closet and took David's picture. But neither paid much attention to David as they went about their business. David went to the closet and found a small suitcase. Then he put on his dad's straw hat, departed by the back door, and began to walk down the mill railroad tracks that ran behind their house and went out of town. Caroline and Tom did not miss him for about an hour, and when they finally realized he had actually left, they were horrified. With the neighbors, they searched the block, but David was not to be found. They extended the search to other blocks and made a pass through downtown Kirbyville. Still no little boy in a straw hat and travel bag. Just as they were about to call the fire department for a townwide search, David returned holding Pete Parker's hand. Pete found Mr. David on the railroad tracks a mile south of town. David did not wish to return, but Pete finally talked him into going back home.

"He say his daddy goin' beat me up if I'se stop him, Mr. Tom." Both men laughed at David's threats. "But I'se just brung him in anyway."

That was the first time the Wilsons had met—even seen—Pete Parker. His reputation preceded his introduction. They were so relieved to have David back they decided no punishment was necessary. From that day on, they considered Pete to be a family friend, and he and Tom would occasionally go hunting together. Pete became the provider of the beer and alcohol consumed at the fire station lounge—at a slight profit, of course. It was so much easier to buy it from Pete—although illegal in Jasper County—than to drive thirty miles across the Neches River and buy it at Frank's Place near Silsbee. Pete liked the arrangement too.

Pete always insisted, "But I'se ain't no bootleggah."

The firemen didn't care.

David wondered why the whites of Kirbyville called Pete's a honky-tonk when Toye Lee said it was a grocery store and café. He looked around at his new surroundings. It was difficult to get a clear picture because the smoke wafted everywhere and they were almost walking in the dark. He also noticed that Pete must have been trying to conserve on electricity because there were very few lights burning, one particularly giving a blue haze to the room. In the corner was a multicolored Wurlitzer jukebox with bubbles rushing through the glass tubing. There was a counter with several customers looking rather curiously at him. A number of tables with chairs lined the walls. In the middle of the room was an empty area which David had never seen in a café.

As David and Toye Lee stood there, not exactly knowing what to do next, a man from behind the counter made his way through the smoke.

It was Pete Parker, the owner. "Mr. David, I'se so glad to see y'all." It was obvious that Pete was expecting him. "How you be doin', Toye

Lee?" he asked. "Ya'll come on in. Heah's a good table right ovah heah." Pete steered them to a corner somewhat away from the other customers. By this time, the attention which had been given to the arrival of a white boy had dissipated and the customers returned to whatever they were doing. Eating, David presumed.

Pete was beaming so broadly that his gold tooth shone like a beacon when it caught the blue light above the dance floor. "Mr. David, how is yo' papa . . . and mama?"

"They are doing fine, Pete," David answered nervously, hoping that Pete wouldn't tell them about his visit the next time he saw them.

"Don't worry. I'se knows what yo' and Toye Lee is up to. Goin'-away party, he say. Yo' be goin' to state university in a few weeks?"

David nodded yes. He was surprised that Pete would know that.

Then he added, "I'se ain't goin' tell yo' folks about this. Yo' just have a good time."

David was relieved and thanked Pete.

About that time, Toye Lee walked over to the jukebox and dropped some nickels in the machine. He still had plenty of nickels in his pocket—the spoils of their Galveston outing. He looked at the selections and pushed the buttons. "Yo' know, them nickels have come in pretty handy. Now, white boy, yo' goin' heah some real music for a change. We's ain't got that Doris Day crap over heah. Or them Ames Brothers."

"The Ames Brothers are colored," David reminded him. "So are the Ink Spots."

"But they's ain't soul . . . or blues. Theys play white man's music . . . to please white folks. They's doesn't sing from the heart . . ."

The jukebox selected a record and flipped it on the turntable.

"This song is Ivory Joe Hunter's biggest hit. Remember I'se told yo' he come from Kirbyville, but he was lucky enough to get out of here. I'se wish I'se be in Holly-wood like him. He got a big house . . . and nice wheels and plenty of gals."

As Toye Lee spoke, the lyrics of the song began to waft through the room in a soft beat to the music.

—

"When I lost my baby . . . I almost lost my mind . . . When I lost my baby . . ."

Toye Lee joined in with the singer. "Ain't that nice?"

As the music played, several couples slithered to the middle of the room and began to dance. It was a slow dance, and they moved around the dance floor, synchronized with the beat of the music and looking like two copulating snakes. When the song was over, the jukebox switched to a fast number. The couples changed tempo. Now they were going to and fro with the beat of the music, waving their arms in the air and swinging their partners out and back again. It was not the jitterbugging David had seen at the Quack Shack, the teen dance hall in Kirbyville.

"What's it called?" David asked referring to the dance.

"Don't know if it got a name. Around heah I'se think theys call it the slithah. They's just pressing themselves together. Yo' whites always says dancin' come natu'al to us . . . what yo' think? Might be called jivin'. Yo' want to try it?" Toye Lee asked.

"You must be crazy?" David was not about to engage in what he thought looked like a voodoo medicine ritual. "If you did something like the slither in the white part of town, you'd be arrested for indecency and be thrown in jail."

"Is yo' kiddin' me?" Toye Lee asked, not finding the dance that offensive. "But sometimes it do give yo' a rise or two."

Pete Parker had reappeared now as they settled in at their table. "What can I'se git y'all?"

Toye Lee took charge. "Bring us two orders of yo' 'all you can eat' ribs. All the trimmin's plenty of bread. And two Pete's Specials."

Pete winked his eye and headed for the kitchen.

"He got the best ribs in the county," Toye Lee assured David.

David was bewildered by what he was seeing and hearing. Everything was happening so fast it blurred his mind. He had forgotten that he had eaten already, but with the anxiety of the moment, he was hungry again.

In a few minutes, Pete returned with two plates heaped with spare ribs, surrounded by beans and potato salad and topped with onions.

He placed them before the boys with eating utensils and plenty of napkins. He disappeared again.

"Looks good," David told Toye Lee. "But I need a Coke or Dr. Pepper to wash it down with."

"Two Pete's Specials on the way."

Before he could ask, Pete had returned and put two bottles of Lone Star beer in front of them.

"Beer! I thought this county was dry," David said.

"Pete has a special arrangement with the constable."

Pete cackled when he heard what Toye Lee said. "Yo' boys enjoy yo' meal."

Toye Lee dug into his ribs like a dog who hadn't eaten in days. "Hmmm . . . Hmmmm. These be good."

It was David who had the dilemma. He had never drunk—even had—a beer in his life. He had been kidded about going to UT supposedly where all the drunks went to college. Baylor students were told that UT students had to take a sobriety tests before they registered. Most of them believed it. Tea-sippers did not drink tea, especially in the fraternity houses. David just passed that off as part of college jesting and would handle it when he got to Austin. But now, staring him straight in the face was a tall brown sweaty bottle of cold Lone Star beer. What was he to do?

Toye Lee raised his bottle and made a toast, "Heah's to yo', Mr. College Boy. Yo' has a good year in Austin and come back next summer so we's can run 'round some mo' and go to Galveston. He tipped his bottle and took a long gulp. It was obvious that it was not his first beer.

David had raised the bottle but could not bring it to his lips.

"What's the matter? Afraid to drink? Yo' white boys are big talkers, but I'se ain't seen no action."

The challenge was laid down before him. David felt like there was no alternative to the situation. If he backed out now, it would disappoint Toye Lee. If he refused, he knew somehow the news might get back to his friends and he would be teased unmercifully. He slowly put the lip of the bottle to his lips and prepared for a disaster. In his first drink—which seemed to take the longest time—he tasted the bitter brew which tickled his mouth and throat. The cold liquid soothed his throat, now dry by the smoke and the anxiety of the moment.

"Now take a bite of ribs," Toye Lee suggested. "Does I'se have to show yo' how to eat, too? Damn, David."

The second swallow wasn't as bad; and he found that ribs, potato salad, and onions seemed to have a symbiotic relationship with Lone Star beer. The third gulp was even less offensive to his palate, and in a few moments, he had overcome his reluctance and pounced on his ribs with gusto.

The conversation between the two boys ranged from baseball and sports and the U.S. involvement in Korea to worldwide news and movies. The clarity of their conversation seemed to be directly relative to the amount of beer consumed. Toye Lee had not felt any effect of it—yet. He ordered another beer.

"Yo' ready yet?" Toy Lee asked David if he also wanted another brew.

"Not yet," David answered. He immediately recognized there may not be another one if his talking and thinking didn't clear up and become coherent.

Toye Lee's tongue became loose with baseball talk. "Yo' see where Vern Bickford of the Boston Braves pitched the first no-hittah since 1948 in the Brooklyn game?"

David answered, but his speech was slurred. "No, I didn't and who gives a damn?"

"And World Series television rights were sold for $800,000?" Toye Lee continued. "Bought by the Gillette Company."

Who cares? David thought to himself. "You don't have a television set, so what's the big deal?" As a matter of fact, few people in Kirbyville had a television set.

Now it was David's time to review the world scene. "Queen Elizabeth had her second baby—a girl."

Toye Lee was puzzled. "Who is Queen Elizabeth? . . . Only *queen* I'se knows is that guy sittin' ovah there in the cornah, and he ain't no gal." Toye Lee threw his head back and roared with laughter. "And I'se don't think yo' wants to meet him . . . her."

David rolled his eyes in disgust. "Turd." *Damn and double damn.*

"You seen them new Packa'd cars?" Toye Lee asked.

"Are you talking about the Patrician model?" David asked. "Only pictures in a magazine."

The automobile companies were introducing the new cars for the year. But Kirbyville only had dealerships for Fords, Chevrolets, and Plymouths. Expensive and fancy cars were sold in Beaumont—not this little one-horse town like Kirbyville.

"I'se goin' buy me one of them Packa'ds one day . . . when I'se leave this shitty town . . . and get rich."

"Yeah, sure." David pooh-poohed Toye Lee's ridiculous statement. "And I bet you'll put a squirrel tail on the radio antenna too."

"Sho' will . . . maybe . . . two!".

The conversation drifted and so did David's train of thoughts. He was beginning to feel a little woozy, but it was a nice feeling.

"Ready for another beer?" Toye Lee asked.

Making such a decision now might become earthshaking to David. On the one hand, he liked the feeling he was getting and he was still eating ribs. Pete Parker had replenished their plates already. On the other hand, he was driving his dad's car; and if he wrecked it or even scratched it, he'd have to give his heart and soul to God because his butt belonged to his daddy.

"One more. That's it. I swear."

Toye Lee's face now looked like all teeth. His grin stretched from one side of his face to the other. He motioned to Pete for another round. David's second, Toye Lee's third.

During this time, the other patrons continued with their drinking, eating, and dancing; but periodically, they looked toward the boys and chuckled to themselves. David had also noticed several young nigrah boys had sauntered in the café in the last hour. They didn't look too friendly. He assumed they were high school students or young workers at the sawmill. He was a bit scared but assumed Toye Lee would protect him. He didn't feel comfortable when they stared at him. He also felt like the whole crowd had known of his venture to Pete's place and had come to witness the event. David Wilson, a white boy, was on display in the Quarters for the entertainment of some nigrahs. David got over his fear when he realized that the customers were more concerned with having a good time and not watching him. He returned to his ribs.

The meal was finally over. David touched the seat of his chair to make sure he was sitting and not flying around the room. This was an experience like none he had ever had. Winning the scholarship was exhilarating but could not compare with the euphoria he was now feeling. But he couldn't—and wouldn't—tell a soul about his night in the Quarters. Not if he wanted to stay out of trouble. He could see that old invisible line running across the dance floor. *Don't break the code!*

Pete Parker cleared the table. He smiled at David as he sought approval, "Yo' like them ribs, Mr. David?"

David was truthful. "They were best I have ever eaten—all ten pounds of them."

Everyone laughed.

Reaching for his billfold, David said, "Toye Lee, let me help pay for this meal—my share." It was almost eleven by now, and David thought Pete Parker might want to close his "café" and head home.

"We's stays open 'til two p.m., Mr. David," Pete informed David. "Yo' stay and has a good time."

"I'se already told yo' that tonight was on me." Toye Lee was adamant about paying the check. "Besides, we ain't had dessert yet."

"I couldn't eat another bite, Toye Lee. Honestly, I am stuffed." David rubbed his stomach. "No dessert."

Toye Lee ignored David's comment as he turned and looked toward the jukebox and motioned for someone to come over. David could not see who he was waving to behind him and the smoke would have probably obscured them anyway. Shortly, three nigrah girls appeared at their table. They appeared to be a little older than the boys.

One was light skinned—what whites would call high yeller. She had freckles and somewhat reddish hair, and it was kinky. She was thin and gangly. Her eyes looked blue, and her breasts were not particularly large.

The second girl was darker and had unusually smooth, soft, and beautiful-looking skin. Her hair was long and wavy, beautifully cut, and no doubt covered in Dixie Peach pomade. From the look of her hands, one would conclude she did not do hard work. Her eyes were almond colored, and her makeup was perfect. Her shape was almost model-perfect.

The third girl, shorter than the others, had very dark skin and a big nose and fat lips. She was heavier than the other two. She had cut her hair very close to eliminate the kinks. Gaudy earrings dangled from her earlobes. And her breasts looked like matching wash pots that David remembered were in his grandmother's backyard.

They smiled so broadly, bearing their teeth, David thought he was about to be devoured.

Each girl had a different hairdo and an array of costume jewelry around their necks and on their arms. They were dressed in very modish clothes—modish, at least for Kirbyville. It was obvious they had not purchased their clothes at Mixson Brothers. The neckline of each girl was barely containing their beasts, which looked like they were just about to declare their freedom and separate from their dresses. The smile on their faces, greatly enhanced with bright red lipstick, and their movements on the floor left no question as to why they were standing there. They were not students from West Kirbyville High School.

"Davey . . ."

He's using that name again. I'll bet he wants me to dance with them.

"Davey, I'se want yo' to meet yo' dee-ssert. Miss Chocolate Pie, Miss Chocolate Cake, and Miss Chocolate Puddin'." Toye Lee pointed to each girl as he introduced them. "Yo' has yo' choice of white chocolate, milk chocolate, or dark bittah-sweet chocolate."

David didn't understand the joke.

"Yo' has always told me you liked chocolate. Heah it is. They's yo' choices for dessert. Now yo' gotta choose the kind of chocolate yo' likes—one or all—it don't make no diff'rence—and go upstairs to one of the rooms above the café for a samplin' contest." Toye Lee was displaying another big grin—perhaps the biggest David had ever seen.

Damn and double damn!

It now dawned on David what all this game was about. He could feel his legs wrap around the legs of his chair and tighten. His face drained of color. His mind became temporarily blank. It was already fuzzy because of the beer. All he could muster in this confusion was a confused and shaky "Toye Lee? What are . . . ?"

The customers at the other tables and at the bar were enjoying this scene as much as Toye Lee. David could not see them, but there were many chuckles from all sides.

Toye Lee was quick to explain. "Us niggers knows what yo' whites say about us."

"What do you mean?" David was completely unaware of what Toye Lee was saying. "What whites are you talking about?"

"Some folks say white men is jealous of us niggers because the white girls like us over the white men. They say we hung like hosses. I'se even was called Ramar, the elephant boy, once by some yo' white friends . . . yo' know. We's s'posed to be big studs and all. We's knows how to cut the mustard."

David didn't see the relevance of Toye Lee's statement.

Toye Lee continued. "We's knows what yo' say about nigger girls too."

"What's that?" His throat was becoming dry. If David's naïveness was ever apparent, it was now. "I don't even know any nigrah girls."

"Well, them whites is always saying they ain't nothing as good as nigger poontang."

David had heard the expression many times in the dressing room of the high school gym. The football team talked most about it. He always passed it off as being male talk of those boys who were acting macho. White males bragged a lot more than they actually performed. He doubted if anyone had ever had sex with a nigrah girl even though it was considered a mark of distinction among the so-called studs of the senior class. As for himself, nothing was more remote from his mind—David Wilson—the boy who couldn't even get a date to the junior-senior banquet.

"Toye Lee," David said, "you know damned well that is a bunch of crap. Guys like to brag. Try to impress each other. I'll bet no white boy I know has ever even touched a nigrah girl."

Toye Lee threw his head back and let out a cackle. "I'se knows yo' right. But heah yo' chance to show them up. I'se givin' you a chance to try some yo'self." Again he flashed a toothy smile. "This is yo' happy goin'-way present."

David's stomach churned at the dilemma he faced. Already the three girls were pawing him and tugging at his shirt and rubbing his arm. They were trying to get him to stand up.

"Make yo' choice. Bessie, Jessie, or Tessie—each a special kind of chocolate. They's all got special talents. Now git up and go upstairs. Proof is in the puddin' . . . bettah make that chocolate puddin'."

David felt faint. But not enough to notice that the patrons at the counter and other tables were enjoying the scene even more. There were chuckles or snickers from all around him.

If the white men of this town heard about this, they would come over here and kill some of these people and burn the Quarters down. My daddy would have to leave town and couldn't say what my mother would do. Damn and double damn.

David was now in the middle of the dance floor completely speechless. The smoke had obscured everybody and everything so that only David and his three desserts were seen. The three girls were still smiling, weaving with the music, and making all sort of suggestive motions that interpreted meant "choose me." David hadn't been so embarrassed and humiliated since the day he sang the church offertory solo one Sunday with his fly wide open. If there was a hole to crawl in, he would have done it—gladly. It was much worse than the roller coaster in Galveston.

If Lena Horne, the most popular female nigrah movie star in Hollywood, was there in a slinky dress motioning for David to go upstairs with her, David would have preferred to be in an armadillo hole outside Pete's Café. So much for his Hollywood dreams.

I think I'm going to puke.

Toye Lee soon saw David's discomfort. With the wave of his hand, the three girls retreated to the exit and disappeared into the night—probably back upstairs on the job. David began to breathe normally again.

Toye Lee was the first to speak. "I'se know'd yo' wouldn't go upstairs with them. Yo' lives too clean a life. Maybe yo' protected too much by yo' mama. But they ain't no way yo' goin' mess around with them gals. I just wanted to tease you a little. But I'se might have ovahdone it."

David couldn't get mad at Toye Lee. He remembered some of the pranks he had pulled on Toye Lee himself. He was sorry he couldn't enjoy the joke like Toye Lee had. But he was so glad the incident was over. "Toye Lee, I guess I don't have what it takes to cut the mustard. Must be that Baptist upbringing. I've always been a little behind in the physical development department—not like you."

Toye Lee was sympathetic, almost apologetic. "I'se thinks with my peckah, I'se guess. Yo' thinks with yo' brain. Yo' is smart, and that's a hell of a lot bettah than screwin' gals and bummin' around—like me—and goin' nowheah."

David could not resist a retort. "Toye Lee, if you exercised your brain as much as you do your pecker, you's probably be a genius."

Toye Lee smiled but made no comment.

"But you've got special qualities that I don't," assured David. "Your health is good. You're really in good shape. You work hard. You're reliable. So don't put yourself down. At least, you don't faint when a girl puts her hand on your thigh, like I almost did. I've probably had more opportunities in the educational areas than you have. But not in the facts of life. You've got me beat there by a country mile. And you are a ladies' man . . . a real stud."

Toye Lee laughed. But didn't disagree.

"I guess I'll have to wait 'til I get married before I'm ready for sex," David concluded.

"Well, not me, Mr. Goody Two-Shoes." Toye Lee was not ready to go that far. "Maybe I'se change if I'se evah get out this prison called Kirbyville, Texas. Maybe the army will turn my mind in another direction . . . maybe . . . I'se doubt it."

"Yeah. And maybe you'll fly to the moon or become a priest," David replied.

Having finished his dinner and declining dessert, David suggested they leave.

Pete Parker saw them rise from their table and came over. "Mr. David, Toye Lee get carried away sometimes. Maybe a little wild. All

—

the boys around here is wild in theys own way. Theys be good boys tho', but sometimes theys feels like animals trapped in a pit full of snakes and theys can't get out of. Theys be like a rat on a treadmill. No futcha for these boys in this town."

"What do they do?" David asked.

"If theys stays here, it be the mill or pulp woodin'. And theys make about half what white men makes doin' the same job." Pete paused a moment, pondering whether he should even discuss this with David. Both David and Pete were straddling that invisible line of the code. "Theys stays here and theys feels likes theys rottin' away. Theys can't get on at the chemical plants except as janitors. Civil service jobs go to the whites. If they want to make it, it's goin' to a big city—Beaumont, Houston, Dallas—or joining the army . . . Most chooses the army. No experience needed . . . or education. Just about anybody can shoot a gun. No chance of getting in the navy or air force. If they get to be sergeants, pay ain't bad."

David began to realize that staying in Kirbyville or leaving it was something that preyed on the minds of a lot of young nigrahs. He also saw that the military—along with music and sports—was the "underground railroad" for midcentury colored people, at least nigrah males.

David and Toye Lee thanked Pete for the evening's activities.

"Pete, I don't think I'll ever forget your good food. And that 'dessert' was something else. And . . . I'm hoping all this doesn't go any further than right here."

Pete replied, "Mr. David. Yo' got my word on it."

David was still light-headed from his two beers although the chocolate incident had sobered him considerably. Now he had to be very careful about driving Geraldine home. "Thank God we're on dirt roads without any traffic," he said.

Toye Lee was also enjoying his moment of "no pain."

"Want me to drive, David? I'se better shape than yo' is."

If Tom knew Geraldine was chauffeured by a colored person, he would have had a cardiac arrest. "Okay, but only to the alley."

David was not even sure Toye Lee could drive. He had never seen Toye Lee driving. Since he didn't own a car, he probably didn't have a license either. But at the moment, it seemed like a good idea.

The ride back was brief. Even so, David shut his eyes for a short rest. When he opened them again, he found they were in the garage beside his house.

"What the hell are you doing, Toye Lee? What if my folks see us? And you driving? My dad would kill me . . . and you."

"David, yo' in no shape to drive. Yo' ain't really drunk—just a little high—but it bettah yo' not drive." Toye Lee quietly opened the car door and deposited the keys in David's hand. "I'se can walk home—it's just a few blocks and I'se okay."

"Thanks."

Before he got out of the car, Toye Lee asked, "What about next week?"

"Next week?" David was puzzled.

"Well, next week prob'bly goin' be the last week we has this summah." Toye Lee hesitated as he consulted his mental calendar. "My school starts Tuesday, the day aftah Labor Day."

David had forgotten that the next weekend would be a long weekend for him, having Sunday and Monday off.

Toye Lee continued. "I thought we might go up to the old fishin' hole and have one last swim." It was the place where they had first gone in the early part of the summer. It had been several weeks since that day. Why not for their last meeting?

"Toye Lee, I can't go tomorrow. I promised Mother and Dad I'd go see some of Dad's relatives after church. Mother wanted me to say good-bye before I left for Austin. What she wants to do is show me off. Her baby's going off to college. Most of Dad's folks never got past high school, I think she wants to rub it in . . ."

Disappointment overcame Toye Lee's face when David declined the invitation.

"But what about Labor Day? I could get away in the afternoon without any problems. I don't have to register until the twentieth of September."

Toye Lee thought for a moment. "That's fine 'bout three?"

David nodded. "Meet you behind the store."

Toye Lee slid out of the driver's seat. David fumbled with the door handle. In a moment Toye Lee had disappeared down the street into the darkness. The only thing that David could think of now was whether his parents were still up. He was pretty sure that they had retired at their regular time. But he was extra quiet as he made his way to the door and past their room. He heard his dad snoring. He closed the door to his room and quickly undressed. He found a note from his mother on his pillow. It read, "Our man won the election. Will wake you for church." David was glad the local candidate had won the election, but politics was the furthermost thing in his mind at that moment. He was just trying to keep his room from swirling about him. *I've got to get some sleep*, he thought as he sank into the mattress. He held on to the side of the bed for a moment. The mattress was spinning around and rolling from side to side. He had never felt this way before, but it was not unpleasant. Why did he ever let Toye Lee talk him into a going-away party? He was asleep before he found an answer.

CHAPTER FIFTEEN

The long dry spell of summer was broken when during the next week it rained two days. It gave temporary relief to people, plants, and animals. This was unusual for Southeast Texas since most people did not expect to see a decent rain until October. The temperature remained steamy.

"God must feel sorry for East Texas," Caroline remarked to David one evening. She had already said "last rites" over her zinnias, marigolds, and petunias and was on the verge of pulling them up. Yet they miraculously awakened from their droopy state and began to bloom again. She noticed that people's gardens were reinvigorated; and some of the summer crops, like okra and tomatoes, given a new lease on life, began to produce again. The San Augustine grass in the yards were taken over by brown patch and chinch bugs. Yards needed lots of water, and since people did not water their yards, they became disaster areas and would not recover until next spring. David did not necessarily see this as a catastrophe—even though the yards were a mess—since he didn't have to mow nearly as much.

Indications of fall were also noticed in other ways. Signs advertising a portable skating rink and a traveling circus had been posted on the light and telephone poles around town. Every year in October, the owners of those outfits would come to Kirbyville—the skating rink for a month and the circus for two days. *Toye Lee would have a fine time.* But again, the skating rink was White Only. The circus was another matter. There were special areas designated Colored around the ring.

—
233

Although he would not be in town during that time, David was going to encourage Toye Lee to go see the animals and ride the midway. He still chuckled about Toye Lee's day in Galveston and the roller-coaster ride. *I think he likes midways now.*

Other indications of approaching fall were high school football practice had started in both schools and school supplies being advertised in the papers. David presumed that Toye Lee would play football his final year, but there was no mention of it yet.

The Baptist and Methodist churches had their revivals earlier in the summer and were now turning their attention to a new year. It was a race to see which denomination could "save" the most people by the end of the year. Methodists never won. Church ice cream socials also began to taper off, and members began to get serious about other matters, like budgets, literature, and revitalizing Sunday school.

And finally, Crawford's Drugstore was processing hundreds of Kodak film rolls. People had been on vacation and now would show their pictures around town.

With the reinvigorating rain, people began to look forward to Labor Day. Labor Day—like the Fourth of July—was not an important holiday in Southeast Texas. Since most of the people were farmers, timber people, or small merchants, the celebration of the American labor movement was insignificant. Only those persons who had gone to work in the chemical plants at Orange and Beaumont during the war were involved in unions and labor matters, but once they retreated to their homes in the country, union loyalty disappeared. They paid their union dues but had no real affinity for the organization. With the air cleaner and the ground now soaked with precious rain, people begin to think about getting outside and celebrating the holiday. Maybe a fall garden. The temperature remained unbearably hot, but somehow the rains had brought a promise that fall was on its way and cool days would soon be upon them. Yet they were talking about picnics, backyard barbecues, and going to Singletary's Bridge for a swim on Monday.

David had seen Toye Lee only briefly during the week. With school beginning, Crawford's Drugstore was one of its busiest periods of the year and everyone needed school supplies.

—

Toye Lee was busy at Parson's Grocery, stocking the shelves with chips and drinks for the holidays and for school lunches. He was amazed at the amount of meat the people were buying. It was going to be some barbecue, he thought, if they cook all the meat they bought.

But both boys looked forward to their swim Monday afternoon. Unknown to each other, each boy also planned to bring some food they could snack on after the swim. It would be their last time that summer they would have to talk with each other. And perhaps the last time ever. And snacks seemed appropriate.

On Monday—Labor Day—David met Toye Lee in the alley behind the drugstore. They quickly made their way down the alley, past the depot, across the tracks, and into the woods on the edge of town. They decided to walk today and enjoy the rebirth of the trees and wild flowers along the banks of the creek. The ground along the creek was still damp from the rains, and the creek had risen a few inches and was dirtier than usual. They noticed tracks of several animals along the trail.

"Them's coon tracks," Toye Lee said, pointing to the impressions in the damp clay. "And those be deer."

David looked in that direction. "Ever eat coon?" He pointed to tracks across the trail.

Toye Lee looked surprised that he should ask that question. "I'se guess all us niggers has eat it some time. I'se didn't like it."

"Uncle Freeman brought some to the store once. I tried it, but I had a hard time getting it down knowing it was coon meat." Uncle Freeman was an old nigrah man who had lived in Kirbyville all his life. David had no idea what his full name was since everyone called him Uncle Freeman. But everybody in town knew him.

"You kno'd Uncle Freeman?" Toye Lee asked.

"I used to wait on him in the store. He told me once he was born a slave . . . in Mississippi, I think."

"Uncle Freeman was mo' than a hunnert yeahs old. And he be po' . . . I mean really po' . . . livin' in that shack ovah in the Quahters. They say he ate anything he'd catch or shoot. Rats, possums, gars, buffalo fish. Heard he eat a buzzard once, but that might be just nigger talk."

David gagged at the thought of devouring the flying scavenger.

"Watch out for that snake on that log," Toye Lee warned David as he quickly stepped over the small, but wiggly animal. He had a sharp eye for everything that moved in the woods. David was thankful for that warning since he probably would have stepped on the snake—and everything else—if Toye Lee hadn't pointed it out.

"Listen to those fussy blue jays!" Toye Lee exclaimed. "And that crow. Something's really got them stirred up."

They made their way north past town and under the bridge north of town on Highway 96. The sun was blistering hot, but they were protected by the thick branches on the trees which lined the banks of the creek. As they walked the trail, David was reminded of the circus due later in the fall.

"Toye Lee, there is a circus coming to Kirbyville in October. You ought to go see it."

"I'se always wanted to go but just nevah did."

"You'll like it—the acts and especially the animals." David assured him. "Remember it's not Ringling brothers which comes to Beaumont each year. But it's fun and they have some rides you'll like. Remember the roller coaster at Galveston?"

Toye Lee's eyes lit up like a rocket. "I'se ain't ever goin' to fo'get that day . . . nevah."

They both laughed as they remembered their day on the beach in Galveston.

Just before they reached to swimming hole, Toye Lee pointed to a vine in a tree. "See them vines?"

David looked but saw nothing unusual.

"Them's scuppernong and muscadine vines. Look at the fruit at the top." Toye Lee stepped off the trail and went to the vines. He shook them vigorously. A number of the grapelike fruit fell to the ground. "Eat these," he said, handing both fruits to David. "Yo' can make wine from these, and it be good." Then looking straight at David, he added, "Yo' does drink, don't yo'?"

David understood the meaning of his question. He tasted the muscadine that had a tart flavor. Then the scuppernongs which were much sweeter. "You made wine before?"

Toye Lee nodded his head. "But most of it exploded before it was ready." He laughed when he remembered the bottles which he had stored under his house exploding and scaring his mama. "Mama thought someone declared wahr on our house."

David was intrigued by Toye Lee's attempt at winemaking. "Maybe we can make some next summer when yo' come home from college."

David did not respond to his suggestion. He still thought of his going-away party and the consequences.

The swimming hole, like everything else around it, appeared to have been taken on new life. The gay feathers and black-eyed Susans on the high banks were aflame with yellow and purple colors, making their last debut for the year. And the goldenrods had begun to replace the other flowers indicating fall and allergies. Chinese elms everywhere were ablaze in tones of red, orange, and yellow. These were about the only signs that fall was on its way. The green lacy maidenhair fern below at the water's edge displayed the beauty of nature when given the right nutrients. The water was a little murky because of the recent rains. Although everybody living around there knew of the swimming hole, David and Toye Lee acted like it was their own special spot and looked upon any other swimmer or fisherman as an interloper. They surveyed the scene as if to see that it had not been disturbed since their last visit. No evidence.

Toye Lee found a spot at the base of a magnolia tree to deposit his cache of goodies. He was proud that he had remembered to bring some snack food. "These give us some energy," he said.

David also placed his sack of goodies beneath the tree. "What did you bring?"

Together they had pooled Hershey bars, potato chips, Tom's peanut butter crackers, Mounds bars, and Cheetos—much more than anyone should eat at one time.

Both were pleased and knew they could consume all their goodies.

David reached into his bag and withdrew a moon pie. "Here's your favorite food," he said with a big smile on his face.

Toye Lee had a big grin for his cookie. "Hmmmmm. Good."

All was quiet for a moment, and each boy looked out to the creek and the woods beyond in a sense of reverie and quietness.

Toye Lee broke the silence by saying, "Only thing missin' is something to drink . . . maybe a ice-cold Lone Star?" He looked to David for a reaction.

"Or a Coke or a RC Cola?" David added. "I don't think I'm ready for the real stuff for a while. Maybe a root beer." He remembered the week before at Pete Parker's place and the following day when his mother practically had to drag him from the bed to get him up for Sunday school.

Toye Lee got a big kick out his comment. He remembered too.

"Want to eat something first?" David asked.

"Naw, let's wait 'til we's swim."

Toye Lee undressed first—as usual. He threw his clothes in a pile as he grabbed the rope and swung out to the middle of the creek and dropped.

David slowly disrobed and carefully folded his clothes and placed them in a neat stack beside Toye Lee's. He avoided the rope swing and slowly made his way down the steep incline of the bank. He had swung earlier in the summer, but when he dropped, he barely missed the huge log which extended into the water. It scared him enough not to try it again but walked down to the water instead. Even so, a misstep on the trail down could lead to a person crashing into the log if he wasn't careful.

They splashed water on each other and tried to dunk each other when the other wasn't looking. Toye Lee was up and swinging again, sometimes diving. David was content to swim around the cypress knees, sitting on the log, and treading water, watching the antics of Toye Lee. After a while, they stopped and just held on to the log, enjoying the coolness of the stream. The swiftness of the flow was therapeutic and the calmness of the afternoon made for a perfect moment of rest.

Toye Lee looked at David and then looked away. "David, I'se gotta apologize for what happened at Pete Parker's place." He slapped a gnat as it lit in the water. "I'se think I'se got carried away and carried the joke too far."

David just shrugged. It was a good joke even if he was the butt of it. "You wanted me to have a heart attack, didn't you?"

Toye Lee continued, "Sometimes I'se lets my feelings git the best of me and do somethin' that might be wrong."

David did not understand. And he did not want Toye Lee to feel guilty about it. "Well, let me tell you that I will never forget the experience as long as I live. It reminds me of a time when I went to see a girl from Buna. Her daddy and brother liked to play jokes too. So one night, after it was dark, they placed a six-foot alligator they had killed earlier on the pathway to the house close to the steps. I wasn't paying any attention to the ground before me—just waiting to get to the door and pick her up. I was on top of that damned varmint before I saw it, and I think I must have jumped from its nose to the top of the steps in one big jump. All the time her family were hiding behind some curtains enjoying me having a heart attack and crapping in my britches. Last time I took her out."

They both laughed at the story.

"Never went out with girls again."

David thought for a long moment and continued, "Our lives have been so different, Toye Lee. You know about things that I've only read about in books. You're a survivor."

Toye Lee looked surprise. He never thought of himself as being different. He turned his face to the opposite bank.

"Look at me. I've been sheltered all my life. My mother has done a lot for me—too much—and there have been times when I should have made decisions myself instead of letting her do it. I have a problem talking to my dad although I feel he would like to talk to me sometimes . . . He acts like he's afraid of me. I'd like to get his advice, but he kinda avoids me. We're not close . . . You and I are closer."

"But yo' does has a dad," Toye Lee reminded David. "That's mo' than I'se got. But sometime my jokes hurt somebody . . . and I'se really don't mean to. I'se takes it out on a person 'cause I'se angry at the way things is . . ." He didn't know how to explain his anger to David. "Coloreds ain't got a chance in this state or in this town. We's goin' be slaves to the whites and to the law and to the system as long as we's be's around heah. That's why I'se got to get the hell away from heah. And I'se be gone already if it wasn't for my mama. But who goin' take care of her. Sometimes I'se get so mad at the way I'se be treated or looked down at that I'se wish I'se could just pick up and leave today. The day I'se turn eighteen, I'se goin' stop doin' what evah I'se doin', grab my bag, and haul ass. I'se goin' send Mama my army paycheck to help her out. But my shoes be headin' one way—out!"

As they were talking, they noticed twigs and leaves drifting down the creek. The water was moving faster than usual and created a small whirlpool as it hit the log they were hanging on to. The leaves—like miniature boats of various colors—were on their way down Cow Creek to the Sabine River and eventually the Gulf of Mexico. The trees blotted a lot of the sun, although it was still trying to pierce the water. And this day seemed to be the day that all insects came alive, especially mosquito hawks.

David could see Toye Lee's point but offered no words of comfort. He did not know how to reply to Toye Lee although he agreed with Toye Lee.

"Tomorrow school start again." Toye Lee looked toward the sky. "That old school building is goin' fall in any day. We's goin' git books which yo' has passed on to us when yo' git new ones. I'se ain't sure our teachers be qualified to teach. And half the time they don't show up. Then classes has to be cancelled. We start football . . . don't know who the coach's goin' be. Don't kno' the schedule. And our equipment? Things the white school has give us when they become old—maybe unsafe."

"But it's your senior year. Isn't that special?" David asked.

"We ain't got no football queen or homecoming. We don't go on no senior day like yo' does. They's ain't no junior-senior banquet. Some of the gals has dropped out to have babies. Boys has to get out of town. Most has dropped out by the end of school. No high school graduation—not enough niggers left to graduate—so they don't botha'. No . . . it just be's another year of hell. And when the year is ovah? What does we's do? Where does we go? Sho' ain't college or to a good job somewheres. We stays heah. Maybe git married and has kids. Maybe just has kids. And it start all ovah again with those chil'ren. Evah see a rat on a treadmill? Go round, round, and round? That's us niggers."

David knew Toye Lee couldn't—or wouldn't—say what he just said to anyone else. He had already stepped over the line that separated the whites from the blacks. He had gotten *out* of his place too many times. He also knew Toye Lee spoke the truth. David could understand his anger and bitterness despite the fact that he had never really experienced anything like Toye Lee had mentioned. The summer months had been revealing to David. He couldn't share those experiences with his friends. And certainly not with his family. And he didn't know how to respond to Toye Lee or encourage him.

Toye Lee saw the forlorn look on David's face and tried to relieve David of his discomfort. "David, I'se didn't mean to dump all the problems of coloreds on yo'. I'se think I'se just got wound up too tight. Yo' ain't supposed to feel guilty about all this."

David looked in the woods with a distant stare. "No . . . Don't apologize. I know what you're saying, and I think all white people ought to feel some guilt. But they don't."

"That ain't true, David." Toye reached over and grabbed David's arm. "Yo' is a good person. I mean really good."

David lowered his eyes in embarrassment.

"Yo' has done mo' for me than any person—white or colored—in my life. Yo' has tried to open doh's that had been slammed in my face. Yo' has tried to educate me and teach me something worth knowing. I'se know yo' doesn't hate coloreds. Yo' couldn't hate nobody. Yo' just caught in the trap like a lot of whites. But yo' trying to understand it and maybe change it—not like most the whites around heah."

The wind suddenly turned brisk, and hundreds of dry and wilted leaves fell from the sky and into the water. Then they were gone swept down the stream. Insects were aroused again and flew into the sun seeking food. Mocking birds and blue jays swept down out of the trees looking for insects. Then all was quiet again.

David couldn't see what he had done or could do to make life better for nigrahs—not at this point in his life. *Maybe as a lawyer.*

"And yo' mama. She be a good woman. Damn good! Yo' gets yo' concern for othahs from her . . . I'se hears lotsa people in the Quahters talk about how she helped them when theys gets bad. And they also talk about yo' grandpa—old Judge Wingate. He was born into the system and was part of it. But in court he be's fair. And many's the time I'se heard wheah he helped coloreds out when they got in trouble. They felt that he done his best for them . . . least the best he could. And yo' grandma. She fix lotsa food for some of them po' folks." Toye Lee hesitated, "But . . ."

"But what?' David asked.

"Yo' daddy. He ain't like the rest of y'all."

"What do you mean, Toye Lee?"

"Well, the workers at the mill respect him. They say he be fair and tries to work with them on they's problems. But he still draw a long line—a long white line—between him and the nigrahs. He ain't interested in doing anything about the system—'cept keeping it."

David had never thought of his dad as a racist. His dad's job required a certain amount of discipline over his crews. As much as he had heard his dad talk about colored people, he never felt that Tom hated them. He couldn't see his dad as a prospect for the KKK or one who would use violence to maintain white supremacy. Tom was born into the culture—the system—and worked to maintain it. Did that make him worse than any other man in town?

"My dad is a good man," he quickly blurted. "To me and my mother." It was hard to defend his dad in racial matters.

"Yo' know," Toye Lee added. "Maybe he be scared."

"Scared of what?" That word didn't describe Tom Wilson.

"Scared of losin' face with his friends and buddies. Scared of not bein' a man in the eyes of othah whites. Or losin' his job."

David thought about Toye Lee's comment. His dad's best friends were his old football buddies. The members of the volunteer fire department were some of the same group as well as his hunting buddies. They were undereducated—some high school dropouts, had dead-ended jobs, and limited in their involvement in community affairs. This was not to say these were bad people—maybe people without vision or compassion for others.

"Maybe yo' dad just can't love . . . or feel anything . . . for po' people . . . or nigrahs . . . or anybody. Maybe he just lookin' out for hisself." He paused for a moment as if thinking, and then he continued. "At least yo' knows who yo' daddy is and that's mo' than I'se can say."

David had no response to that.

Toye Lee had only mentioned his daddy one time before, and David knew absolutely nothing about the man. "But that's okay. About half the kids in the Qua'tahs don't know who theys daddy is anyway. We just thinks of ourselves as cousins. Most lives with theys grandma and forgets the whole damned thing."

David wanted to change the conversation quickly. He moved to a subject Toye Lee was reluctant to discuss. "And what about school?"

"It start tomorrow."

"Hell, Toye Lee, I know that. But what do you plan to do this year?"

"Probably nothing." Toye Lee's answer irritated David.

"That's a shitty attitude!"

"Well, school be shitty anyway."

David was disgusted with the way Toye Lee's behavior dealing with school had been. "Will you do me one favor?" David asked.

"What that?"

"Promise me that you will graduate."

"Why should I's screw around with graduating. I'se goin' in the army anyway . . . and stay until I'se retires."

Toye Lee was on the army kick again. He had a one-track mind when it came to that subject. David tried to reason with him.

"Okay. Okay. But if you graduate, you'll have a high school diploma. That could mean you might get a better job in the army. And . . . promotions might come quicker."

Toye Lee looked at David sideways and slapped the water in David's face.

David continued, "After your army days, you might get the GI Bill like the veterans of World War II. The government will give you money if you go back to school—college. If you have a GED, it's harder to get aid than if you have a diploma."

"I'se keeps telling yo' that I'se ain't college material. I'se has to take two years of English, and I'se can't even speak it, much less study it."

David was trying to think of his best arguments for graduating. "But what about technical school. Like electronics? Or auto mechanics? Or something in the oil industry?"

"Do yo' think I could do that?" Toye Lee asked. He never thought past his induction into the army.

"If you want to bad enough, you can do just about anything. A high school diploma helps you make better grades on the civil service test. And if you're a veteran, chances are you can get a government job . . . say . . . like the post office. They give extra points on the tests to people who serve in the military."

Toye Lee seemed to waiver on his determination to stay in the military—not completely, but new options had been opened to him. "I'se think about it . . . tomorrow . . ."

"I want mo' than think about it," David insisted, trying to sound like Toye Lee. "I want a promise you'll finish the year in school," he demanded.

Toye Lee was at a crossroad. "David, yo's too hard on me. Yo' trying to confuse me . . ."

"Promise?" David exclaimed insistently.

Toye Lee did not reply.

"Promise?" David insisted.

Toye Lee rolled his eyes. He'd rather be discussing something else—or eating a Hershey's bar.

David was looking straight at him, his eyes quivering. His eyes had dilated. His face flushed by his persistence. "Goddam it, Toye Lee, I want to hear you say 'I promise.' Just open your mouth and say it, 'I promise' . . ."

Just as Toye Lee was about to answer him, David put his hand across Toye Lee's mouth. "Shhhhhhhh . . ." he whispered. "What was that noise?"

"What noise?" Toye Lee asked.

"Up there." David pointed up the bank in the direction of the thick undergrowth and near the place where their clothes were stacked. "See, there it is again. You hear it? It sounds like someone giggling."

Toye Lee listened. At first he could only hear the birds as they chirped and flitted from one tree to another and the rustling of the wind through the branches of the trees. Then he, too, heard someone who seemed to be laughing. "I'se hears it now. Who do yo' think it is?"

"How in the hell would I know? Someone is up there." David was nervous at the thought that someone was secretly watching them. "There's only one way to find out." He wasn't about to get out of the water to check it out in his birthday suit. He was about halfway crouched behind the log and half-hidden by the overhanging limbs. Then in his loudest voice, he yelled, "Who's up there? Who's hiding in those bushes?"

There was no answer.

Toye Lee joined him. "Hey yo' up therah, come out so we's can see who yo' is.

Still no answer.

"Guess we'll have to shoot at those bushes," David yelled as loud as he could, hoping to scare the stranger into running away. "Hand me that gun, Toye Lee." He wanted the intruder to hear his threat.

From the bushes came a burst of laughter. Then another. "Who do you think you're fooling, Davey Wilson?" It was a female voice which sounded familiar to David, but he could not readily identify the speaker. "You ain't got no gun, 'cept the one between your legs, and it don't look like it got too much firepower."

Who is that? I know that voice, David kept asking himself. *Why doesn't she come out of hiding?*

Toye Lee yelled, "Yo' be afraid to show yo' ugly face?" His strategy was to chide the person into revealing herself.

The stranger yelled back, "Ain't no uglier than yours—and a lot whiter . . ."

"Guess we'll just have to come up there and see who you are," David said. He really didn't intend to climb that bank bare-ass naked unless he had to, but the threat may work.

"In your birthday suit, Davey?" the voice asked.

"Plan postponed," he muttered. *What next?* David asked himself.

But another plan was not necessary as the bushes parted and the stranger appeared before them.

"My god!" David exclaimed in a voice tinged with shock and embarrassment when he recognized the person. "Dee Dee, what in the hell are you doing out here and up there?" It was Dee Dee Grimes, and she was intruding on their last weekend.

David had not seen Dee Dee Grimes since earlier in the summer. He avoided her as much as he could, but he always ended up waiting on her in the drugstore. She would let no one but David wait on her even when buying the most intimate articles. She was a junior, and they were in the drama club together. For some reason, she had taken a liking to David; and ever since, he had spent time trying to absent himself when she was around. He was not always successful.

Dee Dee was dressed for the weather, not for fashion. She had never been known to wear modest clothing even in school. As a matter of fact, she was sent home once by the principal for wearing "unacceptable" clothing. Dee Dee would be starting school the next day, but today she looked like Jane, mate of Tarzan. Her blouse was sort of a halter which had no buttons down the front and tied in a knot at the bottom using the two corners of the blouse. Her breast were ready to escape from their confinement. Her pants were cutoff blue jeans with frayed edges as far up her legs as they would go. She looked like she had been poured into them. Her sandals might have been shower clogs, but they could easily be taken off if she desired to jump into the water. One might call it an outfit to be worn when relaxing on the banks of Little Cow Creek—alone.

Dee Dee was not an ugly girl, nor was she unshapely. The boys at school admired her breasts, and she did everything possible to see they got their eyes full. Her dark sparkling eyes might have even been mistaken as a lustful invitation, but when she opened her mouth and displayed those threatening cuspids—which to David looked like fangs—people forgot the rest of the face and body and drew back in intimidation. David had always prayed that she would never get a chance to sink those "fangs" in him.

"Davey . . ."

Why does she insist on calling me Davey? David asked himself.

"Davey," she started again, "did you forget I live right over there on the highway?" She pointed over her shoulder in the direction of the highway.

Sure enough. David had forgotten the Grimes lived behind their car repair shop on Highway 96 north of town not far from the creek. There was only an open field and a stand of oaks and pine trees between her house and the creek.

Dee Dee continued. "I come down here every once in a while to take a swim or look for muscadines. Sometimes to cool my hot body." David felt blood rise to his face. He didn't dare look at Toye Lee but could imagine what he was thinking about this.

"How come we've never seen you before?" David asked.

"Bad timing I guess," she replied.

"How long have you been watching us, Dee Dee?" David was naked as a jay bird but underwater and desperately holding on to a slick log.

She flashed her carnivorous smile again. "Long enough to see ya'll horse around and swing from the rope up there and dive off the log." She pointed to the log which was partially hiding their bodies. "And I'll let you know right now, Mr. Davey Wilson, you ought to ask Mother Nature for a refund on your body parts . . . at least when compared with Ramar, the elephant boy, swimming beside you. What they say about nigger men is definitely true."

David was embarrassed, not shocked, by what she said. He had never heard a girl talk like Dee Dee was talking. Toye Lee turned his head so David could not see him smile at her comment and David's discomfort.

David could hear Toye Lee retort to her statement. "Sho' is!"

"By the way, Davey, who is your friend with the summer sausage between his legs?" She laughed loudly and threw a twig at them. "I saw your sausage too, Davey. It looked more like Vienna." She cackled again.

Damn and double damn. That's all David could think of at the moment. He would have gladly shot her at the moment if he had a gun.

Toye Lee was really enjoying the banter between them, but remained as quiet as he could. He was keeping his "place" as much as he could.

Dee Dee had moved to the spot where they put their clothes and goodies. "Do your daddy and mama know you are running around with a nigger boy?"

David looked just about as helpless a person could be considering the circumstances of his situation. And he could not muster a response.

Dee Dee sat down near the stack of goodies and on top of the boys' clothing. "What have you got in your refreshment sack up here?" She picked up same candy bars and moved the chips from one place to another. "How come you don't have some moon pies for your friend?" she asked. "And some chitlins. Ain't that what niggers like the best?" Each time she bent forward, her blouse would open and the boys didn't need an anatomy book to identify the parts. Toye Lee was especially fascinated by their conversation and the view.

"Come on, Dee Dee," begged David. "Don't be so tacky."

Dee Dee laughed again, showing her fangs, which Toye Lee had now come to dread himself. She was enjoying tantalizing the boys. David consider it more sadistic than tantalizing. She had never been this aggressive—or repulsive—before.

"How about bringing us our clothes?" David asked. "On second thought just throw them down here."

"You want these? You will have to come up and get them. You ain't got anything I ain't already seen." She pursued their humiliation with glee. Dee Dee was like a cat playing with a mouse before the kill.

Up until this moment, the whole scene was one of innocence. Dee Dee was teasing David unmercifully. David was trying to extricate himself from an embarrassing and humiliating moment. And Toye Lee was enjoying the banter between the two with delight. He had never seen white folks titter like his before. Then things began to change.

David was getting angry. "Dee Dee Grimes, enough is enough. Please leave so we can get dressed and go home."

"Grimes?" Toye Lee whispered desperately. "Did yo' say Grimes?"

"Yeah, that's her last name. Dee Dee Grimes."

"Do she have two brothers?"

"Yep." David conceded. "And meaner than junk yard dogs."

David could see immediate intense terror written all over Toye Lee's face. Toye Lee had grabbed David's arm and tightened his grip to a point of pain.

The reputation of the Grimes boys was known even in the Quarters, and nobody—but nobody—wanted to tangle with those two, especially nigrahs. Stories had circulated for months about some mysterious deaths of some colored boys. It always appeared that the Grimes boys' name was connected with any investigation of their deaths. But no charges were ever made against them because of lack of evidence.

"I'se gotta get my ass outta heah—and fast!" Toye Lee yelled. The intensity of his panic ran the length of his body.

"How?" David asked. "She is not moving an inch."

"I'se guess I'se just gotta run up the bank, grab my clothes, and run to the woods." Toye Lee accepted this as the only option in getting out. "I'se don't want to be around her or any other white person. What yo' goin' do, Davey?"

"I don't know." He was too embarrassed to come out of the water naked. He was hoping that Dee Dee would soon get tired of her shenanigans and leave.

Dee Dee rose to her feet. "Okay," she announced, "if you won't come up here, I'll come down there for a swim myself."

As she moved forward down the embankment toward the water's edge, she began to untie the knot on her blouse. In another step, she dropped the blouse to the ground and moved toward the creek, her breasts leading the way.

When Toye Lee saw that she was about to take her blouse off, he hopped on the log and bolted past David, pushing him back into deeper water. To get to his clothes, Toye Lee would have to race past Dee Dee, giving her one final chance to taunt the nigrah boy. It looked like the only way of getting out of this predicament.

All this activity remained a harmless prank until Dee Dee heard a limb crack. Dee Dee looked down the trail and, through the undergrowth, recognized her two brothers approaching the swimming hole. Now she became terror-stricken with her joke exploding in her face. She knew the brothers would never understand her joke or her predicament.

Almost instinctively she began to scream to the top of her lungs. "Please don't touch me!" she yelled. "Rape! Rape! Help! Let me go! Help . . . Help!"

Toye Lee ran past her. He had seen the brothers now, and his only hope was that he could scoop up his clothes and outrun them down the trail.

During this time, Dee Dee continued to scream, "Rape!" She reached over and picked her blouse from the bush it had landed on. Quickly, she tore the blouse in several places before putting it back on.

Toye Lee was not fast enough. By the time he reached the top of the bank, the Grimes boys were already there. Both had found a broken limb from a fallen tree and were ready to strike anything coming up the trail.

"You black nigger bastard," yelled one as he swung the limb hitting, Toye Lee in the face and head.

The second brother followed. "Take that, you goddam ignorant coon!" He swung at Toye Lee just as hard, hitting him on the back and neck. The limb broke, and he picked another and continued the beating. They alternated hitting Toye Lee until one swing hit with such force it sent Toye Lee reeling down the bank where he hit the log with his head with a resounding thud. His body was motionless and was half in the water.

The Grimes brothers peered over the bluff above the body. Toye Lee did not move. He lay there, his eyes staring into space and blood running from his nose. One brother looked at the other. "Want to check it out?"

"Let's get the hell out of here."

Dee Dee was already down the trail running toward her house. She was quickly followed by her brothers. "Keep running, sister!" one yelled to her. They quickly disappeared into the verdant foliage.

In those moments of violence, everyone forgot David who was still in the water. He had recovered from his being pushed back into the deeper water and had swum back to the log still hidden by the overhanging branches. He peered over the log and witnessed everything that happened, including Dee Dee shredding off her garment. Even as the Grimes fled the scene, there was no indication they were concerned about David's presence. They never looked back.

Suddenly it was quiet again. Even the sounds of nature seemed muted. David had seen Toye Lee take the whacks and fall backward to the creek below. He heard the loud thud as his head hit the log directly in front of him. He climbed back on the log and moved to a position to look at Toye Lee who was peering vacantly into the woods.

"Toye Lee, you okay? . . . Get up . . . Dammit, Toye Lee, get up and let's get out of here." No movement. David felt tears running down his cheeks. His mouth was dry. He reached down and scooped some creek water and threw on Toye Lee's face. Nothing.

David put his hand on Toye Lee's neck and felt no pulse. There was no movement at all. Toye Lee's eyes showed no movement, only fully open in permanent stare into the woods across the creek. David was panic-stricken—frozen. He was absolutely at a loss as to what to do. One side of his conscience told him to get aid and call the emergency service. The other side was advising him to get out of there—and in a hurry. Unable to help Toye Lee, he climbed the embankment back to the top of the bluff. He found his clothes beside Toye Lee's and the goodies they had placed there for their after-swim snacks. He dressed quickly and took the sacks of candy with him. He looked around to check any other debris. Only Toye Lee's clothes. Realizing there was nothing more he could do, he ran from the swimming hole as fast as he could. He had never moved as fast as he did that day—not even while running track his freshman year.

Refuge took on a new meaning as David walked up the sidewalk and entered his home. The events of the last hour had caused deep anxieties within David. He was sick—his stomach churning madly. His heart pounded so hard he thought it was coming out of his body. The only place that he could think things through was in the solitude and sanctuary of his bedroom.

Tom and Caroline Wilson were sitting in the kitchen trying to keep cool. Tom was perusing the *Beaumont Enterprise* trying to catch up with the world and state news. Most of his free time was spent meticulously scanning the sports section and the classified ads—the section advertising automobiles and trucks. But with the Korean conflict, he had become interested in what the United States was doing in the Far East. Caroline was trying to decide what leftovers she should leave out for the boys before she left for the church's Labor Day recreational prayer meeting. David's return scarcely caught their attention as he entered the kitchen.

Caroline was the first to speak. "Hey, honey," she said. "Want some cool lemonade? It's over there on the counter."

Tom didn't bother to look up. "Hi, son . . . They got the Wildcat football schedule printed in the *Enterprise*, David. Hemphill is the first game of the season." Tom always looked forward to the beginning of the Kirbyville Wildcat football season and the return to the playing field on which he had been the local sports hero long ago.

David did not reply to either. He quickly walked past them into his room and shut the door.

"Wonder what his problem is?" asked Tom.

Caroline shrugged as she looked at the closed door. "Maybe he's getting nervous about leaving here."

David crashed into his bed and lay there as if he were in some kind of frozen state.

There was a knock on the door. Then it opened, and Caroline came in. "Are you all right, honey?" She walked over to him, and seeing the disturbed expression on his face, she sat down on the bed and put her hand on his forehead. It was very warm.

"I believe you have a fever." She felt again. "I hope you aren't coming down with a summer cold. I'll get you some aspirin."

David finally spoke. "I'm okay, Mother. Just hot and tired from the sun and the walk." He didn't say walk from where, and she didn't ask. "I just need a quick nap. I'll be all right in a little while."

Caroline rose and headed for the door. "You rest and I'll have supper on the table when you wake up. Are you going to the church Labor Day recreational prayer meeting tonight?"

"I think I'll skip tonight if you don't mind."

She looked disappointed but was beginning to realize her "little boy" had a life of his own now and she could not expect him to continue to do the same things he had for the last several years. "That's all right, dear." She shut the door behind her.

David felt sheer agony. And nothing—even the University of Texas—seemed important at the moment. Only the thought of Toye Lee lying across a log on the banks of Little Cow Creek. Insects crawling over his body, which was probably bloating now and burning in the sun. *How long will he lie there?* David could not answer his own question. *What will Allie Mae do when he doesn't come home later that day?* It was obvious to David that he couldn't report the accident—the murder—but who else would? He wrestled with these questions over and over. No answer came to him. He was hot, sweaty, and miserable. He wanted to talk to someone, but the only person he felt close enough to talk to lay dead north of town. It was almost unbearable. The world that David was on top of yesterday had suddenly collapsed around him, becoming chain around his neck and his room a prison. *Damn and double damn.*

David lay motionless staring at the ceiling of his room. His body now was just another piece of furniture. In the quiet room, he slowly shut his eyes and finally went to sleep. *Maybe I can sleep forever*, was his last thought. His sleep drifted into a full night.

CHAPTER SIXTEEN

Next day, David went to work as usual although his mother tried to get him to stay home. She felt he was still running a fever. He had dark circles around his eyes. But the room which had been David's refuge last night had become his prison today. He had to get out and breathe fresh air. It was a good thing that business was slow that morning because he went through it with the motions of a zombie. He had to keep reminding himself where he was because his thoughts seemed to keep drifting back to the banks of Cow Creek. He would periodically go to the loading dock, hoping he would see Toye Lee unloading trash. At one fleet moment, he saw Allie Mae standing behind the café, smoking a cigarette, and gazing up and down the alley. She did not see David because he ducked behind some boxes. He couldn't face her anyway. David had no appetite at lunchtime, so he went to Newton's Drugstore for a Coke. Already this morning he had taken half a bottle of Alka-Seltzer. The headache and the pain would not go away.

Around two o'clock that afternoon, the serenity of the town was interrupted by the blast of the wailing fire whistle. As usual everyone working on Main Street went outside to see if they could spot the fire. Today, the whistle didn't stop after five or six blasts. It continued to wail—over and over again. That was a sign that something other than a fire had happened. Not since the end of World War II or the disappearance of the Jenkins child did David remember the prolonged wailing of the siren. He heard the sound of the speeding cars roaring down Main Street as the volunteers arrived at the fire station. Shortly thereafter, the big fire truck with its siren blasting pulled out of the fire station—men on board—turned down Main Street and headed north on Highway 96. Then it was quiet again, and all the people on the street went back to their place of business and jobs, wondering what the emergency was.

At five o'clock that afternoon, David completed his chores and went directly home. It had been an agonizing day. Even the aspirin Mr. Crawford had given him had no effect on a headache which he had borne all day. His mother was busily preparing supper. She greeted him and continued with her business.

"Your daddy is going to be late tonight," she announced.

"How come?" David asked.

"He's got to check some equipment at the planer. He was working on it when the fire whistle went off today and he had to stop work and go to the fire station before he finished the job. He dropped by to tell me he'd be running a little late since he wanted to fix it before tomorrow. He lost time at the mill when he went out on the fire truck."

"We heard the siren at the store. Where was the fire?"

"It wasn't a fire, honey. Some men setting out some trotlines on Little Cow Creek found the body of a nigrah boy at the swimming hole north of town . . . The fire department was called to retrieve the body." Caroline shifted pans on the stove.

"Did he say who it was?" David asked.

"No, he didn't mention any names. He said he looked like he was high school age. I doubt if he would know him anyway."

David's stomach churned, and his headache intensified. He tried to keep from showing any emotion. His mother was so good at reading his face. He was relieved that Toye Lee's body had been found. All day David had imagined the body lying in the sun, covered with gnats and flies, buzzards circling around the body, blood dried by the sun, and the smell of bloated rotting flesh.

David retreated to his room.

Tom came home around seven o'clock. Supper was on the table, and the family sat down immediately.

David asked about the discovery of the boy. "Did anyone know him?"

"About all I know is that he worked at Parson's Grocery. Mr. Parson hadn't reported him missing though."

Caroline winced as she said, "I guess they thought it was just another nigrah who didn't show up for work."

David tried to look stunned. "My god. That was Toye Lee Johnson!" he exclaimed.

Caroline interrupted. "Watch you language."

"You know him?" asked Tom.

"Not really. I would see him dumping boxes in the trash bin every day. We'd wave sometimes or say hi."

Tom continued, "It looked like he was swinging on a rope over the creek, and he lost his grip. Fell directly on a log headfirst. Pretty messy." He spared his family the details. "We found a candy bar wrapper in the brush. There may have been other persons there, but that's just my guess. Nobody came by with any kind of information. And we only found his clothes."

Damn and double damn. I must have missed one.

David's breath was short as his chest tightened at the memory of that scene on the creek. "Where'd you take the body?"

"Over to Coleman's Mortuary in Jasper." There was no funeral home in the Quarters.

"What will they do now?" David asked.

"That will be up to the Justice of the Peace."

David tried to fake his hunger but eventually pushed his plate away and left the table. He did not feel like eating and went to his room.

Caroline was quick to say when he shut the door behind him, "I think he must be coming down with a summer cold. He looks so peaked."

"Naw," Tom replied. "I think he's just getting nervous about leaving for college. The excitement is about to get the best of him. And he's going to miss his mama."

"I hope you're right."

Because of the Labor Day holiday, the *Kirbyville Banner* came out on Thursday instead of Wednesday, the usual day. The edition was smaller than a normal copy also due to the shortness of time to cover the news. Toye Lee's death made the back page in this particular edition. David saw the paper almost immediately after it was delivered to the store.

He stared at the headline first that read, LOCAL STUDENT DIES IN ACCIDENTAL FALL. David was stunned. "Accidental fall!" he muttered to himself. He felt nauseated. Since no one else was in the store at the time, Mr. Crawford and Mr. Arnold, his friend, drinking coffee at Lea's Café, David read the article to himself out loud. "Toye Lee Johnson, 17, a student at West Kirbyville High School was found dead by a fishing party on Little Cow Creek on Tuesday morning. It appeared that he was swinging on a rope on Labor Day when he fell and hit a log below him, causing instant death." David was still shaken by the memory of the scene. He continued, "Toye Lee was a senior at the school located in the Quarters and active in football, basketball, and track. He was employed by Parson's Grocery as a part-time employee. Members of the Kirbyville Volunteer Fire Department assisted in recovering the body when called by the local constable. Justice of the Peace, Judge Darby Powell, has ruled the death accidental based on the evidence and the witnesses of those who were at the scene of the accident."

David threw the paper back on the counter. "Damn and double damn!" he yelled. He could still remember the limb cracking Toye Lee's head. He looked around to see if anyone had heard him. Picking up the paper again, he read on, "Toye Lee is survived by his mother, Allie Mae Johnson. Funeral services will be held Sunday, September 10, 2:00 p.m. at the Pilgrim's Rest African Methodist Church with burial in Evergreen Cemetery in West Kirbyville immediately following. Friends are invited to call at the home of the deceased in East Kirbyville. In lieu of the usual memorials, the family suggests a contribution to a memorial fund which has been established in Kirbyville State Bank to help defray funeral expenses. Services are under the direction of Coleman Mortuary of Jasper."

David read the article again and then laid the paper back on top of the counter. *Poor Allie Mae*, he thought. *She doesn't have money to pay for the funeral costs. What will she do?* He began to think of how he might put some money in the memorial fund without being discovered. If he went to the bank personally, people might suspect his involvement. *An anonymous donation perhaps?* His thoughts quickly turned to anger again. *Accidental death? What kind of investigation did they do? Did the Justice of the Peace even go to the scene?* There were more questions than David could cope with. This whole affair was beginning to get the best of him. He had to get his mind on his job. But how could he?

The rest of the afternoon was a loss. Bessie and Mr. Crawford noticed David as he went through the business of waiting on customers. His usual enthusiasm had disappeared. His friendlessness had turned to curtness. His mind was a million miles away. Both shook their heads in disbelief—it was so unlike David—but neither suspected the reason for his change. David could hardly wait for the hands of the clock to reach five. He had to get away from the store. It had become another prison.

That evening, David and his parents were sitting in the living room. He had remained at home each night all week, mostly in his room, and this worried his mother. She had never seen him to be so remote from everybody. "Your friends have called several times. Wanted to know if you were sick. They were going to the picture show and asked if you were interested." Caroline was trying to cheer him up.

"Just tell them I'm under the weather and will get back with them soon." He was hoping his mother would cover for him without becoming his personal nurse.

"Honey, you need to get out some. Staying in your room just makes you more depressed."

Tom looked up from the *Enterprise* he was reading and asked, "Y'all want to go somewhere? Maybe to Newton's for ice cream?"

They both shook their heads no.

Suddenly, looking at his mother, David asked, "Aren't Justices of the Peace supposed to be smart?"

Caroline was surprised by his question. "Well, your grandaddy certainly was. He had a real feel for law—and life. He was admired by everyone." She never hesitated in praising her father and his accomplishments. That's why she was so anxious for David to do well in school and be accepted into law school. "You are so much like Papa."

Tom wrenched. "What are the qualifications of a JP?"

Tom looked at Caroline who always seemed to have the answer. "The law in Texas says he must be a qualified voter of his precinct and get elected."

"Is that all?"

"Not much, is it?"

"No law degree?" David asked.

Caroline shook her head.

"No legal training of any kind?"

Again she shook her head.

"What do they do—specifically?" Caroline began her discourse. "They preside in criminal and civil cases at the lowest level. In criminal matters, they deal with misdemeanors where the crime involves fine or jail punishment. Like traffic violations, marital disputes, DWIs, disturbing the peace, and things like that."

David could understand that.

Caroline continued, "In civil matters, his court is like a small claims court where the amounts involved are less than . . . a thousand dollars, I think. If someone doesn't pay his bill or rent or maybe won't pay for damages to your car, you can sue for payment in the justice's court."

"I can understand all that," David replied, remembering the many times he had played at the jailhouse where his grandfather held court. There were times when the judge held court in his barn with a bale of alfalfa hay as his bench. "But how can they rule on a person's death? They have no medical training."

"You mean like Judge Powell did in the death of that nigrah boy?" Caroline asked.

"Exactly!"

"The law is strange because it allows Justices of Peace to decide the cause of questionable deaths. Goes back to medieval times in England." Caroline stopped for a moment and then continued. "It's called holding an inquest. But this happens in small counties where there is no medical examiner . . . and remember Texas was a frontier state where there were few or no regular judges."

"But what kind of training do they have to do things like that?" asked David.

Caroline replied, "None whatsoever! In big cities like Houston or Dallas, they have medical examiners. In rural areas, the JP has the final authority sometimes based on the advice of a local doctor or the county coroner who may also be the local doctor. We don't have an official coroner in Jasper County."

"But Dr. McKinnon wasn't called in on that case."

"I heard that," she replied.

David was amazed at her answer. "Now why didn't our government teacher tell us that last year?"

In a rather biting way, Caroline replied, "Remember, honey, he was a football coach and didn't know it." She grinned.

Tom chuckled at her remark but did not comment or look at her.

"Look at Uncle Darby Powell." David was trying to put this together. "He's old and decrepit. How did he ever get to be a Justice of Peace. And how could he have the ability to decide between an accidental death and one which maybe wasn't accidental?"

"Honey, he knows everybody in this precinct. He has been around here so long that everyone votes for him. He ran against Papa so many times I can't remember them. Only after Papa died did he finally win."

David was amazed at what he heard.

"Honey, there was a case a while back . . . not in this county . . . but somewhere else, where a man's body was found in the middle of a cornfield. He had been shot five times in the stomach with a bolt action .22-gauge gun which was lying beside the body. That means he had to cock it each time it was fired. The Justice of the Peace in that county ruled it a suicide."

Again, David shook his head in disbelief.

It was Tom's time to speak. "Reminds me of a story that's been going around here for years." He laughed out loud. "I don't know if its true or not, but people always tell it on Uncle Darby."

"What's the story, Dad?"

"Well, it seems that there was a man over on the other side of the county who got killed. So Uncle Darby wrote 'suicide' on his death certificate. A friend of Uncle Darby's came to him and protested the cause of death. He told Uncle Darby that the man was killed by a jealous husband and Uncle Darby knew it. Uncle Darby replied to the man, 'Yeah, I know. I told that son-of-a-bitch that if he kept messing around with the man's wife, he was committing suicide. The man kept running around with her, so that's how I wrote it up.'"

Tom winked at Caroline who had heard the story too, but only remarked, "Tom Wilson! Watch your language."

David was not amused by the story. He was still disturbed—angry—by Uncle Darby's ruling of Toye Lee's accidental death.

"Uncle Darby didn't even go to the scene of the accident," David said.

Quickly Tom replied, "Probably couldn't climb the banks of the creek . . . too old! Too steep." He chuckled.

"But on the hearsay of others? That just doesn't make sense!"

"Well, honey," his mother reminded him, "a lot of things don't make sense around here. It's the mother I feel so sorry for . . . her only child. How lonely her house must be at nights . . . her life must also be so empty now."

The way the incident was handled confused David as much as it angered him.

Tom concluded the conversation by adding, "Justices of the Peace also have the power to perform weddings, David. Just in case you ever need one." He winked at his son. "Lots cheaper than church weddings. No fuss. Ask for the two dollar special. Takes about five minutes. I have recommended to several men at the mill to go to the Justice of Peace for a quickie. Then there are others who don't see the need for any kind of ceremony at all. Common law marriages don't bother them." Tom laughed. "As one worker told me, 'Mr. Tom, we just takes up.'"

CHAPTER SEVENTEEN

By Saturday, David had finally made his mind up to go across the tracks to Toye Lee's house. He had pondered the matter for four days and thought it was the only decent thing to do. He had borrowed the car from his dad and had planned to arrive at dusk. He drove the car near the Johnson home. It was truly a shack. It leaned to the right. The roof needed patching. The planks on the front porch showed gaps where one could possibly stumble or fall through. The columns on the front porch had long disappeared, and the roof was being held by some metal rods which had been propped under it. Several people were going into the house, and several men stood outside smoking cigarettes. He slowed down for a moment, but when the men looked his way, he sped up again and went around the block. Again, he passed the house, and once again he went by without stopping. *Maybe a Coke at Turner's Café before I go in*, he thought.

After downing a Coke, David once again made his way back to the little nigrah community east of town across the tracks. Darkness had fallen, and had it not been for the many lights in the house, he might have passed it. There were no mourners on the porch now, so he slowed down and stopped in front of the house. David cut the car lights off. This time he was definitely going to stop. He could see through the open windows with no screens and the open door was missing a screen too. On one side of the room were a number of colored people sitting in a chair surrounding Allie Mae. Her face revealed the stress of her bereavement. On the other side of the room David could see a simple casket resting on a bier flanked by a worn maroon velvet curtain. Across the curtain in faded letters was the name Coleman Mortuary. The picture of the half-open casket left him numb. He opened the car door and put one foot on the ground when the door of the house opened—perhaps to greet the next visitor. One of the mourners came outside. He noticed the white boy in the black car and started to walk toward him. It was too much for David. Back into the car, he gunned Geraldine and sped down the street and back home.

Sunday came too soon. David did not want to get up, but his mother insisted they go to Sunday school and church. "Your Father has agreed to meet us for the sermon service, and I'm not going to let him back out now."

David stayed in bed as long as he could. He finally pulled himself from the sanctuary of a firm mattress and clean sheets, quickly took a shower, and dressed. His mother, already dressed, had breakfast on the table that he gobbled down quickly. There was no time to read the *Enterprise*, which had already been opened by Tom who always looked at the sports page first.

"Less than a month before the World Series," Tom announced. He followed baseball religiously and could quote statistics like Toye Lee often did. He would soon be taking his portable radio to the mill so everyone could listen to the play-offs. David never liked baseball, and he saw no real importance in being able to pronounce useless statistics on cue. And he certainly had no interest in what teams were leading their respective leagues. Since Texas had no major league teams, David saw little reason to support any Yankee teams.

"Let's walk today," David said more in the form of an announcement than a request. They only lived a three blocks from the First Baptist Church on Main Street. The sun had begun to blister the sidewalks.

"That's a lovely idea," his mother replied. "David, why don't we go on, and, Tom, you follow us when you finish your coffee."

Tom did not object at all.

David saw an opportunity to talk with his mother without the presence of his dad. The question was how do you go about discussing a matter without being too particular.

"Mother," he began. "What would you do if you saw someone do something wrong and nothing was said or done about it?"

"You mean like morally wrong?"

"Well, like legally wrong—breaking the law." He was looking for an example. "Like you saw someone take something from a store without paying for it."

"Shoplifting?"

David nodded.

"First, it's against the law, therefore a crime. Then remember what the Bible says, 'Thou shalt not steal' . . . Yes, I would report the theft to the proper person."

David was not satisfied with her answer. "What if your best friend cheated on tests in school and the result knocked you out of being named an honor student? Or you saw that same person take some kind of illegal drugs? Would you report it to the teacher? Or to the proper authorities?"

Caroline was not so quick to answer that question. It involved a friend. It posed a more complex question with no easy answer. "I'm not so sure what I would do. I think I would try to help a friend on drugs or alcohol. But I might just have to bite my lip and suffer not being an honor student. Maybe the guilt of the person would be rectified in the end. Maybe ask my forgiveness."

"Sure they would," David said sarcastically. "And the person would write you at Sam Houston College from the university where she got the scholarship you were entitled to." David laughed. "That's noble, but how many people would apologize?"

"Probably none."

David searched for an example. "Would you tell your best friend if you saw her husband trifling on her?"

Once again, Caroline was stumped. Then she ventured an answer, "I suppose it depends on the person and the situation. I see your point that all things are not clearly delineated. What brought on this discussion anyway?"

David could not tell her what he was thinking. "I believe everybody at one time or another is faced with decisions where he or she is torn between doing what is right or legal and maintaining an old custom or which is wrong and breaks the law. Maybe that's why dictators survive. They take advantage of fear and indifference . . . should bad people be allowed to live or go unpunished in order to protect the innocent." David let out an exasperated sigh. "It doesn't seem fair."

They were approaching the First Baptist Church, and the people who were congregating on the steps waved to Caroline and David as they approached the entrance. Before they got within hearing distance of those people, Caroline made one final comment.

"Do what you think is right. Do what makes you feel comfortable. Remember, you have to live with yourself the rest of your life. I would never suggest someone break the law. Papa would turn over in his grave if he heard me say I'd break the law. But sometimes even the law has to be bent . . . or stretched. It was the age-old matter of omission versus commission. You've heard the expression . . . Don't ask, then you won't know." Caroline quickly ended her comments and was ready to greet fellow worshippers.

"Let sleeping dogs lie?" David asked.

By that time, they had arrived at the church and the conversation ended as each person went to his respective Sunday school classrooms.

David could not remember one word of Brother Lewis's sermon that morning. He might as well have been on top of Mount Everest as far as his attention to the morning's services. David could only think of Toye Lee. In a few hours, his best friend would be laid to rest in a cold grave in Evergreen Cemetery. That friend did not deserve to be there—just because some whites hated nigrahs. And David could do nothing about it. Well, he could if he was willing to break the unwritten code between whites and coloreds. If he was willing to subject himself and his family to abject humiliation—and possibly harassment. Perhaps physical abuse. He could report a crime and then escape by going to Austin, but his parents had to face the people of that town every day of the year. And David would return to the city in a few weeks or months. *What am I going to do?*

After eating lunch, David begged to be excused.

"Honey, please don't go back to your room and sulk," his mother said.

David saw a chance to get the car without arousing suspicions. "Can I have the car?"

Caroline was quick to answer before Tom could think of a reason he shouldn't. "Of course you can. Tom, give David the keys to the car." She had no intention of asking Tom if he objected or had plans of his own. "David wants to get out and see his friends."

Tom obliged Caroline, handing over the keys promptly. His only comment was, "Would you fill Geraldine up before you come home?" He handed David some money. It didn't take much at nineteen cents a gallon.

"Sure." With that remark, David was out of the room and out of the house. *Whew!* he thought. *That was easy.* He dashed for the car before his parents changed their minds.

A few minutes before two o'clock, David drove to the Pilgrim's Rest African Methodist Church. He parked Geraldine across the road under an aging cedar tree so that he could see both the entrance of the church and the gate to Evergreen Cemetery which was located next to it. The church looked like the perfect example of a poor colored church. He could see a pile of freshly dug dirt in the cemetery. David had been in the church once before when the youth group from his own church took it on as a summer missionary painting project. Behind one of the front doors was a rope hanging from the ceiling. This rope was attached to a bell in a belfry which was more home to pigeons and dirt daubers than it was to the bell. From the foyer you could enter two Sunday school rooms, one to the right, the other to the left. Also from the foyer you entered the main sanctuary with its aging and creaking floors and pews and decrepit piano with some of its ivory and ebony keys missing. It appeared to David that the building had not been touched since that summer he helped to paint it. Between the church and the cemetery to the rear were two outdoor toilets. From the looks of those privies, you might presume the user would have had to have been desperate to use it or unable to control his bodily functions. It was a perfect place to be the home of black widow spiders. The toilets didn't look too busy.

David sat in the car watching. Some late-arriving members noticed his car parked off the side of the road but thought nothing of a white man observing them unless it was the sheriff. David was somewhat surprised that Toye Lee's funeral was held so quickly. Usually colored people "funeralized" for at least a week, and by the time the funeral was held, the deceased was more than ready for burial. Allie Mae, for some reason known only to herself, chose to have the funeral and burial quicker than usual.

Shortly after two o'clock, the choir and congregation began to sing, which soon turned into claps, shouts, and praises. The choir did not sing in harmony, but everyone sang. They were loud. The only songs that David recognized was "His Eye Is on the Sparrow," "Amazing Grace," and "Jesus Saves." He did not recognize the others, but they sang on and on. By the time the reverend began his sermon, the crowd was warmed up, the church was full, and he was on the "main line." Interspersed in the inspired sermon were many "hallelujahs," "amens," "praise Jesuses," and "sho' 'nuffs"—all seemingly agreeing with the preacher. The grief of the mourners made its way to David through the sounds coming from the church.

An hour later, the singing stopped and the crowd once again poured through the doors of the church. David spotted Allie Mae, wearing a black veil, as she made her way down the steps. She was surrounded by the sisters and friends who helped to hold her up. One friend near her pointed to David's car. Allie Mae looked that way and nodded but quickly turned away to follow the casket as it was carried through the door and toward the cemetery. The mourners followed the casket down a path through the broken gate of the cemetery.

Evergreen Cemetery was one of several cemeteries in the Quarters. Each nigrah church usually had its own burial ground. The few remaining pickets had not seen paint in years. Like most cemeteries in Southeast Texas, the cemetery was dotted by cedar trees some appearing to have been over a century old. David always thought that cedars and cemeteries had a strange affinity. They were the only things Evergreen Cemetery that were green. Everything else was brown, scorched by the sun. He could see the freshly dug grave with its red clay piled high and only partially covered by the artificial grass laid out by Coleman Mortuary. David could not hear the parting words of the preacher, but when he heard one gigantic amen, he knew the service was over. He started the car and slowly drove away. David wished he could talk to Allie Mae who might have invited him to the services. In fact, he felt that they might welcome him. But he never intended to go to the service. Whites just didn't do that—the code, of course. What could he say or do that would comfort a mother whose only son was needlessly killed by white sadists. Only she didn't know what he knew and he couldn't tell. *Or did she?* The truth was David was still overcome with emotion and he could not face anyone at that time. The congregation watched him as he drove down the dirt road back to town, but David did not see them.

Later that evening, near twilight, and long after the last church brethren had departed the church and gone home, when the trees made long, stretched-out shadows across the sparse tombstones and graves, David drove back to the gate of the cemetery. There was still light on this September day although the sun had long dipped beyond the trees. It was quiet now, and the only sounds was the wind whistling through the cedar trees. Birds had now gone to roost for the night, but the crickets had begun their nightly chorus and lightning bugs began to flicker here and there. There were no prominent marble or granite headstones comparable to the white cemeteries. In fact, many were wooden markers whose painted names had faded years ago. David made his way through the small concrete markers and rotting wooden crosses to the newly dug grave some four by seven feet of fresh clay. The red clay had already begun to dry out. David saw two floral arrangements, one from Lea's Café, the other from Parson's Grocery. David was even afraid to send flower for fear of being discovered. The other flowers looked like they had come from someone's backyard. There was little to suggest the end of one's life. David stood there for a long moment. He said nothing. But the tears that slowly made their way down his cheeks gave expression to his feelings. No words were necessary.

Then David knelt before the grave, one knee touching the lumpy red clay already drying in the summer heat. At last he spoke, but the words did not come easy.

"Toye Lee, I wish I could play 'Taps' for you . . . like other soldiers killed in battle . . . but I can't . . . I wish this was Arlington National Cemetery and you had an honor firing squad with a twenty-one-gun salute, but it isn't. I don't own a gun. But you will always be in my heart, and our souls will meet again some day . . . in a place where God's children are not judged by the color of their skins or their material possessions . . . Good-bye . . . my friend . . . I'm so sorry . . ." He reached into his shirt pocket and withdrew two moon pies. He put them on the newly dug grave. "We missed eating these . . . our last meal." A tear or two ran down his cheeks, followed by others and then falling on the drying clay which quickly absorbed them. Then more. *Was it possible to love a nigrah as a friend?*

David rose and slowly turned away, trying to muffle the sobs that continued to come. The sun was down and shadows quickly forming. He got into the car after looking across the cemetery one more time and slowly drove away. *It might be a long time before I come to Evergreen Cemetery again*, he told himself, *maybe never.*

CHAPTER EIGHTEEN

It was Monday, the beginning of the last week of his employment at Crawford's Drugstore. Monday was always a busy day at the drugstore, but on this particular day, McKesson Company of Beaumont had delivered the annual order of prescription bottles and boxes and the Christmas merchandise that Mr. Crawford had bought at the summer Christmas market in Dallas had begun to arrive. It was also the quarterly delivery of their supply of Upjohn Pharmaceutical Corporations' citrocarbonate. Dr. McKinnon prescribed this medicine for all stomach ailments and as well as everything else. By the calculation of Al Murray, the McKesson salesman, every citizen in Kirbyville must have consumed forty bottles of citrocarbonate in the last twenty years. So common was its use that the nigrahs referred to it as Upjohn medicine. David had to find a place for the ten dozen cases that had been delivered. He knew that he would be spending a lot of time in the stockroom marking and stacking the merchandise. He didn't mind working in the back this last full week of employment because he wasn't in the mood to meet people. Besides, it would give him a good chance to talk with Mr. Crawford and feel him out on several matters. David's only problem was the storeroom overlooked the loading dock, and the loading dock was directly in front of the trash bin where so much of his time had been spent with Toye Lee.

By the time Mr. Crawford returned from Lea's Café after having his morning coffee with Mr. Arnold, David had the invoices ready to check and had placed the drugs and sundries which had arrived the last few days on the table. He was ready to write prices. Mr. Crawford would give him the cost which he wrote in a store code number, and then Mr. Crawford would tell him a selling price which he also wrote on the package. When a basket was full of the items they had marked, David would take it to the front of the store where Bessie would put them away in the appropriate shelves or on the islands or wherever they could find a place to put them. The store was always packed with merchandise. One of David's jobs had been to make room for seasonal merchandise, especially Christmas items. He often thought that half of the work in a drugstore was stocking. Selling sometimes seemed secondary. The store did a tremendous business in prescriptions. With a doctor's office just above them, it was hard not to get all the trade—even though most of it was on credit. There were a lot of unpaid accounts in the bookkeeping section of the store. Mr. Crawford did not press people to pay their bills promptly.

"Last week, huh, David?"

"Looks like it." David wanted to sound like he was really going to miss working in the store. Truthfully, however, he was ready to clear out of the town—now more than ever. *I sound like Toye Lee*, he thought to himself.

Mr. Crawford looked at the array of items before him and shrugged. "Used to be that drugstores sold patent medicines, some drugs, and prescriptions. Look at all this stuff. Now we have to have picture frames, gift items, paint, cosmetics, veterinarian supplies, and who knows what else. No wonder this store is bulging at the seams."

Drugstores in small towns often became the source of wedding, birthday, and graduation gifts; and when there was no veterinarian in town, they were center of animal medicine.

David did not remember those days when merchandising was much simpler, but he could imagine. He had become an expert in all kinds of departments—hosiery, perfumes, beauty creams, and horse medicine. He thought of many bottles of dog mange cure he had sold in the last four years. "You gotta lot of money tied up in stock, Mr. Crawford."

Mr. Crawford nodded and put the matter out of his mind. "When daddy owned this store, we sold only the basics. But that was another time and another era. Times change." He returned to the new order.

"So you're packed?" Mr. Crawford asked.

"Pretty much. I'm sending my boxes—sheets, towels, blankets winter clothes—things like that on Friday. Guess I'll be pulling out of the bus station next Tuesday on the nine o'clock special to Austin." It wasn't called special, but it was to David. "I think registration is on the twentieth or twenty-first."

"I think Cleve is leaving this week . . . some time." Cleve was Mr. Crawford's brother with whom David was going to room at the boarding house on San Antonio Street. That's how David got his room so quickly and easily. "I think he's joining a pharmacy fraternity this year and they rush the week before school starts . . . never cared for fraternities myself. Didn't have them at A&M when I was there," Mr. Crawford said and flipped several pages of invoices.

"I forgot he was in pharmacy . . . makes sense though with the drugstore and all,' David said as he unpacked another box.

"His real plans were to go on to medical school in Galveston, but pharmacy was his insurance if he can't get accepted," Mr. Crawford added.

Galveston! David recalled his visit only a few weeks ago, which now seemed like years ago. But he immediately dismissed the thought from his mind. Now memories of the beach, the ferry, the roller coaster only haunted him.

David couldn't imagine Cleve being turned down by the admission board. Cleve had been the valedictorian of his class, involved in all school activities, and had made the dean's list his first year in college. "When Cleve Crawford is turned down by medical school, they'd better just shut it down all together."

"You're absolutely right," Mr. Crawford replied somewhat modestly. The Crawford family was very proud of Cleve's accomplishments and didn't mind telling anyone about them. That alone made it very difficult for Lou, his sister who was still in high school, to live up to family expectations. She planned to follow him to the university. But like David, Cleve was no ladies' man and never dated in school. *I wonder if he had trouble getting a date to the junior-senior banquet like I did?*

As David was finding a place to put the new supply of prescription bottles, he glanced out the back door. There dumping spoiled vegetables and paper boxes was a young colored boy. "Good lord!" he exclaimed, scaring Mr. Crawford who was in deep thought trying to determine the cost of some perfume.

"What's the matter?" Mr. Crawford asked.

"That boy down there . . . I thought . . . that's a new boy!"

"Parson's Grocery has already replaced the boy who died on Labor Day," Mr. Crawford said. "I was talking to Jack Parson a few days ago. Said he had to have someone quick with all his stock piling up and the fruit and vegetables rotting."

David already decided he didn't like the new boy. Seeing an opportunity to bring up the subject, he asked, "What did you think about that boy's death?"

"Things like that sometimes happen. I never thought it was a good idea going swimming alone. Sure wouldn't let my kids do it. To chancey. Something happens . . . nobody there to help you or run for help." Mr. Crawford continued to mark items on the table. "I feel sorry for his mother. I see her every day at Lea's Café, and I haven't seen her smile since they brought the boy's body back to town. She used to be such a cheerful person. Only child too. Now she's got no one. It must be really lonely when you don't have anybody."

David could feel himself tightening up. That feeling, first remorse, was swept away by a feeling of anger. "How do you know he was alone at the swimming hole?"

"No one else was there. No one came forward to give the Justice of Peace information to the contrary. About all he could do is call it an accidental death."

"What do you think of Uncle Darby's report on the death?" David was beginning to pry into Mr. Crawford's conscience.

"That old fart," Mr. Crawford laughed. "That old man died twenty years ago, but someone forgot to tell him. He's on medication for senility problems. Should have never been Justice of Peace."

"Then why was he?"

"You get the job by vote. There are no qualifications other than that he be a resident and a voter. And that guy must be related somehow to everybody in this precinct . . . maybe this county. I couldn't vote for him even though he's a good customer. Nobody would run against him. I haven't voted for JP since your granddaddy died. Now that was a good man."

David was intrigued. "But should his report be based on what the firemen reported they found at the scene?"

It was already known around town that Judge Powell was too old and frail to walk the creek trail and scale the bluff. He made his ruling from the comfort of his office.

"It just doesn't seem fair," David retorted.

"David, old boy, if life was fair, I'd be the president of a gigantic corporation and rich and you would be Clark Gable surrounded by all the starlets of Hollywood."

David smiled, then laughed.

"Based on what they saw, Uncle Darby did the best he could. I doubt if anybody else would have done it differently."

"What if someone came forward and presented a different story with different evidence?"

"Where is that person? Why didn't he come then?" asked Mr. Crawford. "Maybe he has something to hide."

"Maybe that person is scared. Maybe he doesn't want to get into trouble."

Mr. Crawford couldn't understand David's point. "Scared of what? What kind of trouble? Seems to me the law would protect anybody who had credible evidence."

"You don't think a person should withhold evidence?"

"I never admired a person who 'ratted' on another, especially a friend. But if a crime is involved, the situation is different. Besides it's against the law to withhold evidence. You're not a traitor if you're honest and aboveboard and your intentions are good. A man's got to do what is right—if it's the law and maybe, more importantly, if the man wants a clear conscience. That goes for women too. But you gotta live with yourself the rest of your life." Mr. Crawford spoke as if he felt strongly about this matter. David could detect it instantly.

—

David had already heard the same argument from his mother.

"What if your testimony hurt your family—caused a great deal of harassment? Humiliation? Ruined their standing in the community . . . maybe in your case, caused you to lose a lot of business," David asked.

Mr. Crawford frowned for a moment. Rubbing his chin across the graying stubble, he answered, "I can't think of a situation where revealing the truth would cost me business."

"You don't think that if someone came forward and testified you were a child beater or you were having an affair with the wife of the minister of the Baptist Church, you wouldn't lose business?" David asked. "What if people in town discovered you didn't pay your taxes or were getting special tax breaks from the city tax department?"

"You may be right. It could be harmful to the business." Mr. Crawford laughed as he remembered the Church of Christ scandal years ago. That was when the minister's wife ran off with the nigrah janitor. That particular incident was on the lips of everybody in Kirbyville for a long time, and when the shock was over, the anger began. Church attendance dropped off so much and contributions were so meager there was talk about closing the church doors permanently. The church survived because of the efforts of a dynamic new minister who fought to restore confidence in the denomination.

"I guess what I'm saying is should a person withhold the truth if revealing it will cause all sorts of problems . . . It's like saying 'what you don't know won't hurt you.' It was another case of don't ask, don't tell." David was ready to pursue this further.

"That's not an easy question to answer . . . Depends on many things." Mr. Crawford was looking for the easy way out of the conversation. "It's sort of like being damned if you do, and damned if you don't." He tossed David a carton of Carter's Little Liver Pills. "Mark these. How did this conversation come up anyway?"

The conversation with Mr. Crawford, as interesting as it was, did not resolve David's dilemma. He still didn't know what to do or who to go to for advice. Toye Lee's death had not affected Mr. Crawford as it had David. To him it was simply the death of another nigrah. David wondered if Mr. Crawford had known Toye Lee had been killed by the Grimes boys if he would have felt any differently. David began to suspect all the citizens of Kirbyville regarded coloreds as expendable. Nobody wanted to get involved. Ask no question, have no problems.

All the merchandise on the table had been marked and distributed. It would be stocked later in the day. "This is a good breaking point," Mr. Crawford. announced. "I think I'll go home for lunch."

David was ready to quit also. The stockroom was a mess. Packing material and many cardboard boxes covered the floor. He gathered the trash as much as possible and put it in boxes. When it was all sacked and boxed, he carried it to the trash bin across the alley. The new boy at the grocery store was busy sweeping the back of Parson's Grocery. The boy looked like a real worker. Farther down the alley, David noticed the back door of Lea's Café. No customer was going in nor coming out. Business was slow. He thought he might see Allie Mae, but she was nowhere in sight. What would he have done or said to her if she had come out for a smoke? He returned to the front of the store to wait on customers—if there were any. More than anything, he was watching the big clock over the pharmacy doorway waiting for the hands to turn to five.

David had completed his daily chores in record fashion. The trash had been emptied. The cigar humidor had been refilled with water. He had checked to see that there was a good supply of prescription containers. David straightened the magazine rack, which looked like a disaster area at the end of each day. He had done these routinely for the last four years. Now he was in his last week of employment at the drugstore, but he wasn't sure he was attentive to these activities as he had been in earlier times. Time dragged as he watched the hands of the clock slowly move to the five.

Shortly before he was to leave, Mrs. R. C. Allen came bustling into the store fussing to herself. Spotting David behind a counter, she exclaimed, "Thank goodness you're still here!"

David was surprised to see her but always welcomed the opportunity to chat with her when she had the time. She was still his favorite teacher and always would be. He also noticed how upset she was.

"You know how the beginning of school is. Well, it's hectic enough just getting your room ready, but today we had the longest faculty meeting on record. I think the principal was going for the world record." She often mentioned her dislike for faculty meetings. Her philosophy was if teachers knew their business and did their job properly, they wouldn't have to attend faculty meetings every week. Memos could serve the same purpose. Mrs. Allen knew her job and just about everybody else's too. Her patience often wore thin with her colleagues who spent their off-period in the lounge smoking rather than in their classroom preparing their lessons. She also resented the fact that the football coaches were excused from faculty meetings—no exceptions—while all the other teachers had to suffer through the boring sessions.

She continued, "But my big problem is we've run out of ink for the mimeograph machine in the *Stylus* room." The *Stylus* was the school newspaper which was published by the students. Mrs. Allen had been its sponsor for years—so long she considered it her paper. "We have to go to press Thursday . . . And no ink!"

David had been the *Stylus* editor the year before, and he knew the room and equipment well as well as the problems. "I never heard of you running out of ink in all the years I was on the staff, especially at this time of the year."

"The school secretary messed up our supplies order. She's new, and it wasn't her fault. But we need the ink now." She was visibly upset at the dilemma.

Mimeograph ink and paper, along with duplicating sheets, were a teacher's salvation at test time; and that's why Mr. Crawford had always kept a few of those supplies on hand—just in case the school ran out or a secretary "messed" up. He couldn't beat the wholesale prices the school could get, but the goodwill it brought more than offset his effort.

David made his way to the school supply table and found the mimeograph ink beneath it on a shelf. "How many did you want?" he asked.

Mrs. Allen was relieved they were in stock. "Better give me two cans. What we don't use on the paper, we'll use on our tests."

—

Looking at Mrs. Allen, David thought about the past four years and how much effect she had on him and half the students in high school. He admired her integrity and dedication, and often when working on the newspaper, he had sought her advice about college and career. Outside of class, she was very friendly and helpful. She had a real sense of humor, but few people knew it. Only in class did she get serious about her profession—and that was to teach students grammar and literature. It was said of Mrs. Allen by former students that graduated before David that Mrs. Allen had saved them from flunking freshman English in college. She stressed grammar and writing. Students complained about her unreasonable demands on papers and her obsession with grammar. When they completed their first college English course, however, they were singing her praises.

Mrs. Allen reached into her purse to pay David for the mimeograph ink. While standing by the cash register, she reached over and picked up a handful of Hershey bars. "I'll take these too."

Mrs. Allen was a small and thin but wiry woman, dedicated to any activity she undertook. She was not particularly pretty—she often reminded David of his mother—but the character inscribed on her face far outshone its beauty. Her olive complexion blended with her brown hair—courtesy of Middleton's Beauty Shop where she was a regular Friday customer after she left school for the weekend.

Like everyone else, Mrs. Allen had little habits that she thought she concealed. But nothing escapes the eyes of students—some of whom spent more time studying the teachers than they did math and history. She monitored a study hall one period every day, fifth period in the middle of the afternoon. It was here she would indulge in her little habit—drinking a Coke and eating a Hershey bar. As discreet as she tried to be and as she almost succeeded, she could almost chew candy without moving her lips—everyone saw her. But no one dare say anything about it. It was the whole school's secret.

David had been fortunate to have been in Mrs. Allen's English classes for four successive years. That in itself was unusual because she rarely taught freshmen and sophomores. One year, however, she asked to be given a freshman class and teach that class through their senior year. It was sort of an experiment to see if more literature could be taught with one teacher rather than two or three, which was normal. It was David's freshman class, and that was the beginning of her association with David and his classmates. It was an association that he would remember the rest of his life. The effect of her teaching on David was profound.

Mrs. Allen's basic philosophy of teaching was knowing the subject matter and maintaining a disciplined environment in the classroom. You can't teach when the students aren't listening or are preoccupied with other things. No one talked in her class. She was also a perfectionist inasmuch as she expected students to do their best—no exceptions. Like all teachers, she knew everyone was not a genius, especially in literature and grammar. Even so, they would do the best they could with what they had—intellectually. Before the year was over, she had the students asking to study an extra Shakespeare play and reading additional poems. Other teachers were amazed at what she could do with the football and basketball players much to the chagrin of the coaches.

David loved literature, but he equally loved grammar and especially the mundane task of diagramming sentences. It was because of this he was very attentive to the way he spoke—as correctly as possible. He often told himself that best—and most successful lawyers—were those who spoke well and wrote well. Juries were impressed by eloquence. Speaking correctly often became an obsession with David.

Mrs. Allen rarely made mistakes—at least ones the students could detect. She was on top of every activity that occurred in her classroom. She was prepared for her daily classes and was exceedingly prompt in returning papers, properly marked, and with useful suggestions for improvement. David could remember only one occurrence where decorum broke down in her classroom. That particular incident, however, became a school legend, much to the embarrassment of Mrs. Allen and to the joy of her colleagues.

Part of Mrs. Allen's curriculum was to have students memorize poems of the great American and English writers and passages from Shakespeare that were her favorites. They would then recite them orally to the class. The purpose was to recognize classical poetry and important lines from the bard. It also helped the students overcome their shyness. She was cognizant of the fact that some students had difficulty doing this, so she accommodated them as much as possible. One female student could not recite the passages without stuttering. She was a choir member, so Mrs. Allen let her sing the words of the play. That was a rarity—*Macbeth* in music.

It was the second six weeks in David's senior year when English students studied *Macbeth*. During the past three years, they had dissected *Romeo and Juliet*, *Hamlet*, *The Tempest*, *Othello*, and *As You Like It*. They had prepared notebooks with pictures and quotations from these plays—a sort of scrapbook presentation. But it was *Macbeth* with its strong and sinister characters and dramatic lines that Mrs. Allen enjoyed the most with its strong characters and fluid lines. Each year she chose specific lines from the play—those which were significant to the work or characters. The students would recite those passages as part of their test grade. Mrs. Allen chose that particular line where Lady Macbeth, afraid her husband was losing his nerve in the murder of the king, chided Macbeth for losing his courage and becoming weakhearted. The line read, "But screw your courage to the sticking place. And we'll not fail." However, when Bubba Jones, the all-district football and basketball player—heading to Tulane University on an athletic scholarship—ambled to the front of the class for his recitation, it was not the same as Shakespeare wrote. He struggled through the first part of his presentation without any problem, but when he had Lady Macbeth tell her husband "But stick your courage to the screwing place. And we'll not fail," the class nearly fell apart. It was hard not to burst out with laughter especially since it was Bubba, admired for his brawn but not his brains. Yet no one dared break the classroom decorum. There were some who saw Mrs. Allen bite her lips and struggle to hide her smile but to most of the class said she never changed her expression. Bubba just stood there somewhat dumbfounded as his classmates were on the verge of collapsing. He never realized what he had said. From that day on, however, *Macbeth* was out and Mrs. Allen turned to safer classics such as William Wordsworth's "The Daffodils" and Oliver Wendell Holmes's "Old Ironsides." She never made that mistake of requiring Lady Macbeth's speech part of her curriculum again.

David grabbed the two cans of ink and moved to the door. "I'll take these to your car for you. I'm on my way home anyway. No problem." As he opened the trunk of the car and put the cans, Mrs. Allen asked, "Could I give you a ride home. I'm going right by your house."

David was hoping she would make the offer. It would give him a chance to ask for her advice. *But how to begin the conversation?* "How's school this year?" he inquired as he climbed into her car.

"We got off to a good start. My classes are full. And I don't think the senior class is nearly as good as yours was last year." Changing the subject, she asked, "Are you ready to leave for Austin?" She hesitated for a moment. "They have an excellent English department, but I understand the freshman English course is a terror."

"I've heard that too. But chances are, I'll get a teaching assistant my first year."

Mrs. Allen quickly inserted, "I hope not. They're not good teachers. They are more concerned with their own graduate studies to be bothered by some new students on campus . . . But you will do fine. After all, you got the English Award last May. You can compete with any graduate of one of those big-city schools."

David was flattered by her compliment. But it didn't resolve his dilemma. Finally, he brought the subject up.

"Mrs. Allen, are those characters in those stories we read about real? I mean, do heroes exist?"

She didn't know how to answer his question.

David tried to explain. "What if a person knows about a wrongdoing but didn't say anything about it? What he knew was bad—perhaps something legally wrong—but he kept his silence. I can understand a newspaper reporter not revealing his sources for the protection of their privacy and maintaining freedom of the press. But should a person withhold evidence or something he knows would free the innocent? Would revealing the truth make him a hero? Or a traitor?" David was having trouble trying to get to his point.

Mrs. Allen still did not know what he was asking.

David continued, "Remember when we were studying *Cyrano de Bergerac?*"

She did indeed remember. His was the only class in her teaching career that had shown any interest in French literature.

"Roxanne was in love with Christian because he had written such eloquent letters although they had actually been penned and spoken by Cyrano. Cyrano lived his whole life loving Roxanne without ever admitting he was the author of the letters she so dearly loved. Does that make him the hero? Or downright stupid? If he had confessed, he might have lived a happy life and married Roxanne."

Mrs. Allen laughed for a moment and then replied, "But that was fiction and where's the plot if the truth is known?" She thought for a moment, trying to think of a particular scene. "He is the hero, of course."

"He's the hero to the author . . . and to the audience. But not to Roxanne . . . not until the final scene when it's too late. But in real life, should the truth be hidden if a wrong . . . a crime . . . is committed?"

"I don't think so," she answered.

"In *Cyrano* the person who maintains his silence is the hero while the featherweight pretty boy gets the girl." *How many examples could I give without rousing some suspicion?* "But what if revealing the truth might hurt innocent bystanders? Would it be better to remain silent to protect the innocent than to let the guilty go free?"

They were quickly approaching David's home and no answer was forthcoming.

"I do not condone lying in any circumstances," Mrs. Allen said as she pressed on the brakes, slowing the car. "Reality and fiction are different. Yet I realize that the answers to a lot of questions are not easily answered. There are exceptions to every situation. It has been my experience that eventually secrets will be revealed." She smiled for a moment. "Remember Shakespeare wrote, 'The truth will out.'"

David recalled reading that in some play.

"I guess what I'm saying," she continued, "is it's up to the individual to decide for himself. Who else could? Maybe we can learn the answers to some of life's problems from fiction. From literature. College will help you seek out answers to questions like that. Maybe you should take a philosophy course."

David hoped so. But this matter needs to be settled before he left for college. He opened the door of the car now stopped in front of his house. As he was doing so, Mrs. Allen spoke again.

"Do you remember in *Hamlet* in the scene where Polonius is speaking to Laertes?"

David recalled the scene because if was one of the quotations they had to recite before the class. He nodded.

Quoting the lines she had so often taught her students, Mrs. Allen continued, "This above all: to thine own self be true. And it must follow, as the night the day, Thou canst not then be false to any man . . . ."

The message struck David again. He had heard it from his mother, Mr. Crawford, and now Mrs. Allen. He would have to decide for himself.

"Please come by and see me when you come home for Thanksgiving, David. And Cleve too. Let me know how you're progressing. You might have some suggestions to help improve my classes for future graduates."

"Oh, by the way, thank you so much for the graduation present. I appreciate it so much," David replied.

"You are so welcome. Bye now."

Slamming the car door, he agreed he would. "Thanks for the ride. See you on Turkey Day! Bye now." He walked toward the house as Mrs. Allen drove away.

Entering his house, David heard his mother bustling in the kitchen.

"I'm home!" he yelled.

"Aren't you running a little late?" Caroline asked.

"I was talking to Mrs. Allen. She was giving me some advice about school." Mrs. Allen was the only woman Caroline would approve giving advice to David. She was a great admirer of the English teacher, probably because their teaching philosophies were compatible and both endorsed literary and art activities. As she continued to prepare supper, Caroline reminded David of her forthcoming absence. "Don't forget that I won't be here this weekend."

He didn't remember that she would be gone. "Where are you going?"

"Didn't I tell you the choir at the church is going to Waco for a music conference, Friday and Saturday. Maybe I forgot . . . oh well, we are leaving early—real early—Friday morning and coming back late Saturday evening. We should be here for Sunday's services."

"Dad going?"

"Now you know better than to ask me that. I do good just to get him to church sometimes." Caroline shrugged as if she was talking about a lost cause. "I'll put some food in the refrigerator if you like. Or your and your dad could go to Schaeffer's or Turner's Café for a meal out. Sort of like boy's night out!" Caroline alluded to the fact that perhaps David and Tom needed some time together, especially since David would be leaving next week. "You and Dad could get some male talk or whatever kind of talk it is men do while I am gone."

David and his dad had never talked before, David thought, so why would she think they would in her absence? He just shook his head and answered, "Great!" He was very much in favor of letting his mother herself going out of town. The choir was her favorite activity. She rarely got to break her daily routine, and going out of town was a real luxury. This would be good for her. He knew they would survive even if it meant going their separate ways and doing their own things.

The work at the drugstore kept David busy the next few days. It was routine work that he had done every day for the last four years. He was bored, and only the anxiety and anticipation of leaving for the university within the next week kept him going. Fighting the heat and staying cool was work in itself. The gang had broken up for the fall with everyone going back to their respective schools. Cleve Crawford had been gone a week. David was the lone holdout, the university starting a week later than the nearby colleges. Only Sug would remain home and work at the bank.

He had not noticed the man who delivered the *Kirbyville Banner* that morning. In fact, he did not see it lying on the counter near the magazine rack until early in the afternoon. When things had settled down from the morning rush, he sauntered over to the magazine rack to see what new editions had come out that week. David often spent time between customers perusing the current magazines. It helped kill time and rescued him from abject boredom. As he was poring over the various magazines, his eyes scanned the *Banner* as it lay on the counter. He was transfixed by the headlines of the newspaper. It read, SHERIFF REOPENS ACCIDENTAL DEATH CASE. David grabbed a copy of the paper and continued to read. "Under pressure and complaints from the Beaumont NAACP, Sheriff Tolly Humphrey has agreed to reopen the case involving the death of West Kirbyville student, Toye Lee Johnson. Justice of the Peace Darby Powell had previously ruled the cause of death as accidental caused by a fall from a swing on Little Cow Creek."

David felt weak. He hesitated for a moment to catch his breath. Then he read on, "Beaumont officers of the local NAACP felt the investigation of the accident was too superficial and not enough time was spent in seeking more information from would-be witnesses or people who might have knowledge of the incident." The article intimated that there might have been additional people at the scene, but such possibilities had not been considered by the judge in his investigation. David read through the article. Then he reread it to make sure he didn't overlook anything. The article concluded, 'Anyone having additional information on this case is asked to call Sheriff Tolly Humphrey's office, Jasper County Courthouse, telephone number 383-4570. All calls will be held in strict confidentiality.'"

Is God giving me a second chance? Is this a sign that I should do something? David asked himself. *Is the agony that had consumed my mind and body for the last two weeks on the verge of being quelled? Maybe an anonymous letter to the sheriff's office with details and names. But would that hold up in court? Even if it got that far. Circumstantial evidence?* The conversations with Mr. Crawford and Mrs. Allen began to resonate in his mind. He found a blank sheet of paper on the shelf near the newspapers. Reaching into his shirt pocket, David withdrew the fountain pen that Toye Lee had given him for his birthday. He sought the number again in the article and began to write it down, "3-8-3-4-5-7-0." He checked the *Banner* to make sure he had written it correctly.

David was so intent in reading the article and jotting the telephone number down he was unaware someone was standing directly behind him. He was stunned by a voice that spoke his name.

"Davey . . ."

He froze. He couldn't move. He didn't dare turn around. But he knew exactly who it was. He had heard the voice too many times before in his mind. "Damn and double damn," he said, not caring who heard him.

Again, the nonchalant voice spoke, "Reading the *Banner*, Davey?"

David turned and came face-to-face with Dee Dee Grimes. He felt sick and thought he was going to vomit. His legs became elastic as he grabbed the counter for support.

Dee Dee was the epitome of calmness. She smiled in her usual carnivorous way, like she was about to devour him for dinner.

"I have nothing to say to you, Dee Dee," David managed to finally say. The lump in his throat had disappeared. He moved to get past her, but she stepped in his way, almost pinning him against the counter.

Dee Dee was hurt and rolled her sad eyes. "I was just waiting for my brothers to pick me up, Davey. They should be here any minute." She smiled sweetly again. "I heard you'd be leaving here next Tuesday. Thought I would say good-bye and wish you good luck . . . Probably a good idea to get out of town for a while. Don't you think?" Dee Dee acted as if nothing had happened.

"Is that before or after I call the sheriff?" David asked, trying to neutralize her aggressiveness and put her on the defensive. It worked. She moved away from him, her complexion turned pallid and the smile disappeared from her face, her fangs receding into that cavern which had been her mouth. It was Dee Dee that now sought the counter for support.

"What do you mean?" she demanded.

"What the hell do you think I mean? Don't try to play innocent with me anymore . . . you bitch! Just leave me alone and get out of my way." David had never talked like that before, especially to a girl. But this time it felt good. The thought of the Grimes boys going to prison pleased him.

"Is that a nice thing to say to someone who came by to wish you a good school year?" She was trying to put on the charm again. She turned the smile on David.

—

David was aware of her guile. He had put up with her long enough. "Now, if you will excuse me, I've had enough of your horse crap!" He bolted past her and disappeared into the stockroom. He was glad no one had witnessed this scene.

Dee Dee was so unaccustomed to hearing David talk like that she was taken aback. When he disappeared behind the counter, she was left facing an open newspaper and a sheet of paper from a note pad with the sheriff's telephone number on it. She quickly picked up the small piece of paper and, looking to see no one was watching, put it in her purse. She hastily retreated to and beyond the front door to the sidewalk, frantically looking for her brothers.

For the first time in days, David felt relieved even though his face was flushed when he looked into the mirror in the pharmacy department. Finally, he had stood up to Dee Dee and it felt good. No, it was exhilarating. Breathing came a little easier. He was still undecided what he would do, if anything, or how he would do it. But he seemed to have recaptured his old zeal and confidence which he had lost on Labor Day. *To thine own self be true,* he thought. Maybe Willy Shakespeare had a point after all. "Damn and double damn!" he shouted when no one was looking.

David awoke next morning feeling like a new person. He had slept better than he had in days. He bounced out of bed at his usual awakening hour looking forward to a good breakfast. His appetite, also, was restored. He stuck his head out of the bathroom for a moment and called his mother. "Mother!" There was no answer. He called again, "Mother, are you there?"

His dad answered. "She's already gone on the choir trip. They left early. But she left breakfast for you."

David had forgotten it was the day Caroline was to make her trip to Waco with the church choir.

"I thought you would already be gone," he said to his father.

"I'm on my way. Wanted to remind you that Mother left us some food in the refrigerator for tonight." Tom hesitated for a moment. "Unless you want to go out to eat."

"No, let's eat here. She has already prepared it." He was taught to never waste food. David thought instantly that he might have answered too quickly. Maybe it would be a good idea for them to go out and "talk." Too late now.

"I'll be home at my regular time," Tom said as he was about to leave the house.

"I'll be a little late, Dad. The people at the drugstore are going to have a little cake and ice cream for me after five today, so I'll probably be about an hour late. No much more."

"I'll have it on the table, Mr. Joe College," his dad replied. "I'm out of here," he yelled and slammed the door.

David ate in silence. But he felt like a million dollars. Tomorrow was his last day of work. He expected to see several friends in the next two days and tell them good-bye until Thanksgiving. He was flattered the staff at the drugstore were going to honor him with a little friendly going-away party. He would miss them tremendously. After all, they had worked closely together for the last four years. He quickly reminded himself that this was not going to be a wake. For heaven's sake, he wasn't going to Tibet or to the moon but only to Austin and he would be back during the holidays and also working next summer, for sure.

But the most important aspect of the morning was not the breakfast or the prospect of dinner with his dad or the party at the drugstore. David had arrived at a decision—the dilemma had been resolved. And he could live with it. After his conversations with his mother, Mr. Crawford, and Mrs. Allen—the people he admired the most—he had decided to notify the sheriff's office and give them an account of what happened on Labor Day. He would make arrangements to talk with the officers on Monday, the day before he left. He didn't look forward to it because it might embarrass his family. His mother would understand. His dad might have a hard time accepting the fact that he was running around with a nigrah. Tom's friends and the fire truck crew were sure to chide him about it, but at this point, David thought truth and honesty were more important than hurt feelings. Absence would probably heal the hurt after a while and things might return to normal. He thought of what each person had told him, "You

—

have to live with yourself the rest of your life." He could now look at himself in the mirror without hanging his head in shame. David kept reminding himself that omission of information about a crime was as blatant as commission of a crime. A lot of weight had been lifted from his shoulders. If he had wings, he would be flying.

As David rose from the table and put his dishes in the sink, he noticed the calendar on the wall. Clearly marked was Tuesday, the nineteenth of September, the day the bus would depart from Schaeffer's Café and Bus Station for Austin. It really begin to sink in that he was a "short timer." And he was truly anxious to board that bus and proceed with his life now that a burden had been lifted from his back.

The day passed quicker than the days had in the last few weeks. Numerous people had dropped by to wish David well in Austin. Some kidded him about becoming a tea-sip. He enjoyed that, and he expected to hear that for four more years. At five o'clock the staff of the drugstore had their little going-away party in the rear of the store. Bessie gave him a big hug; and Ben, the pharmacist, shook his hand and patted him on the back.

"You and Cleve better behave yourselves," Ben kidded. "And don't get in trouble."

Cleve was his brother also, and he knew perfectly well that neither boy was about to get into trouble.

"How could I go wrong with him being my roommate?" David asked. Two nuns stood more of a chance of getting in trouble than him and Cleve. "We might be accused of living the dullest life in Austin . . . but not trouble. I know how much he studies and how important grades are to his getting into med school. I just hope I can do as well as he has done."

But it was to Mr. Crawford that David had the hardest time saying good-bye. After four years of thousands of boxes and invoices, tons of trash, and many fatherly talks, their relationship was about to end, at least for a while. It was hard for either of them to talk without choking up. Finally they gave up. Mr. Crawford went over to David, put his arm around his shoulders, and said, "We have something for you that all college men need. And this, I know, you'll use."

David had not expecting a gift. Maybe a small bonus, but certainly nothing like a going-away present.

Mr. Crawford went into his office and returned immediately carrying a big box. It was not wrapped, so David could immediately see what it was.

David was overwhelmed. "My gosh!" he exclaimed. "A portable Remington typewriter . . . I . . . I . . . don't know what to say!" he stuttered.

"A simple thank-you will do," Mr. Crawford suggested.

"Mr. Crawford . . . Ben . . . Bessie . . . You guys have been so good to me and put up with me for so long. But the pleasure has all been mine. I've never worked with anybody that meant as much to me as you guys do. I will never forget this day . . . and gift." He was close to welling up with tears and decided that he had said enough.

Mr. Crawford broke the awkwardness of the moment by adding that it was time to either go home—or get back to their chores or customers. It was a good opportunity for David to get his typewriter together and head home. "See you tomorrow!" he yelled as he left the store. Tomorrow was his last day, but a Saturday, and they would be too busy with people paying their water and light bills and waiting on customers to be concerned with his departure.

By the time the party was over, it was after six o'clock. David started home carrying his newly acquired typewriter. His face reflected how proud he was of his gift. How pleased his mother would be when she came home. It took him longer to walk than usual because of the additional weight he carried. The days were shorter now, and dusk came earlier. The sinking sun would soon be followed by the dusk, and the fireflies that still filled the air were beginning to come out for the night. But they would be gone soon too.

CHAPTER NINETEEN

David felt at peace with the world because after talking to his mother, Mr. Crawford, and Mrs. Allen, he had made up his mind to talk to the sheriff's office. But that moment was changed when he saw a strange car in front of his house. He slowed for a moment and then stopped. The car looked very familiar, but he could not remember who it belonged to. A moment later, he heard two male voices talking rather loudly with his dad, using vile words. In fact, they seemed to be warning Tom about something. When David identified the visitors on seeing them, he quickly hid on the side of the house in some hydrangea bushes. The thick foliage covered him, but he could see the visitors. It was the Grimes boys coming out the front door, and they looked as mean as hell and as determined as David had ever seen them—like the time he saw them on the creek bank.

"You better take care of your goddam business, Tom Wilson, or else," one of the brothers yelled. And now, they cursed, slammed the car door closed, and sped away, leaving black tire marks on the street.

David emerged from the bushes slowly as the Grimes brothers disappeared down the street. He made his way into the house, wondering what was happening and why the Grimes boys had come to his house.

Tom was sitting at the kitchen table, his face drawn and blanched and his fingers nervously running through his hair.

"Dad, what's wrong" David asked. "What were those Grimes boys doing here?"

Tom did not answer. He just looked at David with a gaze that was neither anger, shock, nor hurt.

"Dad, are you all right? What's the matter?"

Finally his father replied, "You know goddamned well what's the matter." Tom tried to compose himself. "I've had a very interesting visit with Fred and Howard Grimes. They have informed me of several incidents which occurred on Little Cow Creek earlier this month."

"What do you mean?" David asked, knowing perfectly well what his dad was referring to but being afraid to admit it.

"Son, this is no time to act dumb . . . or lie. What is this all about? . . . I want the truth now from you and not the scum of Kirbyville."

Damn and double damn! David realized that the time had finally come to face the truth and admit his relationship with Toye Lee. Lying would serve no purpose. Yet David did not think the revelation of his friendship with Toye Lee would be so earthshaking that it would change the course of history. So he geared himself to tell his dad what happened.

David began, "I met this boy . . . in June . . . who worked for Parson's Grocery."

Tom interrupted, "A nigrah boy?"

David nodded.

"Damned!" replied his dad.

David continued, "We worked together all summer and saw each other every day. So we decided that on some days or nights we would get together and do some things. Like going to the picture show or fishing or swimming at the swimming hole. He lived across the tracks with his mother, Allie Mae. You remember? I mentioned her one day, and you said she had kept me while Mother was in the hospital that time."

Tom remembered the conversation very well.

David looked at his dad for some kind of response that did not come. "We didn't go out a lot, but we did several things together. No one ever saw us. We would go out of town or wait until night most of the time. Except, when we went swimming . . . I felt sorry for the boy, but I liked him. He had trouble with school . . . He was a good athlete but didn't care much about school. All he wanted to do was join the army as soon as he was eighteen. I tried to get him to stay in school and improve himself . . . Dad, I never realized how bad the coloreds were treated around here—"

Tom quickly interrupted David's discourse, "Sound just like your mother . . . Trying to upset the balance of things around here. David, don't you know that you were just asking for trouble?"

"Trouble? Just for doing something decent? Just for being a Christian for a change or being kind to another human being?"

"It's not a matter of Christianity. There are things you do and things you don't do. Knowing your place in this town is one of them. And your place is with whites. You can't change things that have gone on for years. As long as each side knows the rules, you have no problems. When you break the rules, then you are asking for trouble . . . But maybe you see that already."

David could not agree with his father. "Dad, things are going to change whether people here like it or not. I can see that already. Besides, what harm can come from being friends with a nigrah boy?"

"But when you try to change the situation, you involve other people . . . Your parents . . . Me. Your mother. How do you think this is going to affect my bosses at the mill? Or my crews at the planer. What kind of respect will I get now? And the church and fire station? What will they say knowing my son was running around here with a nigrah boy? People are going to start calling us nigger lovers. How does that sound? And your mother . . . people will treat her differently, maybe even stop speaking to her completely."

David was unconvinced. "But it's my doing—not yours or mother's. My 'sin' doesn't fall on you."

"Oh, but it does . . . man, how it does!" Tom was well aware that breaking the code didn't just affect the offender. It went well beyond that.

David shrugged. "I don't see how."

"How long has this been going on, son."

"All summer."

"And that trip to Galveston? You lied to me, didn't you?"

"That was Toye Lee and me . . . I didn't want to lie about it—and I apologize—but I knew you'd never let me go if you knew about it . . . That boy had never been out of the county. Dad, you can't imagine how much fun he had . . ."

Tom quickly stopped him. "Dammit it . . . not another word. Screw the fun. I don't want to know about it."

David was disappointed he couldn't tell his dad about the day Toye Lee's world opened up. But he knew better than to continue with his explanation.

Tom shifted positions in his chair. He seemed to be having trouble trying to find the right thing to say. "What happened on Labor Day?"

David tried to explain how it all happened. "Toye Lee knew I was leaving for school in a few days, and he wanted to get together one more time. So we decided to go swimming that afternoon—one last time before I left for Austin. Nothing unusual happened for a while. We talked a lot. We swam and played around on the swing for a while. But then Dee Dee Grimes found us and started teasing us. She was sitting on our clothes, so we couldn't get out of the creek to dress. She wouldn't move or give us our pants. Up 'til then, things were under control. Then she started pulling off her blouse and coming down toward us. She said she would going swimming too. Toye Lee was already terrorized, out of his mind, especially when he found out she was a Grimes . . ."

"Oh god!" Tom exclaimed "What happened then?"

"Her brothers appeared on the trail as she was coming down the bank. And when she saw them, she started screaming and hollering, 'Rape.' And the brothers came running to her. Dad, I saw her tear up her blouse when Toye Lee ran past her."

"Son of a bitch!" Tom wiped his brow as sweat beads began to appear and drip off his face. He was becoming more and more tense, and the color in his face had completely drained. "When did he fall from the swing?"

"What?" David asked incredulously.

"Judge Powell ruled the cause of death an accident—a fall from the swing hitting a log. How did that happen?"

"He didn't fall from a swing. The Grimes boys found some limbs there and hit Toye Lee on the head—several times—as he was trying to escape. The last blow knocked him over the bank, and his head hit the log in the water . . . he never fell."

"Goddammit . . . son-of-a—"

Tom didn't have time to finish his swearing because David interrupted his expression.

"Did you really think he fell?" David asked.

"The Grimes boys said he did."

Tom nodded.

"Well, they lied. I saw everything from the water behind the log, and they killed an innocent boy just because of the color of his skin. Just battered his head in. Dad, 'mean' doesn't even begin to describe those murderers."

Tom put his hands to his head, cupping both ears. David had never seen his father so distraught. His words became shaky and sometimes unclear; his face drained of color—looking more like a mask, immobile and waxen. He sat there a long time with his eyes shut, sometimes shaking with emotion. He reached over his shoulder and grabbed an almost-empty bottle of whiskey off the cabinet and had a swig. David had never seen his dad drink before although he knew the firemen always had liquor at the fire station. Finally, Tom dropped his hands and looked at David. "What are you going to do about it?"

"I've thought about it for several days. I couldn't sleep at night, and I think I have lost weight over it. I've looked at the way it will affect me and how it might affect you and Mother. But I keep coming to the same conclusion."

"What's that?" his dad inquired.

"I am going to call the sheriff's department Monday and tell them what happened. His phone number is in the *Banner*."

"But you're supposed to go to Austin Tuesday."

"I know. But I'll tell them about my leaving for college and hope they can come out here Monday afternoon for my statement." David

—

hesitated for a moment then added, "It will probably be months before a trial could be held. I can come home to testify when that happens. No point in sticking around here until the trial."

"Do you know how this will affect your mother?" Tom asked.

"Dad, I think she will understand. She would say I was doing the right thing."

"Have you told her about what happened?"

"I haven't told a soul, except you and that's at this minute."

"Have you made your mind up completely?"

David looked at his father. "I can't think of anything that would change my mind now."

Tom shook his head. "Shit!"

"Dad, you aren't intimidated by what the Grimes boys will do, are you?" David couldn't understand his dad's silence. "What could they do—or say—anyway? They broke the law, not us. We don't have anything to fear or worry about."

Tom did not reply. He looked forlorn and shrugged slightly.

"Surely, you don't think I should not report this, do you, Dad?" David looked at his father curiously. "You can't approve of what they did to Toye Lee . . . even if I was running around with a nigrah boy?"

Tom spoke again, "Maybe sometimes it's best to not say anything. Just let things lie. It's happened before and prevented some racial problems in this town." Tom didn't elaborate when or what he referred to. "Sometimes, a person might avoid a real bad situation by remaining silent."

"Just sweeping it under the rug? Looking the other way? Isn't that the way people solve nigrah problems around here? Just closing their eyes and putting the matter out of their minds?"

"It works."

David couldn't agree with his father. "Silence is the same as approval of what the Grimes boys did. Could you live with yourself if you kept silent? And let the killers go free?" He looked at his dad who made no comment or gesture to indicate how he felt. But David could see that Tom would be more than willing to forget the whole matter—the quicker the better. "Well, I couldn't!"

Tom arose from the table and moved to the pantry. David thought he was now ready to start warming the food left by his mother. Instead, Tom reached into the back of one of the shelves and withdrew another bottle of whiskey. Tom took his glass and poured a goodly amount of whiskey into the glass and filled the remainder of the glass with water. To that he dropped in some ice cubes he took from the refrigerator.

David had long suspected that he imbibed at the fire station—along with the other firemen, Baptists and Methodists—but he wasn't sure. He had no idea his mother would permit whiskey in her kitchen. His eyes grew big as his father brought the glass and the bottle and placed it on the table.

Tom spoke first. "I wish I could pour you a drink so you could join me in a man-to-man discussion," he said. "But it's against the law to give liquor to a minor. I could stand up to the law, but I couldn't face your mother if she found out."

David smiled. He had tried a beer—one time—and under the circumstances would have taken one then. But that information would remain his secret. He was not ready to try the hard stuff. "Dad, drinking is not going to make the problem go away."

"But it makes things easier for me." Taking a large drink and catching his breath as the liquor ran down his throat, Tom continued. "Davey, we need to have a man-to-man talk . . . We never had a chance to talk like a father and son. Guess I was just too scared."

"Scared?" David repeated. "Of your own son?"

"Well, afraid of what your mother might think or say."

David did not know why his dad would make such a comment. After all, Tom was his father and no one could deny that. But it was true that they had never really communicated. He often wondered why they hadn't been as close as many other boys he knew and their fathers. But David had often noticed that in matters dealing with him—or decisions which affected him—it was always Caroline who was to be consulted. And she made the final decision. His mother was a strong-willed person when she wanted to be—when she got her dander up. He had seen how, from time to time, his mother had cowed his father. He always gave in to her wishes. But he had passed it off as his father's belief that his mother knew what was best. He never saw Tom as weak and spineless. His dad was just being practical. David could never remember his parents engaging in a fight, not even a heated disagreement—never harsh words. Maybe, things would be clearer later with an explanation from his dad.

David pulled a chair out from beneath the table and sat down, waiting for his father to continue.

Tom took his time to begin the discussion. "I guess it begins long before you were born," he said. "With Tommy's accident."

Tom and Caroline rarely spoke of the death of their first son, so David was never fully informed what had happened. He knew very little about his brother who died. The only visible fact was the one photograph in his mother's bedroom. All other things of Tommy's were stored in a trunk in the attic. Caroline had given strict orders that no one would open the trunk. His mother was particularly tight-lipped about him, and Tom never mentioned him for fear of upsetting Caroline.

"Tommy was the kind of kid every father dreams about. He was smart, the best athlete in the school, and popular with everyone in his class. I had visions of him going further in athletics than I had ever dreamed of going. Maybe eventually becoming a pro. He was so good in baseball." Tom paused, "Your mother thought he should spend more time on his studies, but I pushed football, basketball, and baseball . . . Then when he got to an age I thought he could handle a gun, I bought him one and taught him how to hunt. Every daddy in town did the same thing. Your mother strongly objected. She didn't think Tommy was old enough to handle the responsibility of owning a gun. But she finally agreed to it, but with a great bit of reluctance. If we ever had a fight, it was over that damned gun."

David had heard there was some disagreement about a gun but had never known the severity of the problem.

"Then one day I took Tommy out to Grandpa's old farm to shoot his gun—hunt some squirrels. Everything was going okay until we stopped to climb over a fence to get back to the tree brake where the squirrels were. Tommy had put his gun against a fence post and was trying to crawl over when our dog, Nubbin, tried to climb over the fence too, hitting the gun causing it to fire. It hit Tommy . . . bad."

Tom's eyes got misty as he looked into space. It was such a long time ago and so far away. The pain of telling David this story was clearly written across his face.

David had never seen his father cry. Yet despite Tom's efforts to stop the tears, David could see the welling of his eyes.

"I did all I could to save him," Tom said. "But by the time I got back in town and to the doctor's office, he had lost too much blood. He died there in Dr. McKinnon's home office." Tom took another long drink. His eyes were beginning to get glassy from the alcohol. "The days that followed were nothing short of pure hell. Your mother never blamed me for Tommy's death . . . But I always blamed myself . . . But after that, your mother seemed to just give up. She gave up everything . . . her friends . . . the church . . . everything. Nothing was important to her anymore. She lived from day to day like she was in a dense fog. Often she was incoherent—she would sort of walk around the house like she was in a trance. She searched for Tommy and called his name at night in her sleep. I think she had a nervous breakdown, though the doctor never said for sure."

David followed his father's story with great attentiveness. He had hardly moved since Tom began his story. He had never heard about his mother's mental problems. "Really?"

Tom's face was taut with grief, his eyes reddened with tears. "God, I thought I was going to lose her—if not to death, to the state asylum in Austin. It was killing me, and I couldn't do a thing about it. I loved her so, but each day, she seem to go down more and more . . . Then . . . one day, for some unknown reason, she seemed better. And in the days that followed, she improved more and more 'til she got back to where she was before the accident. Not quite . . . 'cause I used to see her look down the road to see if Tommy was on his way home. Or look in Tommy's room—your room now—to see if he was asleep. And she looked so lonely when she realized he'd never come home again. But things got better . . . we began to live like normal people again."

Tom stared into space, remembering the horror of that time—and the pain and sorrow he had suffered. He took another drink and continued. "One day, several months later, your mother told me she wanted to have another baby. Old Doc McKinnon had told us when Tommy was born she should never have another child . . . the strain was too much for her body. You know she has a heart problem, don't you?"

"No." David had never known of Caroline's heart condition. He had seen her take medicine, but she passed it off as vitamins. She had been frail most of her life. But a heart condition? It was news to him. "I never knew that, Dad . . . Is she okay now?"

"But she had made her mind made up . . . you know how stubborn your mother is at times . . . I suggested we adopt a baby. That would have been no problem . . . but she wouldn't hear of it. She wanted a child of her own. A real Wilson and a Wingate. Her own flesh and blood. Any argument I could make against it fell on deaf ears. She was going to have a baby . . . even if it killed her. And it almost did."

Tom stopped for a moment as if to get the facts straight. "Well, she finally got pregnant," he continued. "That has got to be the longest nine months of my life. Dr. McKinnon watched her like no other woman under his care. The pregnancy was a hard one. She often spotted . . . bled . . . and we thought she might miscarry at any time. But you know what a strong-minded person your mother can be if she is determined to be. She carried you for the full term even though there were times I thought she wouldn't make it. But she did."

David had never heard the story of his birth. It was too hard for his parents to tell him considering Tommy's death and all the problems his mother had. Yet he found it intriguing and wanted to hear more. "What happened, Dad?"

"The delivery was just as hard as the pregnancy. Your mother was in labor for several hours. It still was not certain that you would enter this world safe and healthy. Finally you came. Born in that bed right in there . . . feet first." Tom pointed in the direction of their bedroom. "You were a healthy boy. We were so proud to have another child . . . and especially a boy. Our family name would be carried on . . . And for a few days, things went well. You were alive and kicking, and Caroline was weak and sore, but seemed to be slowly recovering. Your grandma and grandpa were here to care for her, and I took off periodically from the mill to run home to see how she was doing. But in a few days, things changed . . . for the worse. Your mother started hemorrhaging, and the doctor couldn't stop the bleeding. Her blood pressure fell drastically, and she became very, very weak and was semiconscious most of the time."

The nightmare had come back to haunt Tom, over and over. His face showed all the strain that he must have displayed when they made the call to the mill. "Dr. McKinnon was not prepared for such an emergency. He called for an ambulance, and they rushed your mother to the hospital in Jasper. She got worse and worse, sort of fading in and out, like a coma. She could have died at any time, and no one would have been surprised. She looked like a corpse lying in the emergency ward, hardly breathing and not moving an inch. Dave . . . I thought if she died, so would I. I couldn't face life without her. After about ten days, she improved and then began to get better each day. Finally, she was released from the hospital and we brought her home. She had a slow recovery. Her heart was messed up because of the strain of the baby and the delivery, but she pulled out of it. Dr. McKinnon was amazed. He cared for her like she was his own daughter. He still monitors her heart three times a year to make sure her ticker is okay."

"Is it?" David asked.

"She's in pretty good health. You know she never complains. But the doctor warns about too much stress or excitement. It could really hurt her—maybe kill her. She still could be a candidate for a heart attack anytime."

David was glad to finally hear the story of his birth and the source of his mother's medical problems. He appreciated his dad filling him what happened. "Thanks, Dad, for sharing this story with me. I know it was hard for you to do it. I don't guess I ever really knew the whole story . . . just parts of it. But I still have a question, Dad," he said.

"What's that, son?"

"What does all this have to do with the Grimes boys and the trouble they're causing. And why did they come by here tonight and threaten you?"

Tom arose from his chair and headed for the water faucet. He drew a little water into his glass, got some ice from the refrigerator, and moving back at the table, poured himself another drink—this time a stiff one. It looked almost like straight whiskey to David. Tom took a long breath, then a drink, and looked at David. "What I've told you is only part of the story. I was just setting the stage for the main event."

Main event? What is he talking about? David asked himself. *What kind of story he is talking about now?* He was curious, and he hoped his dad would tell him. For the first time in his life, he was actually having an honest conversation with his dad. But he was not prepared for what he heard.

Tom looked at David for a long minute, then spoke. "Do you insist on talking to the sheriff next week?" He looked like he wanted David to reply no.

David's mind was made up—just like his mother who could be obstinate when she wanted to. Tom could see that. "Dad, it's the thing to do. I couldn't live with myself if I didn't." Three people had convinced him it was the thing to do although they didn't know about Toye Lee. And he was determined.

Tom began to feel the effect of the alcohol. His movements were slower, and his speech a little more slurred. It had loosened his tongue, but he began to worry where things would go from here. David said very little during his discourse on Tommy's death and Caroline's subsequent illness. David was such a naïve person, perhaps just not quite mature enough for what Tom was about to tell him. Then the memory of the Grimes boys' visit earlier brought Tom to reality, and he continued. He had no choice but to tell the truth. He moved his chair closer to David.

"Your mother had a relapse about two weeks after she came home and had to be put in emergency care in Jasper Memorial Hospital. I took off from work and stayed with her for four days. Old Dr. McKinnon called to check on her, but she was under the care of the hospital doctors. They had already told me she had about a fifty-fifty chance of surviving. I would go into her room when visitors were allowed. I just sat there. Her face was like chalk. Her body was so frail and motionless. Her arms so blue from the punctures made by the injections . . . Davey, you can't imagine how depressed I had

—

gotten. If she should die, then I wanted to die also. For a moment I was thinking about suicide."

David could see the scene in his mind. And he could relate to the agony that his dad must have suffered. He had gone through something similar in the grief over Toye Lee.

"During that time, I'll bet I didn't sleep for hours. It seemed like days. I was so exhausted. At times I felt like I was in a trance floating in and out of reality. I lost trace of time. All I could see was the woman I loved so much standing at death's door . . . and I could do nothing about it." Tom wiped his brow. He put the glass to his lips but quickly removed it. "Then," he said, "after four days, your mother began to respond to the treatment. She regained her consciousness. She opened her eyes and smiled at me. She was weak, the doctors said, but if she continued to improve like she had, she'd be past the crisis. Looking back, I think I must have been on the verge of collapse myself. The nurses insisted I go home . . . and the doctors agreed. They told me that what I needed more than anything was a good night's rest. If I didn't get some, I might be Caroline's roommate."

David shifted his position in his chair as Tom stopped to take a drink of the whiskey. He was completely mesmerized.

"I was reluctant to leave her, but as long as she was beginning to improve, I thought I would go home clean up—I hadn't bathed in that time—and get some rest." Again, Tom stopped his story. *Should he go on?* He paused for a long moment. Too much was at stake at this point. He had no choice. Looking into David's eyes, he no longer saw the little boy that Caroline had raised. He now saw David as a mature young man who would be able to cope with adult problems and crises. Tom regretted, however, that this had to be his first real experience as an adult. He continued, "Grandma and Grandpa Wingate had kept you during the day while I was in Jasper. Remember, you were only a few days old. However, they could not stay at night . . . for some reason, I can't remember now what it was, they had other plans. Seems like he had to take care of his stock or something . . . So I hired a young nigrah girl from across the tracks to come in and stay with you at night. Her name was Allie Mae Johnson."

David jerked at the sound of that name coming from the lips of his dad. His mouth sagged for a moment, but he said nothing.

"She was available. She had taken care of babies before. She had been highly recommended And she needed a job." Tom looked away for a moment. "I didn't have time to really search for a nurse. Allie Mae slept in a roll-away bed in our bedroom next to your bassinet. She prepared your bottles, fed and cleaned you, and washed your diapers . . . one of the most important things you have to do when you have a new baby. I . . . I . . . hated changing dirty diapers . . . With a passion!" Tom chuckled to himself. "And you did a pretty good job of messing them up."

David laughed nervously but said nothing.

"When I got home, it was like returning from a desert island after being shipwrecked or being released from prison. I was so happy to get away from that hospital. And so happy to see my new baby son peacefully sleeping in his bassinet. Allie Mae knew I was coming 'cause I had called Mother's parents to let them know the good news. They called Allie Mae. I didn't get home until after dark. But when I got there, Allie Mae had prepared a home-cooked meal and everything was on the table. It was so nice to have real food for a change instead of that stuff served in the hospital."

Tom took a deep breath and slowly continued his story.

"Allie Mae saw how tired I was. She suggested I take a good hot bath before I ate. I never knew how great a hot bath could be until that night. It was like getting a new lease on life. It revived me. Now with clean clothes and a good hot bath, I felt like a new man again. She had placed the food on the table right before my plate . . . just like your mother always did. I don't remember what she had cooked . . . but whatever it was, it was delicious . . . and I was famished. I do remember how surprised I was to see how mature Allie Mae was and how she could prepare such a meal at her age. Seems like she was about seventeen at the time.

"While I ate, she sat at the table holding our two-week-old son. 'He be such a good baby, Mr. Tom. He just eat and sleep all day long as he be full and dry, he be happy,' she said.

"We chatted for a while. She gave you a bottle and put you to bed."

304

David was fascinated by this story of his early days on earth. No one had ever told him anything about his mother's illness, her stay in the hospital, or his having a temporary nanny. "What happened next, Dad?" he asked.

"While Allie Mae cleaned up the kitchen, I went into the living room and found a copy of the *Beaumont Enterprise*. I hadn't read a paper in days. Then I remembered that I had part of a bottle of whiskey stuck in the back of the pantry." Tom stopped talking for a moment. Looking at the bottle before him, he said, "Surely this is not the same bottle."

"I hope not!" David exclaimed. "If it is, then it has aged a lot."

"Anyway," Tom continued, "I fixed myself a drink and sat down to read the paper. There was nothing like being home again. Everything was perfect . . . except your mother was not there. But it was like my life was being restored to better times." He slowly continued. "Allie Mae finished cleaning the kitchen. When she came into the living room, I offered her a drink . . . she was almost an adult and I'm sure she had liquor before . . . but she wouldn't take one.

"'Mr. Tom,' she said, 'that stuff only make me flighty . . . I drinks that hooch and I be wilder than a piney woods rooter.' Allie Mae locked the doors and told me she was going to bed."

"I thanked her for all she had done. She smiled . . . she had a beautiful smile, really infectious . . . lots of white teeth. I had remembered that there were some unpaid bills on the table that needed to be taken care of. I told Allie Mae I'd sleep in the other bedroom after I finished reading the paper and paying those bills. After a while, I fixed myself another drink . . . probably a double, considering how good I was beginning to feel . . . and went about writing checks. My finances . . . or maybe the lack of them . . . brought me back to reality. I saw that I had to get back to the mill soon. But now was not the time to start worrying about how I would pay for all this. I guess it did worry me 'cause I fixed myself one more drink. By now things got a little mixed-up. I was tight . . . I mean really tight. I felt like the king of the mountain! But it was time for the king to go to bed. Before going to bed, I went back into our bedroom to take one more look at you as you slept so peacefully. The night light was on, so I could see you so clearly. I was so proud your health was good. As I turned to leave the room, I glanced toward the bed . . . Allie Mae was not asleep . . . she was lying there in a flimsy nightgown watching me but not making a sound . . . At first I was embarrassed for getting caught looking at you and then her. But the look on her face was not one of shyness. There was nothing innocent or shy about the look she gave me . . . She held out her hand to me and moved over to the middle of the bed . . . Her long body covered by shadows of the room was too tempting. And it was so long since I had slept with your mother. I felt like I deserved it."

The expression on David's face suddenly changed from one of curiosity to one of horror. He moved as if to bolt from the chair, but Tom grabbed him. David tried to wrest his arm from Tom's grip but could not. Then he sat down again but remained frigid. His face drained of blood was as pallid as it could be. His mouth quivered uncontrollably.

"I want you to hear all the story—every damned bit," Tom said. "Then you can decide what to do."

David was terribly uncomfortable at the way the story had shifted. He got up to get a drink of water. He looked into the kitchen cabinet—he didn't know why. There was nothing to tell him how to act or what to do. He would hear his dad out, despite the fact that he wanted to run from the room screaming to the top of his lungs.

Damn and double damn!

Tom continued, "I don't know what happened then . . . or why. But in a moment, I was in the bed with Allie Mae."

David was truly tormented and embarrassed by this revelation. "But why, Dad? How could you do . . . Mother lying in the hospital and you are being unfaithful to her? . . . And a nigrah . . . I know how you feel about coloreds . . . Dad, . . . I—"

Before he could continue, Tom interrupted, "David, I know what you must be thinking. You can ask me a hundred times why it happened, and I would be hard-pressed to give you a logical explanation." Tom's facial expression was that of a man who had been severely beaten. He was having a hard time keeping from crying.

"David, I'm not sure you really understand the situation. You've never faced the real facts of life."

David looked at his father, waiting for an explanation. He rose and got a towel for Tom to wipe his face. He sat back down, but he still wanted to run from the room and out of the house. He waited.

"David, I love your mother with all my heart. But she is not a truly warm person . . . at least not to me. We have never been intimate in a strictly natural way. She accepted my natural desires as a wife's duty. But only at her convenience. After Tommy's death, we often slept in separate bedrooms . . . until she decided she wanted another baby. But when she conceived, it was back to my own bed. I did not touch her during her pregnancy with you. I was afraid of hurting her."

David had never heard his father talk so passionately—or so frankly. This first father-son discussion was turning out to be quite a story—and he wasn't sure he was enjoying it or wanted to hear any more.

"David, your mother is a loving mother and a kind person. She is patient and understanding. Some people look upon her as a saint . . . and I know why . . . She's the most compassionate person I ever met. But, David, she could live without sex . . . without that intimacy of a close marriage." Tom looked the other way for a moment. "But I can't. I'm basically a physical person, and sex is part of my nature. David, you can't imagine lying beside someone you love dearly and never putting your arms around her. A person who aroused your passion but would not respond to your slightest touch. Sometimes I felt that I would get more aroused if I had been sleeping with the Statue of Liberty."

David tried to understand what his father was saying. At least he thought he was. But he was confused. Things were blurred. Tom's analogy was meaningless. Both his parents had toppled from the pedestal he had put them on.

"I just can't tell you how frustrated I was." It wasn't only the alcohol that had loosened Tom's tongue. It was the opening of stifled and hidden emotions suddenly released. "It was years of being married to a woman I would have died for, but unable to touch her like she was a fine porcelain china doll which you put on a whatnot shelf . . . out of everybody's reach."

The agony on Tom's face was so apparent. "When Allie Mae held out her hand and offered me her bed, I sort of erupted like a dormant volcano. And I exploded without any feeling of guilt at all. I kept telling myself it's all right. I deserved this after all I had been through. After I had suffered all those years."

David was having a problem looking his dad in the eye. "How long . . . how many . . ." He couldn't find the words.

Tom knew what he was trying to ask. "Two or three times, maybe four before your mother came home . . . Never after that. I let Allie Mae go the morning of the day I brought your mother home from the hospital. I didn't see her for a long time after that."

"Did Mother ever meet her?" David asked.

"Sometime later she had Allie Mae do some ironing for her at her house. But Allie Mae never came back to this house as far as I know. They never met or knew each other."

Tom had dropped a bomb in David's lap. David was trying to put all this information into some kind of order. There were too many slots and too much information. It just wasn't working out—how could his mind absorb so much at one time.

Tom could see the puzzled look on his face. He felt sorry for dumping all this kind of news on him at one time. But he felt he had no choice considering the circumstances.

"Was that it?" David asked.

Tom shook his head. "No." He continued. "I didn't know until several weeks later that Allie Mae was going to have a baby," Tom said, his grip tightening around the glass he held in his hand and waiting for a reaction.

David looked in disbelief at his father. "A baby?"

Tom shook his head.

"Allie Mae had your baby?" David's face blanched. His voice quivered. "My god! What next?" He felt like his stomach was being ripped open over and over. "DAMN AND DOUBLE DAMN!" He had to say it.

—

Tom thought David was about to faint. He became worried and inched near him in case he did. "You need some water?"

David was sick. He thought he was about to vomit but couldn't. Composing himself, momentarily, he asked, "Toye Lee?"

Tom nodded, then looked away.

"Then that means that Toye Lee was my—"

Tom cut him off immediately. "That's right!" Tom didn't let David finish the sentence.

"Does Mother know about this?"

"God . . . no! And she never will."

"Does she even suspect anything?" David asked.

"David, you know your mother hasn't got a suspicious bone in her body. She takes everything . . . everybody . . . at face value and accepts things the way they are. No questions asked. I'm sure she has no inkling about this matter . . . even while living in this small town with all its gossips."

Tom had tried to break this news as easily as he could, but the revelations were almost too much for David. Too much, too fast. He looked for a way to soothe a very frustrated son.

"Allie Mae never made any demands on me. She never came around. She didn't bother me. And as far as I could tell, she never told anybody. But then she must have told somebody. I never saw the baby . . . I never saw the boy after he grew up at all."

"You weren't curious?" David asked.

Tom shrugged. "Allie Mae moved away after the baby was born. I never saw them. I got her address in Beaumont . . . that's where she moved . . . I tried to help her out . . . financially . . . over the years when I could. I gave her some money to pay for a midwife. It wasn't much. If she needed money to buy school clothes or medicine, I'd help her out. He was such a healthy boy, he never got sick. But with our finances the way they were, I had to be careful. You know Mother keeps the books, and any big withdrawal might arouse her curiosity. I used some of my bonuses from the mill. And every once in a while, I'd win some money gambling at the fire station or betting with the guys at the mill."

"But she moved back a few years later," David reminded him. "How did you not see them then?"

"I wanted to forget the whole sordid mess. I wasn't about to stir up old problems. You can avoid seeing people . . . even in this town . . . if you want too bad enough. I never went to the Quarters again."

David was still curious. "But Allie Mae worked at Leas' Café."

"I don't go to Lea's . . . ever! In fact, I don't go downtown at all unless I absolutely have to.

David knew that was true. He didn't remember his dad coming down on Main Street. "You acted like Allie Mae never existed?"

"Yep."

"And she was raising your child . . . alone?"

Tom did not respond. His guilt was plainly on his face.

"I don't see how Mother didn't suspect something all these years," David said.

"I hope she never does." Tom was now at the point that brought this discussion to a head. "And that's what the problem is, David."

"What problem is that, Dad?"

"If the Grimes boys are brought to trial as a result of Toye Lee's death, they have told me all these things I have told you about Allie Mae and Toye Lee will be exposed . . . will be brought out in the trial. They have threatened to tell his whole county about what I just told you."

"You mean," David said, "that if I turn them in and testify against them, they will blow the lid off your little secret?"

"That's what they told me tonight."

"How did they ever find out in the first place?" David asked.

"I do not know . . . have no earthly idea about that . . . But you know how things can get out in a little town like this. The best I can figure is Allie Mae must have mentioned to some friend in the Quarters and they told someone and it eventually got around to the Grimes boys . . . They whore around a lot over there . . . at Pete Parker's place. I'm surprised it's been as quiet as it has. I have lived for years in terror of being discovered. It's like holding your breath for a lifetime."

David knew the answer to his question, but he asked it anyway, "What does all this mean then for you . . . for me?"

"Another scandal . . . tongues would wag for days, maybe years. I might lose my job at the mill . . . or at least lose the respect that I might have with my crew and my bosses." Tom stopped. He needed another drink. "There's always the possibility of your being charged with withholding evidence . . . I doubt it under the circumstances. But more than anything would be the humiliation to your mother and to her family. She couldn't face her friends . . . or the people at the church. She would become a recluse . . . wouldn't have a thing to do with anybody. Like she did when Tommy died. The stress would affect her heart, and the worst scenario would be a heart attack or death."

David added, "And I wouldn't go to the university because of the lack of funds."

"Possibly." Tom arose from the table and emptied his glass into the sink. He returned the bottle of whiskey to its place in the pantry. He put it in a place, however, where he could readily find it again if he had to. Looking at the food on the stove, Tom asked if David was hungry. After drinking so much whiskey, he was not interested in food.

David hardly felt like eating. "No, thanks." There were too many other things occupying his thoughts now, and food was not one of them. *Damn and double damn!* That was all he could think.

Tom put the food back into the refrigerator and wiped the counter. He had run out of anything else to say. He finally turned to David. "I've laid the cards on the table. I've told you things that I never would have told anybody in other circumstances. I have disgraced myself in front of my son. I have jeopardized the health and well-being of my wife . . . I have admitted to being an unfaithful husband and a lousy father . . . I have shown myself as an arrogant bastard and an insensitive bigot . . . In spite of all these things, however, I still love your mother dearly and I still love you, even if you don't believe it . . . Now the choices are up to you."

"Which are?" David asked.

"To call the sheriff's department, report the killing, and testify in the trial. But in doing that, you might hurt the people who love you the most . . . as well as yourself," Tom answered.

"Or?"

"Forgetting the whole matter and letting things remain as they have been . . . Keeping your silence . . . Pray that the situation will soon blow over and you getting on with a new life in Austin and hopefully us surviving here."

"And letting two killers go without punishment?" David asked. "Like nothing ever happened."

Tom didn't like to say it, but he did, "Yes." He bit his lips as he said it.

"The murderers of your son . . . ?"

"But he was a nigrah."

"Nigrah . . . hell, Dad. Are nigrahs half persons? Nonpersons? You act like they're not human beings . . . Toye Lee was your own flesh and blood. Do you want Fred and Howard Grimes to go free just to protect your reputation? To save your own butt?" David's anger was apparent by his flushed face.

Tom's face was stoic now. His eyes did not shift about nervously as they had. He showed no emotion to the questions David had asked. Without hesitation, he replied, "If need be."

David was startled by the frankness of his father. Tom's insensitivity hurt David tremendously. He was concerned about the murder of a friend—his brother now. His father was unconcerned about the murder of his son. Nothing made sense anymore. The application of the code by persons of separate generations was not enough explanation for David. *Have I missed something?* he wondered. *Am I hearing this correctly?* In an expression of anger, he could only yell, "Damn and double damn!"

Tom did not respond to David's outburst.

For many years, David had overlooked or forgotten his dad's remarks about the colored people. He knew his dad was wrong but only enacting the rules of the code. He could not bring himself to think of Tom as a racist. That word was too harsh. That all disappeared with Tom's last comments. *He is a bigot. He has no feelings for anybody colored. And he won't change his mind. He must live by the code.*

Tom's last few minutes of anguish and fear seemed to be temporary. He had told David what the situation was. He had laid his cards on the table or put the ball in his corner. He had opened his soul to his son like he never had to anybody, even Caroline. Tom stepped in the direction of the bedroom. "I'm tired . . . so tired of this goddam mess! This has been a trying time for both of us. I promise I'll never bring the subject up again. You're eighteen now, David . . . old enough to start making decisions on your own . . . start taking responsibility. I will not question whatever course you might take. Look at the choices you have and the long-range consequences and make your decision. Let's just get it behind us. I'll accept whatever you decide . . . Now I'm going to bed."

"Good night, Dad," David answered without looking at him. *How can he just up and leave like that? No remorse? No guilt?* He wondered if Tom was reacting to the alcohol—after all, he had drunk quite a bit—or was he expressing his true feelings about the matter? Now that he had confessed to his indiscretions, the fear, anxiety, and apprehension had disappeared. Tom acted like nothing serious had occurred. *Is he ready to return to being "good old Tom"?*

Shortly David heard snoring coming from the bedroom. *How can anyone snore that soundly after such an emotional confrontation and confession?* David asked himself. Tom had not put the ball in his corner but a ball and chain around his neck and left him to sink or swim.

David found a comfortable chair in the living room and turned off the lights. Sitting in the dark, David recalled the evening's activities and the things his dad had confessed to him. He turned these things in his mind over and over. They still didn't make a lot of sense to him.

After a while, David got up and went to his room. The bed looked inviting. But sleep did not come early or easily for David. He knew that when morning came again, the problem would still be there. Sleep would not make it go away. David was back to square one. Forty-eight hours ago, he had made his decision to call the sheriff on Monday. After the man-to-man talk with his dad, the situation changed—dramatically. He would have to reconsider his position—and he only had two days to do it. David finally dozed off in the early hours of the morning.

CHAPTER TWENTY

Saturday was Tom's day off, and he was soundly sleeping as David left for the drugstore. This was the last day on the job for David, and it seemed like the longest day of his life—and he had seen several long ones in recent weeks.

"Must have been some party last night, huh, David?" Bessie said as she tugged at his shirt to get his attention. "Maybe you need a dose of Hadacol or Mo-Pep." Looking fresh, she sounded like she was ready for some high jinks.

"Why do you say that?" he asked groggily.

"You've been dragging around here like a cat that's been run over eight times . . . look at that," she said, pointing to his feet. "You've got different-colored socks on. You're already forgetting us already now that you're three days away from leaving Kirbyville."

That comment surprised David. "I'm sorry, Bessie. I'm just not with it today. And believe me, I'll never forget you."

"You're not sick, are you?"

"I just didn't get much sleep last night."

"All the excitement of going to Austin, huh?"

"Must be," David replied. He hadn't thought about Austin in several days. He made it through the day. He didn't know how and didn't remember most of it. After saying his final good-byes at the store, he headed for the house. He could really use a nap.

That idea was squashed immediately when he saw his mother. She was back from Waco earlier than she anticipated and ready to tell him every detail about her music seminar and who she had seen. He hadn't seen her so enthusiastic in several months.

"I see you guys didn't eat the food I left you," she said. "Why not?"

"We ate out." He pecked his mother on the cheek and prayed she would not subject him to some kind of interrogation about what they had done the last two days.

"You'll have to eat it tonight, or it will spoil."

"Fine. I'm as hungry as a grizzly bear." David had not eaten since lunch the day before—a hamburger—and he was feeling gaunt. Tom's revelations to David the night before had all but killed his appetite.

"Wait 'til you hear our choir special Sunday. It is so pretty." Caroline hummed the music they planned to present.

"Something you learned at the seminar?" he asked.

"It was so good . . . so educational . . . so musical." She was tittering like the first bird of spring. "You know, those people at Baylor University think the University of Texas is one step above Sodom and Gomorrah."

"What Baptist doesn't?" David asked. "They're jealous . . . That's why I'm going there. More sin than they've got here. Everybody needs a little sin every now and then. Maybe they ought to do missionary work in Austin." He chuckled.

"David!"

"You know those people at Baylor are just like those Baptist bugs."

"What's a Baptist bug?"

"You know those little black bugs that come around in the spring? . . . The ones that are connected at the tail and fly in pairs?"

"The ones around here every year messing up windshields and things. Why do you call them Baptist bugs?" she asked.

"Well, they hang together under any circumstances, but they can't look each other in the face."

"Like Baptists?" Caroline snickered at his answer. "Have you seen your daddy?"

Tom was not home when Caroline returned from Waco. And he had not left a note telling her where he would be.

"Not since last night . . . Remember you did come back earlier than you told us . . . Mother, I think I'll take a nap before supper."

Caroline stopped what she was doing and came toward him. "Are you sick, honey?" she asked, feeling his brow to see if he had fever.

"Whose temperature you going to take after I leave Tuesday?" He laughed at her concern every time he got hot or tired. "I'm tired . . . didn't get much sleep last night. Wake me up when supper is ready." David departed for the sanctity of his bedroom. When he closed the door, he wondered what condition his dad was in. *I'll bet he's got a hangover. Mother will be angry if he did.*

Caroline said she would. She continued to work on the chores in the kitchen. There was so much catching up to do around the house because of her absence the last two days. At least, that's what she kept telling herself. She looked forward to Tom's return to the house. She was bristling with excitement and could hardly wait to tell him about her church trip.

Tom returned home shortly after David went to his room, looking as fresh as he did every day. There was no visible sign of the previous night's discussion or drinking. He was so glad to see Caroline and quickly embraced her with a kiss and hug.

"Is that a trace of alcohol I smell in your breath?" Caroline asked.

"I've been down to the fire station, playing a little poker with the guys," Tom replied.

"And perhaps having a few drinks," she added.

"Possibly," he answered, embarrassed he'd been discovered. Tom had rinsed his mouth with Listerine, eaten some mouth mints, chewed gum on his way home.

"That's just what a Baptist choir member wanted to smell on her husband after her return from Baylor University."

Caroline and Tom chuckled.

Shortly before supper, David reappeared from his room. "Hi, Dad." He avoided eye contact with Tom.

"Hello, son," Tom replied.

"Have a good nap, honey?" Caroline asked.

"Not bad," David answered. "But not long enough."

"You gonna nap every day at UT?" Tom asked, trying to keep David's mind off their discussion.

"I hope not," David answered. "But I need sleep to be alert in class."

"Anyone hungry?" Caroline asked.

Both men answered quickly and washed their hands. And moved swiftly to the already-set table.

Caroline said grace over the meal. And they ate supper.

Tom and David spent most of their time at the supper table listening to Caroline describe the Waco trip. Neither were truly interested in learning new music methods or what quartet was the best or which music was best for special occasions, but both were courteous and listened as if they were. Neither man looked at each other very much, and no reference to the previous night's discussion was remotely mentioned. Neither responded to Caroline's question about their activities while she was gone.

Tom did comment on Caroline's revived enthusiasm. "That trip was good for her, David. I haven't seen her so excited in years. She'll be like a new woman," he said. "Reminds me of the time she learned she was pregnant with you."

David agreed. He didn't want to be the person to burst her bubble.

After putting away the supper dishes and cleaning the kitchen, the family went into the living room. Caroline broke the silence when she announced, "It would be very nice if we all went to church tomorrow as a family. It will be our last service together for a while."

Tom and David did not find this suggestion very appealing, but again to humor her, they agreed. After church, Tom planned to go to the firehouse and play poker with the boys. David had made no plans, but he needed to get out of the house. He needed some breathing room away from his parents, especially Tom. He would have to decide very soon what course of action he would take in the Grimes boys affair. Caroline was elated that both her men would be sitting in the church sanctuary tomorrow as the choir presented their musical specials acquired in Waco.

"You'll love the program," she announced. "It's so different from the 'Rock of Ages' or 'In the Garden' stuff we usually sing. I think we get in a rut sometimes with our music . . . same old hymns. Tomorrow's music will have a little more beat to it," she said, trying to sound cool and jivey. "Not jivey like they sing over at Pilgrim's Rest African Methodist Church. They get carried away over there. Even that's too much for me."

The mention of that church got David's attention. *Why did she mention that particular church? At this time?*

"Have you ever been to Pilgrim's Rest Church?" David asked.

"No," she answered. "But I heard their choir some time ago—at some community function.

The men looked at each other somewhat indifferently.

Tom shrugged.

"Our music tomorrow is going to be so uplifting . . . and spiritual . . . but modern. It's a new kind of Christian music."

"I hope so," whispered David to his dad. "Is Mrs. McKinnon playing the piano?" They all remembered how hard it was for the doctor's wife to coordinate her fingers on the piano with the notes on the music score.

"Lord no!" Caroline was quick to say. "This is a serious presentation—not a comedy act!"

They all laughed.

Sunday church came and went like so many Sundays before. David was wished well by the congregation, still hoping to save him from the impending sins at the university.

After lunch, the family went its own way, as usual. Tom departed for the fire station. Caroline was expected back at church for another of the many meetings. David saw several of his friends at church and made his good-byes. Most of his gang friends had already gone back to college.

Monday for the Wilson family began like any other Monday in a small Southeast Texas town. It was already hot and sultry by seven o'clock. Tom arose early, as usual, and reported to the mill. He had a payroll to make, papers to complete and account for his crew.

Sometimes a nigrah worker or two would take an extra day off—or come to work late—and he had to make sure a full planer crew was present to do the job. The mill was starting on a new project—a big contract—and they needed a full crew for several weeks. Tom was always exuberant on Mondays. They could talk about the football games played during the weekend. Firemen's practice was also held on Monday nights, and Tom always looked forward to the practice—and the "refreshments" which followed. He was also looking for a bonus from the new contract the mill got.

Caroline, also, had planned a full day. Monday was her housecleaning day—sweeping, mopping, changing the bed linens. To most people, the house looked perfect, but to listen to her was a disaster area which needed immediate attention. She also had to buy groceries for the week. This was the first day for the "specials of the week" at Parson's Grocery, and she wanted to get fresh produce. At the top of her list was some goodies to put with David's carry-on bag. She wanted him to have a snack on the bus when he left tomorrow and have something to nibble on when he settled in his rooming house. She had been told at church the day before that there would be a special-called meeting of the Sunday school officers on Monday, so she had to get her chores done before the seven thirty meeting. Caroline arose early too and finished her cleaning chores quickly. Then she was off to the store and post office.

It was not an ordinary day for David. It was the last full day of his old life in Kirbyville and the day before the beginning of his new life in Austin. By the time David woke and got out of bed, his parents had already gone. *What a luxury*, he thought to himself, to be able to lie in bed until you wanted to get up. But he had no choice since the sun shining in his window had rendered his fan useless. This was his one-day "vacation." He found the biscuits Caroline left in the oven and some strips of bacon on a plate. Bacon—the thick slices from a slab of smoked pork—was a real luxury and always a pleasure for David. Caroline wanted him to have something special today because they might not have time for a big breakfast tomorrow. He savored every moment of it as he devoured the food and flushed it down with a big glass of milk. After dressing, he went to his closet and got the two pieces of his new tan-colored Samsonite luggage. David placed them on the bed and opened them. He planned to start packing in the afternoon. Looking at the size of the luggage, he wondered how he was going to get everything in them. His mother had bought several new shirts and pants—and underclothes. *Where will they all go?* But then he reminded himself—don't worry, it won't make any difference anyway.

David opened the top drawer to his Victorian dresser. It had belonged to his grandparents and had become a member of the family. From behind the neatly stacked shirts, he found his bank savings book. He kept it in a very secret place but looked at it often to keep tabs on how much money he had put in the bank. Quickly, looking at the latest entry, he closed the passbook and put it in his pocket, which also contained the fountain pen Toye Lee had given him for his birthday.

As David pushed the drawer back into place, he casually looked at himself in the mirror on top of the dresser. He stood there for a long time as a myriad of questions raced though his mind. He turned his head to the right and then to the left. *Is there any resemblance at all?* He put his finger on his upper lip. *What if had a mustache?* David looked at his body. The comparison was ludicrous. As much as he tried, he could find no similarity between him and Toye Lee.

The face David saw in the mirror did not look like the same one he saw in May. He was pallid with dark circles around his eyes. His eyes no longer had the sparkle of emeralds as they did on graduation night. *Damn and double damn! Is that me?*

As he looked at himself, he wondered if his decision would have pleased his grandfather, Judge Wingate. The judge, as well as his mother, were the two people he looked to guide him in his search for justice. The decision was made, and now he had to live with it.

David turned away from the mirror with many unanswered questions. What would happen in the future? His well-laid plans had turned to shambles. What a mess his life had become. *Damn and double damn!*

He slammed the screen door behind him and headed downtown— no one ever locked their homes in Kirbyville. He was on his way to

—

the bank on Main Street. It felt so good not to be working today, he thought. He entered the bank—Kirbyville State Bank—and observed the lines. David never went to the shortest line. He preferred to be waited on by Mrs. Elizabeth Townes, a family friend of many years.

Soon he was at the front of the line before the teller window.

"Morning, David," greeted Mrs. Townes.

"Good morning," David replied.

Mrs. Townes had been a teller in the bank as long as David could remember. She was about the same age as his mother, perhaps a little older; but already her hair had turned a beautiful silver, making her appear to be older than she was. She was a widow, her husband also a mill worker had died in 1939, leaving her with three small children to raise. She had experienced a hard life, but no one had ever heard her make one complaint about her condition.

"You'll be leaving tomorrow, I hear."

"Yes, ma'am,"

"I was visiting with your mother yesterday, and she thinks you are about ready to go. She sure is going to miss you."

Mrs. Townes and Caroline were members of the BYKOTA Sunday School class at the First Baptist Church. They were so proud of that class whose initials stood for "Be ye kind, one to another." The class was composed primarily of widows and women whose husbands were somewhere other than church on Sundays. For many of the ladies, it was their primary social life, especially the widows.

David looked at Mrs. Townes and, in a devilish way, asked her, "Are you going to show me the secret sign and tell me the password? This is you last chance before I leave." She and David had a long-running joke between them.

Mrs. Townes laughed at his question. She and Caroline were also in the Eastern Star. David had kidded them for years about their using secret signs and speaking in tongues at their meetings at the Masonic Lodge. He always referred to them as a cult, especially when the sisters donned their pink evening dresses for an initiation and spoke in some kind of biblical language. "What are you and the cult of the vestal virgins going to do without me to keep tabs on you?

Come on now, give the secret sign." He smiled broadly as he made the request.

"You better be careful, you heathen, before I put a curse on you," warned Mrs. Townes. "I'll zap you before you get out of town."

David made an eerie sound and held his hands in some kind of contortion imitating a special sign that some secret fraternity might use.

"What can I do for you, Mr. Wilson?" she asked, getting back to business.

David put his passbook on the counter. "I want to close my account." He pushed the passbook toward her.

She looked perplexed. "I thought you had set up your account so you could write checks when you were in Austin and have your parents cover any funds overdrawn?"

"I did at one time. But I changed my mind."

"But you have decided to transfer your money to a bank in Austin?" she replied, nodding her head. "What bank should we transfer the money to?"

"No. Just give me cash, please . . . twenties . . . and fifties," he said in a tone that suggested she hurry.

"That's a lot of money to be carrying around . . . especially in a new town, David." She was concerned that he did not recognize the danger of carrying so much cash. "I can give you a cashier's check for a dollar and a quarter charge."

"Cash, please, Mrs. Townes. I'm sorta in a hurry."

It was his money, and she tried to be helpful. But she saw the determination in his eyes that he would not change his request. She opened the cash drawer, withdrew a stack of bills, and began to count the money. After a few minutes, she stopped counting as she put the last bill on the stack. "Sixteen hundred sixty-two dollars and seventy-four cents . . . Anything else, David?"

"No, ma'am. Thank you, Mrs. Townes. See you Thanksgiving . . . bye now."

Mrs. Townes watched him as he left the bank. She wondered what had happened to change his mind. Caroline didn't mention any change of plans to her at church yesterday. Maybe she would explain next Sunday. But she had other customers and soon forgot about the incident.

David was touring Main Street for the last time. He had said his good-byes to most of his friends already. He observed the activity on Main Street, looking to the east toward the depot and then west toward the schools and West End. *There's no place like Kirbyville*, he thought. This was the same town four months earlier on the morning after his graduation he thought he owned—had been his own domain. Now this same Kirbyville had become a weight around his neck slowly strangling him, and he wanted to get out as quickly as possible. *I think I know how Toye Lee felt*, he kept telling himself over and over again.

David looked into the barbershop, hoping to find it empty. Sure enough there were no customers, so he opened the door to go into the shop. Suddenly he stopped and retreated. *Why am I doing this?* he asked himself. *No need to do this now. That will be taken care of later.* He didn't need toiletries—his mother had bought Ipana toothpaste and the things he was likely to need, so he skipped going to the drugstore. He looked down the street at the drugstore, but there was no real desire to go back for one last time. *How many times can you say good-bye before you wear out your exit?* he wondered. David finished his business in short order. He checked the mailbox at the post office. He bought some stamps at the window and waved to Miss Bell as he walked out the door and headed home. The rest of his afternoon, he folded his clothes and carefully packed them in the suitcases. His mother said she would do this for him later that night. But since she had a meeting at the church, he decided to do it himself. One more night in this bedroom and a new life tomorrow. As the hours passed, he became more anxious.

Tom, Caroline, and David ate supper in relative silence. They made a few comments to each other, but most of the meal was spent in something that resembled a wake. Perhaps each was thinking of their lives in the future—after David's departure tomorrow. For Tom the house would be emptier—and a lot quieter, but he would have more time with Caroline. Tom still had the problems the Grimes boys had laid on him. He had no indication what David would do, but he was beginning to worry that things might get worse after David left. He was praying for a sign.

Caroline saw her "baby," now a budding college student, leaving her. Who would she wait on now—and worry over? It was like someone snatching her heart from her body. She promised herself not to start bawling when he boarded the bus. But could she live up to that promise?

From David's point of view, however, life was about to change and change drastically. The slow and quiet life of a rural town was about to be replaced by a new lifestyle. Many residents often had problems adapting to a large city and eventually moved back. David's excitement had deserted him.

At seven, the fire station siren began to wail as it always did on Monday nights. Cars and trucks raced down Main Street to the fire station for practice. Practice would follow shortly.

Tom jumped up from the table, grabbed his keys, and dashed for Geraldine. "I'm running late," he said. "See y'all later."

Caroline quickly put the dishes in the sink, planning to wash them later. "Honey, I'm going to my meeting at the church. Will you be okay?"

"*Mother!*" David answered somewhat disgustedly. He didn't think his mother would get over treating him like a little boy.

"Will you be here when I get home?"

"Probably," he replied. "Unless someone comes by and wants to get a malt or Coke at the drugstore . . . but I can't guess who that might be."

Caroline grabbed her Bible and her church material and moved toward the door. "I'll fix you another piece of raisin pie when I get back . . . and some milk."

"I'll hold you to that promise, madam," David said jokingly. He knew that it would be a long time before he tasted his favorite pie again.

Caroline's ride was right on time. She heard the car horn blast announcing its arrival "Bye, honey. That's Liz Townes. She's driving tonight . . . See you after the meeting."

It didn't dawn on David that Mrs. Townes might mention his withdrawal at the bank today. He always assumed that financial transactions were confidential, and he had not worried about it until now. *But in this town, secrets go around very quickly.* As the car sped away, David made his way to his room, going directly to the dresser 7where his clothes had been but were now neatly packed in his new luggage and withdrew the stack of bills which he had gotten from the bank earlier in the day. He moved back to the kitchen. He needed something to put the money in. *A paper sack,* he wondered? *No, too flimsy. An envelope? Yes, an envelope—a big one—is exactly what I needed. Where could one be?* He searched the kitchen drawers and, finding none, made his way to his parents' bedroom. Caroline kept her business correspondence and stationery in her closet. Sure enough, he found one. A manila envelope. Just right. Back in the kitchen, he sat at the table and counted out fifteen hundred dollars that he placed in the envelope. Making sure they were neatly stacked with a rubber band around them, he sealed the envelope and returned it to its secret hiding place. "I'll see you little greenbacks tomorrow," he said, talking to the envelope like it was a person. He closed the dresser drawer and moved toward the front door. He was so glad that his parents were gone. It would be difficult to explain what he was about to do.

David exited the house and walked east down Harris Street toward the railroad tracks. Already darkness had begun to settle in the community and the millions of stars were making their nightly appearance. Early fall in Southeast Texas is something special. The mosquitoes and gnats had already begun to disappear, leaving the lightening bugs as the only insect flying in the evening breeze. Their flickering on and off was like a million Christmas tree lights that graced the Jasper County Courthouse during the season. The leaves on the sweet gums, pin oaks, and Chinese tallow trees were turning brilliant yellow, red, and orange, hanging there for a while until the autumn breezes blew them to the ground and turning the flaming trees into skeletons of winter. There were always shooting stars at this time of year. A few of the more ambitious citizens had already begun raking the ground, sweeping the pine needles and oak leaves into piles which became pyres of the evening. The smoke which arose from these burning fires announced to the nose that the true fall would soon be on its way. The night silence was only interrupted by the quacking of the geese in flight, making their way from Canada to the Gulf Coast. *This*, he told himself as he looked around, *is what I will miss*. Crossing the railroad tracks, David stopped momentarily looking for a particular house—Toye Lee's house. He spotted the home and headed in the direction of the nigrah shacks. It was completely dark now, and even the one single street light could not reveal who or what might be there waiting in the darkness.

Walking slower now, he came to recognize the house that two short weeks before he could not bring himself to enter. David was directly across the street from the house but surrounded by bushes so no one would see him. The front door was shut, but he could see through the open screenless window. He saw Allie Mae Johnson sitting in a chair rocking back and forth. Her face was partially hidden by her hand, and she looked like she was reading something in her lap. The thought occurred to David that she might be crying as he noticed the wetness of her cheeks glistening in the rays of a lamp which rested on a small table beside the chair. David could not tell for sure, but it reminded him of the recent past. Also on the table was a picture of Toye Lee smiling broadly. Beside the photograph was an array of what looked like athletic trophies from past sports events.

David looked in both directions to see if anyone might be in his yard watching him approach. He slowly made his way across the road closer to the front door. He stopped quickly as a dog down the street began to bark ferociously, breaking the silence. Then another dog joined the animal, and within seconds, all the dogs of the neighborhood were engaged in their nightly canine chorus announcing the arrival of a stranger. With the commotion caused by the barking dogs, David retreated to the bushes across the street. He barely made it before the front door opened, spilling its light inside across the dilapidated porch. David could only see a silhouette of Allie Mae as she appeared at the door to look outside to see why the dogs continued to bark. Seeing no one on the porch she, she opened the screen door and walked onto the porch. She looked in both directions up and down the dirt street. The streets were empty—nothing to cause the dogs to continue to bark.

—

"Hush," she yelled. The dogs still barked. "Hush, dammit!" she yelled again. When they stopped, she reentered the house. Closing the door behind her, Allie Mae retreated to her rocking chair. After a few minutes, however, she arose again. She picked up the photograph of Toye Lee, looked at it for a long moment, and returned it to its place of honor on a shelf. Allie Mae moved to the window from which David was observing her and slowly pulled the shade down. A moment later, she turned the light in the room out. The house was completely dark now. His task accomplished, David turned and headed home again. He felt better than he had in several days. His pace picked up, and soon he was briskly walking—then running—down the street, feeling his heart pounding and tears spilling down his cheeks. The lights on Harris Street cast long shadows as he walked up the steps and entered his house.

The house was empty. *Thank goodness.* He would not have to explain where he had been now and why. He went to his room and prepared for bed. David put his clothes in a neat stack on a chair. After brushing his teeth, he pulled the covers back, leaving only the sheet to cover himself. He clicked off the light and slid into the cool, inviting bed. It was a little early for his usual bedtime, but he saw a great deal of benefit in being asleep when Tom and Caroline came home. He would not have to look at his mother's face worrying about tomorrow and his final departure from Kirbyville. Or face her intensive interrogation of his day's activities. And he would not miss the questioning look on his dad's face or smell the liquor and smoke that he acquired at the fire station. *Thank goodness they drank after they practiced rather than before. He wondered if they had ever fought a fire when they were drunk. It didn't matter now anyway.*

David was already in bed when Caroline returned from church but was not yet asleep. She went to his room, and seeing his clothes neatly stacked on the chair, she knew he was home. Quietly she asked, "Are you awake, honey?"

David did not answer, feigning sleep.

Caroline closed the door, but as she did, David heard her mutter to herself, "Must be the excitement of tomorrow."

He heard her walking to the kitchen and shortly thereafter the clinking of glassware and the rattle of pots and pans. *I knew she wouldn't go to sleep without washing dishes. She couldn't sleep a wink with dishes in the sink.* He turned over and went to sleep.

CHAPTER TWENTY-ONE

Tuesday, September 19, 1950—almost four months after his graduation—was Freedom Day. Like most days in August and September, it started hot and became scorching by noon. But weather was not the main item of the day. It was the day that David Wilson was leaving for the University of Texas—a day that was insignificant to everyone except the members of the Tom Wilson family. For them it was historic.

The activities and events going on in the city or the world would normally be discussed by the family. But not today. David was oblivious to the films—*Pardon My Sarong* with Abbott and Costello and *Tea for Two* with Doris Day on the billboards at the Palace Theater—his favorite entertainment. He was not aware that his draft board had released the names of twenty-six draftees to the papers with forty-one more to be called to duty. Among them more boys from Kirbyville. And he had not heard that an eighteen-year-old boy from Call had been wounded and later died in Korea.

On any other day, Caroline would be on the telephone gossiping and discussing events. She would have been interested in knowing that Princess Elizabeth had named her new girl baby Anne Elizabeth Alice Louise and the Sadler Wells Ballet of England had debuted in New York. Also she would have read that Elizabeth Taylor's and Nicky Hilton's marriage was on the rocks and Ernest Hemingway's newest book, *Across the River and into the Trees*, had been published. And she would have already made arrangements at the church to take food to the family of the soldier killed in Korea. But today she had one thing in mind, and that was getting David to the bus station.

Also, Tom's attention would have turned to other matters. He would be raging about President Truman's decision to include married men in the eighteen to twenty-five draft class. And like all men, he would have drooled over the picture of Buick's new model, Roadmaster with Dynaflow drive. And more than anything, he would have plenty to say about the soldiers arriving at Inchon and the brutal beating American soldiers were taking in Korea. And he had a good reason for David's departure as soon as possible.

The Wilsons were up early. It reminded David of those years at Christmastime—so many years ago—when everyone arose early to see what Santa Claus had brought to David. Tom always wanted to sleep late, but Caroline insisted that it be a family affair, so Tom had to be up as well. Sometimes that was difficult for him after consuming so much food and drink the night before and having stayed up late assembling those "simple assembly required" toys. Christmas was Caroline's favorite holiday, and she was already secretly making plans for David's return from the university at Christmas break.

David's traveling clothes had been neatly pressed and were hanging in the closet in his room. Caroline had chosen a new shirt and the best pair of slacks she could find with socks to match. His new twin Samsonite luggage set had already been packed, closed, and properly labeled just in case it got lost. He bathed, dressed, and started to make the bed; but he left it unmade, telling himself that his mother probably wanted to wash the dirty sheets before she remade it. His shoes had been spit polished and reflected the gleam of the light in the ceiling. Checking to see if his mother was watching—she wasn't—he opened the dresser and withdrew the large envelope, which he quickly checked to see that it was still properly sealed. He had pasted more stamps than necessary, assuring that it would be delivered. He put the letter where no one could see it, but a place that could pick it up quickly. He returned his pen to his pocket and gave it an endearing pat. *I'll need this to write letters home—and fill out forms—or whatever.* The fountain pen had become his only connection to Toye Lee now, and he would protect it with all his energy and strength. He then reached back into the dresser drawer and took the remaining stack of cash. Again, making sure Caroline was not looking, he counted the money quickly. About one hundred and sixty-two dollars. He had already decided he would need some cash for "spending money" in case of an emergency. This should be enough until he reached his final destination. He quickly inserted the money into his wallet and his wallet into his pants pocket. David slowly surveyed his room for the last time—the room which had been his refuge, his cave, his sanctuary—his prison—for eighteen years. David knew the room would be exactly like he left it. It would become Caroline's shrine until he came home again. With everything in place, except his rumpled bed, he made his way to the kitchen.

"Morning, honey," Caroline greeted him before he entered the kitchen.

"Morning, Mother."

For Caroline it was a special day also. She had gotten up with Tom and fixed his breakfast. She could now turn her full attention to the real matter of the moment—David's breakfast.

"Dad already gone to the mill?" he asked.

"He had to check some invoices in the office and talk to Mr. Herrington. Thought if he went in early, they wouldn't mind him taking off later this morning," she replied.

"Taking off?"

"Honey, you don't think he's going to miss your departure this morning, do you? He said he would pick us up at eight thirty, and that would be plenty of time for your nine o'clock bus."

David had not been sure his dad would go with them to the bus station, but he was happy to discover he was. It would be much easier going by car than carrying the bags by hand to the bus station.

"Your father seemed much better this morning."

"What do you mean *better*?'"

"He seems to have been under so much stress lately. I guess it was the job. He mentioned budget cutting at the mill . . . That's funny, though, because it never upset him before . . . Anyway, he left this

—
331

morning with a sparkle in his eye, a smile on his face, a whistle on his lips, and a jig in his steps. I don't know what has happened, but he's like a different man."

I know what he's thinking. David made no comment. "Something sure smells good!"

"Honey, I got up earlier than I expected this morning. You know how I can't sleep when I'm excited. So I had plenty of time to fix you a good breakfast."

Then he noticed the food on the stove. "My gosh, Mother!" he exclaimed. "This looks like the last meal of a death row inmate! I'm only going to college, not the electric chair."

Caroline smiled as she pulled a chair from under the table and motioned for him to take his place. "Please sit, Mr. Joe College." The chair had now become his throne.

Joining the fun, David grandly bowed to her and sat down for his special breakfast.

Caroline had outdone herself. First came the fried eggs cooked hard. To David they looked cooked to perfection, and it was the first time he had eaten fried eggs in weeks. He was used to scrambled eggs because that's what his dad ate. David had never acquired a taste for eggs sunny-side up. "Raw" is how he described them. On top of the eggs, he poured a big dab of catsup. He was the only person in the world who liked catsup on his fried eggs, and he quickly reminded himself that there would be no more extras like these for some time to come. Along with the eggs, Caroline had prepared another favorite—country smoked, spiced sausage links, smoked by the Hawthorne family, the same family that "provided" watermelons for them earlier that summer. There was a pan of biscuits—homemade, of course—and preserved figs and pears. Caroline had grown a fig tree for one purpose—to have figs to preserve each year. She got the pears from trees on the old Wingate farm. There was a pitcher of fresh orange juice and a large glass of whole milk.

"I'm so afraid that you won't eat properly. Or get enough to eat at the cafeteria," she said, concerned about his future meals. "Do you have enough, honey?"

"The way you're fretting about my future, this is more like a my 'last supper' than my going-away breakfast . . . or like a prisoner's last meal before going to the electric chair."

"Now, don't be sacrilegious."

"This is a meal fit for a king, Mother. After this meal I won't have to eat for a week. And don't worry." David ate several bites. "The food at the university cafeteria couldn't possibly be as good as this," he added. "I may need a crane to get me on the bus."

She sat down at the table after refilling her coffee cup. "You are my king, honey." She looked at him with such pride. All the joys and sorrows—all the hardship and the pain, all the frustrations—of the past eighteen years seemed to come together at this very moment and disappear. And Caroline to herself said, *It was worth it, every bit of it.*

"Larrapin, just larrapin." David was too busy eating to notice the concerned, but proud, look on Caroline's face. *One of these days*, he thought, *I'm going to find out what that word means.* David tried to smile, but he was more concerned in devouring the meal before him. And any additional comments at this time might result in his choking on his food. "Thanks, Mother."

Caroline didn't mind his silence. She reached over and touched David's arm that stiffened for a moment. "We are so proud of you, son . . . We love you so much. I wish Papa and Mama were here to see this day. He would have been so proud to see his grandson go off to college."

The picture of his mother at that moment—the tears that glistened in her eyes and finally fell to her cheek, the way she swept back a lock of graying hair that had fallen over her forehead, the quiver of her voice as she said those softly spoken words—became a picture in David's memory that he carried with him forever. A picture of a person who, in all respects, had become a saint to him especially in the last few months. David swallowed his food, took his mother's hand, and pressed it to his lips. Their eyes met, but no words were spoken.

"Goodness me," Caroline exclaimed, breaking the silence. "Look at the clock. It's almost eight thirty, and I'm not ready . . . Put the dishes in the sink, honey, and put your bags on the front porch." She scurried to her dressing table for that final touch of rouge and to pin that errant lock of hair back in its proper place.

Tom was on time, arriving precisely at eight thirty and letting them know it by blasting Geraldine's horn. He had no problem getting away from the mill for a few minutes. Caroline and David were ready and waiting, and as she got in the backseat of the car, David put the luggage in the trunk and his carry-on bag in the backseat with his mother.

Caroline was the first to speak. "I hope your boxes arrived in Austin all right."

"Always something to worry about, huh, David?" said Tom.

"Don't worry, Mother. I can always wear this outfit until Thanksgiving if they didn't." David laughed, but Caroline saw no humor in his comment.

"Everybody ready?" asked Tom.

"Dad, would you mind driving by the post office before going to the bus station?" David asked.

Both parents looked puzzled and asked why David had made such a request at this time.

"What for, honey?" asked his mother.

"I forgot to get some stamps. It may be a while before I have time to locate the post office in Austin."

Caroline still looked puzzled.

"You want me to write home, don't you?"

"Tom, drive to the post office!" she commanded. "We've got plenty of time." Caroline was beaming at the thought of receiving letters with news of David's progress. "How sweet, honey," she said to David. "Most boys don't write their mothers . . . but then my boy is a little different than most." She winked at David. "We've got such a good son, Tom."

Tom parked the car in front of the post office. While his parents were checking to see who was on Main Street, David quietly produced the envelope he had grabbed just before he left the house. Trying to conceal it as best as he could, he jumped from the car and hastily made his way into the building. He had been attentive to putting enough postage on it to carry it anywhere. Then with the pen Toye Lee had given him, he carefully addressed the envelope. MRS. ALLIE MAY JOHNSON, General Delivery, Kirbyville, Texas. Once again, checking the address, he dropped it into the letter slot as he made his way to the service window.

Miss Bell was standing behind the counter. "Need some stamps, David?"

"Yes, ma'am."

She tore the stamps from the sheet and handed him twenty stamps. "Sixty cents." He quickly paid for and pocketed them and turned to the door.

"Be good now," she called after him. "And have a good semester."

"Thanks. Bye now." David was out of the post office and back into the car in a flash.

Schaeffer's Café and Bus Station was only about five blocks from the post office, so there was no real hurry to rush. As they approached the bus station, they saw the daily buses had already arrived. The Greyhound buses were parked side by side in front of the bus station-café—one marked Houston heading south and the other marked Austin heading north. The big blue and gray freshly washed vehicles trimmed with lots of chrome glistened in the rising sun and reminded David of some kind of chariot. Shortly, he the gladiator would soon be charging out of town.

Tom parked behind the buses but far enough away so as not to be engulfed by the carbon monoxide belching from their tail pipes as their motors roared in unison.

David jumped out of the car with his carry-on bag. "I'll get the ticket, Dad, if you'll put my bags by the luggage compartment."

"Need any money?" his father asked, reaching for his wallet.

"I've got it." It was the first time ever his dad offered money rather than just talking about it.

David was gone a few minutes but shortly returned with a ticket in his hand. "Got it," he said to his mother, holding the ticket up and then putting it in his pocket with his fountain pen.

Until this moment Caroline had remained quiet. She was trying to maintain her composure and kept telling herself she was not going to cry. "Did you pack your goodies?" she asked. She had placed candy bars, chips, and cookies snuggly in his bag.

"Right here in my carry-on." David patted his bag, which was bulging with the goodies inside.

"I hope you have enough . . . I could have put more in there."

"If I need more, Mother, I'll get some at a stop along the way. These will be fine for the trip."

Tom came from around the far side of the Austin bus. "I just went ahead and put your Samsonite luggage on the bus."

"They were marked good, weren't they?" asked Caroline. "With your address on them?"

David rolled his eyes at his mother. He didn't comment.

They waited by the door of the Austin bus. Passengers were not yet being loaded.

"Honey, why don't you go ahead and put your carry-on bag on the bus so you'll have a good seat," Caroline said.

Since there was no one to stop him, David climbed aboard the Austin-bound bus, deposited his bag in the front seat across from the bus driver, and then returned to his parents. He would now be able to see the countryside on his way.

About that time, the bus driver came from the bus station and climbed aboard the bus. As he ascended the steps with a clip file with some papers, Caroline stopped him. "This is my boy," she said. "He's going to the University of Texas." The driver was taken aback for a moment. "You be sure he gets there all right." She said in a nice, demanding way.

"Yes, ma'am. We'll take care of him real good. We have a special place for tea-sips." The driver was amused at the concerned mother. "We'll be leaving in a few minutes."

David saw the nervousness of his parents. It was becoming infectious. His dad looked in the direction of the mill when the mill whistle blew. The smoke from the burning bark in the slag pit reminded him he was supposed to be working. Caroline was just as tense but afraid to say anything.

David noticed that both were unusually uncomfortable. "Look," he finally said. "Why don't ya'll go ahead. Dad needs to get back to the mill, and I'm sure you've got plenty to do too, Mother. I'll just stand here until we load."

Tom liked the idea. Caroline was not as ready to see her child break the apron strings, but she consented. She was determined to be brave.

"All right," she said, "but be careful." Caroline stepped toward David with her outstretched arms. She was fighting the tears, but she was unsuccessful. "Bye, honey. Write us. You're in my prayers. I love you." They embraced for a long moment, and then she departed for the car not looking back for fear of showing the tears running down her cheeks.

David extended his hand to Tom. He couldn't recall ever shaking his dad's hand before. But he had never left him before either, except for church camp and that was when he was a kid. He was a man now. Tom was equally embarrassed as he reached for David's hand. Their hands met, Tom's grip stronger than David's. For a moment, they held each other's hand; but suddenly; Tom brushed David's hand aside and pulled David toward him and put his arms around David in a fatherly embrace, however awkward. It reminded David of the first embrace that Toye Lee had given him after one of their trips.

As David responded with a hug of his own, Tom whispered, "Thanks ... thanks, son, for everything. Your decision saves everyone a lot of problems. You won't regret it." Tom held David momentarily, and then breaking away, he hastily joined Caroline in the car.

Tom turned to David one last time. He waved and flashed his unforgettable smile.

My god! David was jolted by what he saw. *Why hadn't I seen it before?* He never made the connection—until now. As Tom was smiling at him, David did not see his dad, but Toye Lee—his smile, broad from ear to ear with the gleam of those white teeth sparkling in the morning sun transfixed on Tom's face. *How could I have missed such an apparent similarity?* Tom turned and entered the car.

David watched his parents slowly pull away from the bus station. His mother turned around for that last glimpse. Tom looked straight ahead. On to Highway 96 and to the red light of Main Street. David watched them until the car turned left at the light and he no longer could see them.

There was a tear in his eye, too, which he quickly wiped away. Spotting the bus drivers coming from the station, David hopped on the Austin bus and retrieved his carry-on bag from the front seat. Briskly walking around the Austin bus, he moved toward the Houston bus and got in line with the other passengers. The bus driver was a middle-aged man who looked like he might have driven millions of miles and had carried every kind of passenger in the world. David bet he could tell all sorts of stories about the people he had seen.

"Houston?" David asked.

"Army processing center?" the driver asked, noticing the carry-on bag in David's hand.

David was caught be surprise. Was his secret already out before he left town? "Yes, sir, how did you know?"

"We are seeing more and more young men nowadays . . . especially with this Korean business. More volunteers right now, but the draft is coming up soon." The driver hesitated for a moment and then continued, "The army processing center is just a couple of blocks from the bus terminal in Houston. I'll show you when we get there." That news relieved David considerably.

"Thanks." David boarded the bus and slowly walked down the aisle until he spotted a vacant seat near the rear. *Colored to the rear*, he said to himself with a little bit of irony. He slipped into the empty seat near the window. Momentarily he heard the release from the compression in the pneumatic doors which slammed together. He could smell the fumes from the exhaust pipes. Slowly the bus rolled forward, crunching the gravel parking lot and then on to Highway 96, picking up speed as it moved forward. David glanced out the window for the last time but could only see the water tower with its greeting: KIRBYVILLE: Home of the Wildcats.

Damn and double damn!

LaVergne, TN USA
30 December 2009
168525LV00004B/28/P